M000313135

RON GAMBRELL

Six Little Scars

Rough River Publishing LLC
Louisville, KY

www.roughriverpublishing.com

The novel *Six Little Scars* is based on actual historical events. Dialogue and certain events and characters have been created for the purpose of dramatization.

Published by
ROUGH RIVER PUBLISHING LLC
7819 BRAMBLE LN.
LOUISVILLE, KY 40258

Edits by Larry Myers, Kelsey McKim, and Col. Christopher Smrt

Copyright © 2015 Ron Gambrell
All rights reserved.

Release date: April, 2016

ISBN: 978-0-9908562-2-1

Cover art created by Rough River Publishing LLC

Author photo by Jiniece Goodman

Dedicated to the woman whose quiet strength inspired this novel.

Six Little Scars

PART I

Matthew Smith
Louisville, KY 2007

Sometimes confessions come too late. Sometimes they don't come at all. I always knew my father to be an honorable man, born in the Church, baptized. So in the end, what choice did he have but to bare his scars?

A year ago Thanksgiving Day, Father and I sat watching Miami and Detroit play football. It broke my heart to see him that way, sick and dying, nothing but skin and bones. I could tell he was in pain; the grunts, periodic shakes, and the way his arms and shoulders kept drawing up.

1

"Matthew," he spoke with a rasp in his voice, "I've been writing ... things about the past. Things you should know." Reading my puzzled look, he held his hand up. "Don't ask ... questions," he ordered, struggling through each word. "Just look under my desk.... There's a cardboard box. Take it home and read what's in it, tonight, and then burn it all."

"Burn it?"

"No one else should read it ... and that includes your mother."

I leaned back, wondering what he could have written that only I should read.

"Tonight, Son.... Promise you'll do as I ask."

Father barely made it through dinner. He sat crumpled like old folks I'd seen in a nursing home. While the rest of us shared turkey, dressing, and the usual holiday fixings, he ate nothing.

"Daddy, shouldn't you try to eat?" asked my sister, Christine.

Father shook his head. If he said two words throughout the meal, I don't recall them. But he did listen, and I could see in his bloodshot eyes that he cherished those moments, observing his loved ones together as a family. After a while his weak frame slipped in the chair. I stepped to his side and said, "Come on, Dad. Let me take you back to the couch."

"Take me to my bed," he spoke quietly.

I gathered him into my arms and started down the hallway. While stepping sideways, I said, "Remember how you used to carry me, holding me up with my arms spread wide like I was flying?"

Father's breathing shortened. He buried his wet face into my shoulder. I tried to hold my own tears back but couldn't. After gently lowering him onto the bed, I slid in and held him the way he used to hold me when I was ill or frightened by a nightmare. I remained there until the tension in his shoulders subsided and I knew he was asleep.

Later that night, at home, I waited to read until my wife, Lori—four months pregnant—had gone to sleep. After fixing a highball, I relaxed in my favorite living room chair. The old box was familiar. Father's pointed-toe western boots came in it. Removing the lid, I found yellow writing tablets—hundreds of handwritten pages. *Jesus, Dad, how long you been writing? Surely you don't expect me to read all this in one night?*

By the end of the first page, I was hooked. Whiskey became coffee as I read into the morning. How could the gentle man who raised me do the things he described? So much detail, so many seemingly insignificant events that all made better sense by the time I finished. Father didn't just tell his story; he relived it.

Sunrise peeked through the living room window as I finished. Confused and bewildered, I leaned back in the recliner, closed my weary eyes to think, and dozed off. An hour had passed, but it seemed only seconds later when Lori shook me. "Wake up, Matthew. Your mother just called."

"What?" I said, trying to focus.

"We need to go over there right away. It's your father."

As Lori spoke, I remembered the box on the floor next to my chair, out of her sight.

"Why didn't you come to bed?" she continued. "What have you been doing all night?"

"Nothing. Don't you have to work?"

"I'm off today. Remember? Friday after Thanksgiving?"

Sleepy and without a shower, I leaned against the truck's passenger side window, hugging a microwave-warmed, stale cup of last night's coffee. Lori ran stop signs and caution lights in route to my parents' house. There, we found Father exactly as I'd left him the night before: in his bed. The bed where he and Mother slept practically every night of my life. The bed where he, Christine, and I watched cartoons on that same antiquated 19" television still perched in the corner.

Father's sister, Aunt Sissy, had already arrived and was leaning over whispering to him. She backed away upon noticing us. Father seemed irritated, but then settled down. It nauseated me to see him lying there, mouth hanging open, breathing loudly. Mother sat on the edge of the bed holding his hand. The past six months had taken a toll on her. Normally thin, she'd lost weight and looked exhausted to the point of slumping. Her high cheek bones were protruding, and her eyes had sunk back. I stepped to her, nodded toward Aunt Sissy, and asked, "What was that all about?"

"It's nothing. Nothing for you to worry over."

Aunt Sissy backed up against the wall. Her eyes were red as if she'd been crying. She chewed her nails while watching the hospice nurse adjust a morphine drip. I always knew Aunt Sissy had issues, but never understood why until after reading Father's story. Standing there in a sweat suit, still slim and fit, she suddenly reminded me of a 52-year-old version of Hilary Swank in Clint Eastwood's *Million Dollar Baby*. She caught me staring at her covered arms, and tilted her head as if thinking, *What the hell?*

Lori joined me and asked, "So how is he?"

The nurse leaned our way and quietly said, "His suffering is about over. Should have been on morphine long before now."

"So," I asked, "why wasn't he?"

"His choice," answered Mother. "Didn't wanna be all drugged up when you kids came for Thanksgiving."

Christine arrived looking equally rough; her sleepy, green eyes swollen behind uncombed strands of freshly blonde hair. We hugged, and I asked, "Where's Henry?"

"Already left for work," she replied. "I can call him."

"Well, do it now if you're going to." I turned to Mother. "Did you call Dad's elders?"

She squinted at my comment and said, "Yes Matthew, they're supposed to be on the way."

Father's eyes followed me. I kissed his forehead, and then whispered into his ear, "I read your story."

He nodded weakly and seemed desperate to speak, mouthing words with no sound. I tried to read his lips but could not. When I leaned in closer, he managed a grip on my shirt, pulling me closer, and I could barely make out the words, "promise ... the ... promise..."

Assuming he spoke of my promise to burn his tablets, I said, "Don't worry, I will."

Within half an hour, most of the family had arrived. Lori sat in the living room with some of my aunts. Christine put her arm around my waist as our daddy suffered his final moments. Mother's long hair shrouded his face while she shared his moans and groans. Grandpa and Grandma Smith knelt next to the bed. Aunt Sissy had her face buried into Uncle Ray's chest. Grandpa's brothers—the elders—huddled near the doorway. Never before had I seen so many grown men cry. Finally, Father's breathing slowed, his whole body relaxed, and I could hear Mother whimpering. She pulled her hair away, and then gently kissed Father's forehead. His lips remained open. His suffering had ended. Cancer took him at the young age of 50.

Father's funeral took place on Monday, November 27, 2006. Though he lived in Louisville, at his request, we buried him in the company of his ancestors at a place called Bear Creek, in rural Grayson County, Kentucky. Before leaving the graveyard, Mother said she would be coming by the next morning to talk about something. I figured she had concerns over what to do with Father's tools, guns, fishing equipment, etc. Things she would have no use for.

When I answered the door, Mother looked as tired and distraught as she had the day before. "You alone?" she asked, while walking in.

I yawned and said, "Yeah. Lori's already at work. You want coffee?"

"I hoped you'd have a pot. And an ashtray."

"No one smokes here, but for you, Mom, I do have an ashtray."

As I poured two cups, strong, the way she likes it, Mother lit a cigarette.

"So what's on your mind?" I asked. "You look worried."

"The other day, at the house, before your daddy passed, you used a word I've never heard out of you."

"I did?"

"Not once have I ever heard you refer to your grandpa and your great-uncles as the *elders*."

While spooning sugar into my coffee, I said, "And?"

"And! Your daddy spent the last months of his life writing. Things not just anyone should read. Now I can't find it anywhere."

"Maybe he didn't want you to find it."

"Don't play games with me. Know damn well you have it."

I hesitated. "He gave it to me Thanksgiving Day. Told me to read it and then burn it."

"So did you?"

"Did I read it? Sure I did."

"Shit, Matthew. Did you burn it?"

"Not yet, but I will. And by the way, how'd you know what's in it?"

After a sip of her coffee, she said, "I read parts of it while he slept."

"Did you read enough to know you weren't supposed to be reading it?"

"Read enough to know no one should be readin' it."

"I can't believe you read it without his permission!"

"Matthew Lee, don't talk to me like I'm a child. I took care of your daddy night and day. All he did was sit around scribblin' page after page. About drove me crazy. Think I didn't have a right to know?"

For a moment, she sat silent, a distant look in her eyes. Then, after a deep draw from her cigarette, she exhaled and spoke through the smoke. "So, when *are* you gonna destroy it?"

"I don't know. Won't be easy. It'll be like cremating a part of Dad that I never knew."

Mother smashed her cigarette in the ashtray, stood, and said, "If you wallow in the past, it'll haunt you."

Months passed, and when the sleepless nights came, I began to think my mother might have bene right. I understood why my father told me to burn his story. What I couldn't understand was why I hadn't.

When Lori gave me a son of my own, Daniel Lee, she somehow thought I would suddenly get over my father, kind of like a boy getting a new puppy to replace the old dog that died.

On the first anniversary of Father's death, the entire family visited his grave. That night, though worn out, I still couldn't sleep. My mind kept going back to Father on his deathbed, how he tried to speak. I got up, stepped around the bed and peeked in on my boy, resting peacefully in a bassinet an arm's length from his mother. He moved only in his breathing. Standing in the glow of a nightlight, I whispered, "Look at those itty bitty fingernails on those itty bitty fingers."

Lori rolled over and spoke quietly. "What's wrong, Honey?"

"Nothing. Just checking on my son."

"Is he okay?"

"He's fine. Go back to sleep."

After slipping on a sweatshirt, I quietly left the bedroom, carrying my lingering thoughts to the kitchen. Moonlight fell through the skylight as I removed a shot glass and a bottle of Jim Beam from the cabinet over the range. I poured a shot, and then held it up.

"This one's for you, Dad," Quick as I downed it, I poured another. "This one's mine."

The whiskey's warmth ran through me as I longed for the lost opportunity to share a drink, not with the kind and gentle person who raised me, but with the stranger he wrote about. Clouds dimmed the skylight. I felt tired, alone, resentful. Growing up, other kids bragged about how tough their fathers were. Mine had been mild mannered, rarely raised his voice, and never lost his temper. When confrontation came along, he walked the other way. I once witnessed a madman spit on my father. Enraged over God knows what, the man wanted to fight. Father told him, "I know what it's like to be in your shoes, to wanna go off on someone. But I also know what it's like to live with the results." When I asked him later what he meant by that statement, he said, "I'll tell you when you're old enough to understand." Kids in the neighborhood said my ol' man was a yellow-bellied chicken. Why couldn't I have known then what I know now?

Relaxed by the whiskey, I headed back to the bedroom. Still facing the other direction, Lori said, "Why do you keep getting up?"

"Can't sleep. Thinking about Dad."

She rolled over and said, "Honey, I know you miss him, but you can't keep drinking yourself to sleep every night."

"No shit." Feeling guilty, I bent over, kissed her on the cheek, and said, "Don't worry. I'll figure it out."

"Hope so," she whispered. "It's making you mean."

It's making you mean. It's... Lori's ugly words kept repeating as I escaped back to the kitchen. My hands were shaking, and my stomach was in a knot. Opening the pantry door, I turned on a light and used a step stool to reach the plywood lid to the attic entrance. Cold air fell over me while I pulled myself up into the darkness. Within seconds my eyes adjusted to the light bleeding in. Short roof clearance forced me to squat while stepping across narrow edges of ceiling joists. It didn't take long to reach the spot marked by air ducts. Painfully balanced on my knees, I dug through insulation to remove the box I'd hidden there a year earlier. As I pulled on it, a neighbor's dog began to howl. Chills ran through me. I took a deep breath and scurried toward the pantry.

Back in the kitchen, I searched through a junk drawer for the long-shaft butane lighter we use for candles. "This'll do the trick," I mumbled, while pulling on shoes and then quietly slipping out the back door with the box in hand. My breath became visible in the night air as I placed my burden on a picnic table next to the cast iron fireplace normally used for yard waste. After removing the top tablet, I held it close and could almost feel Father. I had to force myself to strike the lighter. Distant howling continued. By the light of the small flame, I could see words:

It all made perfect sense when...

Teardrops fell. Ink ran, and I panicked, trying to rub the moisture away. That same sick emptiness I'd felt the day we buried Father on a hill in Grayson County overwhelmed me. A cold wind picked up, blowing out the flame. I shivered while attempting to strike it again and again, flick after flick with no luck. Scanning the star-filled heavens, I said, "Why can't I do this? What am I missing? Are you trying to tell me something?" The dog quit howling, the wind ceased, and I felt warm.

Returning to the house, I started coffee before taking Father's writing to the living room. I had missed something, and he wasn't going to let me sleep until I found it.

Family Tree of those involved in
SIX LITTLE SCARS
(as of 2007)

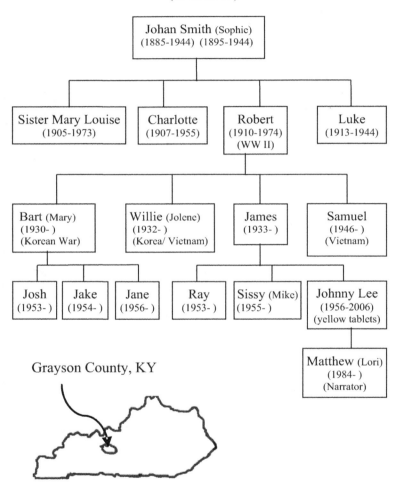

Johan Smith (Sophie)
(1885-1944) (1895-1944)

| Sister Mary Louise (1905-1973) | Charlotte (1907-1955) | Robert (1910-1974) (WW II) | Luke (1913-1944) |

| Bart (Mary) (1930-) (Korean War) | Willie (Jolene) (1932-) (Korea/ Vietnam) | James (1933-) | Samuel (1946-) (Vietnam) |

Josh (1953-) | Jake (1954-) | Jane (1956-) | Ray (1953-) | Sissy (Mike) (1955-) | Johnny Lee (1956-2006) (yellow tablets)

Matthew (Lori) (1984-) (Narrator)

Grayson County, KY

PART II

From my father's yellow writing tablets.

Chapter 1

John L. Smith

April 8, 2006

For my son Matthew

It all made perfect sense when my daddy first said, "Never pick a fight in another man's backyard." On November 11, 1983, I, Johnny Lee Smith, made my daddy's simple wisdom my own as I drove toward a remote destination in the hills of Grayson County, Kentucky. Like we used to say down at the packinghouse, "I had a kill job waiting." The situation wasn't complicated. A ritual of righteousness was about to unfold. My task would be to turn a secluded wooded area into my backyard as I served sentence on a deserving target. The elders considered it an execution, capital punishment for a hideous crime against someone we loved.

My roots are in Grayson County, Kentucky, a place where in the past, simple people, often considered a lesser class by those never acquainted, took not so simple measures when protecting their own. They were hard-working Americans of Irish-German decent who lived through truly tough times while fighting for life, liberty, and when necessary, their own form of justice. They were not nearly as inbred and redneck as some would expect from those in the rural hills of Kentucky. These were reasonable people. They wanted the law to work if and when it could. When it could not, they quietly did what they had to do.

I first approached the elders, confident in my ability to fight for family. When the day arrived, I prayed not only that I was ready, but also that I was doing the right thing. After a night of tossing and turning, I crawled out of bed at 3:00 a.m. All my gear had been prepared the night before. Two cups of coffee set me off like a rocket. An hour passed quickly with me zipping back and forth, double checking everything, chain smoking, and running the plan through my head. Before leaving, I removed eight-month-old Christine from the crib, gave her a squeeze and a smooch, and then placed her in bed with her mother. Bending over, I kissed my beloved on the forehead and whispered, "Love you."

"You too," she replied, gathering the baby in her arms. Standing in the doorway for a moment, looking back, reminded me of my elders' warnings about what I had to lose should something go wrong. At 4:30, I locked the back door and stepped into the cold, dark predawn. My vehicle for the day had been provided by the elders: a gray, 1980 Jeep Cherokee, owned by someone temporarily out of the country. If all went well, its disappearance would go unnoticed until after my need had passed. As planned, upon his return, the owner could report it as stolen. Lexington Police would find the Jeep parked in a conspicuous spot, far away from where I'd be using it. Because it was obviously garage kept, I had dirtied it up a bit. A bucket of water and a few shovels of loose dirt did the trick. As I started the engine and drove away from the house, my heart raced and I thought of what my father had said. "If you're not careful Johnny Lee, you'll become your own worst enemy." He evidently knew how I would be: sweaty palms and my stomach all knotted up.

Were it left up to Pop, he might have taken care of the guy himself, or at least had one of his brothers do it. After all, they'd been professionals, trained by the United States government. Uncle Bart fought in the Korean War. Uncle Willie joined at the end of Korea, and then later, in 1961, he became part of the Green Berets in Vietnam. His second tour ended just before Samuel arrived there in 1966. Born in 1933, my father, James, could not join and never got drafted because of his bum leg. While his father fought overseas in WWII, Pop fell from the barn rafters. He'd been hanging tobacco. His broken leg healed, but he kept a limp.

My experience in killing had been limited to wild game and livestock, neither of which took much skill or discipline. Apparently, the elders were concerned over whether or not I could make the transition from animal to man. At no time on that fateful day did I feel truly alone. The living souls of my father and his brothers seemed ever present as I executed a plan created in part by them. Riding shotgun was the spirit of my grandfather, Robert Smith, and of course, as always, my little friend Gabrielle.

All morning, she whispered things like, *Johnny, it's not too late to turn back*, or *Are you sure you can live with what you're about to do?*

Gabrielle has been in my life since elementary school—a gift from my first grade teacher, Sister Mary Theresa. That lady in black taught me about God and the Church, how to read, write, think, question, and pray. Over time, Sister assumed the role of mentor, giving me private instruction in piano. For six years, that old woman considered me the child her chosen life had denied her. She became my virgin mother and, like any good parent, wanted to protect me from life's uncertainties. In our early days together, Sister spoke often of the world outside and my ability to handle its temptations. Sweet Sister Mary Theresa, despite her abundance of knowledge and talent, feared the world to the point of hiding her life away in the convent. She seemed to think that I too would have problems with the world outside, and so she gave me Gabrielle.

"Johnny," asked Sister Mary Theresa, "do you have a conscience?"

"Don't we all?"

"Have you ever done something wrong, even though you knew it to be wrong before you did it?"

It sounded like a trick question, but after a moment of thought, I did admit to a few times when something inside told me to do one thing, and I did another. Sister advised, "Appears to me you're not listening when your conscience speaks. Perhaps we should name it. Then you'll be more likely to listen."

That day, Sister named my conscience Gabrielle.

Traffic, though light, moved at what felt like a NASCAR pace. Getting stopped by police would abruptly end my trip; therefore, while everyone else drove in frenzy, I stayed only slightly over the speed limit of 55. Between sweaty palms and the butterflies left in my stomach by Gabrielle's nagging presence, smoking a little Kentucky homegrown marijuana seemed in order. If my father had known about me bringing the smoke along, he would have called the whole thing off. Figuring a few hits might settle my nerves, I slightly lowered the window, lit up, took a long hard draw and within seconds began coughing uncontrollably. "Good shit," I whispered between gasps.

Moments later, I had dry palms, dry mouth, and a dry attitude. While I understood the elders' doubts, I had my own recipe for success. Somewhere between Louisville and Grayson County, a regeneration of both mind and body needed to take place. Johnny Lee Smith would have to become a cold-blooded killer, an executioner, a soldier. Even if only for one day. At that moment, it seemed easy to slip off into my own little world, a place described to me by my father's brother.

On rare occasions, especially when he'd been drinking whiskey, Uncle Samuel would speak about Vietnam and how it had stolen part of his youth. How he went from Friday night games and necking

14

sessions in the Dairy Dip parking lot to fighting communism in a faraway country. While his friends hunted deer in Kentucky, Samuel hunted men in South Asia. Ironically, on my drive to hunt a man in Kentucky, I daydreamed of being overseas.

Lighted gauges in the Jeep's dashboard reminded me of an airplane's cockpit. "Tango One, permission to take off," I spoke while merging from one highway to the next. I floored that little V8, and damned if it didn't sound just like a small aircraft rushing down the runway. Gripping the steering wheel, I fell back into the headrest and allowed my imagination to lift off on a support assignment over what Uncle Samuel called a hot LZ in Vietnam—a loading or unloading zone under heavy fire.

I had brought along music, classical pieces compiled on several cassettes. Those tapes allowed me to make-believe my mission was a movie adventure with Mozart and Bach providing the musical score. To this day, my recollections of that trip and the events involved are like memories of a cinema experience. Most of us watch a movie and imagine we are there. I was there and imagined it was a movie.

By 5:00 a.m., Louisville had become a glow in the Jeep's rear view mirror. Through the darkness I navigated southward on Interstate 65, as though on autopilot. While my left brain drove, miles faded by unnoticed, and I began to look back on the beginning of my predicament.

Chapter 2

In June of 1976, I was twenty-years-old and had been working in a meat packing plant for nearly two years. On an otherwise normal workday of pong and blood, I overheard a conversation that would change my life forever. Despite my parochial education, the Ten Commandments, and years of attending Catholic Mass, I found myself wanting to graduate from slaughtering animals to killing men. Not for food or pay, but for revenge.

The day started out well for several reasons. Friday meant a paycheck, the next day would be my family's annual Smith reunion, and Big George Jenkins would be coming back to work on Monday. For two weeks, I'd been forced to fill his nasty, bloody job on the Hog Kill while he vacationed.

Those slaughterhouse days began right after graduation from high school. I'm sure it seemed ironic that a skinny, classical piano playing, honor roll student would take such a job. Truth is, I never intended to stay long. The job started out as a way to make a few bucks and get a break from school and music. Then, like dream episodes, months drifted into years. At times, even I analyzed my participation in such an unusual line of work. On that particular day, it all made sense as I wound up being in just the right place at just the right time; working on the Kill Floor, a place where men who don't mind killing, slaughter, so that others may eat. We spent eight to ten hours a day slaving in hot, humid conditions with a disgusting odor much like that of a gut shot deer, hanging so thick in the air you could taste it. The constant squealing of soon-to-be-dead animals was enough to drive a man crazy.

Six Little Scars

To call me or anyone else at that plant a butcher might be a stretch. We were nothing more than parts of a machine; forty workers collectively slaughtering hogs at a rate of over 400 per hour. Thousands of pigs daily knocked out one by one with an electric shock device and then hung upside down like appliance parts on a chain conveyor. Jugular veins were cut so the still beating heart could pump out enough blood to kill the sleeping beast before it regained consciousness. Hanging carcasses meandered around a room the size of a high school gymnasium so each worker could do his or her small part in a collective process. By the time they reached my job station, hogs that squealed their last squeal 25 minutes earlier had been de-haired, gutted, and reduced to two sides and a detached head.

As those limber sides exited the kill floor toward a chill box, severed heads were slammed onto vertical spikes spaced three feet apart on a waist-high chain conveyor running in my direction. On the way, one man sliced off snouts, another ears, another cheek meat, and so on. Right before reaching me, the skinned heads were removed and placed on a table where two men I grew to hate chiseled jaw meat away from the bone. My job was to reach across the line, grab a head off the table, place it on a machine that ripped off the lower jawbones, and then spike the remaining skull onto another line. Often, that old machine failed to completely detach jaws, in which case I had to manually rip them apart. Down the line, more workers removed remaining meat from the head. Finally, the skulls were split to remove pig brains.

Nearby, separated only by an eight foot aisle, more workers slaughtered beef cattle in a similar process.

To keep my mind off the hard work, I tried thinking about the next day's Smith reunion, a chance to be with family and a few old friends. Then suddenly my good thoughts were interrupted.

The sound of hog screams and the clatter of squeaky chain conveyers limited conversations to those working within a few feet of one another. From my position, that could only be the two men chiseling heads. Their names were Pete and Joe. For some reason, possibly because they worked facing one another, those two characters never shut up. Under normal circumstances I wore hearing protection, as did the whole crew, making it easier to ignore my surroundings. That morning, I'd accidentally dropped my earplugs outside during break. With hair past my shoulders, no one could tell.

When my co-workers began arguing, their elevated voices drew my attention. Each time I turned to grab a head, I heard bits and pieces of a suspicious conversation. Pete and Joe were going back and forth.

"Screw him, don't worry—"

"—sonofabitch thinks *we* owe *him* someth—"

"—need to cool it, man."

"Never shoulda helped him get a job."

"—think you're gettin' too paranoid over—"

"You heard him. He blames it all on us."

"Hell, he did 'er too. What makes you think he'd ever say any—"

At first, their jabber didn't make a lot of sense. Then it dawned on me that they were talking about something they'd done to a girl or a lady. As they continued talking, I continued listening.

"—cause he's a sneaking, lying bastard and you can't trust him."

"—say he ain't really been our friend since that—"

"—believe he was okay with it 'til you started burnin' the bitch's arms."

"—but she deserved it for what she did to Beth."

I stopped in my tracks. Bloody hairs stood up on my arms. My stomach suddenly felt sick, and for a moment I forgot about my job. There was something familiar about what I had just heard. Something gross. The burnt arms and that bitch named Beth. These men were talking about raping my sister. Their words swept me like a witch's spell, revitalizing anger from a past crime that never found closure. During the last four years, my family had longed for the identity of those who had brutalized my sister, and now it seemed that two of the sorry S.O.B.'s were within reach. I could feel a flare in my nostrils, a tremble in my hands, and a desire to attack.

Apparently, Pete and Joe were unaware of my relationship to their conversation. For once, my common name had its benefit. I'm sure no one else in the vicinity could hear their voices, and it seemed as if the

Almighty Himself had funneled those words into my head. Both my knees nearly buckled as I stood, dazed.

"Smith," yelled a voice. "Wake up!"

In a state of shock, I had stopped working. Hog heads were piling up, and workers down the line stood waiting. In what seemed like a scene from a horror movie, I glanced up to see eight people staring straight at me. The looks from Pete and Joe reeked of evil. *Perhaps*, I feared, *they suspect I overheard their conversation.*

Joe shouted, "Hey skinny boy, you need to tighten up!"

"Yeah," added Pete. "Somethin' wrong with you? It's Friday dammit. We got cold beer and a weekend waitin' on us." Both men laughed at me in a nasty tone.

Unsure of what to do, I forced myself to grab heads and continue working. Until lunch I'd be stuck, imprisoned, unable to escape the ugliness that stood only a few feet away. I wanted to speak, to tell someone what I'd just heard, but I knew better. Pete and Joe would surely deny their conversation, and then my life would be in danger. While I worked double-time to catch up, my mind continued to drift.

Chapter 3

The girl named Beth, whom Pete and Joe spoke of, had picked on my sister, Sissy, during school for three years. Pop knew his 95-pound darling liked to fight and had often warned against doing so at school. "Better to take a ribbing in class," he'd say, "than my wrath at home."

Sissy must have taken all she could before snapping that day. Things climaxed on a rainy afternoon right after school. Word that she had finally accepted the challenge spread quickly. I first heard the news while smoking a cigarette in the boys' room between classes.

"Hey Johnny," announced one of my classmates, "hear your sister's finally agreed to take on Beth."

"Who told you that?"

"Donald Nelson told me. Hell, everybody's talking about it. Donald says they're planning to meet out behind the shop."

I snuck out of sixth period a little early, making sure to be there before the fight started. Beth showed up with an escort, like a prizefighter.

"Where's that little bitch at? Been waiting a long time for a piece of her ass!"

Sissy arrived to jeers from several in the crowd. When she saw me, I got a wink of assurance. The crowd grew even though it drizzled rain. Beth's friends started forming a circle. That's when I spoke up. "Hey now, your girl whips Sissy by herself, so be it. But ain't none of you gonna help. Someone steps in, I'll kick your ass myself."

Beth started with words. "Come on, you little whore, let's see what you're made of."

Sissy grinned, chewing her gum hard and fast while moving in a circle.

Beth kept talking, inching closer, "Come on, bitch, come on." She finally took the first swing, popping Sissy a good one right on the chin. Onlookers screamed encouragement. Both girls struggled for footing in the wet grass while throwing wild punches and screaming profanities at one another. Beth grabbed Sissy's long hair and slung her into the crowd. That's when my sister's face began to distort, and I knew things were about to get ugly. In her rage, Sissy began foaming at the corners of her mouth, something I'd seen before. Her fighting style suddenly shifted from girly grabs and smacks to the head-down, fists-up, dancing stance she and I had learned from Pop. She began throwing one-two punches and jabs, and it was a one-sided ass-whipping from that point on.

With a bloody nose and a swollen eye, Beth somehow managed to rip Sissy's blouse half off.

Sissy growled, "You *will* pay for that." Without hesitation, she landed a hard wild hook that dazed Beth, causing her to stumble. Then, to some of the crowd's satisfaction, Sissy began to tear her opponent's wet clothing away piece by piece. Every time the girl seemed to be recovering, Sissy landed another good punch and then continued with her efforts. Someone ran into the school and reported the fight. By the time Coach Jackson and Mr. Thompson got out there to break things up, Beth wore nothing but mud, bruises, and some of her own blood. Coach covered her nakedness with his jacket as the crowd dispersed. Sissy broke loose from Mr. Thompson and ran all the way home. For Beth, it had to be embarrassing, but she'd asked for it.

I always did suspect a connection between my sister being attacked and that fight in the schoolyard. It seemed like some sort of payback, since it occurred shortly after the fight. There were actually three men involved. The bastards held something over Sissy's head while they beat her, raped her, and even took the time to burn marks into each of her arms. Somewhere in the midst of struggle and pain, she passed out. They left her lying there in the dark, branded and unconscious. One of our neighbors discovered Sissy about the time she regained consciousness and took her to the hospital. Because her face had been covered, the poor girl had no way of identifying the attackers. Doctors did tests. The police interviewed Sissy, took photos, and kept samples of clothing. Yet no one ever got arrested for the crime. And Sissy, well, she has never been the same. You can still see it in her eyes. I'd say there's not a day goes by that she doesn't look at her arms and relive that awful, awful experience.

There I stood, four years later, with my desire to attack Pete and Joe making me sick to my stomach. Workers down the line had extra butcher knives laying aside. In my mind's eye, I took a blade and with one effort, ended two pathetic lives. Each unforgiving thought led to another. I began to recall thinking as a child what it would be like to shoot a man. I had killed practically every type of critter living in Grandpa's woods with my .22 caliber rifle, practicing for the day I'd be drafted and wind up shooting at men in Vietnam. Nixon ended the draft before that happened; yet there I stood, a few feet away from two men who had given me reason to kill.

Remembering Pop's words, "Never pick a fight in another man's backyard," I remained silent and listened to learn. Unfortunately, neither Pete nor Joe mentioned the third man's name. I became paranoid; glancing around the room, fearing the person could be close enough to be watching. For the next hour, I struggled with both the job and my thoughts. Each time the line stopped, I threw up in a nearby garbage can. Convinced I was ill, my boss called for someone from the labor pool, and at lunchtime he let me go home.

On the way, I stopped at a liquor store to cash my paycheck and to buy cigarettes and whiskey. A friend of mine worked there and had no problem accepting my fake ID. Most Fridays, I shared a bottle with my friends after work, which was our way of starting the weekend. That day, the drinking began early. I lived alone in an old, small, framed house that I rented. It rested on a half-acre wooded lot at the end of a private lane. A summer shower had begun when I took the whiskey, a short glass of ice, and my concerns to the back porch. The rain's intensity grew and subsided like an ocean's tide as I drank, smoked, and considered all options for dealing with Pete and Joe.

Normally, I would go to my father. For the longest time, his desire to learn the identity of Sissy's attackers had consumed him. However, in light of his recent heart surgery, I feared involving him might not be healthy. It had been less than two years since Grandpa Smith died of a heart attack, and when the doctor said Pop needed bypass surgery, it scared the heck out of the whole family. Taking care of the Pete and Joe situation myself and then telling Pop later seemed a better option.

My brother, Ray, had a college degree, good career, and a family of his own to worry about. While I had street sense, he had book sense. His solution to the problem would likely involve attorneys, lots of money, Pop, and public embarrassment for Sissy.

Grandpa Smith once told me, "A man with no family is a man with no help." I had plenty of family, and I needed help.

For as long as I can remember, there has been a dairy farm in the Smith family. My grandfather built a new house where his parents' place had burned. He and Grandma modernized and upgraded the dairy operation with the help of my father and his three brothers. The oldest, Uncle Bart, married his high school sweetheart right before he went off to war in Korea. Aunt Mary helped run the farm while he was away. When Uncle Bart came home from war, he and Aunt Mary stayed on the farm. Eventually, the other three boys drifted away. It was on that original Smith farm that the family gathered for special occasions. I can recall times when kids were told to stay away while the men went to one of the barns for a talk. One cold December evening, curiosity got the best of me. After a trip to the outhouse, I quietly worked my way around the outside of the barn to the area where my elders met. Slithering close, I squatted in the dark like a baseball catcher while peeking through cracks in the boards.

There they were, Grandpa, my father, and two of his brothers, passing a bottle and talking business. I believe Uncle Samuel was in Vietnam at the time. Hiding in the barn to drink didn't surprise me, Grayson being a dry county.

Boy did I get an earful that night. It seemed someone by the name of Merle Clark had crashed his vehicle into Uncle Willie's truck while intoxicated on whiskey. After sobering up, the man refused to pay for the damage, claiming he didn't recall the accident. In those days, not too many country folk could afford or even cared about hiring an attorney to deal with such a problem.

"Hell, Daddy," said Uncle Willie. "Merle ain't never gonna pay for that truck. He knows damn well he did it. Just too tight to fork up the money."

"Bullshit, boy," replied Grandpa. "He ain't worried none about the money. He just don't wanna admit he did it cause then his woman might figure out where he's been buyin' his whiskey."

Apparently, the night Merle Clark hit Uncle Willie's truck, he'd been on his way home from a monthly visit with a lady named Dora May Evens. Everybody in those parts knew Dora May, a widow woman about 30 years old who'd figured out she could support her three youngsters by making a weekly trip to Louisville, buying whiskey and beer, and then bootlegging it to the boys down home. Dora May Evens wasn't the prettiest woman in town, but she sure had one hell of a body. Sometimes, after a few drinks, she'd sell those married men a little more than the whiskey. Merle's wife thought he and one of his buddies went all the way to Louisville once a month to buy booze. Truth be told, he stopped to see Dora May instead.

Grandpa had a plan. "Tell you what, boys, we pretty much know when Merle's gonna be back over at Dora May's place. There's a spot down round the curve where we can pull us a big ol' tree branch out 'cross the road. When Merle leaves Dora May's, he'll have to get his drunk ass out to move it. That's when we'll work him over. Be interestin' to see if he can remember an ass whupin' after he sobers up."

"Sounds good to me," said Uncle Willie.

"What do y'all think?" Grandpa asked the other two.

"No problem," answered my daddy.

Uncle Bart hesitated. "And what if Merle ain't drunk? Hell, he's liable to pull out a gun or a knife. What happens then?"

"You gotta point, Son, but I'll bet my bottom dollar he'll be drunk. And if he ain't, don't think he'll suspect anything. Damn, boys, if the four of us can't handle one man, we best just stay home."

"Okay," answered Uncle Bart. "It's a deal. But are we gonna wear somethin' over our heads so he don't recognize us?"

"Hell no," snapped Grandpa. "Want that sonofabitch to know who whooped his ass. Just don't need no witnesses. Knowin' Merle, he'd rather take a beating than let his wife know what he's been up to."

I asked my daddy, years later, how that situation played out. He laughed and said, "Ol' Merle came flying around that bend in the road and never even slowed down. We all 'bout busted a gut when he ran into that tree branch at full speed. Left his sorry ass drunk and passed out behind the wheel of his mangled truck, figuring justice had been served."

Many things went through my mind that afternoon in '76, sitting on the back porch trying to decide my next move. I longed for Grandpa Smith's presence. He was the one who taught me how to drink whiskey, and I know he would have been glad to sit there, share a drink, and help me decide what to do about Pete and Joe. Without him I would have to approach someone else in the family. All the elders would be at the next day's family reunion.

Chapter 4

Grayson Springs, Kentucky, is little more than an intersection in the road where KY-88 meets KY-1214. Its main claim to fame is the old, now abandoned, Grayson Springs Resort. The property had once been famous because of its unending supply of mineral waters—mostly sulfur springs. During the late 1800s those waters were considered therapeutic. An old 24' x 60' white-board building remains. Part of a much larger complex that burned in the early 1900s, it had been renovated with Southern-style architecture and became known as the Grayson Springs Inn. For most of my youth, the resort's park-like setting accommodated our Smith Family Reunions.

For that 1976 Reunion, we had a Norman Rockwell day in Kentucky. Sunshine produced a warm, eighty-degree temperature, and the only real noise other than picnickers was the sound of songbirds accompanied by a subtle hiss of leaves moving in the breeze.

There were already several in attendance when I drove through the entrance. My parents and siblings had not yet arrived, which was a good thing. With them around, it would be hard to speak privately to Uncle Bart about Pete and Joe.

The family had become so large I could no longer identify everyone. Children ran about, laughing and giggling. A few old men sat in the shade seeing who could tell the biggest lie while ladies shuffled here and there preparing the feast. At noon we would all share ham, corn, beans, potatoes, and garden salad, topped off with homemade pies and ice cream.

Noticing my arrival, Grandma Smith paused in her preparations. As I gave her a hug and a kiss, she complained, "When you gonna shave that ol' scratchy beard?"

"Don't know, Grandma. Keeps me warm in the coolers at work."

"Does it keep you warm at night?"

"Excuse me?"

"You need a good woman, Johnny Lee. No decent lady's gonna want that thing scratchin' her all the time."

I rubbed my bristles on her neck one more time, growling as I did. She squealed and giggled, then blushed on my release. "Liked that, didn't you? Must mean you're not a *decent lady*."

She swatted me on the butt and said, "Git on outta here. I've got work to do."

On leaving Grandma, I spotted Uncle Bart walking toward the back of the inn. I figured he might be on his way to take a leak, a snort of whiskey, or both. After lighting a cigarette, I grabbed a cola from the cooler and headed that way, rounding the corner just in time to see a deep swig of Very Old Barton.

"Hey old man, how about a chaser?" I asked, offering a drink of my cola.

"Don't mind if I do," replied Uncle Bart, reaching for the bottle with his sun-parched, freckle-covered hand. "Where the hell you been, boy? Ain't seen you in a month of Sundays."

"When you kill hogs all week, you don't feel much like socializing on the weekend."

"Best get your butt on out of that slaughterhouse and into somebody's college. Too smart to be wastin' your life in a place like that."

"I hear ya."

The gleam in his eyes guaranteed it wasn't Uncle Bart's first drink of the day. He offered the whiskey bottle in my direction. "Here you go, might as well have a snort. Know damn well you didn't foller me out here just ta' talk."

After dropping my cigarette on the ground and smashing it out with my boot, I took a rather large swig that caught me coughing a little on the exhale.

"Easy now! They's plenty. No need gettin' all tore up on one swaller."

"Sorry. Got a little carried away."

Uncle Bart stood there a moment, staring at me with his faded red hair fluttering in the wind. Then he asked, "Somethin' ailin' you, Johnny Lee?"

"Well, yeah, matter-a-fact there is something I need advice on."

"You in trouble?"

"No, not me, I mean, I'm not in trouble, but something is bothering me." I could feel my own voice tremble.

Uncle Bart obviously sensed my uneasiness. "Don't be skeered, boy. Spit it out. It's just you, me, and the crickets back here."

After a moment of thought, I said, "You remember what happened to Sissy a while back?"

"Yeah, reckon I do. Boys beat'er up … branded 'er."

"Well there's more to it than what you heard. Truth is those three bastards raped her."

"Got-damn-it. Always did think there was more to that. Wonder why your daddy didn't tell us?"

"Sissy didn't want everybody to know. You gotta figure how she felt. Embarrassed enough without advertising all the details."

"So why you tellin' me now?"

I took another drink for courage. "The other day at work I overheard two guys talking about Sissy. They didn't know I was listening. They were talking about raping her and burning her arms and all that."

My uncle's eyes turned whiskey wild. "Whoa now, boy! You tellin' me you know who done this to your sister?"

"Know who two of 'em are. They mentioned the other guy, but I never did hear 'em say his name."

"What's your daddy say about this?"

"Haven't said anything to him yet and really don't want to, him having a bad heart. It about killed him before."

"So what exactly do you want from me?"

"Before Grandpa died, he spoke to me about justice and family taking care of family. Been thinking about serving Grandpa's kind of justice on those boys, but it seems I'll be needing help."

Uncle Bart reached for the bottle, took another swig, and chased it with the soft drink. Then for a moment he stood scratching his chin. "Just what you got in mind for these fellers?"

"Let me ask you, Uncle Bart. If it were Jane instead of Sissy, what would *you* do?"

Before he could answer, Cousin Jane came looking for her daddy.

"What's goin' on back here? Y'all drinkin' that damn whiskey already?"

"Mind your tongue, girl," replied Uncle Bart while looking at his daughter as though considering my comment. He glanced back at me and sort of nodded up and down.

Jane appeared confused, so I spoke up. "Hey girl, how you been?"

"I'm doin' fine, *stranger*. Where you been hidin'? Grandma says you're gettin' too good to come see us anymore?"

"Blah, blah, blah."

Uncle Bart shoved the whiskey bottle into his pocket. As the three of us stepped around the building and started toward the picnic, I found myself checking out Cousin Jane. She was what my friends in Louisville would call a twenty-year-old babe with an attitude. One hundred and fifteen pounds on a 5'4" frame. Long dark hair, high cheekbones, and eyes so green they almost didn't look real. Jane and I were always close, and if we hadn't been cousins, well...

She caught me looking, smiled, and said, "You do know I can read minds."

"Is that right? So what am I—"

"When you headin' back to Louaval?" interrupted Uncle Bart.

I winked at Jane and then answered her daddy. "Not sure yet, have to work Monday."

"How 'bout you come over to our place and spend the night? That way you and me can finish our little conversation."

"Sounds good. Be hanging around here for a while. Gotta pig out and say hi to everybody, then I'll catch you all later this evening."

Jane said, "If you're planning on seeing Mary Ellen, you'll have to go out to the Davis place."

"Why's that?"

"Cause she married Bobbie."

"No way!"

"You know she couldn't wait on your sorry ass forever. Bobbie's parents even gave 'em the farm."

"You're shitting me. So where'd *they* go?"

"They made a spot for a doublewide out by the road."

I couldn't believe my ears. Bobbie Davis finally talked Mary Ellen into it. Guess you could say he screwed her into it. Apparently, she was six months pregnant when they got married. Everyone assumed *I* was going to marry her. Thing is, while I enjoyed her company, I had avoided the idea of marriage because she was simply too damn bossy. And still, the thought of Mary Ellen White being with someone else brought back the same gut-ache I had to get over when we broke up.

.....One summer, Uncle Willie got me a job working at what they called the Pickle Shed. It was the place where farmers brought in cucumbers to sell. First real job I ever had. I stayed with my mother's parents, Grandma and Grandpa Wilson. And not too far down the hill lived, Mary Ellen White. I'd known of her since we were little kids. That summer, I rode my bicycle past her family's farm on my way to and from work. At first, I just waved on my way by. Then one evening, when the Whites were sitting on their porch, fighting the heat, Mrs. White asked me to stop for a glass of iced tea. When they found out that I had talents on the piano, they invited me in to play their old upright.

Eventually, it seemed that Mary Ellen watched for me coming down the road. She would have a cool glass of tea waiting. I stopped often. By the time summer ended and school started, Mary Ellen and I had become good friends. Mr. White told me I come down anytime to hunt squirrels off hickory and oak trees on the back of his farm, and so I did every time my parents drove down for the weekend.

It seemed the older we got, the more beautiful Mary Ellen became, and of course she knew it. Our talks turned into walks and at some point we snuck off behind those bales of hay in her daddy's barn. Watching Mary Ellen slip out of a sack dress was like watching a butterfly shed its cocoon.....

A really good bourbon-induced fantasy got cut short by the sight of my parents unloading chairs and food from the back of their Chevy pickup. Before I could utter the words, Uncle Bart winked and said, "I hear ya, boy," acknowledging my desire to not include my father in our conversation.

Jane knew darn well we were up to something. She shook her head and said, "Hell no, ain't even gonna ask."

Chapter 5

I left the family reunion that afternoon and headed out to see Mary Ellen, just like Jane said I would. Charlie Pride sang "Kiss an Angel Good Morning" on the radio as I left the blacktop at the entrance to the Davis place. A new doublewide was nested some fifty feet off the road. An acre of trees had been cleared for the lot. It surprised me that Bobbie's folks would give up their hundred-acre homestead for a house on wheels. I guess the new plumbing and being out by the blacktop had its advantages.

Bobbie, the youngest child, stayed on the farm while his siblings drifted into careers. He had a true love for the property. I suppose that's why his parents offered the place as a wedding gift.

No one appeared to be home as I passed the trailer and started up the old road. Most folks wouldn't even call it a road. There were trees on both sides so close you could reach out and grab a limb, and the weeds had grown tall enough to rub the truck's undercarriage. It was a rough ride, but nothing my old Dodge pickup couldn't handle.

Being in the woods at least offered a shaded break from the summer heat. A horse fly, big as a buckeye, flew past my nose on its way in one window and out the other. Halfway to the house, dogs began barking in the distance.

Four of the best-looking coonhounds in Grayson County greeted me at the creek. Their low, deep voices echoed through the holler as I navigated into ten inches of crystal clear creek water. Sunlight filtered through trees and glittered off schools of minnows and small sunfish while they darted away from the truck's intrusion.

I always did like the Davis place. On the way into that holler, one might wonder why anybody would want to live there. Once you reach the clearing it becomes obvious. Some would say it's not much more than a flat spot between two hills. To me it was a paradise surrounded by hardwoods, dogwoods, cedars, pines, and the gentle sound of running water. Much of the timber was virgin or as near as I ever saw. In my younger years, I thought those trees touched the sky.

I first met Bobbie and his folks when my father asked if we could hunt on their property. After that, we all became friends, and on my visits to my grandparents, Bobbie and I would walk the fields and hills for hours on end.

Driving up out of the creek, I could see Mary Ellen standing on the front porch of Bobbie's childhood home, a weathered, two-story whiteboard house with a tin roof and shade trees all around it. Sure enough, she held a baby. That strange feeling returned to my stomach. Bobbie's truck was nowhere to be seen, and Gabrielle warned, *This might be a mistake.* At that point, I figured it would be rude to turn back without at least stopping to say hi.

Mary Ellen recognized my truck and began to wave. I worried she might still be upset. After all, it was me who had avoided her for more than a year.

The truck's wet brakes ground in my struggle to stop. Instead of coming off the porch to greet me, Mary Ellen sat down on the top wooden step with her bare feet in the dusty ground below where traffic had worn away the grass. She flipped her long, dirty-blonde hair back over her shoulders and waited for me to make the first move. I looked for signs in her eyes. Those dark browns that once shone innocent as a puppy's now stared across her freckled nose with an older, more mature look. Getting married and having a baby must have a way of doing that.

Leaning out the window, I said, "I'll be damned Mary Ellen, look at you all shiny like a new penny."

"Don't come 'round here after all this time, actin' like you're gonna sweet talk me. Now get your sorry ass out here and look at my baby girl."

One thing hadn't changed. She was still bossy. "Don't mind if I do," I said, bumping open the Dodge's door. The older pair of hounds had curled up on the porch while the other two begged for my attention.

"Get down, you bad dogs," Mary Ellen shouted while rising to my aid.

Our eyes met, and for a second I felt the old electricity.

She broke the trance, moved close with the baby, and said, "Can you believe this? Her name is Olivia Marie Davis."

"Look at those itty bitty fingernails on those itty bitty fingers," I commented while softly rubbing the child's hands with my index finger. "How old is she?"

"Well, let's see. She'll be four months tomorrow."

"Hot damn, makes me feel like some sort of an uncle!"

"Uncle Johnny. That'll work. And, you can take that worried look off your face. She's not yours. Course she coulda' been iffin' you hadn't been so stubborn."

"So where's Bobbie?" I asked, trying to change the subject.

"Said he was goin' over to Barry Clemons's place to play music. Him and Barry and Billy are trying to put together a group. Shame you ain't livin' down here. You could join 'em."

"Sounds like a good time."

Mary Ellen sat back down, grinned, and said, "It's time for Olivia's feedin'. You mind?"

"Oh no, you go right ahead. I'll wait out here with the dogs."

"That's okay, I can feed 'er right here." She began to unbutton her dress from the top, exposing one of her breasts.

"What the hell ya doin'?"

"I'm about to feed her, silly. Johnny Lee, don't act like you ain't never seen my tits."

"Holy shit," I said, trying not to stare as the little one started its meal. "Looks like having that baby gave you what you always wanted."

"You talkin' about my boobs?"

"Oh yeah," I replied.

"They'll probably go away once I wean this child. Kinda nice though, ain't they?" With that said, she nonchalantly pulled open her dress to expose the other breast.

I nearly lost my breath. "All right now, you shouldn't be teasing me like that, you being a married woman. What would Bobbie think if he should ride up right now?"

"Don't you worry none about Bobbie. That boy ain't laid a lovin' hand on me since well before Olivia was born."

Stunned by her comment, I pulled a new pack of smokes from my shirt pocket and began nervously tapping the end on my hand. "Like a cigarette?"

"No, thanks. Quit em' when I got pregnant."

"Guess that's a good thing," I said, while tearing the foil from the pack. I pulled one out and lit up. "Tell me now, you and Bobbie gonna make it?"

"Yeah, we'll be all right. Just don't think he realizes how much I need his attention. This youngin's takin' up most of my days and nights, and I'm not complainin' cause I love 'er more than life itself..."

While Mary Ellen rattled on, the little one continued nursing. I found it interesting, having never watched a baby breast-feed before.

"...but a girl needs some attention now and then, and you'd think he oughta know that."

In all my days of knowing Mary Ellen, I could never recall seeing her cry. At that moment, it appeared she might. I said, "That baby ain't sucking on both boobs. How 'bout you cover one up so we can talk a little easier?"

"Don't be scared, Johnny. I ain't gonna attack you."

"Damn," I smiled.

Mary Ellen stopped the feeding, tucking away her left breast. "Wake up, sweetie," she said while patting the little one's back. After the baby burped, she was given access to the other side.

"So, she gets to—I mean *has* to, suck both sides?"

Mary Ellen looked up and asked, "Would you milk one side of a cow and not the other?"

"Hmmm. Guess not."

For a few seconds, we stared at one another. I blinked first and said, "Be right back," before walking around the side of the house to take a leak. On my return, I lit another cigarette.

Mary Ellen asked, "You nervous, Johnny Lee?"

"Maybe a little."

"You know, after feedin', Olivia always takes a nap. If you want, you can come in for a while."

Better think twice about that, whispered Gabrielle.

The hounds all lay staring up at me as if waiting for my answer. I remained silent, thinking.

When the feeding was over, Mary Ellen re-buttoned her dress before burping the baby again. I flipped my cigarette into the yard, took a seat on the steps, and asked, "Can I hold her?"

"Well, sure you can." After handing me the sleepy-eyed little creature, Mary Ellen grinned while watching me adjust. I sat there rocking the baby and wondering why Bobbie would be avoiding sex with Mary Ellen. *Surely he doesn't think this is my child.*

My friend leaned back, bracing her elbows on the porch planks. She seemed nervous and inviting as she twiddled her big toes in the dust. I turned to her grin and said, "Listen, I've had a little whiskey, and sitting here right now you sure do look fine. I'm afraid if I go in that house, might do something we'll both regret later on."

"But Johnny—"

"Hold on. Let me finish. This ain't about to be my last trip to these hills, and I know damn well I'm gonna run into Bobbie and his family now and then. Like to be able to look 'em in the eye, just like I am you right now and tell 'em how much I miss 'em. And if your marriage goes to hell, don't want it to be because of something *I* did."

Her tears began to roll. "Damn you, Johnny Lee. When I saw your truck coming up the lane, got so excited I about wet myself. And now here I am actin' a fool and runnin' you off."

"Bullshit. You're not running me off. I'm having a good time. This little baby's doing fine sleeping in my arms, and I'm enjoying your company. Let's just sit here a while, and catch up on old times."

Mary Ellen spoke through her hands while wiping away tears. "You always were the good one. Shoulda held on when I had you."

"Just because it ain't right for you and me to be together, that doesn't mean we can't be friends."

"Johnny—"

"And, if you haven't already had this little baby girl baptized, you better be considering me for a godfather."

Mary Ellen smiled, tilted her head and said, "Hope you know you just made my day. I'll—I'll talk to Bobbie about that real soon.... Hey, look at me bein' a bad hostess. Are ya' hungry?"

"No, not at all. Just ate a while ago at the family reunion. But I could use a cold drink."

"Got sweet tea and some Cokes in the icebox," she chirped while rising from the porch.

"I'll take a Coke, thank you," I replied, feeling relieved.

Mary Ellen scurried off into the house leaving me on the steps with the little one in my arms. Sitting there, I began to somewhat envy Bobbie's situation. He had so much.

Suddenly, for no apparent reason, all four hounds became restless, jumping up and running toward the lane. It could only mean one thing. They recognized the sound of Bobbie's truck. If it were anyone else, they'd be barking. Within seconds I could hear the engine noise myself.

I thought, *Glad I'm not in that house with Mary Ellen.*

When Bobbie's Chevy crossed the creek, he recognized my truck and began tooting his horn. I remained seated, cuddling his bundle of joy, who seemed unaffected by the noise. Pulling up next to the porch, Bobbie smiled and turned off the truck's engine.

Keeping my voice low, I said, "Hey boy, hear you been out pickin' and grinnin'."

"Heeelll yeah," he slurred loudly, still leaning back in the seat. "Wish I'd known you were in town. You coulda' joined us."

"That's what Mary Ellen was saying."

As I spoke, Mary Ellen reappeared with my Coca-Cola in a tall, iced glass. "Hey Bobbie, looky what the cat drug in."

37

Bobbie leaned over, resting both arms on the open window of the truck's door. His long dark hair streamed out from under a dirty Cincinnati Reds baseball cap. "I hear ya, honey. Been so long, hell, I thought we had a stranger. Damn good to see 'im though, ain't it?"

"Sure is," she grinned my way with a wink. "Just made Johnny some Coke. You want some too?"

"Weellll, might as well. Gonna be needin' a chaser here in a minute."

Mary Ellen set my glass on the porch, leaned down, and said, "Let me have Olivia. I'll put her in the crib so's you two can visit."

I took a long drink while watching Bobbie. He gradually opened the truck door, slid his feet to the ground, and then reached back under the seat to get a pint bottle of whiskey. "Check this out, Johnny Boy. Been savin' it for a special occasion. Now, let's you and me sit up there in them easy chairs and have us a drink."

"Sounds good," I agreed.

As Bobbie started up the steps, he stumbled, knocking my cola all across the porch. Fortunately, I stopped his fall.

"Damn, boy, I'm glad to see you, but you oughta stayed where you was. You keep driving in this condition, you'll wind up killing yourself or someone else." I hated to criticize, but he needed it. After helping him to his chair, I asked, "How about a smoke?"

"Don't mind if I do," he replied while slumping into the quilt-padded rocker.

I tapped out a couple cigarettes, lit both and handed him one.

"Thanky, Johnny Boy." Bobbie took a draw. "So what brings you all the way out here?"

"Drove down this morning for the family reunion. Figured I oughta at least come out and congratulate you and Mary Ellen. Still can't believe you talked her into marrying your sorry ass."

"Sounds to me like you're just a little bit jealous."

"You got that right," I replied while taking a seat in the chair next to Bobbie's. "Hell, look around. You've got yourself a woman, a perfect little baby, and a place of your own. Most people work their ass off for years to get all this."

As I spoke, several head of prime Angus cattle grazed just on the other side of the creek. I thought, *Man, what I'd do to have a place like this.*

Before my daydream went any further, Mary Ellen came out with Bobbie's drink. "Well, I'll be," she spoke, while nudging Bobbie. He had passed out right there in the chair, his lit cigarette barely hanging from his lips. "One of these days, he's gonna burn this whole damn place down."

"Shit," I said, removing the Marlboro from his mouth. "You want me to take him in?"

"No, let 'im sleep it off right there. He'll be just fine. Ain't the first time."

"You sure?"

She just nodded.

I took a deep breath and said, "Believe I should leave. Uncle Bart's expecting me over at the farm."

"You stayin' down tonight?"

"Yeah."

"Can you call me later?"

"I'm not sure that's a good idea right now. I'll be back down soon, and I'll come see you and Bobbie. And the baby."

Mary Ellen looked up, wiped her cheeks, and said, "Come on, I'll walk you to the truck."

It felt like two miles instead of thirty feet to the Dodge. I really didn't know what to say.

Mary Ellen spoke first. "I'm so glad you came by, even if it was only for a little while. And let's plan on you bein' Olivia's godfather."

When I climbed into the truck, closed the door, and leaned out the window to say goodbye, she snuck a quick salty kiss on my lips. It felt like more than a friendly farewell. I started the truck, put it in gear, and said, "Tell Bobbie I'll see him next time down."

The two younger hounds escorted me across the creek and into the woods. In the mirror, I could see Mary Ellen waving. My heart ached.

Chapter 6

Most of the Holsteins were grazing away from the milk barn upon my arrival at Uncle Bart's place, indicating a near end to the afternoon milking. Max, a young mixed-breed mutt somewhere between Shepherd and Collie met me halfway down the lane. By the time I got out of the truck, he had that tail wagging a hundred miles an hour—his way of begging for attention.

Uncle Bart's new Ford pickup sat next to the old one he had passed on to Jane. As Max escorted me to the barn, I wished Cousins Jake and Joshua could be there. Josh, having received his degree from the University of Kentucky Agriculture program, had already started at a job for the state. Jake played football for the Western Kentucky University Hilltoppers while working on a Business degree. He'd just finished his junior year and was currently on vacation. He would soon be home to help with summer crops. Jane, two years out of high school and with no interest in college, was the only one left to help with the twice-daily milking chores. I opened the door just in time to watch the last six-cow rotation enter the barn.

"Well now, looky here. Told you Johnny would wait 'til we were done before he'd show up," jabbed Cousin Jane, hair all pulled back in a ponytail, as she poured feed into a trough.

I did in fact feel bad, considering my untimely arrival. "Sorry about that. Tell you what, tomorrow morning you can sleep while I help out here in the barn."

"Hear that, Daddy? You be my witness."

Uncle Bart chuckled a bit and shook his head in acknowledgement.

Watching Cousin Jane work was almost entertaining. In less than two minutes, she poured feed, washed udders, and applied vacuum-milkers for her three cows. I tried to imagine Mary Ellen doing the same. The girl grew up on a cattle farm, but had no desire to get her hands dirty.

Uncle Bart stepped on my thoughts. "Hey Johnny, when was the last time you rode a horse?"

"It's been a while."

"How 'bout you and Jane finish here while I go saddle the mare and 'er filly. One cow short today. Best go out and see what's up. Figured you might wanna ride along?"

"Sure, sounds good to me." It would provide the perfect opportunity for the two of us to be alone and talk business. "Better give me Becca." That would be the older horse, a six-year-old mare.

Jane chimed in, "What's wrong, Johnny? Uncle Willie's colt got you scared?" The girl never missed an opportunity to rib on me. "Daddy, sure wish you'd been there. What was it, Johnny, two years ago..."

We'd all heard the story before, but she just had to tell it again.

"...Boy thinks he can ride, but Star knew who was boss. Threw his ass in a heartbeat. Wouldn't listen to me tellin' him to wrap his arms around the colt's neck and slide off. More worried about showin' off than gettin' off."

"Blah, blah, blah," I complained.

Uncle Bart walked away, leaving Jane and me to finish those last six cows and the post-milking chores. By the time we finished, he had arrived outside the door with two horses saddled and ready to go. When I joined him, he handed me reins for the mare.

Jane punned, "Need a hand up?"

"Ha, ha," I answered, while mounting.

"Don't forget, I'm sleepin' in tomorrow," she sassed while turning toward the house. "And y'all best not be out there too long. Mama and Grandma are gonna be heatin' up leftovers from the reunion. Hell, I'm already hungry."

I lit a cigarette, took a draw, and stared as Jane walked away, pulling the rubber band from her ponytail, shaking loose her long, dark strands. When she stopped and glanced back, I quickly turned, exhaling into the wide-open space. That's when I spotted several buzzards at a distance, circling high in the sky.

"Hey Uncle Bart, see those buzzards? Bet that's where your cow is. Could still be alive," I guessed, since the scavengers were in the air.

"You might be right, boy, but then again, you might not. Wait here a minute. Gonna fetch my rifle."

As Uncle Bart rode toward the house, I sat high on my trusty steed, imagining we were in the old Wild West, about to chase down some dirty, rotten cattle rustlers. Maybe we'd wind up hanging the scoundrels from an old, dead tree. My daydream faded to the sound of hooves as Uncle Bart returned with a .30-30 Winchester in the scabbard on his saddle.

"Gonna shoot those buzzards?"

"Hell no," he answered. "Might have to put the Holstein down, or shoot me a coyote."

"Coyote? I've never seen one around here. You?"

"Yep. And I hear 'em howlin' at night. Could be wild dogs. Either way, if it's chewin' on my cow, I'll kill it deader-n-hell."

Reaching in his pocket, Uncle Bart came out with a twist of Mammoth Cave chewing tobacco. He cut off a plug and pushed it into his mouth. "How 'bout you, boy?" he offered.

"No, thanks. Mammoth Cave's too strong. Chew it while I'm riding, might get sick."

He put the twist back in his pocket and said, "Gid-up." Off he went.

I pinched out my cigarette, kicked the mare in gear, and followed.

Those buzzards, high in the air, didn't seem affected by our approach. At one point we rode through the woods for a couple hundred yards, destroying a multitude of spider webs along the way. Before reaching the clearing, my commander slowed his mount to a walk, and I followed suit. Both horses announced relief with a blow. Uncle Bart seemed a bit too cautious for someone trying to scare off a coyote. He pulled up his horse, looked back, and raised an open hand like he wanted me to stop, then one finger to his lips as if to say, "Be quiet."

It reminded me of when Pop taught my brother Ray and me to use hand signals while squirrel hunting. We had it down pat to the point of knowing exactly what the other was trying to say without speaking a word.

Again, my uncle slowly raised his hand, pointing in a northeastern direction as though he wanted me to see something out in the field. Between tree limbs, I caught a glimpse of movement around a hundred and twenty-five yards out. Couldn't see the entire object because of its position in a shallow ravine. One thing for sure, it wasn't a Holstein. Glancing upward through the tree canopy, I could see the buzzards still circling.

My mind began reeling, considering what might be dead and what might be alive out in that field ahead. I pulled the cigarette pack from my pocket with intentions of lighting up. Uncle Bart shook his head. Knew right then he was serious about something. Keeping my eyes focused on the movement, I nudged Becca forward a couple steps to get a better look. "Believe it's a horse," I whispered.

"Horses don't eat dead stuff," he replied quietly.

That's right, I thought. *A horse don't get around anything dead unless it's ridden there by a man.* Then it happened. A man's head bobbed up and then back down. My heart skipped a beat as I whispered, "There's a man out there."

Uncle Bart nodded in acknowledgement as though he had seen the same thing. We sat in saddle for what felt like an eternity. Then, in short, careful movements, he began to dismount. I followed suit. Once on the ground we both tied off our horses, and I gingerly moved around to my elder's side.

He leaned to my ear. "Surely that sonofabitch ain't butcherin' my cow."

I lost my breath for a moment. Hadn't felt that way since I got buck fever with my first whitetail deer. While I stood perfectly still, waiting for Uncle Bart's next move, my mouth became cotton.

43

"We need to get closer," he whispered. "Follow me and don't make a sound."

When he reached over the saddle for his rifle, I worried, *Holy shit. Is he gonna shoot a man?*

We carefully moved toward the edge of the woods to get a better view. With each step I became more anxious. My hands began to sweat. In less than a minute, we worked ourselves into a spot with a better view of the ravine. I could see a man all right and enough black and white to identify what appeared to be a dead Holstein. After squinting, Uncle Bart drew close. "My eyes ain't what they used to be. Can you make out what's going on?"

The intruder's knife blade flashed in the sun. "Believe he's cutting up the cow," I whispered. "What should we do?"

"I want you to shoot his ass. Can you do that?"

"Me? Why not you?"

"Cause I can't see that far. Here," he bossed, shoving the gun into my hands. "Hurry up now, before he moves out of sight, and make it a head shot."

"Head shot?"

"Yes, a head shot, dammit. Just do as I say."

I waited for Gabrielle's advice but got none.

Uncle Bart placed his fingers in his ears and said, "It's got one in the chamber."

Shaking, I slowly pulled back the hammer until it clicked. Bracing against a tree, I steadied the gun, aligning its bead on my target, and then began squeezing the trigger. Each time the man moved I held what I had until he came back in my sight, then continued the squeeze. Sweat began running down my forehead and across my brows. After what felt like an eternity, the hammer dropped. Kabooooom! Percussive shock waves echoed through the woods. The man's horse jumped but then stood still. There was no sign of the man.

"Did I get 'im?"

My uncle held his finger up, demanding silence as he scanned the area. I stood there, ears ringing and heart beating like a bass drum, thinking, *What the hell did I just do?*

Uncle Bart got close again, "You okay, boy?"

"Yeah. Let's go see if I hit 'im."

"Hold on now, that ain't no deer out there. That's a man. He might still be alive, and he just might have a gun. You wanna galley-wag on out there and find out the hard way?"

Good point, I thought. Never before had I shot at anything that could shoot back. Not knowing what to do, I waited like a dummy for directions, worrying, *What on earth are we gonna do with the body?*

Finally, Uncle Bart said, "Get on your horse, boy. Might as well go on out there and see what kinda damage you did."

"What happened to 'he might still be alive?'"

While mounting his ride, he said, "Can't see anything. Ain't movin'. Reckon you got 'im. Give me that gun just in case."

When I handed over the .30-30, Uncle Bart pulled down the lever and injected a fresh round. He held the rifle with one hand, reigns in the other, as we approached. At about thirty or forty yards out, the man's body came into sight, lying on the ground next to the cow. I mumbled, "Looks like I got 'im," while trotting the horse on in.

"Slow down, boy," my uncle said from behind me. Then all of a sudden, the body jumped up and started screaming.

"Boy, what in the world are you doin'?"

"Oh my God!" My Uncle Willie stood there skinny as ever with a shit-eating grin. Totally pissed, I screamed like a crazy man. "What the hell's going on? Are you nuts? I could have killed you!"

Uncle Bart placed the rifle back into the scabbard, rode close, and then grabbed me, darn near shaking me off the horse. "Easy now. Settle down, and I'll explain."

"Settle down, my ass! What kind of a stupid game is this?" Never before had I been so disrespectful to my elders, but it seemed they deserved it. "I've pulled some dirty jokes in my life, but never—"

"Dammit, boy," hollered Uncle Bart, "said I'd explain, but by hell you gotta settle down first!"

I slid off the mare and stepped next to the carcass. From the smell of things, it had been there for some time. Swelling had begun in the summer heat, and flies were trying to beat the buzzards to a meal. "Okay, somebody explain this to me."

Uncle Willie began. "Johnny, you came down today with some news that knocked us for a loop. Bart tells me that those men who attacked Sissy, raped her, and that you might know who they are. That's somethin' we need to talk about."

"So if you wanted to talk," I snapped back, "why'd we have to go through all this? Why couldn't we just talk?"

Uncle Bart offered, "Because, boy, you spoke like you had some serious revenge in mind for them two fellers. Talk's cheap, you know, but actually pullin' the trigger on a man is a whole 'nother ball game. And I'd say you pulled the trigger a bit too easy."

"You told me to."

"Sure I did, but that don't make it right."

"At least you know I'm willing to shoot a man."

"Yeah, that's true," admitted Uncle Willie, "but that's not the only thing we were lookin' to find out. Boy, you gotta have a good reason to go shootin' someone."

By then I'd grown tired of the lecture. "So what'd you do, put blanks in that rifle?"

"Hellll yes," Uncle Bart grinned. "You don't think I was gonna let you kill my brother, do ya?"

"Well," I huffed, "if it was a real bullet he'd be dead right now."

Uncle Willie said, "No, I wouldn't. Only reason you got a shot at me was because I let you. Heard y'all coming in the woods long before you got close enough to shoot me. Then you come trottin' out here like I was some kinda deer or somethin'. Damn, boy, coulda' shot you three or four times…"

"Hey, I only came out here when Uncle Bart told me to."

"So if he tells you to jump off a bridge, you gonna do that too?"

"What he's tryin' to say," added Uncle Bart, "is that when you're ready to do this kind of thing, you'll know what to do and what not to do, and you won't do it just because someone else says to. You'll do it because you know it is the right thing to do. And you won't be so quick to give up your gun. Don't mean no disrespect, but you got a lot to learn about huntin' men."

My elders seemed to be waiting for a comment. When I didn't speak, Uncle Bart pushed strands of stringy hair back off his sweaty face and said, "Let's get the hell away from this stinkin' cow. We can talk more later. If we don't get back soon, Jane's liable to eat all the leftovers."

No sooner than he spoke, a dinner bell rang in the distance.

Uncle Willie grinned and said, "Girl is impatient, ain't she?"

After spitting out a well-chewed wad of tobacco, Uncle Bart looked me in the eye and said, "Boy, what we done here today ain't nobody else's business. So there's no need for you to be talkin' about it. Understand?"

"Yes Sir, I hear ya."

On our ride back to the house, I got to looking at Uncle Willie's horse, a big Appaloosa, and asked, "How long you had that gelding?"

"About six months."

"No wonder I didn't recognize it. And by the way, Uncle Bart, do you know what killed your cow?"

"Died in the night, tryin' to calve. Bitch of it is, I lost 'em both."

"So you just let the buzzards have her?"

"Yep."

Chapter 7

As usual, I ate too much. Grandma wore her apron proudly and was the last one to sit down. While transferring leftovers from the stove to the table, she said, "What don't get ate is goin' to the hogs."

After the meal, as in the past, I helped with the cleanup. Doing so never really bothered me, yet it seemed like men in the country frowned on such behavior. The old guys were already sitting outside rubbing their stuffed bellies when Jane and I finished drying dishes. We rewarded ourselves with a Coca-Cola from the icebox and then followed Grandma and Aunt Mary to the front porch.

Uncle Bart jabbed, "Nice of you *ladies* to join us."

Instinctively, I struck back. "Well, old man, while you been out here telling lies, Aunt Mary's been in there telling me how pretty you was in lady's underwear."

Grandma about swallowed her teeth, and Uncle Bart growled, "What the Sam hell you talkin' about?"

I said, "Don't go getting all fired up. Just messing with you, like you were messing with me."

Actually, Aunt Mary and Cousin Jane found my comment amusing. Jane played along. "Now Daddy, you know it wasn't me that told him all that stuff, 'cause I promised not to tell."

Grandma had a seat in a rocker and said, "Reckon I need to get me a hickory switch after two youngin's."

Couldn't really tell if Uncle Willie found it amusing, as he seemed to be having a hard time keeping his eyes open. Max, hoping for more attention, kept beat with his long, hairy tail against my chair. Giving in, I made his day. It didn't last long, though. Something else drew the dog's attention. A vehicle I'd never seen before turned off the blacktop, heading up the lane.

"Expectin' Danny Dawson?" Uncle Bart asked.

"No, Daddy," replied Jane. "That there's his sister Paula."

Uncle Willie raised his sleepy head. "Can't believe Danny let 'er drive that car."

"Paula's home for the weekend. She sweet-talked Danny into it. Me and her's gonna run over to the Boone place. They're havin' a little git together for Sheila's birthday. She's twenty-one today."

"Well, you best not be drinkin' over there, young lady," ordered Aunt Mary.

Jane shook her head in disgust. "Mama, I ain't your baby girl no more. I'm almost twenty-one."

"Don't make no difference how old you are. Long as you're livin' under my roof, you'll live by my rules."

Thought to myself, *Same line my parents used.*

"How's come you didn't just meet 'er over there?" questioned Uncle Bart. "Ain't the Boone place a right smart closer to the Dawsons' than it is here?"

"Yes Daddy, but she said she'd pick me up. Besides, think maybe she wanted to meet Johnny."

"Oh well, figured as much."

They spoke of me as though I wasn't there. Didn't matter though, long as I got a good look at this newcomer. She drove a candy apple red, two-door 1972 Chevy Nova with deep-dish chrome reverse wheels.

When the dust settled, I saw my first preference on a woman, long dark hair. *So far so good*, I thought. It only got better as she stepped out of the car. "Daaamn," I uttered at the sight of those tight-fitting Levi's.

"Easy, Johnny," advised Uncle Willie. "There's enough woman there to kill a young boy like you."

"Oh, but what a way to go," I added as the long-legged beauty approached.

"You boys be nice now," advised Grandma.

Jane spoke bluntly, "Grow up, Johnny. You don't gotta act like Daddy's bull. Invited her to meet you, not to be another notch in your." She cut herself short and stepped off the porch.

Surprised and confused at what sounded like jealousy, I downed the rest of my Coca-Cola, trying not to stare. This Paula girl looked to be in her mid-twenties, 5'8" tall and about 125 well-proportioned pounds. Began to think, *Maybe I should be going to the party.* As she stepped up on the porch, I stood and offered, "Would you like a seat, ma'am?"

"Ma'am?" she sassed with a cute country accent. "Hell, I'm not your elder."

"Sorry 'bout that, it's just that we haven't been properly introduced."

"Well, I'll be damned," spoke Jane in a singsong voice. "Let's git proper all of a sudden. Paula, this here's my cousin Johnny. Johnny, meet Paula. That better?"

"Thank you, Jane. Thank you very much. Now Miss Paula, would you like to sit?"

"That's okay. Don't wanna take your seat."

"No, no, I'm fine. Been sitting way too long already."

Uncles Bart and Willie grinned ear-to-ear watching my young ass trying to impress. Grandma gave Paula a good stare, then got up and went into the house.

"How's your folks?" Aunt Mary asked.

"They're just fine and dandy. Mama's gittin meaner, Daddy's gittin fatter. And how 'bout y'all?"

"We're doin' all right," butted in Uncle Bart. "Did Jane say you girls were goin' to a birthday party?"

"Yes, sir. Sheila Boone made twenty-one today, and I reckon we're all gonna celebrate a bit."

The more Paula talked, the more I liked her.

"Johnny, if you're gonna get all bug-eyed, you might as well come with us," Jane suggested in a slightly aggravated voice. "We'll get ya home in time to milk them cows in the mornin' like you promised."

"Yeah, come along," echoed Paula. "Jane talks about you so much, feel like I already know you."

"Sounds good."

"Afraid you won't have time for that," huffed Uncle Willie. "We got business out in the barn. Remember?"

Damn, I thought, *you guys are gonna make me give up an evening with this girl.* The look on their faces said yes. "Uncle Willie's right," I admitted. "Guess I'd better take a rain check."

Jane stepped up on the porch and sassed, "Paula, you come on in the house with me. Gotta run a brush through this hair and I'll be ready to go. We'll let these old men take care of business."

Two seconds after they entered the house, Paula stuck her head back out the door and said with a smile, "Nice to meet you, Johnny."

"You too," I replied.

After she was out of sight, I turned and said, "Believe she likes me."

My uncles laughed.

Aunt Mary stood. "If you men are goin' to the barn, you'd best go now. Hee Haw's fixin' to come on in a little while."

It somehow felt like I was giving up Jane and Paula for Buck Owens and Roy Clark on TV. Didn't seem like a fair trade.

Uncle Bart stopped rocking, stood, stretched, and said, "Wake up, Willie. Mary's right. We need to get started."

"Reckon you're right," admitted Uncle Willie, rubbing his sleepy eyes. "Let's get this done."

"Honey, could you call over to Samuel's and tell him we'll talk later? Tell him me and Willie's gonna be in the barn for a while."

"Sure," she replied on her way in the door.

As we walked to the barn, Uncle Willie said, "Don't blame you a bit, Johnny. If I was a mite younger, I'd be tempted to chase after Paula my own self."

I grinned and said, "Didn't think old men like y'all still had such desires."

"Boy, you gotta lot to learn," snapped Uncle Bart. "In a few years you'll realize we ain't near as old as you think."

By the time we reached the barn, Jane and Paula were hollering, "Bye!" A warm summer breeze feathered my face as I exhaled heavy and watched that bright red Nova roar out of sight.

Chapter 8

I'd been in the barn on many occasions, but never for a *family meeting*. This time, I would be on the inside with the men instead of on the outside, peeking. Adjacent to the milk shed, the old worn structure was used for storing hay and stripping tobacco. That evening, the barn served simply as a meeting place for family matters. I didn't realize just how seriously my uncles took this situation until we were inside. The summer's first cut of hay had already been stacked wall to wall, fifteen bales high. Uncle Willie secured the door while his brother Bart opened a wooden cabinet that hung on the wall. It appeared to be empty except for a quart-size Mason jar.

"Boy, you ever had any 'shine?"

"No sir, but I've heard lots about it."

"Well, this here's the real deal. We're gonna take us a little shot now and another later, before we leave. It's kind of a pact. But first, let me make it clear that what's said and done in this barn stays in this barn. You understand?"

"Yes sir, I do. Hell yes."

Uncle Bart removed the lid from the jar, raised it, toasted, "Here's to the barn," and then took a snort. After just one swallow, he shook his head and said, "Now that's gooood."

Uncle Willie followed suit and squealed, "Ooooweee," before passing the moonshine to me.

"Now you take it easy there, boy," Uncle Bart advised. "This ain't like drinkin' good bourbon. It'll fool ya. Goes down easy, then it burns."

I made no comment, but heeded his wisdom. It did burn. "Damn," I said, shaking my head and holding back a cough.

Uncle Willie smacked me on the back and said, "Welcome to the barn, Johnny Lee. Now let's pray."

Pray? I thought. *In a barn?*

"Bow your head, boy," ordered Uncle Willie as his brother began.

"In the name of the Father, and of the Son, and of the Holy Ghost," he started as they made the sign of the cross and I quickly followed. "Lord, we thank you for this day as we come together to discuss family matters. Give us wisdom, knowledge, and understanding in our endeavors. And please forgive us for any mistakes we might make along the way. Amen."

"And one more thing, Lord," added Uncle Willie. "Help Johnny here understand that in a man's darkest moment he just needs to have faith and follow directions. Amen."

What a strange statement, I thought as we again made the sign of the cross, this time silently, to end the prayer.

I started to light a cigarette, but Uncle Bart said, "Hold on, Johnny Lee. You'll need to wait on that."

Heeding his order, I stood baffled while he returned the moonshine to its cabinet. Uncle Willie had begun tugging at a bale of hay near the bottom, right-hand side of that enormous stack of fescue. He had hold of the grass strings that held the bale together, working the whole thing back and forth as he pulled. Eventually, the bale's removal created an opening.

"I'll go first, you follow me, and Bart can come in behind," said Uncle Willie as though commanding a platoon in Vietnam.

"Hope you ain't scared of the dark," Uncle Bart added as he turned out the lights.

It got dark, but not totally, since the evening sun bled through gaps between the barn boards. "Don't worry about me," I answered. "I'll be okay."

By that time, Uncle Willie had already crawled his way inside the opening. I got down on all fours, but could barely see him as he moved on, allowing me access. "Damn, it *is* dark," I commented while crawling in.

"You ain't seen nothin' yet," chuckled Uncle Willie.

It only took a few seconds to find out what he meant. After sliding in the tunnel backwards, Uncle Bart reached out, grabbed the extracted bale of hay and tugged it into its original position. What little light there had been totally disappeared. "How's that?" he joked.

I felt trapped, wondering, *Where in the world is all this leading?* "So what now?" I whispered.

"You don't have to whisper," said Uncle Bart. "Just follow Willie and be aware there are some turns. First left, then two rights, then left again. Just feel your way through. Eventually, you'll come to a door in the floor. Below the door, there'll be more, but things won't be the same unless you wind up on your back. Then it'll be the same as the way you came."

I began to think the moonshine had gotten to Uncle Bart. He seemed to be talking in riddles. *Is this a game or for real?* After all, these were the same two who had staged the cattle-thieving scenario just a couple of hours earlier.

If not for the overwhelming smell of fescue, I might have imagined I was in some labyrinth beneath a medieval castle. The tunnel had just enough height to crawl and barely enough width to turn around. "This must be how a groundhog feels."

"You'll get used to it," Uncle Bart answered.

Since the first turn would be on my left, I kept patting my left hand along the bales in search of the gap, and soon found it after about ten feet.

Not so bad.

It only took another eight to ten feet of crawling to find the first right. That's when I realized I could no longer hear Uncle Willie ahead. Obviously, he moved on faster because of familiarity with the way. *Hopefully he'll have the door in the floor open for me. Surely, there'll be some kind of light.*

I stopped to wait on Uncle Bart, but heard nothing. "Uncle Bart? Where are you?" Still nothing. No sound at all. "Bullshit. Hope you guys aren't messing with me again." Being alone gave the blackness a new dimension. "If you guys are playing, I'm not impressed." Still nothing.

On many occasions, I had walked into the woods before daylight, in search of a tree stand for deer hunting. With a cloudy sky, it would be dark, but nothing like that lightless maze beneath tons of hay. "You guys are pissing me off!"

For a few seconds, I hesitated, listening, thinking, and wiping a gritty mixture of dust and sweat off my forehead. So far there had been one left turn and one right. I didn't see any reason to doubt Uncle Bart's directions. Continuing like a test rat in a maze, I found the second right and then the final left. *Now,* I wondered, *how far to the door, and will it be obvious?* One thing for sure, there wasn't any light at the end of the tunnel. Then I heard something. Pausing and remaining quiet, I heard it again, this time recognizing the sound as one from the stock pens at work. It was that squeaky little noise a rat makes. "Shit!"

So I'm not the only rat in this maze. Had it been light enough to see, that wouldn't bother me nearly as much. *Just keep moving.*

Moments later, my hand found wood. By rubbing across its surface, I found a small hole, just big enough for one finger. Looking through it revealed nothing but more darkness. "Damn!" No light and no sounds. With my right index finger, I used the hole to pull up on the wood. It hinged up and against the end of the tunnel.

I turned around to drop in feet first. My nose began to tingle from breathing too much dust. "Aaaawwwcheww." From the direction I'd just crawled, there came that rat noise again. They were following.

My feet found ground and it felt good to be standing upright. After a few seconds of stretching my legs, I squatted and began feeling for the direction of the tunnel. This time the walls were dirt and rock. "No shit, Sherlock. You're underground." Another wooden board kept me from moving forward. When I pushed, it hinged upward easily, opening one pathway while apparently sealing the other. Reaching up, I found the door above me had not only closed, but also locked, thus limiting travel to one direction. Turning back would no longer be an option. For a moment, I sat slumped against the cool wall, anxiously reassessing the situation. *Wouldn't be here if they had doubts about my surviving this stupid test.*

Scratching noises above the wood sent me back to my knees. Moving forward, the tunnel became smaller in both width and height. What felt like little pieces of root protruded here and there from the cool, damp walls. It seemed too much a perfect setting for insects and snakes. Eventually, what had to be tree roots hanging in my face, forced me to crawl on my stomach. Inching along with my elbows, I found an intersection. "Now what? Which way?"

Trying not to panic, I recalled Uncle Willie's words, '...in the darkest moment you simply have faith and follow directions...'

But what were the directions?

'Below the door there will be more but it won't be the same unless you wind up on your back. Then it's the same as the way you came.'

So what the heck does that mean? They expect me to do this on my back...or is it just a way to get directions? It seemed worth a try. Listening carefully for rats, I rolled over on my back, tried to relax, and closed my eyes to think. *If you wind up on your back, it's the way you came. So how did I come? One left, two rights, left again.*

"Holy shit, Batman. I get it." A right turn on my knees would be a left turn on my back. That would make it the same as the way I came. One left, two rights and then one more left. "Bingo." Remaining on my back, I decided to take the turn on my left, all the while wondering where the other path might take me. In trying to visualize my exact location, the turns suggested somewhere behind the barn, possibly near an old storm cellar built into the hill.

Finding the next turn relieved some of my worry. It at least felt like I was traveling in the correct direction. From there the ceiling clearance grew closer with every inch scooted. Small stringy roots brushed my face. I tried to roll over on my stomach but there simply wasn't enough room. Moist soil above me broke loose, falling on my face. Spitting dirt, eyes closed and arms stretched ahead, I tugged forward. The tunnel had become so narrow it felt like a coffin. With barely room to wiggle, I could no longer raise my knees to get a good push with my heels. Even retreat seemed impossible. Breathing became difficult. *Stay calm, stay calm,* I repeated as my outstretched hands reached some sort of opening. Forcing my way through caused clods of dirt to fall. Something moved on my arm. Another, then another. *Ants?*

Within a matter of seconds, the tingling movements were under my shirt and up my pants legs. I couldn't reach down to rub them off, and I damn sure couldn't stay there while they ate me alive. Painful, pinching sensations moved up my thighs. In a panic, I growled and snarled, clawing forward with every ounce of my remaining energy. The tunnel sloped downward, offering more headroom. After ten feet or so, I had enough space to stand and reach my Zippo cigarette lighter. In the flickering yellow light, I could see and feel ants all over me: my hair, my neck, my back. I pulled off my shirt and boots, dropped my drawers and went at the little shits, smacking and scraping like a crazy man. By the time I plucked and flipped away those that had locked to my skin, the lighter dimmed. Thankfully, I'd gotten away from the source.

Closing the lighter, I stood exhausted, using my fingers to examine whelps on my legs, buttocks, and torso. I ran my fingers through my hair, shook and beat on my jeans, hoping to make them bug free, and then put them on. Did the same with my shirt. At that, I was grateful to be upright. After a couple deep inhales, trying to get my breathing back to normal, I continued and soon found the next turn.

Determined to save the lighter for absolute necessities, I felt my way with one hand while rubbing wounds on my neck with the other.

Beyond what I estimated to be the final turn, there were several indentions in the walls—nothing more than cubbyholes for God knows what. Uncles Willie and Samuel had both told me stories about the Cu Chi tunnels around Saigon. I never dreamed they were building their own.

The smell of hay again found way to my nostrils, and that made no sense. The walls became less dirt and more rock. Several feet later, I ran into a knotted rope hanging from the ceiling. Lighting the Zippo revealed a pit ten feet wide, spanned by a single 2x6 board turned on its edge and notched into the dirt.

"What the hell?" I couldn't tell the hole's depth, but noticed that the rope looped through several large roots in the ceiling. *Well now, do they want me to use the rope to hand walk this wobbly thing? Maybe they're just testing to see if I'm dumb enough to try.*

With no other options in sight, I closed the lighter, and inched my way onto the contraption. What first seemed difficult turned out to be rather simple. *Why go to so much trouble to dig a pit if it's this easy to cross?* After reaching the other side, it dawned on me that by cutting the rope and pushing the board into the pit, crossing would become virtually impossible.

Feeling more confident, I moved on. Seconds later my face crashed into a dead end, smashing my nose. "Son of a ... this is bull." As blood trickled over my lip, I stuck my tongue out, accepting the warm taste.

There had to be an exit, yet feeling both sides revealed none. Reaching above my head, I discovered one. "Praise the Lord."

Chapter 9

By pushing the door open, I found a rat's reward, a room complete with uncles. Someone turned on a light and it about blinded me. "Welcome to the family room," congratulated Uncle Willie. "What took you so long?"

Squinting, I recognized my father. "Uncle Bart, you weren't supposed to—"

"Now, now, boy, before you go gettin' upset, let me explain. I know you didn't wanna include your daddy, and for good reasons, but that would be a mistake. Earlier today you asked, 'What if it were Jane?' Believe me, if it were Jane and my brothers left me out, I'd never forgive 'em."

Uncle Samuel offered me a hand. "Come up out of that hole."

I gladly accepted. Pop took my other hand and the two lifted me up. "What's with the bloody nose?" Pop asked.

"It's dark down there. Ran into the wall. Believe you guys are trying to kill me."

"Did you learn anything about yourself?" probed Uncle Samuel while surveying my bug-bitten arms and scuffed elbows.

"Yeah. Learned that in a man's darkest moment he should keep faith and follow directions."

"Good job," Uncle Bart replied while smacking me on the back. "Hoped you were payin' attention."

"Also learned I don't like piss-ants. Ran into a nest of 'em and they about ate me up."

"I can see that," acknowledged my father. "Got whelps on your arms and neck."

"Got whelps in places you don't wanna see."

They all laughed as Pop brushed dirt and a couple stubborn ants off the back of my shirt. The room was no bigger than 12 x 14 feet. Cluttered about were a couple metal cabinets, what looked like a gun safe, four lounge chairs, and a wooden spool used as a makeshift table. Uncle Samuel moved the spool to cover the door in the floor. Both ceiling lights had clear incandescent bulbs controlled by pull strings. Only one was lit.

"Why couldn't y'all at least give me a doggone flashlight?"

Uncle Willie said, "Shoot no, that would take all the fun out of it."

"And by the way," I asked, "how deep is that pit?"

"Deep enough to scare your ass if you'd fallen in," he continued. "Like to say it's full of snakes, the way they were in 'Nam, but it ain't. Filled the bottom with hay in case you fell."

Uncle Bart said, "Hey guys, we can talk about the tunnels later. Right now it's gettin' late, and we need to take care of business."

My father started. "Son, hope you understand why I have to be involved. Be more likely to have a heart attack if I found out my brothers didn't include me."

"So, why'd you keep it from them about Sissy being raped?"

"Back then we thought the police would find whoever did it. If I'd said something, these guys woulda wanted to get involved. By the time I realized the police weren't gonna arrest anyone—well—I decided to keep it private for Sissy's sake. It was an awful thing what happened to her, and she still ain't got over it. Never will, I suspect. And I'm sure she'd rather the whole family didn't know what happened to her."

Pop glanced around the room at his brothers and then continued. "Things have changed. Before, we didn't have a clue as to who did it. Reckon now we do. Now we have a reason to work together. And I feel certain no one in this room is gonna spread Sissy's grief."

"But what about Ray?" I asked. "He knows about the rape. Should we tell him what we're up to?"

"No, Johnny, you were right not tellin' your brother. It's better that way. Same goes for your mother and Sissy."

Uncle Samuel offered his opinion. "The fewer people who know about what's goin' on, the better."

"Someday," added Uncle Bart, "we might let 'em all know how proper justice got served, but first we have to figure out what we're gonna do, how we're gonna do it, and when. For now, you just start from the beginning and tell everyone here what you told me this morning."

I found out that day what family was all about. I repeated everything said by the two men at work, gave their names, Pete Metcalf and Joe Simpson, and what I knew about them.

My father then made it clear to me that I should have nothing to do with whatever had to be done. "Do not associate with these two guys. If they speak to you, just be polite and move on. Don't want anyone to be able to connect you with them in any way."

"But Pop, I'd like to be in on whatever gets done."

"Hell no," he snapped. "Not yet. Done heard about your little episode in the field today. Ain't tryin' to run you down, son, but from what your uncles told me, you've got a lot to learn."

"Just doing as I was told. Guess I got caught up in the moment."

"You said the right word, son. *Caught.* Man goes after those two guys you work with like you went after your Uncle Willie, guarantee he gets caught. This ain't easy stuff. Huntin' down another man is somethin' you have to live with the rest of your life. This ain't Vietnam, and this ain't Korea, and if you kill someone, dammit, the law's gonna be lookin' for you from now on."

"I hear ya."

"Don't make light of what I'm sayin'. If we decide to take out the sombitches that raped my daughter, it'll be because we know they did it. If we know they did it, and there ain't no way the law can take care of 'em, then *maybe* we will. But by God, if we do, there can't be any room for mistakes."

"He's right," added Uncle Bart. "Stay as far away from this thing as possible. Especially since you work with 'em."

Uncle Willie tapped his boot, shook his head, and said, "Damn, guys, seems pretty cut and dry to me. James, your boy done heard those two men talkin' about what they did. I say we git 'em off somewhere, talk to 'em ourselves, and if they did it, we do 'em right then and there."

"Easy, brother," butted in Uncle Bart. "If Daddy were here today, he'd tell you, 'Don't go killin' nobody if the law can take care of 'em.' No need for rushin' in."

"It ain't about rushing in, dammit. Do it now and nobody will suspect us. Get the law involved, that means dragging Sissy through court. Ask me, the girl's been through enough already. And then what if they don't get convicted? Our hands'll be tied. Anything happens to 'em, we'll be the first ones the law comes looking for."

"Good point," replied my father, "but I'd still like to see if the evidence collected after Sissy got raped can be connected to these two men. If it can, they'll go to prison."

"Go ahead," Uncle Willie snapped back. "Just walk on in there and ask the police if they can do somethin' about them boys. If they do, it'll surprise me. If they don't, then what are we gonna do?"

Pop stood there scratching his chin and said, "Samuel, our friend at the Louisville Police Department. Reckon she can look into things without connecting us to it?"

"Don't think she'd mind doin' us a favor, but the question is can she?"

"Hold on, boys." Uncle Bart had his concerns. "Having her check out the license plate of those idiots who were dumping garbage on Samuel's place is one thing. What we're talking about here is a whole lot more serious."

"Dammit, James," scorned Uncle Willie, "why you wanna get that girl involved?"

"Seems to me she was the one who came to us about getting' involved. Wasn't our fault our old friend slipped up and told her to come see us."

"Hey now," said Uncle Bart, "None of us minded helpin' her out. At least she got her car back, and everything in it."

"Yeah," finished my father, "and I'll bet those little punks never steal another vehicle."

I had no idea who they were talking about.

Uncle Samuel said, "I'm confident we can trust her. Just need to make sure she knows where this could lead. If we end up taking care of those bastards ourselves, can't have her fallin' apart." The elders all nodded in agreement. "Regardless of whether or not we use *her*, we gotta do something. Those two men Johnny described, they're some real wackos. Considerin' all they done to Sissy, my guess is they've done it again since and will continue until someone stops 'em."

"See there, that's what I'm sayin'," snapped Uncle Willie. "Hell, James, you always said, 'If it was my kid, know what I'd do.' Well, this here *is* your kid. Believe we oughta stop 'em right now, or as soon as we can."

Everybody looked at Pop, and Uncle Bart asked, "James?"

Father hesitated. "Willie's right. But dammit, we're gonna check things out. Wanna be sure that they are the ones who did it. And I want the third man's name. We find out there's indisputable evidence linking them to the rape, we'll let the law take care of 'em. Don't necessarily wanna put Sissy through it, but we might have to. On the other hand, if we find out it is them, but there's not enough evidence, we'll go Willie's route. Samuel, you check with our girl. Talk to her about how to do this without getting herself or us in trouble. We'll wait and make a decision after we hear back from her. Whaya say, Willie?"

"Guess that'll work. Just make sure the girl fully understands our intentions."

I stood there listening. Not once did they ask my opinion. And they seemed to be going out of their way to avoid saying the girl's name. To confuse me even more, they all stuck their fist out to touch, sort of like a toast without glasses. Then they looked my way and waited for me to join them. I did.

Pop spoke first, "Together?"

Everyone repeated at the same time with me chiming in a little behind: "Together." It seemed we were done discussing family matters. By pushing on a portion of the wall, my father exposed the second entrance I'd anticipated. Thankfully, this tunnel was short and had been built tall enough to walk through.

After his brothers entered and opened the door at the other end, Pop pulled the string, turning out the bulb above. Light bled through from the other end. I entered, and he followed, closing the door behind us. The tunnel opened up into the storm cellar, just as I had suspected. A tall pantry, complete with dusty can goods and a few Mason jars, hinged into position, hiding the tunnel's opening. These guys were extremely thorough in covering their tracks. Again, there were two lights on the ceiling. "Hey dad, what's the second light for?"

"It's connected to the light in the barn. If someone turns it on, this light and one in the family room both come on as a warning."

We all left the storm cellar together and entered the barn through its back door. Once inside, Uncle Bart opened the cabinet and extracted the jar of moonshine. He took a swig and then offered it to me. "Never," he said, "are you to come here and open this cabinet or enter those tunnels or the family room without first discussing it with one of us."

Before we exited the barn, Pop told Samuel, "When you find out something, let me know. We'll all meet back here."

As the five of us marched away from the barn, I began whistling Elgar's "Pomp and Circumstance."

Pop said, "You've got it backwards, son. That wasn't graduation. More like initiation."

Chapter 10

When Willie and Samuel left, Uncle Bart went inside the house to watch Hee Haw with Aunt Mary. Pop and I took a seat on the porch. We both sat quietly for a moment, and then he asked, "Whatcha' thinkin' about, Son?"

"Everything. It's been a hell of a day."

"I'd say." His hesitation told me Pop had something on his mind. Finally he said, "You told Bart that your grandpa talked to you about justice and family. What exactly did he say?"

"Not much. He was just giving advice, or at least that's what it seemed like at the time."

"Did he ever tell you about this house and how we came about living here?"

"No. You mean you weren't born here?"

"Samuel was. Me, Bart, and Willie, we were born over there where Willie lives now. It was all part of the original Smith property. My grandparents, your great-grandparents, Johan and Sophie Smith, they lived here. This is where my father and his sisters were born. In the old house. When my father got married, Granddad deeded him a hundred acres. Willie's place. During World War II, while my father was over in Germany, there was a fire in the night. Burned the house, and killed both my grandparents and Uncle Luke."

"Luke?"

"Uncle Luke was a good ol' boy with a weak mind, incapable of making adult decisions. He dropped out of school early. Never did learn how to read. Man was happy just living here, working on the farm. Shame they all had to go that way. Daddy's sisters took care of all the funeral arrangements. Problem was, with him overseas, wasn't anyone here knew anything about Grandpa's financial affairs. Practically everything, including the farm's deed, got lost in ashes. Realizing the situation, some asshole banker took it on himself to draft a mortgage note listing the Smith farm as collateral. His name was J.P. Garrett Jr. No one knew better, and the bank claimed all of the Johan Smith property. When my father came home from the war, he protested the note, but was unable to prove his case. Law wouldn't return the farm to its rightful heirs.

"Now this J.P. fellow, him and your grandpa never did get along. More than once, they wound up in fisticuffs down at the schoolhouse. J.P. didn't mind bringing attention to the dissimilarity between his new clothes and my daddy's worn, sometimes torn, hand-me-downs.

"J.P's. father, John Garrett Sr., was a good honest man. Did well in the farm implement business. Because of his poor roots, he had a sense of respect for those in need without immediate means. If a man needed a plow, a disk, or even a tractor but had no money, John Garrett would work a deal for credit according to the purchaser's ability to pay back. He often allowed farmers to be late with payments. His style of business brought more business. Problem was, he spoiled his son rotten.

"Once J.P. Jr. figured out the process of lending on time and interest, he chose a career in banking. Unfortunately, his spoiled ways had hardened his young heart. Man saw only the bottom line profit in lending money. Developed a reputation for lending to those who likely couldn't meet payment requirements, thus leading to easy acquisition of collateral properties. When he forged my Granddaddy's mark on that note, most folks figured the old man had fallen on hard times and mortgaged the property.

"Now there was another farm, not far from here, that had been repossessed through much the same process when its owner, Henry Dawson, died in the war. Henry was survived by his widow, two sons and four daughters. The oldest boy turned eighteen right after my father returned from the war. When he got wind of the Smith farm being taken, Darrel Dawson came by our place. I remember him and

Daddy standin' out in the cold, talkin'. After a few swigs of moonshine, I reckon they decided to pay a little visit to Mr. J.P. Jr."

For the next thirty minutes, Pop sat there on Uncle Bart's porch telling me the story that I'm sure he was told by his father.

In 1945, J.P. Garrett Jr. lived on a 40-acre plot off Highway 88 near Bear Creek. He and his wife Jenny would likely be alone on a cold Saturday morning and hopefully wouldn't get company until later in the day. Robert Smith, medium height, strong and thick, and the taller, thinner Darrel Dawson hid in the dark. Both men leaned their double-barreled shotguns against the back of the small barn where J.P. garaged his shiny black 1940 Ford Coupe. Expecting the hound might cause a ruckus, they brought along a warm, meaty hambone to keep Buck busy. It only took a few seconds for the old dog to catch wind of it. Darrel quietly smooth-talked while teasing with the smelly bait. Moments later, he had ol' Buck tied to a fence post, lying down, and contentedly chewing on that bone.

Reaching in his coat pocket, the elder man pulled out a plug of tobacco. "How 'bout a chew?"

Darrel shivered a bit, blowing on his hands to warm them, adjusted his cap and said, "Don't mind if I do."

Lights came on in the house. "Won't be long now," whispered Robert.

About a minute later, the back outside light came on. "Hey Buck, here boy," hollered J.P. as he stepped to the edge of the porch and took a leak.

Young Darrel held the dog's snout tight so it couldn't bark.

"Damn hound's done gone and run off again," complained J.P. as he gathered several pieces of firewood off a stack on the porch and entered the house.

Ten minutes passed, a distant rooster crowed, and the soon-to-rise sun broke the darkness. "So what we gonna do if he don't come back out?" worried Darrel.

"If that ornery sombitch don't come out shortly, I'll just have to send you in after him," teased Robert. "Course I expect he'll be out soon to take a shit. Don't you always have to go in the mornin'?"

"Depends."

"On what?"

"Depends on whether or not I eat me a big meal before goin' to bed."

"Well I figure that asshole eats good every night."

As Robert spoke, the back door opened again. This time J.P. exited with a hot cup of coffee in one hand and a fresh roll of paper in the other.

"Bingo," whispered Robert, reaching for his shotgun. "Hold on to that dog."

Darrel again held and comforted the hound until J.P. walked the hundred-foot path between the porch and the small wooden outhouse. From behind the barn, the two men were only about 45 feet away. Darrel whispered, "Now what?"

"Grab your gun. We're gonna sneak on up there. When I nod, you open the door, and I'll have 'im in my sights. Then just do as I say."

"But what if his ol' lady hears us?"

"That's why we gotta be quiet, stupid. We'll keep an eye on the house."

The two moved away from the barn and toward the outhouse as quietly as possible, boots crunching slightly in the morning frost. As they got there, that old dog, still tied to the post, began barking. Robert nodded. With his shotgun in one hand, the teenager reached for the door.

"Who's out there?" called J.P.

Startled, the boy hesitated and glanced back. When Robert nodded again, Darrel grabbed the wooden handle, pulled open the door, and backed away a couple steps.

"What the hell?" yelled J.P. as he stood up, pants still at his ankles and the steaming cup of coffee in his right hand.

"Shut your mouth, J.P., or I swear to God I'm gonna kick your ass right here in the shitter," demanded Robert in a low voice.

69

"What the hell you want?" J.P. asked again.

Without a word, Robert swung the butt of his gun up, striking J.P. in the chin and knocking him backwards. Hot coffee flew out the door and all over Robert as the stunned, fat-bellied man fell back onto the wooden seat. "I told you to shut your mouth. You understand?" insisted Robert quietly, aiming the shotgun at J.P.'s chest.

This time J.P. just nodded while reaching for his pants.

"No, leave 'em down and git your sorry ass up. Come on out here real slow. Me and you and young Darrel here's gonna go in that barn and talk a little business."

J.P. almost fell when he stumbled down the single step, blood dripping from his busted chin. Buck continued to bark as his master shuffled forward, closely followed by his captors. Nearing the barn, Darrel nudged Robert, glanced at the house, and then back toward the dog.

Robert whispered, "You open that door and then go untie the dog. Bring me the rope."

As J.P. waddled in, Darrel took off.

"Git on over there by the car," ordered Robert.

J.P. attempted to talk again. "Hope you don't think you're gonna get away with this."

Robert hesitated, peeking out the door at the house. When the dog quit barking he said, "You cheated us out of our farms, J.P. We intend to get 'em back."

Darrell came in the door. "Dog's bone was out of reach."

"Gimme the rope. Keep your gun up in case he tries somethin'."

Robert leaned his shotgun against the grill of the Ford and began tying J.P. to one of the tall cedar posts that supported the roof rafters. Desperate, J.P. tried to reason with Darrel. "Boy, you gonna let this crazy man get you put in prison?"

Darrel snarled and then spit tobacco juice in J.P.'s face. "You think Robert's crazy, wait 'til I get done with ya'."

Robert finished tying the final knot while J.P. bent his neck, wiping spit juice mixed with drying blood off his chin onto his shirt.

Darrel continued, "Just wish my daddy was here to kick your big, fat ass."

J.P., in his half-naked state, began shaking in the cold.

"Now as I was sayin'," said Robert. "Before we leave this here barn, you'll either figure a way to give us back our farms or someone else might have to service Miss Jenny, 'cause I'm gonna make a steer outta you."

"You're out of your mind."

"Might be, but you stealin' my daddy's farm made me that way. Know damn well you forged his mark on that mortgage note."

"You don't know that," snapped J.P.

"Sure I do. My daddy saved ever spare dime he ever made. Just cause he didn't trust your bank ain't no sign he didn't have money."

"Times were hard while you were away, Robert. Your daddy ran out of money and came to me."

"Bullshit! When I came home, Daddy's money lay right where he hid it. He saved up to help take care of Luke and Momma, case something should happen to him. You're a liar and a thief, J.P."

"You gotta understand, Robert, I thought you were dead," pleaded J.P., "and with your parents and that retard brother of yours gone, who was gonna run the farm, anyway?"

"Oh, I see," interrupted Darrel, "you figured Robert was dead like *my* daddy. You's just screwin' his family like you did ours. My daddy never got no money from your bank. When he needed money, he borrowed from Uncle Charlie in Chicago. You faked both them mortgages. I oughta kill you right now."

"Easy, Darrel. J.P's gonna get our farms back. Ain't that right?"

"There's nothing I can do, Robert. The bank's done foreclosed, and it's all about to be sold at auction."

Robert pulled out his pocket knife and said, "Well then, looks like I'm gonna have to follow up on my promise. Darrel, reckon you can hold J.P.'s little pecker out the way while I geld 'im?"

J.P. began squirming and shouting, "Don't do this, Robert. I'll figure something out!"

"Hold on there!" shouted a voice from behind. "Ain't nobody cuttin' on *my* man." In the open doorway stood Jenny Garrett, hair sticking out all wild, wearing a winter coat over her night gown, and holding up a shotgun of her own.

Seeing his wife with the upper hand, J.P. began pleading, "Jenny, these crazy bastards were about to kill me. Make 'em untie me so I can call the Sheriff."

Robert knew Jenny from school. "Jenny, it ain't what it looks like. I can explain."

"First I want you to put that knife back in your pocket. Then both of you step away from those guns."

Darrel and Robert looked at one another.

"I mean it, Robert," insisted Jenny. "Don't make me do something I don't wanna do."

Robert moved away from J.P., leaving his double barrel against the '40 Ford. Darrel followed suit, lowering his shotgun to the ground.

"God I love you, baby," grinned J.P. "Now get me untied!"

"Not yet. Ain't turnin' your sorry butt loose until you explain to me what I just heard y'all talkin' about."

Darrel looked at Robert. Robert winked.

Jenny continued, "You forged those notes, didn't you?"

"Now honey, you never heard me say that!"

"Believe I heard enough."

"But they were about to cut me."

"You know, J.P., always knew you were capable of lying, but I never thought you'd go this far. I've known Robert ever since we were kids. Tell you right now, he ain't no liar..."

"But honey..."

"Don't 'but honey' me. And how can you call his brother Luke a retard? Man's dead, for Christ's sake."

"But Jenny, I'm freezing. You gotta untie me so I can pull my pants up. Then I'll explain."

"No, not yet. You'll be fine right there until these two are gone. Don't want anybody gettin' hurt."

"Dammit, you can't just let them walk out of here after what they've done to me."

"J.P., after what I just heard, you're lucky *I* don't cut your balls off."

Darrel couldn't help but laugh.

Jenny snapped back, "This ain't funny, boy."

"Sorry, ma'am."

Jenny lowered her shotgun slightly and said, "Okay Robert, want you and this boy to go on home and leave those guns here. I'll see to it you get em' back later on."

"Now Miss Jenny," spoke Robert, "me and Darrel, we came here with a purpose. We need them farms back, and that ain't about to change just 'cause you make us walk away."

"Robert, I swear you ain't heard the last of this. I'll call J.P.'s daddy. He surely can figure a way to keep y'all from losin' your property."

Satisfied that Jenny would be true to her word and that things would be set right in the end, Robert nodded at Darrel.

Still tied, cold, and shaking his head, J.P. complained, "I swear to God, can't believe you're doing this."

"Shut up, J.P. Now Robert, y'all get on outta here."

On his way through the door, Robert expressed gratitude. "Jenny, hope you know how much this means to me and my family."

"Mine too," added Darrel.

When Pop finished his story, he stood to leave and said, "Eventually, John Garrett Sr. bought both farms at auction. Man turned right around and sold 'em back to us and the Dawson's for one dollar each. In return, both families agreed not to press charges on J.P. When the bank fired him, he and Jenny moved away, somewhere up in Indiana."

I stayed on the porch while Pop said his goodbyes to Uncle Bart and Aunt Mary. Couldn't help but wonder how long the Smith family had been taking matters of justice into their own hands. How easy it seemed for Uncle Willie to consider ending the lives of the two men who had participated in the inhumane attack on my sister. How even my father had agreed to do so in the event the law could not provide legal justice. At that moment, sitting on the porch of the house that my grandfather had built, lived in, and died in, I felt sure that were he there, he would feel the same. On his way back out, Pop ruffled my hair and said, "You have questions, call me. And, stay the hell away from those two boys at work." The sun inched below treetops across the field as I sat there watching his pickup disappear. In the distance, a groundhog nibbled its evening meal while Uncle Bart's Holstein bull wailed in desire for one of the cows. *What a day,* I thought. *What a day of initiation.*

Chapter 11

It sure seemed like a dream that dark Sunday morning, sleeping in Cousin Jake's bed. Already warm, wearing nothing but boxers, I felt as though I was wedged between two hot bodies.

"Wake up, Johnny," whispered the voice on my left, which I easily identified to be that of Cousin Jane. No doubt the sweet-smelling thing on my right had to be Paula.

My first choice would be to snuggle with the girls for a couple more hours of sleep, but that wasn't going to happen. "What time is it?"

"Almost time for you to start milkin' them cows, Johnny Lee," answered Jane in a quiet, sassy voice.

Paula licked my ear and whispered with vodka breath, "Can you come outside and play? We'll make it worth your while."

Jesus Christ, I thought, *they should bottle this stuff.* I rolled over on my stomach to avoid embarrassment, and said, "Y'all get the hell out of here, and I'll be down in a minute."

"Okay, but don't be too long," insisted Jane. "That old rooster's gonna be wakin' everybody up in just a little bit."

The two of them slithered out of bed and down the stairs. They giggled their way out the front door while I forced myself to rise for fear of dozing off. After slipping on a tee shirt and my jeans, I tiptoed barefoot down the steps. Just outside the front door, Jane and Paula sat chatting patiently. Easing out onto the steps, I said, "Excuse me a minute. Gotta make a trip around the corner."

While taking a leak in the morning dew, I could hear Jane and Paula's whispers, but not enough to make out what they were saying.

On my return, both girls stood and headed toward the tobacco barn. "Follow us," mouthed Jane.

And I did. Like a puppy on a chain, I followed two well-shaped silhouettes. We wound up next to the barn, where Uncle Bart had an area for cutting firewood. Jane stopped and said, "Check this out, Johnny." From a cigarette pack, she extracted a skinny joint. "Can you handle some?"

Jane took a seat on a piece of a tree trunk normally used as a chopping block. Paula joined her, placing an arm around Jane's waist to keep from falling off. Together they looked like sisters.

I had smoked with Jane before, but not in front of strangers. "Probably shouldn't do that," I said, staring into Jane's eyes.

"Shit, Johnny, you don't have to worry about Paula. I've known her since we were kids."

"Well, that ain't been too long now has it?"

"Ha, ha. You can kiss my butt."

"So y'all done tried this stuff?"

"No, not yet, been waitin' on you. Paula can't smoke 'cause where she works they're gonna make 'er pee on Monday. She thought you might want her part."

"Is that right?" Truth be told, I was more interested in Paula than the joint. "Well that's mighty considerate, and I do appreciate it, but..."

The old rooster began crowing. Dawn had reached Grayson County enough to see cows gathering out by the milk shed.

"But what?" Jane asked.

"But, I don't need to be reeking. Your daddy might smell it."

"Ain't like he never smoked this stuff before."

Hoping Paula wouldn't see, I shook my head slightly as if to say, "Keep quiet." Figured Uncle Bart had done some crazy things in his day, but that didn't need to be any of Paula's business.

A talker the night before, Paula sat quiet. With heavy eyelashes and a mischievous grin, she stared. Finally, she whispered into Jane's ear.

"Stop that," Jane snapped as she stood, pulling loose from Paula's hold.

When the rooster crowed again, Jane peeked around the corner of the barn and said, "Light's on. Daddy's up. Guess I oughta be gittin' in. Paula, you look like you can drive now."

"Hey," I said to Paula, "I'm gonna be making coffee in a minute. Want me to bring you out a cup?"

Jane glared. "She ain't got time for all that. Needs to get Danny's car home before he wakes up."

Paula rose, obviously disappointed. "She's right. Best get on home." Then she winked and said, "Shame we didn't leave the party earlier."

With Jane leading the way, we walked toward the house, stopping at the Nova. Paula gave Jane a hug and a quick kiss, strangely, to the lips. The sight of that gave me an odd feeling.

Paula climbed in, started the engine, and, before closing the door, said, "Call me later."

"Will do," Jane answered.

As Paula backed out, she rolled down the window. "Hope to see you again real soon, Johnny."

"Sounds good," I answered while walking along side of the car as it pulled away. "Maybe we can go down to the jamboree and watch 'em play music."

When the Nova reached the creek, Jane let me have it. "What the hell's up with you, Johnny? First you act like you don't trust her. Then you wanna ask her out?"

"Ask her out? I was asking you both out."

"Bullshit," she jabbed while walking to the house.

"And besides that," I continued, "does your daddy know you go around talking about him smoking weed?"

Jane stopped on the porch, and asked, "Are you really that paranoid?"

"It's not about *me* being paranoid. Old people I know who smoke weed don't go around advertising it."

"Okay. I get your point. Just don't go say anything to him about what I said."

Changing the subject, I asked, "So, what kind of job does Paula have?"

"She works at the Louisville Police Department."

"You're shitting me! And you want me to smoke with a cop!"

"She ain't no cop. She's a clerk. Does office work."

"And by the way, what's with the kiss on the lips?"

"What's that supposed to mean?"

"Guess that's what I'm asking. What does it mean?"

"It's just a girl thing, Johnny. Nothing more. You men are all alike," Jane mumbled as she opened the door and headed off to the bathroom.

If my grandmother never taught me anything else, she taught me the simple art of making coffee. Hot and strong was all that really mattered. Running water from the sink, I thought about how lucky Uncle Bart and Aunt Mary were to have indoor plumbing, remembering days when they did not. My mother's parents lived nearby, and they still didn't have running water. For them and their children, walking downhill a quarter mile to the closest well had always been a daily chore. Early on, I accompanied Grandpa while he carried a bucketful with each hand, some of which would splash out on the way back.

I remember asking Grandpa why he didn't have the well at the top of the hill and the house on the bottom. That way it would be easier to carry the full buckets downhill. He just laughed and said, "A lot of things in this world seem backwards until you get old enough to understand."

As time went on, I made trips to the well by myself. Being such a little fellow, I had to stop to rest along the way. To me, what others took for granted became a world of beauty and adventure. There were cardinals, robins, mockingbirds, doves and bobwhites. Sometimes I got lucky and would startle a young cottontail rabbit or a black snake as I made a turn in the path. An oak stump about midway provided a resting place. Perched on that stump, I'd look down at the ground in wonder at a world of plants, insects and the like, items most would overlook. Nature indeed had been my first love. I enjoyed all the different forms of vegetation, even the chigger weed with its intricate color and structure, admirable but untouchable.

It was during one of those trips to the well that I first met Mary Ellen. She also had come for a bucket of water. When I offered to pull the heavy full bucket up for her, she refused, saying, "You think I can't do it."

We were young and didn't say much to one another. As we parted I glanced back only to see her doing the same. That night, when Grandpa Wilson and I stood admiring the Clarkson town lights on the distant horizon, I asked, "Grandpa, am I too young to understand women?"

He shook his head and said, "Believe it or not, I'm still too young to understand women."

Before Jane could return from the toilet, Uncle Bart joined me in the kitchen. "Didn't expect to see you up so early."

"Well, you can thank Jane for that. She woke me up a while ago."

"Wonder what time she got home?"

Jane entered the room just in time to answer his question. "Don't worry, your little girl got home before daylight."

"Thought I heard Paula pullin' out a few minutes ago."

"Yeah, she went home to get some sleep."

"So how was the party?"

"Good, and yes, I did have me a beer."

"Oughta keep that little bit of information from your mother. You know how she is."

Uncle Bart turned on the radio. A kitchen in the country always had a radio. Being Sunday mornings, the family's favorite station aired some preacher man, busy reading scripture, saving souls, and asking listeners to send money. "Jane, what's that station that plays music on Sunday morning?"

"Believe it's twelve-eighty."

After a little adjustment, Patsy Cline filled the room with "Crazy." Jane started singing along with the radio, "Craa-zy, craa-zy for lu-uv-vin yooooo."

"Sure do hope to hear you singin' with that much enthusiasm at Mass this morning," preached Uncle Bart.

"Now Daddy, you know I been out all night, and since Johnny's gonna do my part of the milkin, I was plannin' on sleepin' in this mornin'."

"You're welcome to sleep while we milk, but stayin' out all night drinkin' and partyin' ain't no excuse to miss church. Gonna be wakin' you up in time for breakfast."

"Oh, all righty then," sassed Jane on her way out the door. "I'll go to church and I'll say me a prayer that God won't punish you for bein' so mean to me."

Uncle Bart and I talked about a lot of things that morning over coffee and chores. He never brought up the subject of Pete and Joe or anything that occurred in the barn the day before, so neither did I. When he asked about Mary Ellen and her baby, I filled him in and described my concerns over Bobbie's drinking.

He simply said, "Some can handle it, some can't," and left it at that.

By the time we finished in the barn, Grandma and Aunt Mary had made breakfast fit for a king. A sleepy-eyed Jane joined us.

After breakfast we all attended eleven o'clock Mass. To my surprise, Jane did sing. For a while, my mind remained on Paula. During the sermon, Jane moved close, leaned her sleepy head on my shoulder, slipped her hand into mine and gripped snuggly. Her warmth felt good. After a few minutes, Grandma noticed the situation. When Aunt Mary saw Grandma's glare, she reached over, pinched Jane's hand, and gave us both a look.

Chapter 12

On Thursday, June 24, 1976, the week following my initiation into family business, Uncle Samuel made a trip to Louisville. He had a meeting with the family friend my father had spoken of. Turns out his inside contact to the Louisville Police was none other than Jane's friend Paula Dawson. Their rendezvous took place in the city's south end at Iroquois Park and went something like this:

Halfway up to Lookout Hill, a small parking area accommodated recreational runners and walkers. Paula had already arrived and watched for Samuel's cue. As planned, both exited their vehicles and began stretching exercises.

Uncle Samuel, thirtyish, lean and strong, started his run uphill by way of the winding road. As he ran out of sight, Paula used the walking path, a more direct route to go straight up through the woods. Eight minutes later they met at the top, a spot overlooking the city.

"Nice view," started Samuel as he took a seat on the rock ledge next to Paula.

Instead of answering, she leaned on his shoulder.

"Bad day?" he asked.

"Just got better."

"Let's walk a trail. Be easier to talk."

The two rose and entered the woods for a private stroll. Paula reached to hold Samuel's hand and then said, "So how come we couldn't talk when I was down home the other day?"

"Some things don't need to be said around family. For their own good. And that's why you can't mention these little meetings to Jane, or anyone else for that matter."

81

"What about Jane's cousin, Johnny?"

"What about him?"

"Is he involved in family business? Does he know that I know?"

"Yes and no. He knows about what we do. But far as I can tell he's not got a clue about you."

"Should he?" Paula asked.

"Kinda thought we'd let you make that decision. Definitely don't want Jane to know, and I'll tell you right now, Johnny's really close to her."

"No shit. She talks about him a lot. You see the way she looks at him? It's disgusting, them being cousins."

"I wouldn't worry about that. Hell, they've been like brother and sister all their lives."

"Oh well," continued Paula. Then, in her sexiest voice, she said, "So why didn't you send Johnny to see me? Doesn't he live up here somewhere?"

Samuel released Paula's hand and stopped walking. "Didn't drive all the way up here to talk about Johnny. Need you to get serious. We could use your help. If you're willing, fine. If not, we'll understand. But you need to know we don't play when we do business, and we can't afford screw-ups. Got it?"

"Sure, Sammy, I get the message, but tell me this: what is it you can say here today that you couldn't say when you called? You really that worried about talkin' on the phone, or did you drive all the way up here 'cause you wanted to see me?"

"Little of both, I guess."

"How nice."

"Be glad to talk to you down home, but if you and me go sneakin' off talkin', someone's liable to get the wrong impression."

"Is that right? Wouldn't want *that* to happen, now would we? So, since we *are* together, what *does* the family want of me?"

Samuel hesitated, digesting Paula's sarcasm before speaking. "Four years ago, my niece, Johnny's sister, got attacked. Bastards beat 'er, raped 'er, and then branded her arms, leaving scars. Some kind of cigarette burns it would appear." Samuel pulled a small envelope from his pocket and handed it over. "Details are all inside. Don't pass my note on to anyone else. Burn it. To our knowledge, police never interviewed any suspects. A few days ago someone overheard two guys talkin' about it. We'd like to find out if there's any way to connect evidence from the initial investigation to those two men."

"You sure there is evidence?"

"They tell me there is, or at least should be. Surely they kept something."

"Well, keep in mind I'm just a clerk, and clerks don't have access to evidence in the property room."

"So what *can* you do?"

"Not a whole lot, but if you don't mind, I do have a detective friend who might be able to check it out."

"Can you keep our name out of it?"

"Guess so, but hell, if it goes anywhere, someone may connect the dots. Who but family would inquire after all this time?"

"I hear ya. Just be discreet and let me know if you hear anything."

"Sure. That all?"

"Paula, I need to know that you understand the seriousness of what we're asking you to do. There's a chance that if the law can't take care of these guys, we will. That happens, how you gonna feel about it?"

"Considering what you said they did to Johnny's sister, somebody needs to do something. But answer me this, Sammy, you guys ever do anything bad to anyone without just cause?"

"Never. And we don't do anything until we're sure the law can't or won't. Like your car."

"Still like to know who took it."

"You don't need to know their names. Just four young boys screwin' up. They knew we were lookin' for 'em. When we caught up, they had a backhoe burying your car so we couldn't find it. We made 'em dig it out by hand with shovels. Tell you right now, those boys'll never steal another car, especially not yours."

"And that's one of the reasons I don't mind helpin'. Mama and Daddy wouldn't be where they are today ifin' it weren't for your family."

Samuel stood silently, staring into Paula's eyes. She slid her hands around his back, pulled him close, and they kissed.

Chapter 13

That next morning, in all the normal hustle and bustle at the Louisville Police Department, 32-year-old Detective Kelly arrived to find an anonymous envelope on her desk. On the outside were the words, "Attention Detective Kelly, PERSONAL." She held it up and asked, "Anyone see who left this on my desk?"

Few paid attention, and when no one answered yes, she held the envelope down with a tissue, opened it with a letter opener, slid out the folded note, and read;

In 1972, a girl named Patricia Smith was beat, raped, and branded on her arms several times by three men. Apparently, no one ever became a suspect. Recently, two men, Pete Metcalf and Joe Simpson, were overheard talking about the crime. Both men work at the packinghouse on Mellwood Ave. Please check to see if either can be connected to any evidence collected at the time of the crime.

After reading, she lowered the note and recalled, *Hell, I remember that. My first rape case. They wouldn't let me follow up then, now some chicken-shit puts this on my desk, and I'm just supposed to jump.*

The phone rang, interrupting her thoughts. She grabbed the receiver as if wanting to slam it on the desk, but answered instead. "LPD, Detective Kelly speaking."

"Hey cutie, how are you?"

"Busy. Told you not to be calling me at work."

"Can't help it. I'd like to see you."

Ron Gambrell

"See me, to do what? Seems we've been down that road enough."
"It's never enough when two people care about one another."
"You're so full of shit."
"Kelly—"
"I'm serious. Don't be calling me."
"Don't do me like this. I miss you. Just wanna talk."
"Bullshit. Tell you what, give me your word you won't call me here anymore, and I'll meet you. Just to talk."
"Sure, where and when?"
"At the boat dock."
"The boat dock?" asked the man with disappointment. "Thought we could get a room."
"That's not gonna happen. Just meet me there at six. Okay?"
"Whatever you say. See you then."
Kelly's partner, Detective Lantz, walked in from the Captain's office just in time to hear the end of her phone conversation.
"Trouble?" he asked.
"Nothing I can't handle."
"Hope it can wait. We have a body in the West End."
"It'll wait. Let's go," replied Detective Kelly as she opened her desk drawer and tossed in the envelope.

Later that evening, Detective Kelly met Carl Jacobs at Cox's Park, a public facility on the banks of the Ohio River. A few picnickers gathered at tables while children played softball in an open area nearby. Several vehicles waited in line to either launch a boat or bring one out of the water. Kelly left her car and got into Carl's.

The two had met during his rookie year on the force. They became friends and eventually intimate, even though she was married and had no intentions of divorce. When the rookie lost his job for disciplinary reasons, it seemed like a good time for Kelly to cut ties. Unfortunately, Carl refused to take no for an answer, and she couldn't bring herself to put a stop to it.

As Kelly climbed into Carl's sedan, he said, "Good to see you. Appreciate your coming."

86

The detective avoided answering as she pulled out a cigarette.

"Can I have one of those?" Carl begged.

"Don't you ever buy your own?"

"Trying to quit. Afraid if I buy a pack, I'll smoke too many."

"How about you buy *me* a pack. I'm sure you've bummed at least that many."

"Ha, ha."

While the two sat smoking, the impatient Carl put his hand on Kelly's leg. Without resisting, she said, "I'm not here to fulfill your fantasies or to be teased. Don't know if I feel for you or just feel sorry for you, but you calling me at the department has got to stop."

"Why?"

"Already told you, I don't need anybody downtown associating me and you together. I've got too much to lose."

"What kind of bullshit is that?"

"You know what I'm talking about. People think bad cops hang out with other bad cops. And I don't need that reputation."

"What I did wasn't that bad. If I hadn't been a rookie, the guys would have taken care of me."

"Maybe. Maybe not. Ask me, most of those guys didn't like you to start with."

"Screw you."

"You wish."

Carl took his hand off Kelly's leg and said, "You know what your problem is? You think you're better than me."

"No I do not. I just see things how they are. I'm black baby. I'm used to seeing through the bullshit when it comes to how people treat one another. Some of those guys don't like you because you hung out with me, you being white."

"Fuck 'em."

"That's easy for you to say. Your job doesn't depend on getting along with a bunch of sorry ass, white ass mother fuckers that think they're better than me because I'm black."

"You worry too much."

"Damn right I worry."

"You might have gotten hired because you're a black woman, but that's not why they keep you. You're good at what you do. They're not gonna get rid of you."

Kelly hesitated, then after staring out the window for a moment, she asked, "So, why are we here?"

"I want you to know I still care about you."

"You need to move on, Carl. Things are not gonna change between us. You know that."

"You gotta be patient."

"You don't get it, do you? I can't keep putting myself through this, and you *are* gonna quit bothering me about it."

Carl drew off his cigarette, exhaled, and said, "So how you and Detective Lantz getting along these days?"

"David's okay."

"David? First name basis now. You sleep with him yet?"

"Fuck you Carl! No I'm not and will not sleep with my partner. Man's got a wife and two little girls! You're a fucking asshole just to say—"

"Calm down baby."

"Why would you even say such a thing?"

"Because I'm jealous."

"Jesus."

"I'm jealous that he's with you while I'm stuck in a shithole packinghouse with a bunch of hicks. Swear to God, some of 'em can't even read the newspaper."

"Oh, that reminds me, I've been asked to look into a couple guys who work at your plant."

"For what?"

"Someone overheard 'em talking about a rape case from four years ago."

"No shit? What're their names?"

"Pete something and Joe something. Got their last names at work. If you want, I can call you later."

"You can call me anytime, but I'm not really interested in who those guys are. Hell, half the men up there could be rapists. So, when do I get to see you again?" Carl asked as he leaned over, trying to get a kiss.

"You don't ever get up, I mean give up," replied Detective Kelly while pushing the door open.

"Thanks smart ass."

"And, I'm serious, don't call me at work."

The following day, Detective Kelly went through old case files until she found the folder for Patricia Smith from 1972. According to the file, an evidence box in the property room contained photos, clothing, and blood and hair samples that she herself had collected.

After jotting down the case number, the detective made her way to the Property Room. "Hey, Charlie."

"Well, how *you* doing Kelly?"

"Fine, and you?"

The old guy behind the cage just smiled and said, "Better now that you stopped in. What can I get you?"

"I need a box. Let's see," she said while pulling out her notes, "number 156-1972. Name is Patricia Smith."

"Seventy-two? That's the year before I started down here, but I should be able to find it. Be right back."

Charlie left in search of the case box. In about a minute, he returned. "Here you go, good lookin'. Just need you to sign for it."

"No problem," Kelly answered.

After signing, she slid the box down the counter a few feet, mainly for privacy, and opened it. "Son of a bitch."

"What's wrong?" Charlie asked.

"There's supposed to be several pieces of evidence in here. Put 'em there myself. All I see is a rock wrapped in a towel."

"That would mean someone stole the contents."

"But why the rock?" asked Kelly.

"Whoever took the evidence replaced it with the rock so it would weigh the same as when the clerk brought it out."

"Clever," reasoned Kelly, "But wouldn't that person have to be a cop?"

"Sure, or possibly the evidence clerk himself. But the clerk wouldn't worry about the weight. I'm guessing it was a cop."

"So then the cop had to sign it out. Suppose we can find his name?"

"Tell you what. Give me some time, and I'll go through the old sign-out logs and see what I can find."

"I'd sure appreciate that, Charlie. Check back with you later."

"May take a while."

"That's okay, it's been four years. No need hurrying now. Sure do appreciate your help. Oh, and do me a favor?"

"What's that?"

"Can you keep this between you and me until we see who signed the book?"

"No problem. You can count on me. Ain't like the rest of those guys."

"What's that supposed to mean?"

"Well, you know how it is. Most guys round here don't think it's right having women on the force. Me, I don't really give a damn."

"You're saying they don't like me because I'm a woman? Not because I'm black?"

"Honey, you're about the prettiest black girl I ever met. And I'd say you got some white in you. Hell, if I was a single man, I'd be hittin' on you right now."

"Thanks, Charlie." As Kelly left the Property Room, she mumbled, "I hate men."

Chapter 14

After a weekend in the country, I always dreaded returning to work. Monday, June 28, 1976 was no different. The elders had made it clear that I should avoid Pete and Joe. The head machine job I'd worked the previous two weeks would never be considered a desirable position. Low seniority had forced me on it. Unfortunately, my only job choices for the following week were on the kill floor. Therefore, in order to stay clear of Pete and Joe, I volunteered for the Daily Labor Pool. The company used this position to fill daily vacancies, primarily due to illness or injury. Five minutes after the six o'clock starting time, I got sent to the tank house department. They were having trouble with an auger, and my job would be to assist. That didn't sound bad until I got there.

The auger in question, located on top of one of the buildings, carried inedible materials from a grinder to a cooking system. All items coming from the slaughter or production departments that were unfit for human consumption got ground, cooked, and sold as fertilizer. Bones and guts made up most of the load. Occasionally, there would be an entire carcass that needed grinding, having been tagged by USDA inspectors for one reason or another. One job, which I had performed on multiple occasions, consisted of dumping those inedible parts into what we called the "pit." Any item dumped would be pulled by the pre-auger up and into a grinder. That loud, bladed machine could reduce an entire hog into mush in a matter of seconds.

Product exiting that grinder traveled up another story via the secondary auger to a level where additional grinding and cooking took place. The problem had been in the performance of that secondary

91

auger. Because of structural inadequacies, the product would only travel up the auger when just the right mix of bones and guts was present. Several times an hour, there would be too many guts and not enough bones. When this occurred, I would have to help the product along by shoving an oak stick into the auger behind the guts and in essence walk them up the hill. Often, the contents of the auger would spill out, causing me to have to work in a 6 to 8-inch-deep slur of hog and beef entrails. When I say my job stank, I mean it literally.

For three months I spent my workdays on that rooftop while company engineers designed a solution to the auger problem. Early morning hours were not so bad, but once the sun got high, it was hot as hell. On rainy days, I wore a plastic poncho. My feet and legs were protected from the waste material by rubber boots that were tall enough to cover my calves.

Each morning, I arrived well before daylight, changed into work clothes, and then purchased a breakfast sandwich and a cup of hot coffee from the vender's truck in the alley. After punching the time clock, my day was spent being pretty much by myself. Even the tank house boss stayed away from that roof unless something went wrong. Long as things kept moving, he left me alone.

In my spare time I carved a small pipe from one of the oak sticks that broke while shoving guts. Before the kill started, I'd sit alone on top of the building and smoke a little pot. Getting a buzz took my mind off the blood and guts. It also made a greasy egg and sausage sandwich taste like rib-eye steak.

From atop that roof, I could watch the sunrise erase headlights trailing up and down the interstate. Thousands of people driving toward jobs they hated. My rooftop job sucked, but in a strange sort of way, I enjoyed it, and it did keep me away from Pete and Joe.

The auger system worked well for at least 10-15 minutes whenever an entire vat of beef bones were dumped into the pit. After a quick cleanup of spillage, I could relax. Occasionally, an old black man would sneak out and have a cigarette with me. He called himself Henry Smith. Henry had recently moved in from Detroit, Michigan, where he worked in another meat packing plant.

One day I said, "You know, me and you having the same last name, people might think we're related."

He laughed and said, "Don't worry. Smith ain't really my name."

The old man liked to tell stories, mostly lies I figured, but they were always interesting. On one hot day near the end of summer, I asked, "Hey Henry, if a man were to fall into the pit, think we could tell the difference when he came past here, all ground up?"

"Doubt it. Guts is guts, and bones is bones."

"So you suppose it's ever happened?"

"Oh yeah."

"Really?"

Henry kept a half-pint of vodka in his pocket. He pulled it out, took a drink, and said, "I'll tell you somethin' boy, but you gotta keep it to yo-self." Henry started nearly every story with that same line.

"Sure."

"Well, you know, back in Detroit, they was this old fella worked third shift in the tank house. He told me secret meetings took place in the middle of the night. Called 'em union meetings. Said he knowed when one was about to take place 'cause boss man would come and tell him to take a break. Go lay down in the locker room. Nap for an hour. One night last summer, my friend woke up from sleepin'. Hadn't quite been a whole hour, but he figured he best get back to work. When he got to the tank house, he heard voices, someone bitching about how hot it was and how much the place stunk. Peekin' around the corner, he seen two well-dressed men taking clothes offa some white fella. Man was layin' on the floor, looked to be dead. They took off every stitch of clothes the man had on. When they pulled off his ring, it dropped down in the pit. Could hear it bouncing on the metal, all the way to the bottom. One man told the other he ought to crawl down in there and fetch it. His partner told him to go to hell. Anyway, they shoved the naked man in, turned on the system and stood there watching while the auger carried him up to the grinder. It chopped that unfortunate feller into pieces just like a big fat hog."

"So what'd your buddy do then?"

"What could he do? Took his ass back to the locker room and pretended like he was still sleepin' when the boss came to get him."

"What about the ring?"

"Later that night, when the boss went to lunch, I, I mean my friend, went down to the hide cellar where the lower end of the auger sits. Took the back plate off, and sure enough the ring fell right on out. Put it in his pocket and took it home. Next night, boss had some maintenance people down there a-lookin' for it."

"And?"

"And that's it. Ain't no more to tell."

"Wow, Henry, that's one hell of a story."

"Yeah, and if you tell anybody what I just told you, same could happen here. I'll throw your young ass in the pit."

"Sounds to me like it was you, Henry, seen all that happen."

"You heard what I just said, boy."

I could tell the old man was serious. Not like in his other stories. I tried to play it off. "Shit, Henry, wouldn't anybody believe a story like that anyway."

By the end of that summer, Old Henry was gone. Someone said he moved further south to be with family.

Every day after Henry's story I imagined shoving Pete and Joe live and kicking down into the tank house pit. Offering to stop the machine in return for information would likely provide the name of Sissy's third attacker, after which I could restart the auger and serve long overdue justice. Within minutes, their very existence would be equal to that of the bones and guts of dead animals. Like fertilizer, Pete and Joe could be spread on the ground with a promise that whatever they helped produce from the soil would be more worthy of this world than they were.

Chapter 15

My preoccupation with sex, religion, college basketball, and hunting left little time for news. Therefore, on a cold Monday morning, January 3, I entered the plant after a three day weekend completely unaware of the previous day's events. We'd been given Friday off for New Years since it landed on Saturday that year. The cafeteria buzzed with talk of some sort of accident involving two of our co-workers, Pete Metcalf and Joe Simpson. My heart began racing. I tried to hide excitement while inhaling my cigarette and as much information as possible. Apparently Pete and Joe had been out in Shelby County hunting quail when the incident occurred. Both had been hit square in the face with birdshot. Neither survived. The property owner became worried when Pete's bird dog returned to the house alone. As evening approached, he and his son ventured out and found the bodies.

"Maybe," one man guessed, "when the birds flushed they flew right between 'em. Could they have shot at the birds and hit one another?"

"No way," one guy intoned. "I've been hunting with Pete and Joe, and I can't see either one being that careless."

Others in the cafeteria asked, "Were they drinking, stoned, or both?"

"Maybe they were mad at one another," someone speculated.

"What do you think, Johnny?" my friend Darrel asked.

"Don't know. Didn't know 'em very well. Guess a man would have to be there to know what happened."

"Really sucks," added someone from another table. "Joe's wife just had that baby girl not long ago. Now the poor kid's gotta grow up without a daddy."

I wanted to say the baby would be better off without *that* daddy, but held my tongue.

An hour later, I learned more. The entire lower level of the plant served as a refrigerated warehouse, referred to as the Order Room. Processed meat products were stored there until shipping. As a variety of boxed meats rolled down a conveyor from the upstairs production, my co-worker Richard Barns and I stacked them on wooden pallets. While doing so we were able to listen to a radio. At around 6:50 a.m., the station announced that at the top of the hour, they would be talking about a police investigation into the deaths of two hunters in Shelby County.

Police investigation? Nervously, I stuffed a wad of Red Man chewing tobacco into my mouth, chewed up some moisture, and then used the nearby floor drain as a spittoon.

Within minutes, Richard passed the word on to most in the area regarding the upcoming news story. Several came to listen in on the broadcast. Those last few moments of waiting seemed to take forever, as the station crammed advertisements in one after another. Several guys stood around jabbering while they waited. Right before the hour, our boss, Carl Jacobs, spotted the crowd and came to inquire. Carl, a twenty-three-year-old, had only been with the company for about a year. Being made supervisor at such a young age had gone to the man's head. He apparently met the company's criteria for supervisors: tall, loud, and obnoxious. "What the hell's going on over here? Don't you guys have work to do?"

Richard filled him in quickly. "Don't worry, boss, we'll only be a minute. On the radio they're gonna talk about those boys that got killed yesterday."

"What do you mean, got killed?"

"They said there's a police investigation."

"Thought someone said it was an accident," Carl replied.

96

"Well," continued Richard, "*you* oughta know, police investigation usually means foul play."

Just the sound of their conversation increased my anxiety. With sweaty palms, I anticipated what might be reported, all the while wondering if the elders were listening. Could I call them? *No way.*

Finally, we heard the familiar musical intro used to introduce the news. A reporter's voice began: "It's seven o'clock at your news station, WHAS. I'm Donald Chapman reporting. At the top of the news, two Louisville men, both employees of a local meat packing facility, were shot to death yesterday while on a hunting trip in Shelby County. Their bodies were found in a field. According to autopsy reports, the fatal wounds were caused by shotgun blast at close range, ruling out an accident. Further details have not been released pending police investigation. In other news..."

My co-workers immediately began commenting on the story. "Sonofabitch," one man said. "Why would anyone want to shoot Pete and Joe?"

Carl almost spit on himself, saying, "Damn those boys. They must have pissed somebody off pretty bad, and you can bet your sweet ass it took more than one man to do it."

"You're right about that, boss," added a guy named Harry. "Someone had balls to attack two men carrying shotguns. Think maybe they snuck up behind 'em?"

"Don't make no sense," commented Billy Wells. "How the hell do you sneak up on two guys out in the middle of a field and shoot 'em in the face?"

Richard, a former MP in the Marines, kept speculating. "Could be they ran into some other hunters. Maybe they had a squabble over dogs or something. Or, who knows, they mighta been friends with whoever shot 'em."

Carl, looking a little disturbed by Richard's comments, said, "Okay guys, that's enough. We've got work to do. You fellows can play homicide detective on your own time."

With that, everybody dispersed to individual job assignments. As Richard resumed working, I mentioned, "Boss seems a little shook up over those boys who died."

"Sure does, but you gotta understand … Pete and Joe are the ones who helped get him hired on here. Believe they all went to school together."

Billy Wells drove a dolly, hauling pallet loads to and from the dock. Seemed every trip he had something more to say to Richard about the deaths. Me, well, I took the elders' advice, staying as far away from the topic as possible. "If you don't speak, you can't say the wrong thing," they would say. By lunch, my co-workers had gossiped Pete and Joe into the mob, the militia, local drug rings, and a multitude of other possible criminal factions. Their guesses were wrong, or at least I felt sure they were.

When the guys at work took up a collection for the families of Pete and Joe, I gave five dollars. My hope was that things would get back to normal after the funerals on Wednesday. That didn't happen, though. The next day, homicide detectives came to the plant as part of their investigation. Someone saw them observing the area where Pete and Joe worked. Luckily for me, I had an assignment in the Order Room. Otherwise, they might have forced me to fill one of the kill floor openings. The police scheduled interviews with each of the co-workers from that immediate area.

On that Friday during lunch break, my friends and I were playing pinochle in the locker room. Carl Jacobs stood at the top of the steps and hollered, "Hey guys, Johnny Smith down there?"

"Yeah, I'm here. Whatcha need?"

Carl walked down the steps and into the room. "After lunch break you need to report to personnel. Someone up there wants to talk to you."

Confused, I asked, "You want me to go now, before the line starts back up?"

"No, don't worry, they sent you a replacement."

"Really? So what's going on?"

Carl spoke hesitantly, "Not sure I should say in front of all these guys."

"Bullshit," I said in frustration. "These guys all know me. What's up?"

"Oookay. You know those detectives that were here investigating that shooting? Seems they wanna talk to you."

"No way! Why me?"

"Well, don't quote me on this, but I heard they were talking to anyone who had worked with those two fellows in the past six months. Evidently, you took somebody's place up there for a couple weeks. Is that right?"

Gabrielle's whisper scolded me. *Now you're in trouble.*

Without thinking, I mumbled to myself, "Am not."

"Am not what?" asked Carl as the rest of the crew stared.

"Sorry man, just talking to myself." Trying not to lie, I said, "Sure, I worked up there for two weeks when big George Jenkins went on vacation."

"Hell," replied Carl in his inquisitive, detective-like manner. "You were right there with Pete and Joe. No wonder they wanna talk to you."

Suddenly realizing the seriousness of the situation, I needed to get my act together quickly. "Well that's cool," I said. "Don't mind talking to 'em. Who knows, maybe they can fill us in a little on what happened to those guys. Didn't really know 'em, but everybody says they were all right."

Because it was already nearing the end of lunchtime, I decided to start toward the office. Wanted to grab a cup of coffee on the way. As Carl followed me up the stairs, chatter emitted from the room below. I figured if the guys had something to say behind my back, Richard would fill me in later upon my return to the line. Near the top of the stairs, just inside the will-call lobby, I fed three nickels into the coffee machine while acknowledging Carl's presence. "Would you like a cup, boss?"

"Sure. Thanks," he replied. "Make it black with sugar."

After pushing the appropriate button, the little paper cup fell into position. Five seconds later, fresh java began squirting down like a cow pissing on a flat rock.

"Tell me, Johnny, you know something about what happened to those boys that got shot?"

"What's that supposed to mean?" I asked, as if offended.

"Well, you seemed a little upset down there a minute ago," he replied as I handed him the cup of coffee.

Calmly, I deposited three more nickels and lied, "Listen, Carl, just found out Saturday that the love of my life got married to one of my best friends. Last couple days ain't been easy. Got this ugly feeling right in my stomach."

"Oh, sorry, didn't know. Love'll do that to ya, won't it?"

He seemed to buy it hook, line, and sinker. *Boy, you're good*, I thought.

Good liar, scolded Gabrielle.

My cup finished filling, and we continued. Carl insisted on coaching me. "When you go up there, just be straight with the cops. If you act like you did downstairs, they'll become suspicious."

"Suspicious of what? How the hell could they be suspicious of me? I didn't even know those guys!"

"Calm down, man," he advised. "They probably just want to see if you might have overheard anything that could help in their investigation. Anything at all could be significant. Did you?"

"Did I what?"

"Did you hear anything out of those boys when you were up there working?"

"No. Hell no. Why you asking?"

"No reason, just trying to help you out here."

Help me out? Then why does it feel like an interrogation?

Chapter 16

I walked into the personnel office nervous but confident. Other than my desire to see Pete and Joe die, I hadn't done anything wrong and shouldn't fear being questioned. Hester, the cute Italian receptionist, looked up from her desk and said, "Hey Johnny, how you doing?"

"I'm great, and how about yourself?"

"Fine, thank you. And what can I do for Johnny today?"

"I'm looking for whoever's doing the interviews."

She looked surprised. "You mean the detectives? Are *you* on their list?"

"Yes, ma'am. At least that's what they tell me."

Hester, a 30-year-old married hottie, spoke with a seductive smile. I had the feeling she gave that look to all the guys.

"The detectives went to lunch. They should be back soon."

"I'll just wait, then."

Hester stood up, showing off her tightly covered curves, and asked, "Can I get you a refill on that coffee?"

"Sure, that'll work." I handed her the cup and lusted as she walked away.

Taking advantage of her absence, I moseyed into the conference room where the interview would take place. In my mind, it became an interrogation room. The large wall mirror reminded me of those one-way windows used in police stations. My reflection revealed a bad case of red eye—too much partying and not enough sleep. An idea came to mind. On my way in, I'd seen a little bottle of eye drops, the kind that "gets the red out," on Hester's desk. Returning to the receptionist's area, I quickly borrowed a couple drops, placing them in my left eye only, then recapped the bottle and set it back in place just before Hester returned with my coffee.

"Got you a better cup. It'll stay hot longer," she explained.

"Thank you," I said, reaching for the steaming ceramic cup. "Thank you very much. Guess I owe you one."

"Careful, Johnny. Might hold you to that," she replied with a wink.

Being nervous had me craving a cigarette. "Believe I'll have a seat in the conference room."

"That's fine."

Walking into the room, I said, "Be alright to smoke?"

"Sure. They have been all morning."

I lit a cigarette and waited for the cops, restlessly tapping my fingers on the chair arm and contemplating what kind of questions would be asked. It crossed my mind that the cops might not expect much intellect from a packinghouse worker; therefore, my best approach would be to politely meet their expectations.

Just as I finished my smoke, they returned. There were two, as I expected. It surprised me that one was a woman. Jim Wrong, the personnel manager, accompanied them. After introducing me to Detectives Kelly and Lantz, Jim excused himself and shut the door. *Good*, I thought, *at least Hester can't listen in.*

On one hand, I felt extremely anxious. On the other, I was strangely excited.

"Have a seat, Mr. Smith," motioned the man, as he and his partner sat down on the opposite side of the large oval conference table.

"Mr. Smith, can we just call you Johnny?" started Detective Kelly, a butch-looking cop with a slight northern accent and no wedding ring. She wore pants, a white shirt, and a blazer that resembled a man's suit jacket. Her hair was all pinned up. No makeup at all. I remember thinking, *she must be mixed, because no one has that good a tan in January.* "Sure ma'am, that'd be just fine."

Her partner, Detective Lantz, a young guy who seemed to be less masculine than she, butted in as I was butting out my cigarette. "Okay Johnny, I'm guessing you know why we're here. We just want to ask a few questions about your relationship with two former co-workers who were recently shot to death." While he spoke, he stared straight into my eyes.

"My relationship, sir? What exactly does that mean?"

"You did know them, didn't you?"

"No sir, not really," I replied, purposely keeping my answer short.

"But Johnny, according to the records we saw, on occasions you fill vacation vacancies up on the kill floor. Didn't you work next to those guys a few months ago?"

"Sure did. Around June, if I remember right."

"So," Detective Kelly interrupted, "Did you not get to know them during that time?"

Instead of answering her question, I squinted and began rubbing my right eye.

"You okay, Johnny?" she asked after glancing at her partner.

"I'm fine ma'am, why do you ask?"

"You were rubbing your eye and—"

"Oh, sorry ma'am, it's just that I got something in my eye this morning on the line. Cleaned it out at lunch time but it still smarts. So, what was your question?"

"First of all, you can call me Detective Kelly, if you wish. And I asked about your getting to know Metcalf and Simpson while you worked next to them."

"Knew 'em by name. That's about it."

Detective Lantz asked, "So, how long did you work up there this past summer?"

Figured they already knew the answer. "Worked the head machine for two weeks."

"And in two weeks you never talked to those guys at all?"

Before speaking, I removed a cigarette from the pack in my pocket. I placed it in my mouth and just let it hang there unlit. "Not really. When you have to handle 400 hog heads per hour, there's not a lot of time for socializing."

"We understand that, but what about when the line stops for whatever reason?" added Kelly, revealing her knowledge of the kill process.

"What about it?"

Impatiently, she replied, "What *do* you do when the line is stopped? Don't you ever talk to anyone during that time?"

"Usually try to get a drink of water first thing. If there's time, I pick up about me. You know, the jawbones that fall off the machine and hit the floor. Gotta keep things up so the government inspectors don't shut 'er down."

"So, tell me this, Johnny," she asked. "When you're working up there, can you hear what other people are saying to one another?"

"Not really. You can hear people talking, but unless you're right next to 'em, you can't hear what they say. Company makes us wear earplugs."

She continued in a more forceful voice. "So let's get this straight, Mr. Smith. Are you saying you were not at all an acquaintance of Metcalf and Simpson?"

At that point, I slipped a little, lost my patience. Seemed they were asking the same damn thing over and over. I dug into my pocket, found the Zippo, and lit my cigarette. After a long draw, I began speaking and exhaling smoke at the same time. "All I can tell you about those two is what they looked like and their names. Ain't never been out with 'em, or even seen 'em other than here at work. I know they're dead now, just like those hogs we kill every day."

"Just like the hogs?" questioned Detective Kelly.

I raised my eyebrows and said, "Ain't but two good reasons to kill an animal. One is if you plan on eating it. The other is if it goes mad and hurts somebody. Since ain't nobody gonna eat those boys, reckon they musta' hurt someone awful bad."

For a moment, the two seemed astonished at my outburst and remained silent while jotting notes. Finally, Detective Lantz spoke. "Why is it people here don't seem too upset that two of your co-workers died?"

Hmm, I thought, *So I'm not the only one with the who-gives-a-shit attitude toward Pete and Joe.* "Mister, we kill thousands of animals here every day so people like you and me can eat meat. Animals die. People die. It happens."

104

Lantz said, "You compare men dying to animals dying. Kind of cold, don't you think?"

"Let me ask you a question, sir. When you look at the obituaries, do you feel sorry for all those folks who died? Or do you just close the page and move on to the sports?"

Leaning back in his chair, Lantz replied, "Now that *is* an interesting point of view, Mr. Smith."

Just when I felt comfortable being obnoxious, Detective Kelly stood, walked around to my side of the table, and blew me away by asking, "Johnny, do you have a sister named Patricia?"

Almost shit my pants right there. *How the hell did she know that?* I took a long draw off my cigarette and tried not to sound nervous in answering. "Yes, ma'am, I do, I mean, that's her name, but we call her Sissy."

"And did your sister get brutally raped some time back?"

This time I even saw surprise in the face of her partner. A lump formed in my throat. "Yes, ma'am, she did. But what's that got to do with those guys that got killed?"

"Are you sure you never overheard Metcalf and Simpson talking about what happened to your sister?"

Against Gabrielle's advice, I lied, "Detective Kelly, I'm glad you're still looking for whoever did that to my sister. And believe me, if I heard somebody talking about it, I'd be calling the police myself."

"Or perhaps shoot the sonofabitches yourself?" she pushed.

"No ma'am."

"Johnny, do you own a shotgun?"

Detective Lantz sat silently while she drilled.

"Sure, got several," I replied."

"Can you tell me where you were on January 2nd, the day Peter Metcalf and Joe Simpson were murdered?"

Now I felt like a suspect: nervous and scared.

Lantz spoke up, "Well, Mr. Smith, where were you on that day? It was a Sunday."

Feeling the presence of my elders, I thought, *Slow down, speak slowly and you'll be okay.* Then it dawned on me. "On Sunday, Sir, I always go to church."

"The coroner says the time of death was around noon that day. What time did you go to church?"

"I play piano at the eleven o'clock Mass."

"You play piano?" questioned Kelly.

"Yes, I do. Is that a problem?"

"Sorry, you just don't look like a church-going piano player."

"Well, ma'am, with all due respect, you don't look like a cop either."

Lantz almost laughed while interrupting. "So, Johnny, what time is church over?"

"Around noon."

"And you're sure you were there that day?"

"Yes sir. It was the Epiphany. Matter of fact, after Mass, I helped take down the Christmas tree in the church."

"And that can be verified?" Kelly asked.

"Sure can, just call Father Tom at my church."

"Which is?"

"Which is what?"

"She wants to know the name of your church," blurted Lantz.

"Oh, St. Michael's. It's out in the southwest."

After writing down the information, Kelly asked, "Johnny, do you know of anyone who might have overheard Metcalf and Simpson talking about your sister?"

"No, ma'am. Can I ask why you think they were talking about my sister? Were they suspects?"

Lantz also, seemed interested in her answer.

"Just a hunch. Nothing concrete. Johnny, I believe we're done for now. We'll check out your alibi. Could be we'll have to talk to you again later, but for now, we appreciate your cooperation."

"Thank you for your time," added Detective Lantz as he folded notes and stood to join his partner.

"And thank you for yours," I replied politely, while smashing my cigarette into the ashtray. I stood and said, "Detective Kelly, if you discover anything more about my sister's attack, I'd appreciate the information."

"I'll keep that in mind," she said while shaking my hand with the grip of a man.

Detective Lantz offered his handshake on my way out of the conference room. I walked away, not sure what to think. One thing for certain, they knew way too much, and that simply did not make sense. The elders would need to know about Detective Kelly's comments.

Hester eagerly waited at her desk. "Well, how'd it go?"

"Okay, I guess. They seemed like nice people." Then I remembered leaving Hester's coffee cup in the conference room. Turning that way, I caught sight of Detective Lantz picking up the cup with a handkerchief. *Good move*, I thought. *Won't get you anywhere.* Looking back at Hester, I said, "Probably oughta be gettin' back to work."

She smiled back and chirped, "Don't forget, Johnny, you owe me one."

Yeah, I owe you one all right. You switched the coffee cups. Bitch of it is, can't trust anyone in this world.

Chapter 17

The thought of those two cops trying to connect me to the shootings of Pete and Joe scared me. I called my father that night to let him know of my need to speak with the elders. Most likely, he would figure I had cold feet after hearing the news about Pete and Joe. "There's a problem, Pop, and I should only talk in the room," got his attention.

"You sure about that, boy?"

"I'm sure."

He sounded upset. "You didn't go and do somethin' stupid, did you?"

"No, Pop. Everything's under control. Just need to tell y'all something."

His voice cracked, "Son, we were already plannin' to call a meetin', but..." His words were cut short, evidently by my mother entering the room. "Can't talk now. Just be down at Bart's tomorrow 'round noon."

Before I could say "bye," he hung up. *Damn, the old man's pissed about something.*

After a long night of tossing, turning, and worrying about Father's uneasy attitude, I rose early, drank coffee, played piano, showered, and then left for the country. Cigarette smoke and classical music filled the truck's cab as I left the blacktop at Bear Creek to have a drink with Grandpa Smith. He's buried in a quiet little graveyard at St. Augustine's Church, high on a hill under the branches of a giant tulip poplar. With frost still covering the ground, I wrapped myself in an army blanket. Sitting cross-legged like an Indian, back against the tree, I uncapped a half pint of 80 proof bourbon. "To you, Grandpa."

Recuperating from a long swig, I cupped my hands to light a cigarette, relaxed, and waited for the medicine to take effect. A gentle, crisp, breeze slid by tainted with the smell of fresh cow manure. Not far off in the winter blue sky, several buzzards seemed to float in peaceful circles. *Why did my parents leave this for the city?*

Rising to my knees, I took another swig and said, "Remember that day when I was a kid, and I asked if you were a hillbilly? You said, 'Define hillbilly.' Well Grandpa, here I am, long hair and a beard, smokin' and drinkin' and soakin' up the sun like an old hound dog. Should I pull off my shoes?"

By then, those buzzards were directly above. It felt as though they were looking down on me, waiting. "Can't have me yet," I mumbled. "I'm still alive." The birds moved on, and so did I.

Back in the Dodge, I started the engine, stick shifted into first, and then waved goodbye to Grandpa as if he were still alive. "I'll give Grandma a kiss for you."

Creeping down the hill, my old truck whined loudly with backpressure. Once on the blacktop, I searched the radio for a country station and began singing along. The drive to Uncle Bart's would be about ten more miles. Along the way, I waved at everyone in sight. Didn't matter if they were sitting on a porch or a John Deere tractor, in a car, coming or going, I waved, and they all waved back. That's just the way country people are.

Driving up Uncle Bart's lane, I could see my father had already arrived. His Chevy truck sat parked next to the milk shed. He and Uncle Bart were cleaning squirrels under the big sugar maple that stood between the house and the barn. Obviously, Pop used the trip as an excuse to hunt. He always loved to shoot squirrels, and Uncle Bart's farm had its share. By the time I got out of the truck, Grandma stood on the front porch waiting for her hug. Passing Pop and Uncle Bart on my way to the porch, I said, "Hell, if I'd known you were gonna hunt, I'd have come down earlier and went with you."

"Yeah, and I'd been glad to let you clean 'em," Pop replied.

On the porch, I gave Grandma a kiss on the cheek. "That's from Grandpa."

She puckered her wrinkled lips and kissed me right on mine. "Pewee, you must have shared whiskey with him."

After a big hug, she went inside while I joined Pop and Uncle Bart in their labor. "Warm for January. Y'all see that groundhog feeding down past the mailbox?"

Uncle Bart spit tobacco juice and said, "We seen it. Need to shoot the little varmint and fill in its hole so the cows don't break a leg."

"I hear you."

Uncle Bart looked at Pop and said, "If he was a good boy, he'd sneak on down there and take care of that for me."

"Sneak down there!" I laughed. "Why would a man walk all the way down there when he could just shoot it from here?"

"Whatcha got that'll shoot that far?" asked my father in that same uneasy voice he had the day before.

"Traded for a .243 a couple weeks ago. Shoots pretty flat at 150 yards. Believe I could hit that groundhog from here."

Uncle Bart spit again and said, "Tell you what, Johnny. Got ten bucks says you can't hit it first shot from here."

Pop stood quiet. He knew my shooting capabilities because he was the one who taught me. I returned to the truck and pulled my gun case out from behind the seat. Had me one of those fancy hard-shelled cases. Couldn't help but gloat when I opened it up on the ground. Dad and Uncle Bart started checking out my Remington Model 788, complete with fold-out bipods and a Weaver 3x-9x scope. My rounds were 100 grain hollow points.

Lying on the cold ground, I scanned the area with the scope and quickly found my target, still in search of a winter meal. "Hey Pop, count to three and then whistle."

With his hands over his ears, my Father cooperated. "One, two, three." When he whistled, that groundhog stood straight up as if to say, "Shoot me." I aimed at the center of its neck and squeezed off a round. "Ka-boom-splat," was the sound of the cartridge firing and the bullet tearing meat in the target's throat.

"Sounded like a hit to me!" I exclaimed.

"Damn, that thing's loud," complained my father.

"Good shot, Johnny Lee," admitted Uncle Bart. "Guess I owe you ten."

As I put the gun away, Max jumped up, tail wagging, announcing the approach of a pickup truck. It looked like Uncles Willie and Samuel.

"Well now," announced Uncle Bart, "believe it's about time for a shot of that 'shine."

"Sounds good," I said.

Pop gave me a funny look. Unlike his brothers, he didn't care much for drinking early in the day.

"Y'all head on up to the barn while I take this game in the house," spoke Uncle Bart. "By the way, Johnny, if you want some of this squirrel, you'll have to stay and help with the milkin'. Jane and Paula rode down to Nashville with Joshua. He got 'em all tickets to watch the Cats play Vanderbilt."

"So why didn't Josh get me a ticket?"

"Believe he did. I told him you were gonna be busy."

Chapter 18

On our way up to the barn, Pop never said a word. We met his brothers where they parked. After howdies, we entered the barn. I tried to read the minds of my uncles to see if they were pissed about being called to meet. They too seemed unusually quiet.

When Uncle Bart got there he handed me a ten dollar bill. "You boys just missed Johnny's *execution* of a groundhog. Hell, it was 20 yards down past the mailbox. One shot from the maple tree."

"Reckon he's become a killin' machine," Uncle Samuel replied with a glare.

For some reason, the comment didn't sound like a compliment.

"Well, let's get this thing started," Uncle Bart said, "Got other things to do."

Uncle Willie opened the cabinet for the moonshine as Pop latched the barn door. The Mason jar, which appeared to be just as full this time as the last, got passed around one swig at a time until we all had our bellies warmed. Uncle Bart led us in the same prayer used on my last visit. At the end, however, he added, "And, make sure this youngin' knows that in the barn, we don't lie to one another. Amen."

We all echoed, "Amen."

As I made the sign of the cross, I thought, *What the hell does that mean? Why would I lie to my elders?*

Additional hay had been stacked in the barn. Would that make the first leg of the tunnel longer? Before having the chance to find out, someone said we'd be using the short trip to the room. After turning off the light switch, we all exited the back door of the barn and walked single file into the storm cellar.

Using the tunnel, we were soon in the family room. All eyes were on me.

"Well, son," said my impatient father, "you've got the floor. Let's hear what ya got to say."

Suddenly I found myself wishing for one more shot of that moonshine. "Contrary to what you guys might be thinking, I didn't come here to talk about what happened to Pete and Joe. I'm A-Okay with that." The elders exchanged glances. "But, I do think you should know I got questioned about their deaths by some homicide detectives."

"And why you reckon they'd be talkin' to you?" questioned Father.

"My boss said they were talking to anyone who worked around Pete and Joe in the last six months. That put me on their list."

"So what'd you tell 'em?" asked an anxious Uncle Bart.

"Nothing. Don't worry. Made sure they knew I was never acquainted with Pete and Joe. But there's more. Something you guys gotta hear."

"Well, spit it out, boy," blurted Uncle Willie.

"One of the detectives who interviewed me asked about Sissy. Dammit, guys, she knew everything. All the details. And she even asked me if I overheard Pete and Joe talking about raping my sister."

"Good God," mumbled my dad. Then he looked at Willie. "Looks like you were right. I screwed up. Shoulda kept it to ourselves."

Uncle Bart said, "James, you had no way of knowing. Didn't expect somebody to go off and do somethin' stupid."

Confused, I asked, "Somebody wanna fill me in?"

"Later, maybe," said Pop. "But first, is there anything else you need to say?"

"Yeah, there is one thing." You could have heard a pin drop. Everyone seemed to be listening anxiously. "Didn't you guys say that Uncle Samuel would check out Pete and Joe before we did anything to 'em?"

"Yes Son, we *sure* did."

"Well, what came of that?"

Everyone seemed confused, standing silently until finally my father looked at his younger brother and spoke. "Samuel, you tell him what he needs to know."

It sounded like I wouldn't be getting the entire story, but I listened.

Uncle Samuel held his hands up and said, "There's not a lot to tell. I talked to a friend of ours who works at the Louisville Police Department."

"You mean Paula Dawson?"

"Now who the hell told you that?"

"Jane."

"Shoulda known," Samuel replied as his brothers shook their heads.

"You didn't say anything to Jane, did you?"

"Noooo."

"Good. Anyway, Paula was supposed to have a detective friend look into it. Judging from what you just said, it would appear maybe you ran into that detective. And so far, we ain't heard back from Paula about what her friend found out."

"You're shitting me," I said, "So you guys just killed those boys on my word?"

"Oh, my God." spoke Pop, glancing around the room.

"I'm not likin' this, boys," Uncle Willie complained with a weird expression. "Somethin' ain't right."

Uncle Bart said, "Hold on, now. We might have this boy all wrong. Ain't never known him to be ignorant."

I got pissed. "Would someone here please tell me what the hell's going on?"

Uncle Bart said, "Johnny, we didn't kill 'em."

"Buuulllshit. Don't be messing with me. This ain't funny."

"Son," my dad spoke, "we're not kiddin'."

"So, if you guys didn't do it, then who did?"

My father's forehead wrinkled as he frowned and said, "We thought you killed 'em."

"No way! And you guys thought that's why I wanted to meet today? Son of a... Dad, it wasn't me."

"Well if Johnny didn't do it, we're damn sure gonna have to find out who did," complained Uncle Willie.

My father said, "Son, you do realize what we meant when we said no one lies in the room?"

"Pop, swear to God, I didn't have anything to do with it. Hell, I figured it was you guys."

Pop looked at his youngest brother. "Double-check with Paula. Find out exactly who she talked to."

"Can't believe y'all trust someone like her. She ain't even part of the family."

Uncle Samuel said, "Johnny, Paula might not be family, but her family and ours go way back. It was her daddy, Darrel Dawson, who helped our daddy get back the farms after they were stolen by the bank. Take my word, we can trust Paula."

"So why didn't you tell me about her before now?"

"Because Jane doesn't know about Paula, and we don't want her to. We were afraid you might slip and say something. That's all there is to it."

"Why don't you want Jane to know?"

"She's not involved, Johnny, and therefore, she's better off not knowing. Besides, girl talks too much. Might slip."

Things were at least starting to make sense. "Maybe we don't know who killed those bastards, but one thing's for sure, the cops suspect me, and I'm not too happy with that."

"You're right," said Uncle Bart. "And if they can't pin it on you, they'll be lookin' at your brother Ray, and then your daddy, and then the rest of us. We'll all need to be careful. Don't make any phone calls about this. We'll be gettin' together from time to time anyway. We can talk then. Meantime, Samuel, when Paula brings Jane home this evening, I'll try and tell her she needs to speak with you. Hell, *she* probably thinks we killed them boys."

Pop spoke again. "Johnny, it's now more important than ever that we don't speak about this to anyone. You understand."

"Yes, sir."

"And after dinner, you best leave before Josh and the girls get back. Bart can take care of things better if you ain't here. Paula might even be thinkin' you did the killin'. No need for you to be around her 'till Samuel has a chance to explain things."

"Whatever you say," I replied, at the same time wishing for another chance to see Paula.

Uncle Willie, who had been unusually quiet, said, "Hope y'all know we done got ourselves in a pickle. Been better off taking care of this thing ourselves."

"Do me a favor, Willie," said Pop. "Save your *I told you so* for later. Right now we just gotta figure out what's goin' on. Hell, if ain't none of us done anything wrong, we got nothin' to worry about. Right?"

"He's gotta good point," added Uncle Samuel.

"True," admitted the ever-cautious Uncle Willie, "but that don't mean we ain't suspects, and it don't mean they ain't watchin' us."

"Another good point," replied Pop. "So we do need to watch our backs."

"Okay then," said Uncle Bart, "we still together on this thing?"

We all reached in, touching fists and gave a united, "Together!"

"Good," finished Uncle Bart. "Now let's get the hell out of here."

Everyone left the way we came in. While walking the short distance from the cellar to the barn, I sensed each of the brothers nonchalantly analyzing the visible terrain. Seemed the Special Forces were on alert. I learned a lot that day about the elders. Guess they learned a little about me too.

Chapter 19

An hour after dinner, Uncle Bart started glancing at his watch. I took the hint and excused myself.

"Where you off to so quick?" asked Grandma Smith. "Thought you'd wait and see Josh, and Jane, and the Dawson girl."

"Promised Mary Ellen I'd stop by."

"Best stay away from Mary Ellen. She's married now. That Davis boy gets jealous, he's liable to shoot you."

"He's my friend, Grandma."

"You didn't say you were going by to see him," added Aunt Mary. "Grandma's right, them Davises are a rough lot."

Better listen, whispered Gabrielle.

I drove up in front of the Davis' doublewide just before sundown. Bobbie's truck sat in the drive behind his daddy's. Figured stopping in would kill two birds with one stone: a chance to see my old friend and his parents. It being Saturday evening, Mary Ellen and the baby would most likely be there with Bobbie.

Reaching into the glove box for a full pack of cigarettes, I noticed a small glass bottle of cologne. I poured a couple drops on my hand and rubbed it into my beard. Still had that morning's *Courier-Journal* in the seat. I had intended to give it to Uncle Bart, but, forgot. Bobbie's dad would appreciate it.

Mrs. Davis must have heard my tires crunching in the gravel. She opened the front door and stood there looking the way I always remembered her: homemade dress and gray hair up in a bun.

"Come on in here out of the cold. Ain't seen you in a while."

The delicious aroma of dried beans cooking drifted out the door. On my way in, Mrs. Davis gave me a big hug and said, "Boy, you sure do smell sweet. Shame I ain't about thirty years younger."

"Thirty years?" I joked. "Hell, you ain't that old, are you?"

"Who is that sweet-talkin' my woman?" ribbed her better half, who was sitting at the kitchen table along with Bobbie and a half a dozen empty beer cans.

I said, "Sure is a nice place y'all have here."

"Still don't feel like home," complained the old woman. "So how's your grandma doin'?"

"She sweeter than sweet potato pie."

Mr. Davis said, "Boy, that sounds good. Bring any with you?"

Mrs. Davis read my face and said, "Don't worry about him. He only hears what he wants to hear."

Bobbie's dad had changed considerably since my last visit. More weight and less hair. He gave me a friendly nod and said, "Damn, check out the mane on that boy. Looks like Jesus Christ just walked in."

"Easy, old man. It'll take a whole lot more than hair to put me in His ranks."

"You got that right," came a surprised comment from Mary Ellen, walking in from a back bedroom. Everyone laughed except Bobbie. He sat quietly, elbows leaning on the table.

When my eyes met Mary Ellen's, she glanced away. She seemed worried about something.

I offered the newspaper to Mr. Davis.

"Well looky here," he said while spreading it out on the table. "Johnny done brought us some big city news."

My old friend still hadn't spoken, so I decided to break the ice. "What's going on, Bobbie?"

Slowly looking up, he said, "Not much. Good to see ya. Sorry 'bout passin' out on you at the house."

"Don't worry about it. Been there myself a time or two. Looks like you've had a few today."

"Yeah, but I'll be all right," he answered while struggling to rise. Making it to his feet, he leaned forward to give me a hug. "Damn Johnny, you do smell good. You fixin' to go out on a date?"

Caught off guard, I lied a little. "Well, I did sort of meet someone last time down. Hoping to see her again later."

Bobbie, slumping back down into his seat, said, "And who might that pretty lady be?"

"Believe I best keep her name a secret. Start telling everybody, it might wind up in the next *Gazette*."

Mary Ellen turned from the sink and kicked the cat clean out of the kitchen. "Git out from under my feet!"

After an awkward moment of silence, I said, "Where you hiding that baby?"

"Back there takin' a nap," answered Mary Ellen. "Afraid I'm gonna have to get 'er to the house pretty soon."

Mrs. Davis said, "Now dear, might as well spend the night. I'm fixin' supper right now, and Bobbie ain't in no shape to be drivin' back there anyway. You and me can go to church in the morning."

"I'll leave that up to Bobbie," replied Mary Ellen.

"I'm okay right here," Bobbie acknowledged.

"Well that's fine, but I still need some things from the house for Olivia and somethin' decent for me to wear in the mornin'."

Mrs. Davis suggested, "Daddy, why don't you run Mary Ellen back to the house?"

The old man had already become interested in the newspaper. "Believe my truck's blocked in. Johnny's probably in the back. Why don't you let him take 'er?"

I shrugged my shoulders and said, "That's okay with me if it's okay with Bobbie."

Bobbie got a little sarcastic. "What, you think I don't trust y'all?"

"Listen here, Bobbie Davis," snapped Mary Ellen, "don't think you have to worry about Johnny, but your sorry drunk ass better start worryin' about me."

Wow, I thought. *What a mouthful.*

119

Even Mr. Davis left the news long enough to acknowledge what was said. "Damn, son. Sounds like you ain't been doin' your homework."

Bobbie stood up and said, "Y'all can all kiss my ass," as he headed off toward the bathroom.

I could see the pain in his mother's expression.

Mary Ellen grabbed her coat and started toward the door. "Come on, Johnny, let's go so I can get back and look after the baby *and* him."

Glancing back at the Davises, I asked, "Sure this is okay?"

"Don't worry about it," spoke Mr. Davis. "Just don't be too long."

Mary Ellen said, "Mama, can you keep an eye on Olivia? We'll be right back."

"Sure, Honey," she replied while giving me a look.

Neither of us had a word to say as I maneuvered the old Dodge into the woods. The further we drove, the blacker it got. I nearly hit a huge owl as it flushed up from the weeds with a rabbit dangling from its talons. By avoiding the bird, I damn near left the road.

"Careful, Johnny," warned Mary Ellen. "You know you can't get in no hurry on this old road at night."

The whole situation had me nervous. When I pulled out my cigarettes, Mary Ellen grabbed the pack. "Gimme one of those."

"Thought you quit?"

"Just now started again. Hand me the lighter."

"What, you think I can't drive and light a cigarette at the same time?"

"Just keep your eyes on the road."

I handed over the Zippo. Mary Ellen lit one for me and then one for her. After a long hard draw, she exhaled, put her hand over mine on the stick shift, and said, "Just like old times."

I said nothing.

As the truck whined along in first gear, all four hounds showed up in the headlights. They escorted us right through the cold creek water.

At the house, Mary Ellen jumped out of the truck so fast you'd have thought she was in a race. "Come on, Johnny, help me out here." She grabbed an armload of firewood from a stack on the porch.

I got out, picked up a few pieces, and followed her in the front door.

She quickly stoked the woodstove, filling it with new kindling. "That'll do for now. Just put yours in the bucket. Bobbie'll be up at daybreak. He can feed the fire when he comes to feed the cattle."

She turned on lights in the kitchen. I could see her running around grabbing this and that. On her way back through she handed me the bag and said, "Here's the stuff for Olivia," before bouncing up the stairs, two at a time.

A minute later, she came back down with a dress draped over her arm. In what seemed like one movement, she laid the clothing across the back of a chair, took the bag out of my hand, placed it on the floor, and then shoved me toward the couch. I didn't resist.

Before you could say lickity split, she was on top of me, gripping my hair, and kissing me like a mad woman.

The whole world disappeared. *Forget Gabrielle, forget God, forget Bobbie, forget everything and just do what needs to be done. She has a need. It's not your fault her husband won't take care of it. Why resist?*

What happened there in my friend's living room might have been wrong, but it sure felt right at the time. Neither of us said a word. We just did what lovers do. Most awesome twenty-five minutes of my life. Until it ended. Suddenly I felt like Adam—exposed, naked in the Garden of Eden. There I lay with another man's wife, thinking, *What the hell did I just do? And what am I gonna do now?*

"Hey," I whispered, "We best get up and out of here before someone gets worried."

"Don't wanna leave," she whispered back. "Just like to lay here for the rest of my life."

Finally, I could hear Gabrielle. *Now look what you did.*

"Where have you been?" I mistakenly whispered as if to take the blame off my shoulders.

"I've been right here all along," replied Mary Ellen. "Why couldn't you be here instead of Bobbie?"

Oh, my God. She thinks I was talking to her. I softly said, "Come on, we gotta go. We can talk on the way."

Mary Ellen said nothing but slid off the couch and out of sight, clothes in hand, covered only by her waist-long hair. While pulling up my Levi's, I began talking to myself: "God, what a mess. Damn you Gabrielle. Why didn't you stop me?"

Clothed and brushing her hair, Mary Ellen reappeared. "Who were you talking to?"

"No one, just myself."

"Daddy says when a man talks to himself, he's talkin' to the devil."

"And if I keep doing what I just did, I'm gonna be spending some hard time with the devil."

"Bullshit, Johnny Lee. What you just did was the nicest thing anybody's done for me in a long time, so don't go beatin' yourself up. Now let's you and me get back before Mrs. Davis gets suspicious. And I want another one of your cigarettes on the way."

Hmmm, this woman has the same coolness in a crisis as my father and his brothers.

"Can you zip me up?" Mary Ellen asked while turning her back to me.

"Sure." But then as she pulled her hair over I noticed a bruise on her back. "What the hell's this?" I inquired, pulling the garment open, exposing four more dark purple fist-sized marks. "What's with all these bruises?" Couldn't believe I hadn't noticed while we were on the couch.

"Don't worry about it, just zip me up and let's go."

"Did Bobbie do this to you?"

"Said don't worry about it!"

"No way," I complained while zipping up the dress. "We're not going anywhere until you tell me what's going on."

"Damn you, Johnny Lee. You just gotta hear it, don't 'cha? Sometimes when Bobbie's drinkin' he don't know what he's doin'."

"Don't give me that. He knew enough to keep it on your back so no one could see it. Do your daddy and brothers know about this?"

"No! And don't you go tellin' 'em. They all warned me about marryin' Bobbie. Maybe I shoulda listened, but I didn't. So it's *my* problem. I'll straighten Bobbie out soon enough. Right now let's get back."

"But Mary Ellen, you don't have to put up—"

She put her hand over my mouth, looked me in the eye and said, "Please don't ruin what just happened. Ain't felt this good in a long time. Just let me enjoy the moment."

It looked like I might as well drop it for the time being, but I damn sure wouldn't forget. "Come on, let's go." I grabbed the bag from the floor while Mary Ellen checked the fire one last time. She gathered her dress from the chair and then shut the door behind us.

The oldest hound lay there on the porch, staring at me sadly as though he knew his master had just been betrayed.

After starting the Dodge, I got an idea. "Get out of the truck, Mary Ellen."

"Do what?"

"Trust me," I said, leaving the cab. "I have a plan."

She got out and said, "What are you doing? We need to hurry."

"Just come over here by the steps in front of the headlights."

She did.

"Now sit down on the ground for a second."

"Are you nuts?"

"Humor me. Just do it."

She did. Then I kicked some dirt up on her.

Jumping up, she complained, "What the hell's wrong with you?"

"Just trying to cover our asses. We've been here a little too long. Now we can tell 'em you slipped and fell coming off the steps, and of course you were dizzy so you had to sit a few minutes." With that said, I picked up a bit of dirt and tossed it on her church clothes.

"My God, Johnny, aren't you the smart one," she replied while climbing back into the truck. "Girl might get the impression you've done this before."

"Not really, just trying to cover all the bases."

Backing out, I turned on the radio and we both lit a cigarette for the short drive. About halfway down the old road, Mary Ellen leaned over, kissed me on the cheek, and said, "Thank you, Johnny."

We both remained silent from that point on.

When we parked in front of the doublewide, Mrs. Davis stood at the front door holding Olivia in her arms. "There's your moma," she said on our way in.

"Did my little girl miss her mommy?" asked Mary Ellen in one of those singsong motherly tones.

As we walked through the door, her mother-in-law immediately noticed the dirt on Mary Ellen's clothes. "What on earth happened to you?"

"It ain't nothin'. Took a spill back at the house."

"Seems she can't walk down her own steps," I quickly added.

"You okay, honey?"

"Yeah. Made me dizzy for a few minutes. Worst part is I got my church clothes dirty. Stepped on the end of my dress, and that's what tripped me."

Good job, I thought.

One lie leads to another, whispered Gabrielle.

"Come on back to the bathroom," offered Mrs. Davis, "and I'll attend to you and those clothes. Johnny, you go on in the kitchen and get you somethin' to drink. We'll be eatin' in just a few minutes."

"No thank you, ma'am, can't stay that long. Gotta be somewhere soon."

"That's right," said Mr. Davis, still buried in the newspaper at the kitchen table, "got yourself a date with that pretty girl, don't you?"

Avoiding Mary Ellen's eyes, I placed Olivia's bag on a chair in the front room and walked toward the kitchen to say my goodbyes. Though I didn't want to see Bobbie, much less talk to him after what I'd seen on Mary Ellen's back, it might appear strange if I didn't at least say goodbye. Fortunately, Mr. Davis sat alone with a fresh-brewed cup of coffee, reading the obituaries.

"I swear, it's hard to believe all these people died in Louavall in just one day."

"I hear ya. Reckon that city life's hard on folks. Where's Bobbie?"

"He done went to bed. Boy's a mess, ain't he?"

"Kinda looks that way. You know, Mr. Davis, with all due respect, you folks allowing him to sit around here drinking isn't gonna help matters."

"Done talked to that boy 'til I'm blue in the face. He's took to drinkin', and I don't believe he'll stop 'til it kills 'im. If he ain't drinkin' here, he'll be drinkin' somewhere else."

I turned around, and there stood Mrs. Davis and Mary Ellen with the baby. Both women gave me a look as if to say, "Drop the subject."

Feeling uneasy, I said, "Gotta get going. Just tell Bobbie I'll stop by to see him later."

Mary Ellen held the baby out, saying, "Here Johnny, you best say hi to Olivia before you go runnin' off."

Holding the little angel, I considered asking about baptism but decided it might not be the best time. Then I noticed an odd stare from Mrs. Davis, watching me run my fingers through the baby's silky, red-tinted strands of hair, almost as if she resented my holding her grandchild. After a good snuggling, I handed Olivia back to her mother and made my way out the front door.

While driving away, I could feel Mary Ellen watching. I drove non-stop back to Louisville, obsessively glancing in the mirror at the red tint in my beard.

Chapter 20

By the first week of February 1977, gossip at work had Pete and Joe as victims of a professional hit. I had been filling a second shift position for the week and decided to stop on my way home for some live music. They called Wednesdays hump night at the Phoenix Hill Tavern—no cover charge and lots of live music. Only a week before my 21st birthday, it would be my last need for a fake ID. Since no one at work wanted to join me, I decided to go alone.

Next to my truck, two co-workers were sharing a bottle of Jim Beam in a car. Donnie and Jerry both had wives, so they did their partying in the parking lot rather than going out to the bars. I joined their married man's ritual long enough to get a good whiskey buzz.

On my short drive to the tavern, WUOL provided classical music, a unique contrast to the rock I would soon be listening to. Phoenix Hill was packed, and I had to parallel park on one of the side streets a block and a half away. Two guys stood on the corner between the nightspot and me. The fact that they just stood there in the cold seemed strange. Were they simply talking, or were they waiting for trouble? Either way, I suddenly felt a desire for my Smith & Wesson. Normally it stayed in the truck, but I'd left the little .38 at my brother Ray's place for a repair.

Opening the noisy truck door alerted the two men. They both turned my way momentarily and then went back to talking. Wearing jeans, western style boots, and a John Deere cap must have given me a hick look. As I walked their way, one commented, "Well what do you know? Farmer Joe done come up to the big city."

The other one said, "Hey boy, you got any of that good green? Can you share a little with us?"

The sarcasm in their voices suggested trouble. I wouldn't mind taking on one, but even whiskey didn't make me brave enough or dumb enough to fight two. I needed a plan and knew my first statement would likely determine the outcome. In my shirt pocket, I had a large ballpoint pen—the one used to fill out order papers at work. Both men stared as I reached under my jacket. "Sure guys, got it right here, but I don't like sharin' with strangers." While speaking I clicked the button on the pen, slowly, creating a sound similar to that of a hammer cocking. Judging from their wide-eyed expressions, it worked. They thought I had a gun. Both stepped back quickly.

"Take it easy, dude," said one of the assholes. "Didn't mean you any harm."

I glared at one, then the other, for a few seconds and then started walking, backwards, hand still hidden under my jacket. From a distance, I added, "Anything happens to my truck, I'll find you two and butcher your asses like a goddamn hog."

"Man, you're a freak," the second man commented as they crossed the street and headed off into the night.

Pleased with my performance, I walked the final fifty yards or so to Baxter Avenue, turned left in front of the building, and found a few patrons chatting near the main entrance. Once I was inside the large wooden door, waves of live rock vibrated through my clothing.

The bouncer, engulfed in the company of an evil-looking redhead, only forced a two-second glance at my passing. He didn't even bother checking my ID.

As I moved down the corridor leading to the main stage and bar room, it all just got louder and louder. Colored lights, bouncing bodies, and a smoky haze painted the scene for my night's entertainment. I bumped elbows with half a dozen people in route to the bar. Standing room only forced me to find a leaning spot at the end. Benson, the bartender, knew me well.

"Johnny Lee Smith. Whatcha been up to?"

"Nothing too exciting," I answered. "But that could change any minute at the Hill."

"I hear ya, brother. So what's it gonna be?"

Didn't see any reason to change whiskies. "Jim Beam on ice, and make it a double." Benson fixed me right up, and I sucked down about half the drink in one swallow.

Next to me sat a decent-looking blonde being wooed by a man at least ten years her elder. I thought she might be a hooker, but then she spoke of a nursing position at the Methodist Hospital. *She can nurse me anytime.*

The man she spoke to wore designer jeans and a nicely-pressed shirt. Figured him to be married, since no man I knew ironed his own shirts. He ordered, "Another round." Both were smoking; the ashtray had five butts, three of her Virginia Slims and two of his Kool menthols. The lady's fragrance seemed expensive.

The band began playing one of my favorite ZZ Top songs, "La Grange," drawing attention toward the stage. My radar honed in on another couple near the dance floor. Of all people, it was Cousin Jane's friend Paula Dawson and Detective Lantz, both dressed casually. From the bar, I began to monitor their behavior while considering the possibility they were watching me as well.

Paula looked just as fine there as she had in Grayson County. I wanted to say hi, but I couldn't. *What if she goes back and tells the elders about me socializing with one of the detectives investigating the Pete and Joe case.* Moving up to the building's next level, where a solo act performed, would be wise. I downed the rest of my drink and then saluted Benson while turning to walk away. Three or four steps later, I found myself face-to-face with Lantz's partner, Detective Kelly. She at least pretended to be surprised, and damned if her feminine appearance didn't knock me for a loop.

On our first meeting, the woman dressed and acted butch. Yet on this night, she appeared just the opposite. Shoulder-length hair fell strikingly across her forehead, partially covering one eye. Unlike before, this time she wore makeup: dark red lipstick, rosy cheeks and mascara. Diamond earrings glistened through strands of hair. She wore a white dress, low cut and short, that accentuated her dark skin and her long, well-proportioned legs. No doubt, she noticed my scan.

"Hey, Detective Kelly, almost didn't recognize you."

"How you doing, Johnny?" She glanced at my cap and said, "Nice to see you again," as though we were friends. Then she leaned toward me and requested, "Tonight you can just call me Kelly, okay?"

Her warm breath did wonders for my mood. "No problem," I replied. "So what brings a..." I leaned toward her ear and whispered, "Homicide dick to a place like this?"

She leaned back and said, "Probably the same thing that brings an underage butcher to a place like this."

Wow, witty and on top of things. "Would you like to see my ID?"

"No, that's okay. They should have done that at the door."

"So, you here alone?"

She hesitated, "Not exactly, I'm supposed to meet up with David and a girl from work. Haven't seen them, have you?"

"Your partner? No," I lied, "but that doesn't mean they're not here. Can I buy you a drink while you wait?"

She paused before saying, "Sure, why not."

I seemed to be playing with fire, yet my old buddy Jim Beam had me ready for the challenge. We maneuvered ourselves back to the bar just as the blonde and her friend got up, vacating two stools. With an English accent I said, "For you, my lady," while motioning Kelly to her seat. Fortunately, our backs would be to the area where I last saw Lantz and Dawson.

"And a chipper thanks to you, good fellow," she played along, to my continued pleasure.

Dangerous as it may have seemed, Detective Kelly's after-work personality struck me as enchanting. While waiting on Benson, I inquired, "Mind a personal question?"

"Depends on how personal."

"The tough guy personality you portrayed at the packinghouse doesn't match what I see here tonight. Which is really you?"

"Which do you prefer?"

Whoa, trick question. "To be honest, kinda like both."

"Both, now how can that be?"

"Well, gotta say your tough side's good, since I don't care for submissive women."

"Oooh, I like that," she butted in. "And?"

"And, on the other hand, I also like your feminine side."

"My feminine side? What're you saying, Johnny? You thought I was manly?"

"To be honest, you did come across a little butch."

"You mean as in lesbian?"

"Hey, you asked."

"Damn, I'm a cop. Cops don't wear skirts."

Trying to change the subject, I said, "One more question and I'll quit."

"Jesus, Johnny, you writing a book?"

"No, but I have to ask, why do you want me to call you by your last name?"

"Oh, that's easy," she relaxed, "Kelly is my first name. Go by my first name on the job because I don't want strangers to know my last name."

Every time this lady opened her mouth, I liked her more.

Benson made his way to us. "Mr. Johnny, like another Jim Beam?"

"Sure, and whatever pleases the lady."

Still looking at me, Benson asked, "Double?"

"No, not this time."

Detective Kelly grinned as if to say thanks, looked at Benson and said, "I'll have the same, please."

Hell yes, I thought, *a whiskey drinking woman.*

We both watched in silence as Benson flipped the bourbon bottle in the process of pouring our drinks. When served, I paid the bill plus a two dollar tip.

"Good habit." said Kelly.

"Benson's a fine man. Always tip him double. He works the railroad during the day and here at night, trying to feed six kids."

"Wasn't talking about your tip. I like the way you watched him make your drink. Good habit," she repeated before taking a sip. "So, now that you've written *your* book, maybe it's *my* turn to ask questions."

"Fine, but should this be considered an interrogation?"

"No, nothing like that. Just wondering why a smart guy like you would waste his life in a packinghouse."

"Hmm. Some days I get out of bed and ask myself that same question."

"Hey, what's going on here?" interrupted Detective Lantz.

"*Damn*," I thought.

Kelly said, "Hey, David."

"Thought you were meeting *us* here tonight," complained Lantz.

"I am," she explained. "Looked around, but didn't see you guys. Then I ran into Mr. Smith, and he offered to buy me a drink."

Paula stood behind the detective and remained silent. Guess she didn't quite know what to think of the arrangement. Lantz, apparently unhappy with my presence, said, "Ooookay, so how are you, Mr. Smith, or Johnny, isn't it?"

"I'm good. How about you?"

He forced an, "I'm cool," with a dose of that, 'Hey, I'm a cop' attitude. There he stood with one of Grayson County's hottest babes and acting like he owned Kelly.

With the whiskey doing my talking, I jabbed, "So, Detective Lantz, which of these fine ladies *are* you dating?"

He looked pissed. "My relationship with this lady standing behind me is none of your business, and I'm just looking out for my partner."

"From what I've seen, I'd say she's more than capable of looking out for herself."

Finally Paula spoke up. "Been back down home to see Jane lately?" Her heavy country accent seemed out of place.

"Couple weeks ago," I replied.

Lantz seemed surprised. "You two know one another?"

"Sure do," I said, shocked that Paula had even mentioned knowing me under the circumstances. "Already had the pleasure of meeting Ms. Dawson."

"My, my, small world isn't it?" commented Kelly with a smile.

Rather than trying to explain my relationship with Paula, I decided to get the hell out of Dodge. *Let her explain,* I thought. *She brought it up.* "Guys, I hate to leave good company, but I've got to go. Let's do this another time."

Lantz looked relieved, but commented otherwise. "Don't run off on our account."

"Don't worry, I'm not."

Paula didn't speak, but Kelly did, as if she were reading my mind about our sudden loss of privacy. "You're right, Johnny, we should do this again sometime."

"Sounds good," I replied, saluting a long distance goodbye toward Benson.

"Be sure and say hi to Jane and her family," spoke Paula, with a, *Glad you're leaving* look.

Kelly reached over, drink in hand, and said, "To our next meeting."

I tapped her glass and replied, "The pleasure will be mine." We both downed the drinks and then popped our empties on the bar. Picking up my cigarettes from next to the ashtray, I turned to walk away. A business card had been slid between my cigarette pack and its cellophane wrapper. *Louisville Police, Detective Kelly Rauschenberg.*

No wonder she goes by her first name. Glancing back, I caught a wink from Kelly. She knew I'd seen the card.

Chapter 21

Cold night air sobered me some as I walked past the end of the Phoenix Hill building and started across the street. After crossing the side street where I'd earlier encountered the two strange fellows, I could see that the Dodge's passenger door stood partially open. "Sonofa...," I cut my whisper short. A slow scan of the area revealed no other people. I moved forward quietly as though stalking game. Eventually, reaching the front of the truck and squatting for a few seconds, I listened to what sounded like someone stealing my brand new radio. Such audacity infuriated me to the point of physically shaking.

Peeking around the front of the truck revealed a leg sticking out and a foot on the curb with the door pulled against it. Rage boiled in me as I lunged forward against the Dodge's heavy door, smashing that leg at the shin. Muffled screaming came from under the dash as I yanked the door open.

"Please, mister, don't hurt me!"

"What the hell?" I said, looking into the face of a kid. He had a knife in his hand, which was most likely intended for cutting the radio's wiring harness. His injured leg hung out of the cab as he lay twisted between the dash and seat. The boy's hands were shaking. Tears were forming as the whites of his eyes glowed bright against his dirty, almost girlish face. He looked scared to death.

"Best put the knife down, unless you want me to go ahead and break that leg."

Without hesitation, he dropped the knife out the door.

"You by yourself, boy?"

"Probably," he grumbled.

"What's that mean?"

"Think my friend ran away. He was supposed to let me know if anyone was coming."

I scanned the area again, and didn't see anyone. My catch appeared harmless.

"How old are you?"

"Fourteen."

"Well, get your thievin' ass out of my truck."

The kid raised up, looking down at his bloody pants leg as if to say he couldn't walk.

"Don't even go there. You're not hurt that bad. Now get out before I grab that leg and drag you out."

Reluctantly, he used his good leg first, then his right. "It hurts."

"Pull that pants leg up, and let's take a look." Sure enough, the door had broken the skin, but not the leg. The bleeding had already stopped. "You'll live."

"Gonna let me go?" the kid asked.

"Right after you fix my radio."

"You mean like, put it back the way it was?"

"That's exactly what I mean."

The boy broke a smile and said, "That's all I have to do?"

Relaxing and feeling a little bad about injuring his leg, I said, "Sit down on the curb."

"Why?"

"Because I wanna talk about what you were doing in my truck."

"You gotta be kidding," he answered in disbelief.

The little thief hesitated, but he finally sat on the curb. Taking a seat next to him, my breath steaming in the night air, I asked, "You cold?"

"I'm okay."

"Not even gonna ask why you were in my truck. Obviously, you somehow convinced yourself that you need my radio more than I do. But I would like to ask about your conscience."

"About my what?"

"Your conscience, boy."

"My conscience? You on drugs, mister?"

I ignored his comment. "Didn't something inside your mind tell you that it's wrong to steal somebody else's property?"

The kid looked confused but answered, "Suppose maybe I knew better."

"But you did it anyway. That means you didn't listen to your conscience, or at least you ignored it. Let me ask you something. If you were walking down the street and passed two strangers, one of whom was talking, would you listen to what he had to say?"

"No, not really."

"That's right. But, if you knew the person's name, you'd probably listen, wouldn't you?"

"Yeah," he replied slowly as if ready for the punch line.

"That's what I thought. So tell me, what's your favorite name?"

The kid hesitated. "Boy or girl?"

"Leave that up to you."

He tilted his head a bit, like a confused puppy. "Sarah."

"There you go. From now on your conscience's name will be Sarah. And now that you know her name, maybe you'll listen when she speaks. Make sense?"

Before the boy could answer, a police cruiser pulled up to the corner. Seeing us, the officer turned our way, stopped, rolled down the window and asked in a low voice, "There a problem here?"

I could see the boy shaking with nerves or cold or both. "No, sir. This little feller come running across the street and slipped, skinning up his leg. Just making sure he's all right."

"How 'bout it kid, you okay?" the officer questioned.

Relieved, the boy answered, "Yes, sir."

"You live close?"

"Next block over."

"That's what I thought. I've seen you hanging out around here before. Now you get on home, and don't let me see you again tonight."

"Yes, sir."

"What about you, mister, you walking?"

"No sir, that's my Dodge."

"This old truck belongs to you?"

"That's right."

"What year is it?"

"'49."

"Cool," he said. "You have a good night. And young man, you get your butt on home."

"Yes, sir," answered the boy as the cruiser moved on.

I stood up and asked, "You able to walk all right?"

The kid rose and tried his leg. "It's okay."

"Now you remember what I said about listening to your conscience, and don't forget that I coulda turned your ass in."

As I moved toward my truck, he said, "Hey mister, don't you want me to put your radio back in the dash?"

"No, don't worry about it. I'll do it when I get to the house. Got better light there. You just get on home. If you don't, I hope that cop hauls your ass in." I picked up his pocket knife from the curb, folded it closed, and said, "Here. You might need this."

When I pitched it his way, the boy caught it with both hands and said, "Thanks, mister." As I climbed into the truck and started the engine, he hollered, "Hey, mister..." Waiting until I lowered the passenger side window, he finished, "Sarah says thanks too."

I tipped my cap and lit a cigarette while watching him limp away.

Chapter 22

For an entire week, I entertained the idea of sharing another drink with the off-duty version of Kelly Rauschenberg. No doubt, the lady had me by several years; nonetheless, I did find her attractive both physically and intellectually.

Working the day shift, I decided to see if Wednesday might be Kelly's regular party night. Using a pay phone at work I called the number on her business card. After several rings, a man answered. "Louisville Police, Jackson speaking."

"Sorry sir, just trying to reach Detective Kelly."

"This is her desk, but Detective Kelly's unavailable at the moment. Is there something I can do for you?"

Caught off guard, I said, "It's nothing important. Just wanted to speak to her. I can call back."

In a polite tone the man said, "That's fine, sir, but can I tell her who called?"

Should I? Why not? "Tell her it was Johnny Smith. She knows me."

"Okay, Mr. Smith, I'll give her the message when she returns."

Disappointed, I hung up the phone and relinquished the idea of seeing Kelly that night.

At lunchtime, Carl Jacobs interrupted our pinochle game. "Johnny Smith, you have an outside phone call in my office."

"Is that right? Did they say who it is?"

With a voice obviously intended to capture the whole room's attention he said, "Yes, *she* did. Her name is Kelly. Sounds like a real cutie."

"Holy shit," I said while jumping out of my seat. "Take my hand, Carl, I'll be right back." Without explaining, I scurried up the steps, proud of myself for having stuck the boss with my hand at cards. That way he couldn't follow to listen in on my conversation.

As I trotted toward Carl's office, my friend Richard hesitated from palletizing Wiener Room products and said, "Slow down, birthday boy. The lady'll wait!"

How does he know it's a lady? I wondered while picking up the phone receiver. "This is Johnny."

"Hello Johnny, this is Kelly."

"Hey girl, what's up?"

"Shouldn't I be the one asking that question?"

At least twenty things must have flashed through my mind before I said, "You're right. I called to see if you're gonna be out tonight. Thought we might get together for a drink, celebrate my birthday."

"Oh, guess this means you can throw away that fake ID," she said jokingly.

"That's right, you knew, didn't you?"

"I'm a cop. It's my business to know. Anyway, what time do you get off?"

Bingo! "I'll be off at four o'clock, but probably won't be able to get away until about five. Some of the guys bought me a bottle for my birthday. They'll wanna have a drink in the parking lot."

"Best not drink too much before driving," she advised.

"I hear ya."

Then to my surprise, she suggested, "Maybe we should meet somewhere close to where you work. Perhaps a little less crowded."

"Hey, I'm open. Remember, I can get in anywhere now."

"How about that little place right down the street from your plant?"

"You mean the Rush Inn?"

"That's it. We can go somewhere else if you like."

"Hey, it's okay with me if it's okay with you."

"So let's meet there, say around five-fifteen?"

"That'll be great," I replied. "See you then."

"Okay, gotta go. Bye," and she hung up.

I walked out of that office on cloud nine. Going out with Kelly would be everything I wanted for my birthday and then some. Her suggestion for a more private atmosphere was perfect. Richard, still unloading boxes on the line, waved me over. I couldn't help but think back to his comment, "the lady'll wait."

"Hey, whatcha need, Rich?"

He spoke in a concerned voice, "Tell me something, Johnny. Who was that on the phone just now?"

"And why would you be asking?" I snapped back, as if to say it's none of your business.

"Easy boy, not trying to pry. Just happened to be in the office warming up when the phone rang, so I answered it. The lady didn't ask for you, she asked for Carl."

"No way."

"It's none of my business, pal, but something seems fishy here. I gave the phone to Carl and then left, but on the way out I heard enough to know he had an acquaintance with the person on the other end."

Richard's right, I thought. *Something's up, and I've done walked right into the trap.*

He continued, "I kept watching, Johnny. He never hung the phone up before he came and got you."

"Thanks, dude. Thanks for watching my back."

"My pleasure. Listen, little buddy, don't know what's going on here, but you'd better watch your ass. You know what Carl did before he came here, don't you?"

"Nope."

"He was a cop."

"No way!"

"And a dirty one, they say. Got fired in his rookie year for kicking the shit out of some black guy he had in handcuffs. Even took the man's money."

I thought, *Oh my God, no wonder he acts like a cop. He was a cop.* "Do me a favor. Keep this all to yourself."

I stopped for a cup of coffee on my way back to the locker room. It took me back to the night when I bought Carl a cup and he talked to me like a friend. Thinking about it made me angry, and a more fearful question came to mind. *Should this matter be taken to the elders?* My allowing these events to occur sure wouldn't make them happy.

Officially, lunch had just ended. Unofficially, everybody took their time getting back on the job. During that first sip of coffee, I heard voices coming up the steps from the break room. Heading the pack, of course, would be Carl.

"Thought you got lost," he spoke in his usual smart-ass tone.

"Sorry about that."

"So what's up with the lady?" he intruded further.

Like you don't already know. "Let's just say I'm gettin' over my broken heart."

One of the guys started in on me. "So who is this Kelly girl who makes you jump?"

If Carl hadn't told them, why should I? "Just some girl I met last week."

"Oh yeah," pushed Billy Wells. "Is it good stuff? Can I have a little bit?"

"Not as good as your wife."

Everyone laughed.

Billy turned red and shook his fist at me. "Funnnny, Johnny. How'd you like an ass whoopin' on your birthday?"

"Just kidding, Billy. But you deserved it. You know if Sherri catches you messing around, you'll be the one gettin' your ass kicked."

Carl stared without speaking.

Getting back to work gave me time to think things out. I wondered how the elders would approach this. Having the one up on Kelly could give me an advantage. Who knows, might even be able to enjoy the evening while covertly reading her intentions. One thing for sure, I couldn't afford to create a long-term relationship. Somewhere during this meeting or soon thereafter, my ties with Kelly would have to be cut forever. *What a mess.*

When the shift ended, my friends cracked friendly jokes, watching me clean up and change shirts. "Must be special!" "Somebody's in love!" "Need one of my rubbers, lover boy?" were just a few of their comments.

Let 'em think what they wanna think.

In the parking lot, the guys gave me a fifth of Jim Beam for my birthday. Between five of us, we drank it all. I decided to hang out until everyone else left, then make my exit. Had I gone first, they'd see my truck at Rush Inn. Knowing them, they'd all stop just to check out my date. It struck my mind that Carl might have communicated further with Kelly, in which case he would know the location of our meeting. Fortunately, his drive home was in the opposite direction.

Chapter 23

I got to the Rush Inn a little early and, not knowing what kind of car my date drove, went on in. A quick scan of the room revealed two guys playing pool, an older couple sitting at a table, and three men at the bar, but no Detective Kelly. I approached the bar to order a drink. The barmaid, a nice-looking forty-something, said, "Can I help you, sonny?"

"Yes ma'am, I'd like a drink."

"Ma'am?" she almost laughed. The whole room stared as the lady asked to see my ID, which I proudly produced.

In a sensuous voice she asked, "Well, birthday boy, what'll it be?"

"I'll have a Pabst Blue Ribbon, please."

She smiled and said, "Would you like a nipple on that, sweetie?"

"You got one?"

With everyone in the room watching, she pulled up her blouse, revealing two rather nice-looking boobs. Biggest darn nipples I'd ever seen. "Will one of these do?" she asked.

Everyone in the room participated with some sort of whistle, "ooh," "ah," or funny comment.

Feeling myself blush I replied, "Can you put one on the bottle?"

Damned if she didn't oblige, rubbing the mouth of that beer bottle against one of her nipples before handing it to me. The coldness caused a reaction as her nipple stiffened to attention. Impressed, I said, "Thank you very much, ma'am."

"Anytime, sweetie, but you're all grown up now. You can call me Beverly."

"That ain't what some of us call 'er," joked one of the guys at the bar.

As the bartender pulled her garment back down, I got the feeling most everyone in the room had seen those tits before.

During my first drink from a wonderfully scented bottle, the entrance door opened. Kelly entered wearing a short, denim skirt and vest, highlighted by a white ruffled blouse and tall boots. As she model-walked my way, every eye in the room watched. I thought, *Bet none of these folks would guess she's a cop.*

Nearing me, Kelly asked, "Drinking beer tonight, are we?"

"At this point, yes, but we can order whiskey if you like."

"No that's fine. I like beer too." Then she turned to the barmaid and ordered a Budweiser.

"And," I added, "she won't be needing a nipple, thank you."

When I started to pay, Beverly winked and said, "That's okay honey, first round's on the house. Consider it a birthday present."

I could feel Detective Kelly analyzing the comment. She asked, "Where would you like to sit?"

The best choice seemed to be a secluded booth in a dark corner. When I motioned in that direction, Kelly tilted her head in agreement. I led the way and waited for her to sit. In typical police fashion, she took my first choice, the side facing a majority of the patrons and the door. Reluctantly, I sat across the table, facing only Kelly. Noticing my frequent turns to look back, she asked, "Why don't you sit next to me, that way we both can see the door?"

"You can tell, huh?"

"Sure, I'm the same way," she answered with a smile.

The old couple across the room stared as I slid in next to Kelly. What a predicament. I'd seated myself next to a beautiful woman, one who might be trying to stab me in the back. Her relationship with Carl could only mean bad things.

Kelly sipped her beer and broke the ice, "So, did you pick this dark corner so we could be alone, or do you not want to be seen with a black girl?"

143

"I'm sitting with the most beautiful woman in the room. The color of your skin is irrelevant to me. Most wouldn't know you were black if you didn't tell 'em. But, let me ask, are you uncomfortable being seen with a white guy?"

"Trust me, Johnny, I'm used to being with a white guy. And, my mama's white. I do have to admit, most of the white men I work with are assholes. Mainly interested in how I can advance their careers. But, you seem different, Mr. Johnny Lee Smith."

"Really? I'll take that as a compliment."

"Please do. So how is your birthday going?"

"Same ol', so far. It sucked having to work. Always thought my twenty-first birthday would be more of a special day."

"Day's not over yet," she commented with a sexy tinge.

As I sat there wishing Richard had waited a day to tell me about Carl knowing Kelly, she asked, "What's with the nipple comment at the bar?"

Kelly found amusement in my short synopsis of how the woman, old enough to be my mother, had acted. Feeling brave, I asked, "By the way, may I ask just how old *you* are?"

"Well, I'm not old enough to be your mother, that's for sure. Actually, I'm thirty-two."

"Hmm, about what I figured. Let me say you're the best-looking thirty-two-year-old I've ever had the pleasure of sharing a drink with."

"And you drink with a lot of thirty-two-year-old women?"

I just smiled. We small talked during two beers and several cigarettes. Kelly suggested a shot of peppermint schnapps along with our third.

"Never had that combination before."

"Try it, you'll like it."

I began to wonder, *Is she trying to get me drunk, or is she trying to get that way herself?*

To my satisfaction, Kelly never mentioned Pete, Joe, their deaths, or anything remotely police oriented. She did mention Paula. "You said you'd already met Paula Dawson. What do you think?"

"Of her?"

"Yeah."

"Really don't know her that well. Met once, briefly, at my cousin's place and then again that night at Phoenix Hill. How long you known 'er?"

"Just since she came to work at the LPD. Year and a half, I'd say."

"So," I asked, "what do *you* think of her?"

"She's cute."

The more we drank, the more magnetized our bodies became. Somewhere around the second shot of schnapps, I felt a warm hand on my leg. Trying to keep my reactions to a minimum didn't keep them from showing on my face. "What's wrong, Johnny, can't a girl be nice to a guy on his birthday?"

Her ploy worked. She had successfully intoxicated my young ass. Without hesitation, I accepted Kelly's peppermint kiss. From there, it went downhill all the way. Gabrielle's warnings became muffled by a drunk state of mind. Somehow, my police friend managed to drive us to a local motel. There, in complete privacy, one of Louisville's finest gave me a birthday present I would never forget: two hours of love lessons from someone who obviously knew the ropes. Though the room was dimly lit, flashing neon lights from across the street bled through a crack in the curtains like a slow motion strobe. Kelly was beautiful, and she knew it. I guess it was because of her profession, but the lady liked being in control. While I hardly said a word, she whispered little directions in my ear. I obeyed. It was good. And it did wonders for my ego.

Kelly kissed me on the lips, whispered, "Happy birthday," and then sat up in bed to light a cigarette. As she leaned back against the headboard, I lay there in euphoria, listening to Gabrielle fuss about what I'd gotten myself into. When Kelly offered me a draw, I accepted and then handed it back. As I stared up at the sweat between her boobs, she grinned and spoke nonchalantly. "Hate to leave good company, but I need to get home soon."

"You gotta work in the morning?"

"No, I'm off on Thursdays, but my ol' man will be back in town, and I need to have all my ducks in a row."

"Your ol' man, as in husband?"

"Oh, I'm sorry, thought you knew about that," she answered, knowing damn well the subject had been avoided. "Hope you don't let that spoil your birthday present?"

The flashing neon light seemed slower and redder, Kelly's grin less enchanting. I sat up and complained, "How would I know? Where's your wedding ring?"

"Are you shitting me? Where the fuck do you think I got a name like Rauschenberg?"

"Hell, I don't know. Thought maybe your mama was a Jew."

The mistake I made with Mary Ellen had been my fault. I knew her marriage status and still allowed it to happen. With Kelly, had I known about her husband, I never would've put myself in such a position. Though I wanted to give her hell, I decided to leave it alone. At least she had given me an out to the relationship. In my mind I knew I would never spend time with her again. Her infidelity only reassured my distrust. *Bitch probably did the same thing with Carl.* Kelly sensed my silence as I slipped out of the bed and into my Levi's.

"So can I count on seeing you again sometime, when my husband's out of town?"

I lit my own cigarette and said, "You know what, Kelly? You might be the best piece of ass I ever had, but there ain't enough beer and schnapps in Kentucky to get me back in bed with you. How the hell could you *not* tell me about being married? I never would have done this had I known...."

"Fuck you, Johnny Smith. You're no better than me," Kelly huffed while smashing out her cigarette and then crawling out of bed. "You think my sins are greater than yours?"

Wow, I thought, having no idea what she meant or might be trying to insinuate. *Does Kelly think of me as a criminal? Am I in fact a suspect in the murders of Pete and Joe?*

For some time, my naked adulteress stood silently, nervously chewing the nail of her pinky. No longer the strong woman of moments ago, her hands shook while lighting another cigarette. Wrinkles formed around her mouth as she took a draw.

I could tell she wanted me to speak, but I really didn't know what to say. What could I say? When I slipped into my shirt, Kelly began gathering her clothes and venting at the same time. "You might not care, but you should know my marriage came about for all the wrong reasons. I slept with a man much older than me, and damned if I didn't get pregnant by a white ass Jew. When he found out, he insisted we get married. I was young and stupid, and didn't know what else to do. So there you have it...." She began dressing.

I started to speak, but she wasn't finished. "After four months, I had a miscarriage. Lost my baby, but I can't seem to lose the old man. And you're right about me not telling you on purpose. As for the ring, I never wear it and never will."

Damn, I thought. When she sat on the edge of the bed to pull on her boots, I said, "Kelly, we all make mistakes, but making excuses doesn't make this right."

She closed her eyes and pressed her lips together as if analyzing. "Sometimes," she said calmly while opening her eyes, "sometimes what I need is stronger than my desire to do what's right. You're young and single, and you can go out and have a good time with people your age. I got married before all that happened. Today I convinced myself to meet with you because of your suspicious behavior during the interview. Truth is I've wanted to be with you ever since Phoenix Hill. I liked your attention, the way you looked at me, the way you talked to me, the questions you asked, and the answers you gave. Johnny, I'm not trying to make excuses. I'm just asking you not to judge me until you know me better, and I'll do the same for you."

Gabrielle had no comments. Kelly wasn't lying. I stood there feeling sorry for the woman. "So you don't want me to judge you ... but you judge me. What'd you mean by my suspicious behavior? You think I had something to do with those guys that got shot?"

Kelly stood and said, "If I really believed you were guilty of murder, we wouldn't be here right now. But you did make some damn peculiar statements at the interview."

"What statements?"

"All that shit about killing animals vs. killing people." Her confidence returned. Kelly slipped back into cop mode. "Let's see, how'd you say it? 'Ain't nobody gonna eat those boys, so they must have hurt someone awful bad.' You have an odd way of stating things. It's easy to see why David or anyone else for that matter might be suspicious."

"I swear to you, I didn't kill 'em, and I don't have a clue as to who did."

"I believe you, Johnny, but I also believe there's a connection between their deaths and your sister's rape."

"So you think those two guys were involved?"

"Yes, I believe they were."

"So what makes you think that?"

"Can't say, at least not for now. But I am checking it out."

Glancing at her watch she said, "Hey, I seriously do need to go," and then she started out the door.

Just as I thought she'd left, Kelly popped back in and said, "Right or wrong, I do appreciate your attention." She snuck one more kiss before leaving for good.

I stood there dumbfounded, watching Kelly leave me stranded over a mile from my truck. *When it comes to love, I've got buzzard luck. Can't kill nothing and nothing won't die.*

Chapter 24

On October 7, 1977, I drove the old Dodge west on US-62 toward Grayson County. At around 7:00 p.m., I crossed the invisible line between Eastern Standard Time and Central Time. Could almost feel that extra hour re-entering my body. A surprise birthday party for Grandma Smith's 70th had been planned for the next day. Everyone else would arrive on Saturday around noon. Driving down Friday night would give me a chance to spend some time with Cousins Jake and Josh. They'd come in for the party and were expecting me.

When the Louisville-based station I'd been listening to began to fade, I plugged in an 8-track, classical tape. After seven minutes of Harpsichord Concerto #1 in D minor, Bach's aggressive notions became mine. At one point, I nearly lost control of the Dodge as my mind's eye stared at the bruises on Mary Ellen's back instead of the twists and turns of that old two-lane road.

Bobbie Davis, an otherwise likable person, had allowed Grayson County's number one disease to ruin his life. Getting drunk and rowdy with the boys is one thing. Getting drunk and beating your wife is totally unacceptable.

Sunrise peeked over the tobacco barn as I pulled into Uncle Bart's lane. A beautiful morning had begun. Jake and Josh's vehicles were parked in the gravel next to the milk shed. Max recognized my truck and began lobbying for attention. My plan was to help with the milking, but I needed a trip to the house first. Upon my entering the front door, Aunt Mary hollered from the kitchen, "That you, Johnny Lee?" She must have heard my truck.

"Yes ma'am, it is. Be right there, gonna wash up a little."

Entering the kitchen just as Aunt Mary popped homemade biscuits into the oven, I joked, "Hope you got enough for Josh and Jake."

"Figured you might be here in time for breakfast," replied my lovely aunt. "Weren't you supposed to get here last night? Boys were lookin' forward to seeing you."

"Yeah, me too. Got tied up."

"Well, you're here now and that's what matters."

"Where's Grandma?"

"She stayed over at Willie and Jolene's last night."

"Think she knows what's going on?"

"Probably. Can't get much past her."

"Jane in the barn?"

"No, she's sleepin' in this morning. Ain't too often the boys are here to do the milkin'. Why don't you go wake 'er up so she can get ready for breakfast."

"Be glad to." Stepping like an Indian on a hunt, I quietly snuck up the steps and into Jane's room. Paybacks are hell, and this would be my first opportunity since she and Paula Dawson slid in on me a few months earlier.

I thought, *It's a damn shame we're related,* while sneaking around the bed and crawling in next to Jane's fetal position. I'd already slid under the cover when it dawned on me she might be naked. Turned out she wore a night shirt.

As I tried to position my arm over her body, Jane whispered, "Johnny Lee Smith, you ain't foolin' nobody."

"Damn," I uttered. "Can't pull a thing over on you."

"Heard your loud mouth when you came in the front door," she bragged in a ragged morning voice.

"So why didn't you come down and greet your favorite cousin?"

"Yeah, right, you can kiss my ass. Not too often I get to sleep in." Then she turned over, wrapping her warm leg across my body and, without opening her eyes, said, "Now you get the hell out of my bed before I pretend we're not cousins."

With her face only inches away, she had to hear me lose my breath. I longed to stay and hold her, run my fingers through her hair, kiss her like she was someone else, but it just couldn't happen. Jane remained still as I slid out from under her leg and off the bed. *Is she asleep or waiting for me to say something?* My voice cracked when I asked, "You gonna get up for breakfast?"

Instead of answering, she rolled back to her original position, partially exposing her bare buttocks. I stared for a second, took a deep breath, and then adjusted the quilt to properly cover her.

I asked again, "You coming?"

Still no answer. When I gave up and started out the door, I heard Jane's soft voice. "I love you, Johnny. Tell Momma I'll be down in a few minutes."

Those four words I'd never heard before stopped me. They sounded real, so sincere. The unexpected words filled my insides with butterflies. I turned but could see only her back, no movement other than the quilt's rise and fall with her breathing. Cautiously, I replied, "Love you too."

Halfway down the stairs, I had to stop. A feeling somewhere between good and bad swept over me. I took a seat right there on the steps. Logic seemed to be absent as the swelling from within leaked out the corners of my eyes. My stomach ached with that same strange feeling I got when first learning of Mary Ellen's marriage to Bobbie, only more intense. While my mind searched for an answer, my senses slipped away one by one until I could no longer even feel the steps. I sat there, silent with wet cheeks, waiting for the truth like a judge's sentence. Then it came, a vision, an old door with a skeleton key protruding from its lock. The key turned and the door began to open. From the other side came a blinding light and a voice. For once, not Gabrielle. For once, not advice or criticism, not the devil or God or Sister Mary Teresa. They were the words I'd been waiting to hear for such a long, long time. *I love you Johnny. I love you Johnny. I love you...*

"Johnny—Johnny you okay?" The sound of Aunt Mary's voice startled me. She stood at the bottom of the stairwell. "Somethin' wrong with you?"

Suddenly, I could feel the steps again beneath me.

"What's going on out here?" asked Jane, already peeking out her bedroom door.

"Looks like he's had a spell of some sort."

Jane hurried down and sat next to me on the steps. She put her arm around my shoulders. "You all right?"

"I'm fine," I said, drying my face.

"You need to come down here and let me take a look at you," commanded my concerned aunt.

As I stood and started down the steps, Aunt Mary tore into Jane. "Girl, let me see them eyes. You been crying too?"

"No, Mama."

"So why they all swollen?"

"Maybe it's because I slept so long. Your eyes get that way when *you* sleep in."

"If I didn't know better, I'd say you two been arguing."

"No Mama, we've not been arguing."

"Well something ain't right. Now get your butt up in that room and put on some decent clothes."

Jane defended herself—"I'm not a child"—before stomping up the steps and into her room.

Aunt Mary turned to me and asked in her normal motherly voice, "When's the last time you ate?"

"Guess it was yesterday evening before I came down."

"Well there you are." She hesitated and then said, "Thought you said you didn't come down 'till this morning."

"Didn't say that."

"So where you been all night?" After a moment of thought, she continued, "Never mind. Ain't none of my business. Now, you come on in the kitchen and let me fix you a cup of coffee and a biscuit with jam 'til breakfast. That'll put sugar in your system."

In the kitchen, I took a seat at the table. Aunt Mary pulled biscuits from the oven and said, "Gonna have to let 'em cool." Then, as she poured my coffee, Jane popped into the room, clothed in Levi's and a flannel shirt.

"This proper enough?"

"Don't come down here being a smart aleck."

"So is he okay?"

"Believe he'll live, providing we get some food in his belly."

Jane began pouring her own cup. "You mean he's just hungry?"

"Would you two stop it?" I complained. "Quit talking about me like I'm not even in the room."

As Jane stood next to her mother sipping coffee, I realized for the first time their lack of resemblance. Aunt Mary, a dishwater blonde, had freckles, brown eyes, and a sunburned nose. Jane had high cheekbones, green eyes, an even tan, and hair so dark it would make a Cherokee jealous. I began to think her gene pool had come from Uncle Bart, but that too seemed a bad fit.

When she noticed me staring, Aunt Mary turned to prepare my biscuit. In the process she took a better look at Jane. "Jane Marie Smith, you *have* been cryin'. Now will you tell me what's going on here?"

Jane's face wrinkled, and tears began to flow freely as she gave it right back, "Is it against the law for me to cry? Everybody else around here cries, why shouldn't I?" She started out of the kitchen.

"Come back in here so we can get to the bottom of this," insisted Aunt Mary.

Jane ignored the order and continued her exit. Walking up the stairs, she spoke loud enough to hear from the kitchen. "Doesn't anybody care how *I* feel?"

Aunt Mary handed me my biscuit and a glare, the kind a disobedient child gets from its mother. I shrugged my shoulders and took a big bite.

She said, "Why do I get the feeling you know what's goin' on with her?"

As if to save me, my uncle and cousins came in the front door.

"Y'all best be leavin' them dirty boots on the porch," preached Aunt Mary. She glanced back at me and quietly said, "I'll talk to you later."

Still trying to calculate the comment, I crammed the rest of my biscuit in my mouth and then rose to greet my cousins. On his way in Josh slapped me on the shoulder and said, "You feelin' all right, Johnny Lee? Lookin' kinda puny."

"You know me, I'm always skinny."

"Well you're right about that," he replied.

I grinned and jabbed back. "Can't say the same for you guys."

Jake rubbed his belly and said, "It's the beer."

"Figured that much," sassed their mother.

Uncle Bart said, "From the looks of what's on that stove, we oughta all put on a pound or two."

Josh glanced around and asked, "Jane still in bed?"

"She's been down. Just went back up," explained Aunt Mary.

"What's wrong with her?" he asked.

"Who knows?"

Uncle Bart had that *something's going on around here* look. He probably got curious just seeing me in the kitchen with Aunt Mary. Normally, I'd go straight to the barn if they were milking. When he glared my way I said, "Good morning."

"Can't say yet," he replied.

Aunt Mary dropped a pan in the sink and started rattling dishes. Uncle Bart turned to his sons and said, "You boys go wash up first while I grab me a cup of coffee."

Josh and Jake left the room, frowning in their confusion and glancing back at me.

Before the old man could speak again, I said, "Hey Uncle Bart, you got anything good to drink?"

He squinted and said, "A little early for that, ain't it?"

"Might cure what ails me."

"And what might that be?"

"Not sure."

"Found him sittin' on the stairs, all flushed, wipin' his eyes," added my aunt. "Think the boy needs some sugar in his system. Says he ain't ate since yesterday."

Uncle Bart scratched his chin and said, "Tell you what, let's me and you step out on the porch while your Aunt Mary finishes up breakfast."

"That'll work," I answered.

As we were heading toward the door, Uncle Bart hollered, "You boys come on out and join us on the porch."

After taking a seat in the morning air, my elder began fishing for information. "Might not be the sharpest nail in the bin, but that don't mean I can't sense a problem. You got somethin' you wanna talk about?"

"No sir, I'm okay."

"Sure about that?"

"Yeah, I'll be okay."

"Let me tell you somethin', Johnny Lee. You can paint over rust, but it always comes back."

"So what's the solution?"

"You get rid of the rust before you paint."

"Sounds easy enough."

"First you gotta admit there is rust."

"What's going on out here?" asked Jake. Josh followed him onto the porch.

"Me and your daddy's talkin' about rust."

Josh said, "Bet he told you to get rid of it before you paint."

I just smiled.

Jake changed the subject. "Hey Johnny, hear you ran into Paula Dawson up in Louisville."

"Now who in the world told you that?"

"You know how it is, word travels quick in these parts."

"Well, I did see her at the Phoenix Hill Tavern one night, but that's been a while. She was with some guy."

"Really," said Josh, "You mean Paula has a boyfriend?"

"Can't say for certain, but it sure looked like they were together."

Uncle Bart seemed interested, but said nothing.

Jake said, "You reckon Paula's gonna be a cop some day?"

"Couldn't say," I replied. "Only she would know that."

"So Johnny," asked Josh, "what do *you* think about Paula?"

"What do I think? Not sure what you mean."

"You know, do you think she's hot?"

"Jesus Christ, Josh," I said, elevating my voice. "You think I'm blind? Sounds to me like maybe you've got a little crush on Miss Paula."

Just as I spoke, Aunt Mary opened the screen door and said, "Y'all come on and eat."

Chapter 25

We were barely seated at the table when Uncle Bart asked, "Jane not gonna eat?"

"I don't know," answered Aunt Mary. "Something's got her all upset. Woman stuff, I guess."

"Never mind," replied Uncle Bart. Obviously hungry, he started grace. "Thank you oh Lord for these thy gifts, and the bounties we are..." His prayer got cut short by the telephone. "Damn thing never rings 'til you sit down to eat."

Josh jumped to answer. "Hello? Well, good morning to ya." Then came silence, long enough to make everyone at the table uneasy. "Oh, my God!"

"What's wrong?" asked Uncle Bart.

"Dad, here, you talk to Aunt Jolene," said Josh as he stretched the cord in his father's direction.

Uncle Bart popped up and took the phone. While he spoke with his brother's wife, Josh filled us in. "Aunt Jolene says on the radio they talked about findin' Bobbie Davis dead, shot in the head."

"Oh Lord," grimaced my aunt.

"Said Mary Ellen found him out in the barn this mornin'. Can you believe that?"

"No," Aunt Mary replied, "I can't." As she spoke, she stared right through me. Finally, Uncle Bart hung up.

"So what exactly happened?" asked Jake.

"Jolene says the news talked like it was a suicide. Guess the boy had problems." As Uncle Bart spoke, he noticed Jane perched near the bottom of the stairs, listening to our conversation. He raised his voice, "Best come on in here. Got some bad news."

Jane entered the kitchen mumbling, "Done heard what you said about Bobbie." Her hair looked brushed, but her eyes were still red. I could sense Aunt Mary watching me watching Jane.

Josh asked, "Johnny, didn't you used to have a crush on Bobbie's wife?"

"Yeah," I answered. "Guess maybe I should ride out and see how she is."

"Young man, you don't need to go nowhere 'til you get some food in that belly," preached Aunt Mary. "You got no business over there right now anyway."

Uncle Bart gave me that look from hell. "I'm sure there's plenty family over there. You best stay away. Besides, we can't let this unfortunate thing ruin your grandmother's birthday party. Hell, your whole family's gonna be here in a little while."

"Yeah, but—"

"Why don't you just stick around here today and tonight? They'll probably have him laid out by tomorrow. After church we can all go pay our respects. Right now, let's eat." He bowed his head to finish praying. "Lord, bless this food we are about to receive, bless Bobbie's soul, and look down on his family in their hour of need. Amen."

"Amen," we all chimed in.

As everyone resumed serving themselves at the table, Jane remained unusually quiet. I shoved down a helping of scrambled eggs with milk gravy and two sausage patties while listening to gossip about Bobbie.

Aunt Mary commented, "At church these last few weeks, I've been hearin' rumors about Bobbie leavin' bruises on Mary Ellen. Reckon there's any truth to that?"

"If it is true, he deserves to be dead," added Josh.

"I'll second that," said Jake.

"What's wrong with you people?" snapped Jane, obviously upset. "You talk about Bobbie Davis like he's a stranger. We've known him all his life. I've never known him to do anything bad."

"Now that's enough outta y'all," scorned Uncle Bart. "Jane's right. Let the boy's soul rest in peace."

Jane rose from the table and headed off toward the front door. Concerned, I stood to follow.

"Johnny!" said Uncle Bart.

"Leave 'em be," jumped in Aunt Mary. "Just leave 'em be."

I reached the front porch as Jane rounded the corner of the house. "Hold on a minute." She didn't stop. Following, I found her with her head hung low and arms folded. She stood there in the morning sun, next to the big maple, looking more like a child than a soon-to-be 21-year-old. I walked up and put my arms around her. She held me tight and we stood quietly for a moment. I broke the silence, "What's the matter, girl? This Bobbie thing got you that upset?"

She leaned her face against my chest and said, "Why does everything have to be so screwed up?"

"Life's kinda funny like that. But generally things happen for a reason. Good or bad, it all works out in the end."

"But it don't seem fair."

I couldn't tell if it was Bobbie's death or something else bothering Jane. "What's going on with you? You in some kind of trouble?"

"No, I'm not in trouble. There is something wrong with me though, but I can't talk to *you* about it. It ain't right."

"What ain't right?"

"Can't say, not now. Just hold me for a minute, please. I'd like that."

So I did. I stood there in the sun, feeling more comfortable holding my cousin than any girl or woman I'd ever held before. When the front screen door slammed shut, we both were startled and released our hold. As I turned to walk away, it sounded like she whispered, "I love you."

I stopped and looked back. Jane stood there using her shirtsleeve to wipe away tears. *Say it again*, I thought. *With me looking right at you, say it again*. She didn't. I took a deep breath, turned, and walked away.

At the front of the house, it surprised me to see Jake on the porch. Figured it would be one of the parents. He asked, "She okay?"

Jane walked around the corner and, with no eye contact, answered for herself, "Don't worry about me. I'm all right. Just got a lot on my mind right now." She entered the house alone.

When I pulled out my cigarette pack, Jake asked, "Can I have one of those?"

"Thought you quit."

"Did, but I could use one right now," he answered with a sigh. "Johnny, can you and me take a little walk? Need to get something off my chest."

Handing Jake a cigarette, I thought, *Holy shit, is everybody in this house screwed up today?*

Chapter 26

Jake and I began walking toward the lane side by side. Pausing next to my truck, I said, "Hold on a second, need to get something." Opening the door, I reached under the seat to retrieve a pint bottle of bourbon, over half empty. "Popped the top on this last night, sitting up at Grandpa's grave."

"You drink that stuff this early in the morning?"

"Not normally, but this day don't seem normal so far. How about you?"

"Sure, why not?" he answered, reaching for the bottle.

Jake's taking a drink that early in the morning meant whatever he wanted to get off his chest must be big. He only left one good swallow, so I finished it, capped the bottle, and stuck it back under the seat.

"Well, let's walk," I said, closing the truck door. We continued down the lane, and I waited for his words. My worried cousin remained strangely silent, drawing heavily on the Marlboro. "Alrighty now, we're all alone. Let's hear what's bothering you."

"You know, Johnny, me and Josh have been talkin' about this for some time, and we wanted to say something to mom and dad, but we were afraid to, and I just thought maybe I could ask your opinion on it, and—"

"Jake, get to the point."

"Well, okay. Do you think Jane likes girls?"

"Do what?" Damn near swallowed my cigarette.

"We think maybe she don't like guys."

I couldn't believe my ears. It never occurred to me to question Jane's sexuality, except that is, when she kissed Paula on the mouth.

And what about her comments 'There is something wrong with me but I can't talk to you about it,' and 'It ain't right.'?

I said, "Come on Jake. What makes you think such a thing? Did she say something to you to make you believe that?"

"I'm not saying she's that way, but you gotta wonder."

"Why? What gives you that impression?"

"Hell, Jane's almost twenty-one years old, and far as I know she doesn't even have a boyfriend. She's barely dated. Not saying it's a bad thing, but I bet she's still a virgin."

A need to sit down overwhelmed me, the way it had earlier on the stairs, and so I did, right there on the dusty ground of Uncle Bart's lane. I sat there emotional and frustrated, not wanting Jake to see me the way his mother had. It would be too embarrassing. Turning my head didn't work. He read right through me.

"Damn, this is messin' with you, ain't it?"

When I turned and looked at my cousin, he spoke frankly. "Sonofabitch, you act like you're in love with my sister!"

His words scared the hell out of me. Ever since we were kids, I'd felt the humility of having a crush on my cousin. I had always hoped no one would notice. "Don't put words in my mouth."

"I'm not. Just callin' it the way I see it."

My cigarette became wet. I threw it on the ground and began nervously digging for another. "Sorry man, I'm really sorry," was all I could say. While lighting up, I noticed Jake didn't seem upset. He actually had a smile on his face and was almost laughing, and it pissed me off. "Up yours. You think this is funny? Don't be laughing at me."

"Easy, Johnny. I'm not laughin' atcha. Hell, you're making my day."

Confused, I stood up and asked, "What's that supposed to mean?"

Jake hesitated. "What I'm about to tell you, you gotta keep to yourself, at least for now. Before it can go any further, I'll have to talk to Mom and Dad. Won't be easy, but it needs to get done."

Impatient, I said, "You're killing me. Just say it."

"Jane ain't really my sister."

I couldn't speak.

He continued, "According to Mom, after I was born, doctors told her she couldn't have any more kids. Said Jane's real mama died while giving birth, and since her and Dad wanted a little girl, well, they adopted Jane."

My heart began thumping like a drum. "Does Jane know this?"

"Not to my knowledge, and *damn* you if you tell her before I get a chance to talk to my folks. If anyone tells her, it should be them. They've earned that right. Now you swear to me that you'll wait on this. I mean it!"

"No problem, but if you're pulling my leg, I'll strangle your ass."

"Ain't lying. Let's shake on it," he said, reaching for my hand.

As we performed the pact, I asked, "So how'd you find out about Jane?"

"Overheard Mom and Dad talkin' about it a while back. I said something to Grandma. Her and Mom told me everything."

Glancing toward the house I could see Jane standing at her window, upstairs, looking out. "Do you really think she could be one of them, you know?" Couldn't even say the word.

"Hell, I hope not. But you need to know, that's what Josh was gettin' at when he asked you about Paula Dawson. He's scared she might be Jane's girlfriend. Don't recall ever seeing *her* with a man."

"Bullshit. Don't see her like that. Girl flirts too much. I'd bet money she likes men."

"Well, I hope you're right."

I stood there dumbfounded, having absorbed too much information. "Damn Jake, this has been one hell of a morning. How about we find us another shot of whiskey?"

"Sounds good," he answered.

Walking back up the lane, I asked, "Does Josh know Jane ain't his real sister?"

"No, he doesn't; but let me and you get somethin' straight. Jane might not be my real sister, but she *is* my sister. Know what I mean?"

"Yeah, I hear ya."

"And," he added, "I'll still kick anyone's ass that hurts her."

"Me and you both, buddy. Me and you both."

"But tell me, do you love 'er?"

My eyes watered again, "Hell, I love all y'all. You're my family."

"That ain't what I'm talkin' about," pressed Jake. "You know what I mean."

"You ask too many questions."

In my mind I thought, *If it ain't love, I don't know what love is.* Still, the whole idea of Jane not being my cousin needed some time to sink in. I knew what Jake wanted to hear, but I wasn't quite ready to say it. One thing was for sure, nobody else could light me up like Jane. Just seeing her smile made my day.

Jane no longer stood at her window. By the time we got to the house, Uncle Bart sat on the porch with a bottle of 7 Year Old Jim Beam and an RC. "Damn Jake, sometimes I think your daddy's psychic."

"I hear ya."

Stepping up on the porch, I said to Uncle Bart, "See you've got the good stuff today."

"Sure do. Special occasion. You boys ready to start celebratin' Grandma's birthday?" As he poured three fingers into each of four short glasses, Josh joined us on the porch.

Uncle Bart stood and passed out drinks. "Hate to start without her, but I believe I'll make a toast to my mother on her 70th and to all the fine people who're gonna be gathered here today." We touched our glasses and sipped some of Kentucky's finest.

Raising my glass again, I said, "To my friend Bobbie Davis, may he rest in peace."

"Amen," chimed in the others as our glasses met once more.

Uncle Bart leaned to my ear and whispered, "Hope what's ailing you ain't got nothing to do with Bobbie's being shot."

At least thirty people showed up that day for Grandma's party. She seemed surprised. Even Sissy and Mike drove down from Indianapolis. They lived there because of Mike's job with the state. That evening as things began to wind down, I found Sissy sitting alone on the front porch, smoking a cigarette.

"Mind a little company?"

She looked up. "Not at all. Just waitin' on Mike. He's out back talking to Ray about work stuff." When I sat down next to her, she said, "You know, sometimes I wish me and Mike lived down here. It's so much more peaceful and quiet, no traffic."

"I hear you. Feel the same way."

"Ever wish you could start your life over? Do things different?"

"You and Mike having problems?"

"Oh no. That's not what I mean. Mike's the best thing ever happened to me. He understands me. I was just sittin' here thinking how Grayson County might be a safer place to live and raise our kids someday if we get that lucky."

She smashed out her cigarette and then leaned her head onto my shoulder. I tried to remember the last time we sat so close. As children we were inseparable. After what she went through, she became withdrawn and distant. It surprised me when she married Mike. He's a great guy, just figured it would take longer for her to trust a man, any man.

"So," I asked, "How's work treating you?"

"Not too bad. Don't plan on staying there long. Can't stand my boss."

Sissy had taken a position at a warehouse in Indy; some kind of distribution center for a mail order catalog company. "Why don't you like your boss?"

"Asshole talks down on me. Treats me different than the other women because I won't buddy up to 'im. I just wanna do my job and get the hell out of there. Don't bother nobody and don't want nobody bothering me. Not about to suck his you know what just to get the easier jobs."

"Is that what the other women do?"

"I don't know. Believe some of 'em would. They're always smiling and cutting up with him. And of course, because they do, he takes care of 'em. Gives 'em the easier assignments."

"You know you're not being fair Sissy—"

"What the hell does that mean?" she huffed while pulling away from me.

"Easy now," I said. "Just because you don't like to smile and cut up on the job doesn't mean everybody else has to be the same way. Keep in mind that they've not been through what you have. Maybe they're not as guarded as you."

"You saying I ain't right?"

"I'm saying you need to relax a little. Quit walking around with a chip on your shoulder—"

"Screw you Johnny Lee!"

"Listen to me, dammit. It's okay to smile, be nice to people, speak to 'em. Then maybe they'll be nice to you."

"How can you sit there and tell me how to act at work. You don't even know those people. They're nothing but a bunch of assholes!"

"I know you, Sissy. I know what you've been through and I know how it has affected you."

Sissy stood and shouted, "You have no idea! No one knows! Not you, not Dad, not Mike, no one!"

"I'm sorry Sissy. Didn't mean to upset you."

"You're sorry?" she shouted down at me. "Well I'm sorry too! I'm sorry I'm not the same person I was. I'm sorry them bastards did what they did to me!" Holding her arms out, she continued. "I can cover these up, little brother, but I can never ignore the ones *inside*! Do you know what it's like to not be able to walk alone without the fear of being attacked? Do you know what it's like to flinch in a fucking sexual moment with the man I love, knowing how it ruins it for him? Jesus, Johnny Lee, I'm afraid to kiss my loving, sweet husband because I'm scared he will bite my lips or try to suck my tongue down his throat! Do you *fucking* know what that's like?"

As I sat there silent, staring at her arms, she repeated herself. "Do you?"

"I ... I just don't know what to say."

She stared for a second, squinting at me, and then shouted, "You think you know everything!" while stomping off toward the car. As she did, Mike and Ray came around the corner of the house.

Mike asked, "What's going on?"

"She's pissed."

"Dammit, Johnny! She was having a good day! What did you—?"

"She got mad because I got on her."

"About what?"

"Her attitude. It sucks man. Mike, she doesn't get along with people, and look how she does you."

"Excuse me?"

"Look at you. All those scratches and bruises. Hell, the whole family's noticed. Looks like you've been fightin' with a cat, and you guys don't even own a cat."

"You have no right, Johnny."

"Hold on now, Mike," interrupted Ray. "Johnny's not trying to get on you. We know how Sissy can be, and why. It's not *your* fault."

For a second there I thought Mike might cry. He held back though and finally said, "Sorry, Johnny. Sissy holds all this shit inside and then some little thing pisses her off and she ... she just goes off."

I said, "Mike, we know. And we understand."

He turned his back to the car and said, "When we got married I knew about Sissy's issues, and I thought I could somehow help her get over them. Problem is she *can't* get over it. Woman might look tough, but she's not. I can't get her to go anywhere where there's a crowd. She knows those guys are still out there somewhere. Sometimes she thinks they're watching her. She wakes up in the middle of the night kicking and punching and—"

"Mike!" Sissy shouted. "We gotta go!"

Mike spoke as he walked backwards toward the car. "Sorry, guys. Didn't mean to vent. It's just not easy."

"Don't worry about it. We understand," Ray said. "Anytime you need to talk, you call one of us."

I said, "Mike, she loves you. She trusts you and leans on you. Just keep on being there for her."

Mike nodded, turned, and joined Sissy. As he started the car, Sissy leaned out the window and shouted, "Dammit, Johnny Lee, we all have scars! Some are just more visible than others!"

Ray sat down next to me, offering a cigarette. We both lit up as we watched Sissy and Mike drive down the lane. Ray asked, "Suppose she'll ever get over it?"

"Don't know. Still bothers me. Can't imagine how she feels."

Chapter 27

That same night, after only a few hours of sleep, I awoke to the sound of Cousin Jake "sawing logs." He lay there next to me, still dressed, making enough noise to wake the dead. I didn't really want to get up, but between the snoring and a full bladder, I did anyway.

After gathering my jacket, boots, and cap, I quietly slid out of the room. When I passed Jane's door, promiscuous thoughts entered my mind. How nice it would be to sneak in and let her know we weren't really cousins. Wouldn't happen though. I'd made a promise and intended to keep it.

I lit a cigarette before stepping off the porch into the arms of darkness. It felt nice out, temperature in the mid to upper 60s, not bad for early October. Clouds had moved in, and for some reason none of Uncle Bart's lights were on, not even the one at the barn. Couldn't see shit if it was right in front of you.

Max nudged me for attention, but moved away when I began wetting the grass. Around half a mile away, there was a lonely, dim incandescent glow at a neighboring farm. The sound of a distant hoot owl suggested I wasn't the only nocturnal beast about.

While finishing my business, I heard what sounded like a man coughing. Up near the dairy barn, a small glow disappeared. Thirty seconds later, it reappeared. *Cigarette*, I guessed. Then suddenly, the light seemed to be heading in my direction. I remained perfectly still, cupping my own smoke to hide its light. There were footsteps in the gravel. My heartbeat increased in anticipation. At about twenty feet away, the sound became a silhouette, and then it turned into Uncle Willie. "Up early, ain't you boy?" he asked on his approach.

"About to say the same for you. Didn't you go home last night?"

"Naw, Jolene tired out right after you, so she went on home. Hell, me and Bart sat on the porch 'til midnight."

"You haven't slept?"

"For a little bit. Laid down on the couch, but woke up a while ago and couldn't go back to sleep."

"Couch too lumpy?"

"No, not that. Seems every now and then I have me a nightmare. Shit left over from the war. Damn things are so real, they make it hard to go back to sleep."

"That sucks."

"Sure does. Then I get to thinkin' about other stuff, and before you know it, I'm up and about. Lose a lot of sleep that way."

"Ever tried sleeping pills?"

"Thought about it, but Doc says they're too addicting."

Then out of nowhere, Uncle Willie said, "Tell me, Johnny, is there somethin' you need to say about Bobbie Davis?"

"Excuse me?"

"I'm askin' do you have anything you need to get off your chest?"

"Damn, Uncle Willie, sounds like you expect some sort of a confession."

"Last night Bart said he thinks maybe you know more about Bobbie's death than you're willing to say."

"Is that right? What, y'all think I went over there and shot Bobbie in the head?"

"Now who told you he was shot in the head?"

"Seems to me that's what Josh said yesterday morning when he got off the phone with your wife."

"Oh."

"You really think I'd do somethin' like that?"

He laughed and said, "You didn't have a problem pullin' the trigger when you thought I was cuttin' up Bart's cow."

"That's different, and you know it. Besides, I never should have."

"Never should have what?"

"Never should have shot at you."

"How come?"

"Because a man cutting up a cow ain't enough reason to kill him. Might be the only way he can feed his family."

"Whoa, impressive," replied my elder. "Looks like somebody's grown up a bit."

"So you guys really didn't want me to shoot you that day? Thought you said you were trying to see if I was willing to kill a man."

"Exactly, Johnny. We wanted to see if you were willing to kill a man just because we told you to. A wise man would ask questions. Don't matter if it's me or your daddy or someone else tellin' you to, if it ain't right, it ain't right, and you don't do it. And from what you just said, I'd say you're a better man today than that day."

"Oh well, if you say so," I replied.

"So," he asked, "you still gotta crush on Bobbie Davis' wife?"

"Damn. And why you asking?"

"Because if you do, think maybe you need to stay clear of 'er, at least for right now."

"You know what, you're worse than my daddy. Bobbie was a friend of mine, and I'll miss him. But at least he won't be beatin' on Mary Ellen any more. And how I feel about her is *my* business. She's always been my friend. Always will be, I hope."

"Easy, boy. Gettin' all upset makes you sound guilty."

"Guilty of what?"

Instead of answering, he just stood there as though analyzing my actions.

"Done told you, I didn't kill Bobbie. Why can't you accept that? And I'm not after Mary Ellen. Got my eye on someone else."

"Anybody I know?"

"Yeah, right. Don't think so! I tell you her name, you'll say stay away from her too!"

"Keep it down, dammit. Wanna wake up the world? I'm just trying to help."

"Bullshit. First, you practically accuse me of killing my best friend, now you act like I ain't got enough sense to stay clear of his wife while she grieves."

Uncle Willie pulled out his cigarette pack and said, "Believe I have somethin' here that'll settle you down." He then slid a finger in and pulled out half a dooby.

"You're shitting me," I said out loud.

"This stuff does wonders when a man gets too wound up inside."

Suddenly things got clearer. "So that's what you were doing up by the barn."

"Yep."

"That mean you're too wound up inside?"

"Was a few minutes ago."

"Oh, the nightmare thing. So smoking pot helps?"

"Sure does. It's about the only thing that does. Drinkin' don't help matters, just makes you start feelin' sorry for yourself, and that ain't no good."

I took a deep breath, trying to digest my uncle being a pot smoker. "You smoke it in Vietnam?"

"No, believe it or not, I somehow managed to avoid it. Lotta guys did, but I always was afraid it would make me too relaxed at the wrong time and get me killed. Friend of mine smoked it before guard duty. Don't know if he fell asleep or just got careless, but he got his throat cut by a sapper."

"Sapper?"

"Yeah. That's one of the Vietcong's Special Forces. Little shits could sneak right through the barbed wire."

"So when did you start smoking marijuana?"

"Couple years after Samuel got back he turned me on to it. Said it would help me sleep without having all those nightmares."

"So it really works?"

"Sure does. What about you, Johnny, you ever smoke any?"

"Yes sir, had my share. The packinghouse is full of it. Some of the guys smoke it every day."

"Well, let's me and you walk back up by the barn, that is *if* you feel like hittin' on this."

"Why not? Let's see what you got."

We moved up to where Uncle Willie stood earlier. When he lit the joint and took a hit, I said, "First time I ever saw someone your age smoke weed."

"Is 'at right?" He said, holding his breath. "You'd be surprised."

"Uncle Bart smoke this stuff?" I asked as he handed me the joint.

"Believe it or not, he has tried it. Same reason as me. Says sometimes Korea keeps him up at night."

I could only imagine how bad things must have been in the wars. Guess I was lucky not to have to go. My uncle's pot tasted green, homegrown. The first hit made me cough.

"Easy, boy. That ain't your run-of-the-mill smoke. And it'll sneak up on you."

I took his advice and hit easy. "Uncle Willie, you think my daddy ever tried this stuff?"

"Not to my knowledge."

We passed it back and forth until the joint got too small to hold.

"So," I asked, "you grow your own?"

"Yep, sure do."

"Where?"

For a moment, he just stood there. He pulled out his Winstons and offered me one. As he lit mine, Uncle Willie spoke. "You and me both know there's people in these parts growing pot for a living. Believe me, ain't nobody 'round here sellin' it. But now, that don't mean we can't grow a little for our own use. Hard to keep it a secret if you're out there buyin' from somebody."

"That makes sense, but if you guys are growing pot, how come I've never seen it?"

"Because we don't intend for you to see it. Ain't got but three plants, and they're not out in the open."

"So can you show 'em to me?"

"Can I rest assured you'll never go out lookin' without me?"

"Yes, sir."

Chapter 28

My asking to see Uncle Willie's pot plants was comparable to asking a moonshiner to show his still. "None of the kids know about us smokin' except Jane," he warned. "She knows 'cause she caught me and her daddy red-handed. Made 'er swear she wouldn't tell."

My mind skipped back to Jane's comment the night she and Paula tried to get me to smoke. *'It ain't like daddy never smoked this stuff.'*

"Stay here," ordered my uncle. "I'll be right back." After disappearing into the barn for a couple minutes, he returned with a pouch strapped over his shoulder. He didn't volunteer the contents or purpose, so I didn't ask.

That night my Uncle Willie took me on an interesting hike. As though on a mission, we walked carefully to and from three different locations, each of which harbored one marijuana plant. Like a wildcat, Uncle Willie navigated through the darkness with me, suddenly stoned to the bone, following closely. He seemed to have the pathway memorized. It reminded me of following my dad into the pre-dawn woods for a deer hunt.

"Uncle Willie, how the hell can you see where you're going?"

"Too dark for you, boy? How'd you like to be doing this on your hands and knees, lookin' for booby traps along the way?"

"No, thanks."

"Been there."

Uncle Willie's property bordered Uncle Bart's. Like most farmers, they allowed a thicket to grow at the intersection of fencerows. These vegetative oasis generally provide haven for small game and a variety of plant life. Within three of the intersections, they hid their cannabis.

174

Pruned to be no more than four feet tall, the plants had a somewhat similar appearance to cacti and were sticky to the touch. By rerouting the existing electric cattle fence, they had provided protection from animals such as cattle, deer, groundhogs, and rabbits. A passerby would have to look closely to identify the unique little plants. Having no trees around allowed for maximum amounts of sunshine, and, being farmers, they knew exactly how to water and fertilize for the utmost results.

The third plant sat high on a hill. Unlike the other locations, a single large black oak stood just north of the plant's hiding place. This time I actually knew when we were close because, like the other two, it reeked similar to a skunk. Thus the nickname *skunk weed.*

"When do you harvest?" I asked.

"I've been splittin' the buds for a few weeks. Won't pull 'em up until after the first heavy frost."

Uncle Willie invited me to sit Indian Style on the ground. I felt like a young Sioux Brave being educated by the tribal elder. He entertained me with stories about his childhood growing up in the country. Told me the one about his father and Paula Dawson's daddy getting the farms back from J.P. Garret, Jr. Some of what he spoke about had already been told to me by my father; however, Uncle Bart's personal twist made it even more interesting.

Stoned and comfortable, I revealed a few inner thoughts of my own that night. I expressed my love for time spent on the farm, learning and exploring in ways that most from the city would never experience. How Jake, Josh, Jane and I used to swing from grape vines in the woods. Me pretending to be Tarzan, with Jane of course being Jane. How we searched the fields for Indian arrowheads and stone tools. Then, for some reason, I told Uncle Willie about one of the weakest moments in my life.

"One day when I was about sixteen, me and Jerry Godfrey, this boy I grew up with, drove down to his grandparents' farm to hunt squirrels. They lived over there by Rough River. Every weekend, during squirrel season, we hunted from daylight 'til noon, and then again in the evening 'til dark. On that particular morning, we'd been out huntin' for a while when four young puppies came trudging through the woods. They were mutts or wild dogs we figured, separated from their mother by some tragedy. Or maybe they had been dumped by a city slicker who no longer wanted 'em."

Uncle Willie listened patiently as I told my story.

"The pups followed us for some time down a logging road. Those little dogs made enough noise to alert every squirrel in the area, messing up our hunt. We desperately needed to get rid of 'em, but all our efforts were in vain. They thought we were playing a game. Each time we walked away, they followed like little ducks behind their mama. Finally, we had an idea. A small cliff near the logging road provided a spot where we could drop the pups, one by one to the soft bed of leaves below. Hopefully by the time they got out, we'd be long gone.

"Ten minutes down the road, still thick in the woods, we prepared to part for hunting. Then Jerry said, 'Damn!'

"One of the puppies, the largest of the four, had followed our scent like a miniature bloodhound. Seconds later the mutt stood at our feet, tail wagging fifty miles an hour. Of course by then we were both becoming annoyed. Something needed to be done or our day's hunt would be wasted. Jerry looked at me with a frown. 'You know one of us is going to have to shoot the little bastard.'

"Don't know to this day what possessed me to do so, but I simply turned, pointed my double-barreled Stevens 20 gauge at the pup's face, and pulled the front trigger. A full load of number 5 shot mangled the little black dog. Nearly a minute passed before it finally quit jerking. I felt instant remorse.

"Never told my friend Jerry how bad I felt about shooting the little dog. We continued our hunt that day, but I didn't enjoy myself. Spent more than an hour sitting against a tree, sulking over my sin."

Uncle Willie wisely waited for me to finish my story before giving his reply. "Kinda felt that way first time I killed a man. Got to Korea late and never had to fire my rifle. In 'Nam, wasn't even a week. We's guardin' a hill just about like the one we're sittin' on, only it was thick with trees and brush. Sun just rose and there was a fog liftin' up out of the bottom. Reconnaissance done warned they were coming. Lieutenant had us all posted thirty feet apart, waitin'. Heard a quiet shuffle of footsteps long before seeing the bastard. Sounded 'bout like a deer movin' in the woods, one quiet step at a time. Had myself hid in the weeds. By the time he came into sight, my heart was beatin' so loud I think *he* heard it. The little guy stopped about twenty-five feet away, then scanned until he saw me. Already had a bead on his head and he was lookin' right down the sight. He froze, and we stared into one another's eyes just like me lookin' at you right now. He couldn't been much more than a teenager. After a few seconds, he began to move his rifle up, forcing me to pull the trigger. Johnny, I watched that bullet go right through the boy's head. It was an ugly feelin', but I soon got over it. Suggest you do the same. That shot started a firefight where three of my friends wound up looking like your little black dog. Had to get over it or die. What you did to that pup seemed wrong because it could have been avoided. At least your sense of guilt proves you have a conscience. But now it needs to be put behind you. Day ever comes when you need to act quickly, having such thoughts clutterin' your mind could gitcha killed."

In a moment of silence, pondering my uncle's story of Vietnam made me think about the tunnels between the barn and the family room. "You mind my asking why you guys dug tunnels under the barn?"

"Huh, that's a good one. Started out when Daddy decided we needed a bomb shelter. He'd been listening to all that talk about the communists coming over here and startin' an atomic war. He had us dig back as far as we could from the storm cellar. Wanted the shelter to be big enough for the whole family. By the time we dug out the room, we were sick of diggin' and draggin' all that dirt out."

"So, the shelter became the family room?"

"Eventually. We used to just meet in the barn. As Daddy got older, reckon he got a little paranoid. Said he was afraid someone might hear us talking. Decided we should hide out in the shelter. That's when he had us make the tunnel taller so he didn't have to crawl. Years later, I got home from 'Nam just as Samuel went over. Couldn't stand knowing what he'd be goin' through. Got to drinkin' one day and just started diggin'. Don't know why. Guess I thought it would take my mind off of Samuel. Before you know it, the tunnel done went clean back under the barn."

"Man, that's a lotta digging."

"You're tellin' me. But you know, back then it seemed like somethin' that needed to be done. There were times when I'd go down there and just sit, all alone. Reminded me of being over there. Can't explain wantin' to feel that way, but I did. Some days I'd sit down there drinkin' and cryin' like a baby. By the time Samuel came home, had the damn thing coming up in the barn. When he first saw it, he cursed it. Told me I was sick in the head. Six months later, he started diggin' his own tunnel off of mine."

"You mean the one I didn't go through."

"You'll see it later," he explained. "Samuel also came up with the idea for diggin' that crazy pit. He said we ought to have snakes or spikes down in it, but we all knew better than that. Bart came up with that contraption to get across."

"So did my father help with the tunnels?"

"No, not really. He did help us when we were kids, diggin' the shelter and all that. But after that he really didn't know what went on 'til we had it done. Besides, him not goin' to 'Nam, he wouldn't likely appreciate it the way we do."

"So since it was a bomb shelter, does that mean Aunt Mary knows about the family room?"

"I'd say your Aunt Mary knows a lot more than she lets on to know. But the fact that she never speaks about it says a lot. Therefore, we never bring it up in her presence. You understand?"

"Yes, sir, I do."

"Good."

The two of us traded stories for a while, and then Uncle Willie surprised me for the second time that night. From the pouch he had been carrying on his shoulder, he removed several items including a piece of cloth, a block of cedar, one small candle, a crucifix, a small bottle which turned out to be wine, and what looked like one of Aunt

Mary's homemade biscuits in a sandwich bag. I watched in silence as he placed the cloth over a nearby rock, creating a makeshift altar. He positioned the cedar block in front. It had two holes in it, one for the crucifix, and one for the candle. He set the wine and biscuit on his altar.

The little candle brought a glimmer of light to the otherwise vast darkness. Its small flame dancing under the image of Christ on the cross created an inspiring sight.

"Johnny, I've been on this earth for a long time. Crossed the oceans, climbed mountains, seen desert sands, and survived jungles. Something tells me this ol' Earth's been 'round a lot longer than what they taught us in school and church. Saw a lot of things in 'Nam that made me question my religion. With nothin' better to do, I began readin' the Bible. Took me over a year to get all the way through it. Been tryin' to figure it out ever since."

A whooshing sound broke my uncle's train of thought. Looked like that old hoot owl from earlier had found our place on the hill. It landed on a lower branch of the nearby oak. *Maybe,* I thought, *it had been attracted by the candlelight.*

Uncle Willie nodded quietly at the big bird as though accustomed to its presence.

"Say hello to your Grandfather."

"Grandfather?" I asked.

"Indians in these parts had a story about the owl. Said whenever a warrior conducted a spiritual ritual, if an owl flew in, it contained the spirit of the warrior's dead father."

Seemed a little far-fetched, but interesting.

Uncle Willie continued. "Sittin' on this hill, meditatin' life's meaning, I've come to peace with my existence. Decided religion is a personal thing. Each man has to come up with his own version of the truth. And if them little people overseas wants to honor their Buddha, that's fine with me. 'Til God comes down here and tells me different, I ain't gonna criticize nobody else's belief. And I don't want them criticizin' mine. Johnny, you ever read the Bible?"

"No sir, not yet."

179

"Well, you ought to. Then you won't have to rely on nobody else to tell you what it says."

It sounded like my uncle had put a lot of thought into his religion. We shared his bread and wine. Uncle Willie's rendition of the Eucharist, while unsanctioned, seemed innocent enough. I participated respectfully but had to ask, "Uncle Willie, how come you do Communion without a priest?"

"Wasn't always a priest around overseas. Had what they called padres, even brought 'em out in the field, but it wasn't the same. Some of 'em didn't even offer Communion. Figured I was better off doin' it myself than not at all."

My uncle and I became good friends that night. I learned that he and his brothers were terribly affected by what they went through in the wars. How hard it must be to keep faith in God while participating in such ugliness. It made the killing, guts, and blood of the packinghouse seem trivial.

I could only imagine Uncle Willie sitting down in that tunnel drinking whiskey and crying, worrying about his younger brother in Vietnam. And who would ever have thought Uncle Bart might smoke pot to stop his Korean memories? I smoked pot to create daydreams; they did so to stop nightmares.

Chapter 29

By the time Uncle Willie and I finished our walk, robins chirped, and the barnyard rooster called both man and beast for the morning ritual. With a cold front moving in, the wind picked up and a light shower began. Rather than make him walk in the rain, I drove my sleepy-eyed uncle to his place. On my return, Uncle Bart had coffee ready and we started our Sunday morning. Jake and Josh looked rough from the night before as we recruited their help in the barn. Jane, of course, got another break. After chores were done, we all cleaned up, ate breakfast and headed off to Sunday morning service.

In the churchyard after Mass, the rain had stopped, and, as usual, several folks stayed around to talk. Many spoke of Bobbie's passing. Some speculated as to the motive for his taking his own life. It surprised me to hear others talking about Bobbie beating up on Mary Ellen. Sad to say, a few old women felt the world might be better off without Bobbie, since he had fallen to a life of drinking and abuse. Drinking seemed to be a way of life in Grayson County. On our way back to the farm, we drove back an old logging road to see a bootlegger.

After lunch, we prepared for our trip to the funeral home in Clarkson. I planned to head home from there after paying my respects. When Jane asked if she could ride with me to the funeral home, Grandma gave Aunt Mary a look.

Aunt Mary frowned and said, "Jane, honey, Grandma and I need to talk to you a minute. Rest of y'all wait on the porch. We'll be right out." Uncle Bart led the way, eager to avoid something.

On the porch, Jake winked at me but said nothing. Josh shrugged his shoulders and asked, "What's going on?" No one answered. Uncle Bart sat silently, whittling on a stick. I didn't have a clue. We were like four men waiting on a childbirth. Even Jake smoked a cigarette. After a while, Josh stood and began pacing, eventually getting on his father's nerves. Just when it seemed my uncle might unleash a few expletives, the door crashed open and Jane came running out. She didn't even stop as she passed everyone and went straight to my truck.

"Whoa," said Josh, "she's pissed."

Leaving the porch, I went to the truck, opened the driver's side door, and just stood there looking in at my teary-eyed cousin. She leaned against the other door, not crying out loud, but with tears running down her cheeks. Never before had someone else's pain hurt me so. Glancing back at the house I saw that Aunt Mary and Grandma had joined the others on the porch. Rather than standing there looking useless, I climbed in the Dodge. Jane turned her head away, staring out the passenger side window.

I asked, "Would you please tell me what the hell's going on?"

She remained facing the other direction and only shook her head as if to say she didn't want to talk about it.

"Come on now, if you can't talk to me, who can you talk to?"

Finally, she turned. "My mother just told me I'm not really her daughter. Daddy's not my daddy and Jake and Josh are not my real brothers..."

I couldn't imagine Aunt Mary wording it in those exact words. Afraid of saying the wrong thing, I just listened.

"...said my mother died when I was born and they don't know who my daddy is. I'm, I'm adopted. Thought all my life they were my family and now Grandma's not even my grandmother."

"Hold on. Finding this out might be a shock, but don't go thinking Aunt Mary, Uncle Bart, and Grandma don't love you like their own. Jake and Josh too. At this point, *they are* your real family."

Jane sat quietly, with that sad look on her face.

I asked, "So why'd she tell you this now after all these years?"

"Because of you."

"Because of me? What'd I do?"

"She says she told me 'cause of the way you been actin'. Thinks you got feelings for me."

It appeared Jake had spoken to his mother about our conversation the day before. "So what else did she say?"

"Don't know, didn't give her a chance. Just ran out. It ain't right, me goin' all these years without knowing something like that."

"Don't you think you should have given her a chance to explain?"

"You don't understand how I feel. It's like I been lied to all these years."

Had it been anyone else, I might have said, "Get over it," and left it at that. But it was Jane. Searching for the right words seemed worthwhile.

"If it were me, I'd want to learn all there is to know about where I came from and who my birthmother was. Hell, *I'd* like to know what she looked like. Been wondering myself why you don't favor Aunt Mary or Uncle Bart."

Jane, upset by my remark, left the truck and ran back to the house. She passed up everyone on the porch, storming through the door without a word. I felt terrible. With all my effort, I'd still said the wrong thing. I considered starting the Dodge and heading on home, but couldn't leave Jane in such a condition. I got out of the truck and forced myself back to the porch. On my way up the steps, Jake spoke.

"Damn, Johnny, what'd you say to her?"

I looked at Jake and said, "Have a feeling you're the one got this started."

"Now, now," interrupted Grandma, "Don't go blaming Jake. This thing's been coming on for some time."

Uncle Bart suggested, "Josh, how about you and Jake head on into Clarkson without us. We'll be that way soon as we straighten out this mess."

Grandma said, "I'll ride in with them."

"Golly, Grandma," commented Jake, "you mean you don't wanna stay for all the fireworks?"

"That's exactly what I mean," she replied, while stepping off the porch.

Chapter 30

"Jane Marie Smith," hollered Aunt Mary, "you get on down here so's we can talk this thing out."

Jane didn't answer. I knew she wouldn't. The girl couldn't stand anybody telling her what to do. After a few seconds of silence, Uncle Bart spoke up.

"Jane, we're gonna sit down in the kitchen, have ourselves a drink, and talk about this ... me, your mama, and Johnny. If you're interested in hearin' what little we know about where you came from, you best come on down now 'cause we don't plan on chewin' our cabbage twice." He hesitated a few seconds, and then said, "Y'all come on. Let's go sit down."

The three of us headed to the kitchen. Before we took a seat, Uncle Bart pulled out two glasses and a whiskey bottle.

My aunt surprised me by saying, "Best get a glass for me too."

I said, "No way! Didn't know you drank whiskey."

"Don't, but I'm about to start."

Uncle Bart shook his head. "Lordy, lordy. Shit's gittin' deep now."

Before he could fill the glasses, my aunt got up and pulled an ice tray out of the Frigidaire. "Can't drink it hot like you guys." It sounded like she had at least tried whiskey.

My uncle began pouring and talking at the same time. "What we're about to say here—"

"Hold on a minute," said Jane as she walked into the kitchen. "Ain't gonna sit up there while y'all talk about me." She went straight to the cabinet and pulled out another glass.

Uncle Bart waited until she added some cubes, then poured. As Jane took a seat across from me, he said, "Well, since we're all here now, let's make a toast." He held his glass out over the table. "To my daughter Jane, that she might always know how much we love 'er."

Aunt Mary and I put our glasses out with his. Jane finally raised hers and said, "I'll drink to that, providin' you tell me everything you know about my *real* parents."

I had to laugh at what followed. My uncle downed his drink, and damned if Aunt Mary and Jane didn't follow suit, coughing and gagging all the way. Figured I might as well do the same.

Uncle Bart immediately began pouring a second round. When Jane started to down hers, he said, "Easy girl, that'll sneak up on you." In her stubborn state she took about half anyway as Aunt Mary started her story.

"First of all, the reason this whole mess came up is because of the way you two been actin' over one another."

"Aunt Mary," I said, "you might need to explain that to me."

"Johnny Lee Smith, don't you sit there and act like you don't know what I'm talkin' about. I've been on to you since that spell on the stairs. You think I'm too old to recognize love. You a-cryin', Jane a-cryin'. It's almost enough to make a person sick."

"Bullshit!" Jane sarcastically butted in.

"Now dammit Jane," scolded Uncle Bart, "if you wanna do this, you gotta give Mama a chance. Ain't no easier for her than it is for you. And what she just said sure as hell ain't nothin' new. We been talkin' about this for some time. Seems to us there's something goin' on here. Ain't sayin' it *is* love, but ain't sayin' it ain't. Your brothers now, they been worried about you not datin', thinkin' maybe you like girls more than boys."

"Oh, my God! My own brothers talkin' about me like I'm a queer woman. That right there's enough to tell you they ain't *my* brothers."

"Stop it, Jane," I scolded. "I won't sit here and let you talk about those boys like that. They love you and you know it. And it's not too hard to see where they're coming from. When was the last time you had a boyfriend?"

Jane stood. "Didn't come down here to listen to this shit. Thought we was gonna talk about my parents."

"Sit down," said Uncle Bart. "We'll get to that."

"Well I don't need to hear all this other stuff about me and Johnny, or me likin' women. We can talk about that later. Just tell me what I wanna hear."

The whiskey sure worked fast on Jane. Knew she could be feisty, but I'd never heard her talk like that to anyone, let alone her parents.

Uncle Bart said, "Jane honey, your mama's gonna tell you all we know about your birth parents, and believe me that ain't a whole lot. And we ain't tryin to hook you and Johnny up. That's somethin' you two gotta figure out. We just don't want you feelin' guilty about carin' for one another. You understand?"

Jane glanced at me, sat back down, and quickly finished her second glass of whiskey.

Uncle Bart nodded and said, "Go ahead, Mama, tell 'em what you know."

Aunt Mary looked as if she were afraid to speak, but did so anyway. "In 1956, on a night in November, phone rang right about bedtime. With Bart being outside takin' care of business, I answered it, fearin' something bad had happened. Scared me even more when old Father Joe from down at St. Anthony's spoke on the other end.

"He said, 'Hey Mary, hate to bother you this late, but knowing how much you'd like to have a little girl, I just had to call you. There's a little baby girl in my old parish, in bad need of a family. Tragic thing, the mother died in childbirth this morning.'"

Jane began crying again. Aunt Mary did too, as she asked, "You want me to stop?"

"No," Jane pleaded, "keep goin'."

"Well, I asked Father Joe, 'What about the daddy?'

"He said, 'They tell me nobody knows. Some soldier they think; left his seed, then left town. Girl ran away from home when she found out she was pregnant. Didn't wanna shame her family. The nuns took her in. They were letting her stay at the convent. Poor thing went into labor early while the nuns were all at the school. Delivered by herself and then bled to death. One of the nuns came in from school and heard the baby crying. Said they didn't really know how long the mother laid there. I asked if the baby was all right and Father Joe said, 'Far as I know, and if you and Bart would like to ride down there with me in the morning, you could take a look and see.'"

I couldn't tell if it was the whiskey or the moment, but Jane looked rough. I moved my chair next to hers and put my arm around her. She didn't resist.

Aunt Mary continued in tears. "Didn't know if Father Joe just happened to be the best damn salesman in town, or if God himself had designed the situation. One thing for sure, the man had my attention. Jane honey, we wanted a little girl so bad. Loved my boys, but still wanted a little girl. And I swear to you with God as my witness, I believe the Lord made me barren just so I could find you. Couldn't of made my own baby and been any better. You were beautiful then and you're beautiful now. Me and Daddy both fell in love soon as we laid eyes on you. You were everything we wanted, and still are. Honey, you looked so alone, laying there in that little crib."

By that point, Uncle Bart and I both were fighting tears.

Jane wiped her face and said, "But Mama, why'd you wait so long to tell me all this? Didn't you think I had a right to know?"

"Honey, we were just so used to you being our baby girl, didn't seem worth the trouble. If your birthmother hadn't been dead, mighta been different. And God knows that poor girl took the name of your daddy to her grave."

"How old was my mother?"

Uncle Bart answered, "She was but a child herself. They told us she'd just turned sixteen, right before you were born."

Jane wanted to know, "Where is this place you had to go to get me?"

"We drove all the way down the other side of them Smokey Mountains. Place called Saint John's Church in Waynesville, North Carolina. That's where Father Joe came from. Believe they said your mama was from somewhere in the Cherokee Indian Reservation."

"You sayin' my mama was a Indian?"

"Yes, honey," answered Aunt Mary, "That's where you got them high cheek bones and all that beautiful dark hair."

"And that mean streak too," I joked.

Ignoring my comment, Jane stood and stumbled slightly on her way to Uncle Bart's shaving mirror hanging on the wall. While staring at the reflection, she began stroking her long hair. Without turning around, she wiped her face dry and then asked, "So you sayin' I was only one day old when you came and got me?"

"That's right," answered her daddy. "Knowing how far we drove, and since Father Joe vouched for us, they let us bring you home that night. We filled out papers later for adoption."

In those few short minutes, my teary-eyed cousin had discovered what little her parents knew about her roots. Turning back toward the table, she stumbled again, woozy from the drink.

"You all right, there?" asked Uncle Bart.

"I'm fine," Jane replied while sliding back into the chair. "By the way Mama, y'all wouldn't happen to have a picture of my mother, would you?"

Aunt Mary bent over, covering her face with her hands and shaking her head. Then, raising up, she looked at Uncle Bart a few seconds before speaking to Jane. "Honey, I've a confession to make. Hope you won't hate me for it."

Jane glanced at me as Aunt Mary continued. "That priest down there, Father Christopher I believe it was, showed us a picture of your mama. Said we could have it, but me being so young and just not thinkin' right, I said no. Everything happened so fast and it seemed best to erase that part of your life. Baby, you don't know how bad that makes me feel today. God knows I'd love to show it to you."

Aunt Mary, in obvious pain, wept profoundly.

"Hold on, Mama. Got me somethin' here." Uncle Bart began digging in his wallet. Behind one of his other pictures, he had the little black and white photo of Jane's mother.

"I can't believe you kept it," said Aunt Mary, wiping her eyes.

"Sure did," he said. "Figured some day you might change your mind."

I sat quietly as Uncle Bart handed the worn picture to Jane. She marveled at the image.

"She's so young."

"Told you."

"Can I keep the picture?"

"It's yours," answered Uncle Bart.

"She's so pretty. Looky, here Johnny, she does favor Pocahontas."

"Jane," I said, "you look just like her."

Jane turned the picture over. On the back it had hand written letters, "*Little Rose.*"

"My mama's name was Little Rose?"

"Reckon so," replied Uncle Bart.

For the first time that day, Jane smiled as we both enjoyed the picture, something she'd keep forever. Uncle Bart asked me outside to finish our drinks. It appeared he wanted to give Jane and her mother some time alone.

I stood there on the porch in the fresh air thinking about the fact that Jane had suddenly become legally and, more importantly, morally available. "Boy, life sure has its strange turns, don't it?"

"And you're just now gettin' started."

In the sky above, several buzzards flew, circling. I said, "You know, sometimes it feels like they're after me."

"Who's that?"

"Those old buzzards up there."

"See 'em every day," he replied, "even when you're not here."

"Really." I thought for a second about those buzzards flying around every day, looking for something dead to eat. *Nature's garbage men.* Then I asked, "Uncle Bart, you really been carrying that ol' picture around all these years?"

"Sure enough."

"So why'd you wait this long to show it to Jane?"

"Been waitin' for the right time."

"Uncle Bart, you sure are a patient man."

"To tell the truth, it's more about being scared than being patient. Worried how she might react."

190

I reached out and offered a handshake. "You did good, sir, and I don't believe Jane could have had a better father. Or mother."

He accepted my grip and said, "Ain't my place to try and sway your feelings one way or another, but I do want you to know, if you and Jane should wind up together, you got my blessing."

Not knowing how to answer, I simply nodded my appreciation. When it came to Jane, I believe Uncle Bart understood me better than anybody. In that silent moment, he became more than an uncle.

When Jane eventually joined us on the porch, she still had a buzz from the whiskey. Uncle Bart shook his head at her clumsy approach and then entered the house, giving us some time alone. As we stood there looking out across the front acres, Jane said, in an honest voice, "Thanks for being here today."

"You're mighty welcome."

I had no idea as to what was said between Aunt Mary and Jane when they were alone. At least for the moment, her frown had turned to a smile, and I thanked God for that.

Ron Gambrell

Chapter 31

After the initial shock of finding out she'd been adopted, Jane for the first time discovered her low tolerance for liquor. As we stood on the front porch, ready to go to Clarkson and Roger's Funeral Home, she appeared tipsy from the whiskey.

"Johnny, how come I'm woozy and you're not, when you drank just as much as me?"

"Could be because you don't weigh much, then again it might be because you're Indian."

"What's that got to do with it?"

"I've heard it said that American Indians can't handle alcohol."

"Why's that?"

"Some say it's because Europeans have been consuming alcoholic drinks for thousands of years while the Indians never had any until the settlers brought it over. Not sure I believe all that, but it kinda makes sense."

"You're so smart," Jane said as we took a seat on the porch waiting for Aunt Mary and Uncle Bart. Within a few minutes, they came out together.

"Y'all wanna ride with us?" asked my uncle.

"Jane can if she wants, but I'll still need to head on in from the funeral home."

"So now you don't want me to ride with you?" whined Jane.

"Didn't say that. Be glad to have you ride along."

"Might give us a chance to talk about things," she added.

"On second thought…"

"Damn you, Johnny Lee," Jane said in a slur.

"Easy now, just joking. Come on, let's get out of here. We'll follow you, Uncle Bart."

The two of us climbed into the Dodge and waited for the LTD to move first. Having never seen Jane intoxicated, I didn't really know what to expect. For a while, she sat quietly as we followed Uncle Bart. I wondered if I'd again said something to upset her.

"You all right?"

"Yea. Whiskey's gotta wear off soon."

"That's not what I mean. I'm talking about all that family stuff."

Her voice elevated. "How can I be all right with that? It's a shock finding out you're not who you think you are."

I didn't say a word.

Realizing my silence, she asked, "You reckon people's gonna think different of me when they find out I'm a Indian?"

"Doubt it. You're still the same to me."

"Really, you still think the same of me now that you know I'm not your cousin?"

I hesitated. "You know, I'll have to think on that one."

"Is it that difficult to say how you feel?"

"Jane, I spent my whole life wishing you weren't my cousin. Now that you're not, seems a little weird."

After sitting silently for a moment, she said, "Remember yesterday, me saying I had a problem?"

"Yeah."

"Well, the problem's you."

"Now what have I done?"

"You ain't done nothin'. I just think about you way too much. Always have. That's why I don't date other guys. Get to thinkin' about you and—"

"And, it drives you crazy because we're cousins."

"Right, because we're cousins, only now we're not."

It sounded like the whiskey talking; nonetheless, Jane sat there describing my exact feelings. She continued: "Seems every time I got to thinkin' you might feel the same as me, Mary Ellen popped up. And now that we find out we're not cousins, she's all of a sudden single again."

"Jane Marie," I scorned, "Is that why Bobbie's death upset you so?"

"No, silly. Always liked Bobbie in school. Seemed like a nice boy to me."

"I liked him too, but he apparently had his problems."

"So, you still think about Mary Ellen?"

"Gettin' a little nosy now, aren't you?"

"No, I'm not. Just wanna know."

By then we were over halfway to Clarkson and the funeral home. It surprised me that Jane had so much to say under the circumstances. I tried to take the attention off Mary Ellen and me.

"So all that stuff from Josh and Jake about you not liking men, you saying we don't have to worry about that?"

"Believe me, I ain't interested in sleepin' with no woman."

"Well that's good to hear, but what about Paula?"

"What about 'er? Don't tell me they think *she's* that way?"

I laughed a bit and said, "Believe it or not, they thought you two might be a couple."

"Oh, my God! Them boys are so full of shit. Paula's man crazy as she can be. Hell, just look at her."

"That's what I told Jake. Woman that looks like that's just gotta like men."

"So you been checkin' out Paula? You look at all the women, don't you?"

Another trick question? It seemed impossible to open my mouth without saying the wrong thing. "Don't tell me you're jealous of Paula?"

"What'd you expect?"

I let off the gas a little and watched the LTD pull away. "What do I expect? I expect you shouldn't be jealous of Paula. Hell Jane, you're pretty as she is. Maybe just a little less sure of it."

I lit a cigarette and blew smoke out the window, waiting for Jane's reply. It came slow.

"Johnny, how much you care about me?"

"A lot. You know that."

"But, I mean, *how* do you care about me? Is it like a man cares about his cousin, or like a man cares about a woman?"

While my heart knew the answer, my lips were hesitant—too much too quickly. "Can't sit here and say I've never thought about you in a womanly way. Hell, I had a crush on you when we were kids. But, you gotta remember, believing you were my cousin made me feel guilty about thinking that way."

Still sitting against the passenger door, looking my way, Jane asked, "So how 'bout now? Now that you know we're not cousins, how do you think about me?"

"Jane Marie Smith, that's not a fair question. Shouldn't even be asking, us on our way to pay respects to Bobbie and all that."

"Never mind. You don't have to say it. I can read your mind."

"But, Jane?"

"Forget it. Don't wanna talk about it anymore."

My daddy always did say women were apt to change their mood in a split second. Seemed that applied double when whiskey got involved. For the next couple miles I tried to figure out what I'd done wrong. The tomboy cousin from my past had suddenly turned into a woman. Truth be known, I loved her to death and wanted to say so, but considering all that had occurred that day, I felt it better to stay away from the subject. In a matter of minutes, my attention would be switching from Jane to Mary Ellen. Both were going through life-changing experiences.

Finally, I could see the stop sign at the end of Highway 88. A right turn would put us only a couple hundred yards from Roger's Funeral Home. Jane remained quiet. Then out of nowhere, she asked, "Johnny, you ever thought about kissin' me?"

I didn't say a word, just grinned and nodded. That's all it took. As we came to the stop sign, Jane slid my way, put her left hand behind my neck, and pulled me to her lips. Her warmth and the smell of sweet perfume surrounded me, and the kiss lasted until someone honked a horn, startling us apart.

"Now, you take that back to Louaval and think about it," Jane sassed as I began my turn.

Chapter 32

Aunt Mary stood waiting for us outside the funeral home. I had no idea what to expect from her. She watched me park behind the building and then headed our way.

Jane slid back across the seat and said, "Here comes trouble."

I just barely had the door opened when Aunt Mary started in, "You two okay?"

"Yeeesss," Jane answered.

"So why'd you slow down?"

"Mom, we're not babies."

"Well please don't go makin' a scene in the funeral home. Not the time or place to shock the world with what's goin' on between the two of you. Much rather explain it under different circumstances."

Don't you just love the way people assume things.

"No need to worry, Mama. Believe Johnny's more interested in Mary Ellen anyway."

I got out of the truck, slammed the door, and said, "The woman shouldn't drink," while leaving both behind.

On my way into the funeral home, I believe half the folks there wanted to shake my hand and say hello. The room where they had Bobbie laid out was crowded with family and friends. The casket remained closed, since his head had been half removed by the shotgun blast. Pictures of my deceased friend were placed all around the casket. While staring into the memories, two arms reached around me. I turned and my eyes met Mary Ellen's. We embraced. Over her shoulder, I saw Jane and Aunt Mary making their entrance. Aunt Mary joined Grandma and the other womenfolk on the far side of the room.

Jane stood near the door, looking pitiful. *At least in a funeral home it's normal for people to look that way.*

The whole room stared while Mary Ellen and I had our moment. Considering Uncle Bart's advice, I'd planned to show my respects and nothing more. Mary Ellen whispered softly in my ear, "Need to talk to you when we get a chance to be alone."

Just the way she said it made me uncomfortable. When Bobbie's parents joined us, Mary Ellen walked off.

Mrs. Davis gave me a hug and whimpered, "How could our Bobbie do this to himself?"

I took her hands in mine and said, "Only God can answer that." Without thinking, I turned to Mr. Davis and asked quietly, "Have they determined for sure that he did it himself?"

"How come you ask that?" replied the grieving father.

"Because it just don't make sense. The boy had everything a man could want."

Mr. Davis, looking tired and in need of a seat, invited me to join him in the lounge for a cup of coffee.

When we were alone, he asked, "You think there's any way this coulda been done by someone else?"

"You mean as in murder?"

"Well, you asked, and I'm like you in that it just don't make sense him doin' such a thing. Hell, we gave the boy everything he needed."

"You're right, but you've got to understand, Bobbie wasn't himself for quite some time. Ever since…"

"Go on and say it boy. Ever since he married Mary Ellen."

"Didn't say that."

"But that's what you started to say. Right?"

"No, sir. I was going to say ever since he took to drinking."

"It was her caused that. My son wasn't no drunk until she came along."

"Mr. Davis, we're all having a tough time with this. Let's try not to say things we might regret later."

"But he was always such a good boy, and so happy, until…."

"Bobbie was a great guy and a good friend to me, but what's this stuff about him leaving bruises on Mary Ellen?"

"I ain't seen no bruises. If it *is* true, maybe he had good reason."

"Come on, Mr. Davis, there is no good reason for a man to be beatin' on his wife."

The old man grimaced and said, "Don't quote me on this boy, but Mama says she thinks Mary Ellen was a cheatin' on Bobbie."

I could have fallen out of my chair. If Mr. Davis knew of my mistake with Mary Ellen, things might get ugly. Gabrielle whispered, *Told you so.*

At that moment and to my pleasure, Bobbie's siblings entered the room and joined us. I paid respects to each and then escaped Mr. Davis' line of questioning by returning to the parlor. Jane had left the room. Her mother still sat with the other women. Mary Ellen stood in front of the casket. After waiting until the person she spoke with walked away, I approached to say my goodbyes.

"Hey girl, where's Olivia?"

"She's with my niece. You might get to see 'er at the funeral."

"You mean if they'll let me off from work."

"Don't ask. Just take off. You know I'm gonna need a shoulder to cry on."

I stood there silently, digesting her comment. Mary Ellen leaned close and whispered, "You ever think about movin' down here?"

"Sometimes. Why?"

"Thinkin' you'd make a good farmer," she said, still whispering. "Sooner or later, you know I'll be lookin' for me a good man. Knowin' how much you love that Davis farm, well, it could be yours, if you were *my* man."

No way, I thought. *Did she just say that?* Bobbie hadn't even been laid to rest, and already Mary Ellen was shopping for another man. Her attitude made me nauseated. I felt like walking away without speaking, and probably should have, but didn't.

I whispered back, "Mary Ellen, you should know me well enough to realize ain't no piece of land gonna decide who I spend the rest of my life with. And how can you stand here in front of Bobbie's casket talking that way. Where's your respect?"

"Come here a minute." Mary Ellen took my hand and led me away from the casket to a spot in the back of the room where we could be more alone. One of her brothers, concerned, headed our way. "Go on, Billy. Need to say somethin' in private." Billy backed off but cautiously watched from a distance, as did the rest of the room. Mary Ellen continued, trying to keep her voice down. "Now you listen to me, Johnny Lee. Dead or alive, that boy don't deserve no respect. He took a swing at me and knocked Olivia clean out of my arms. That's why she ain't here today. Didn't want nobody seein' the bruises on her little face."

"Holy shit, I had no idea. Is she okay?"

"She'll be fine, but that don't make it right."

"Girl, you didn't shoot Bobbie, did you?"

"You can bet your ass I thought about it. Like always when he beat on me, Bobbie run off to the barn to have him another drink and feel sorry for himself. I made sure Olivia was all right, then put 'er down for the night. Loaded up that old shotgun myself. Swear to God, I went out there plannin' to shoot the bastard. There he sat on a bucket, cryin' like a baby. Started telling me how bad he felt and how he might just as well kill himself. Hell, every time I threatened to leave 'im, he'd say he was gonna kill himself. The boy was so pitiful, shit, I couldn't pull the trigger. Left the gun there and told him he didn't have the balls. For once I reckon he did, and now I've been standing up there in front of that casket like I'm sorry he's gone, but God knows I ain't. I'd love to pull this dress off and show everybody in this room why I ain't sorry, but you and me both know that wouldn't be right by his family."

"Mary Ellen, I don't get it. Why'd Bobbie even feel the need to beat on you?"

"Why? Remember how Bobbie used to brag on himself when we were teenagers, you know, how good a man he was? Well, believe me he wasn't all that, and I let him know it. Took that boy about 30 seconds to get me pregnant, and it never got no better."

"Jesus, all this over that?"

"You don't understand. All he ever done was tease me. Satisfied himself. Left me layin' there wishin' I had you instead. Can't you see? You and me were made for each other."

I stood there speechless, trying to digest it all. Then Mary Ellen, in a sick, cool way, said, "Just think about it. Instead of bein' Olivia's godfather, you could be her daddy. I get you, you get me and Olivia, and the farm comes along with it."

Her words made me sick. I didn't need or want any part of Mary Ellen's shenanigans. I'd always known her to be bossy, but this attitude went way over the top. While I would never beat a woman, Bobbie's shameful actions began to make a little bit of sense. From my point of view, the farm should belong to the Davis family. Their heart and soul built that place, and I prayed it was still in Mr. Davis' name.

Out of nowhere, Jane came to my rescue, "Hey Mary Ellen, you doin' all right?"

The two hugged, and Jane gave me a grin over Mary Ellen's shoulder.

"I'm fine, at least for the moment."

"Well, if there is anything we can do, you just call."

"Thank you honey, but it looks like Bobbie's family's takin' care of everything for now. Appreciate the offer."

Jane continued, "Hope y'all know the whole room is watching, wonderin' what's goin' on over here."

"They can all kiss my ass," growled Mary Ellen. "If I feel like sayin' somethin' to Johnny in private, that's my business."

Jane looked at me. "Daddy wants to know if you got any extra cigarettes in the truck. He's out, and the stores ain't open on Sunday."

"Tell him I'll be right out. Gotta head home soon."

As Jane walked away, Mary Ellen squinted and said, "That girl worries me."

"How come?"

"Well, for starters, she smells like whiskey, and I sure don't like the way she looks at you. Girl don't seem to realize you two are cousins."

I leaned close and whispered, "Can you keep a secret?"

"No, but tell me anyway."

"She's not my cousin."

Mary Ellen's jaw dropped as I turned and walked away. I winked at Grandma and Aunt Mary on my way out.

Jane, Jake, Josh, and Uncle Bart were all on the front porch of the funeral home. There were several folks standing around smoking. I pulled out my pack and offered one to Uncle Bart.

He said, "No thanks, got my own." Jane sat there on the bench next to her daddy with a shit-eating grin.

Jake and Josh were full of questions about what went on at the house. Uncle Bart told 'em to hush up.

When I was about to say my goodbyes, a different notion crossed my mind. "Jane, can you take a ride with me?"

"Sure you want me to?"

I didn't ask again, just reached out and took her by the hand. With no resistance she stepped down off the porch and said, "You know Mama wouldn't like this."

"Oh well, she'll get over it."

Chapter 33

On our walk to the truck, goose bumps came up on my arms. No matter what anybody else thought, Jane's hand felt right in mine. Truth was, I'd waited all my life for a chance to be with her. Wasn't any sense in denying it.

On my way out of the parking lot, I pondered where we might go to be alone. I wound up driving down past Uncle Samuel's place to a dead end where the road got cut off by the Western Kentucky Parkway. I turned around and parked facing away from the highway. To the sound of meadowlarks, katydids, and an occasional passing tractor-trailer rig, we tried to speak our feelings.

"How's your buzz?"

"My head's hurtin'," she answered while rubbing her forehead. "Don't think you'll see me drinkin' no more whiskey."

"Probably wouldn't be so bad if you hadn't made such a hog of yourself."

"Don't go lecturing me."

Thought to myself, *Woman sure can't stand criticism.*

Jane started looking around. "How come you decided to park here?"

"No particular reason. Seemed like a good spot to be alone."

"Don't you know people down here calls this lovers' lane?"

"Is that a fact? Well, hope you don't think I'm planning to take advantage of you."

"Bet you would if I was Mary Ellen."

Already knew that would never happen again. "Jane," I said, "Ain't now, and never again will there be anything between me and her, and I'd appreciate it if you'd quit acting like there is."

"But you did sleep with 'er."

"For crying out loud, like you ain't never slept with nobody?"

Instead of answering, Jane turned away. Suddenly Jake's words came back to me. 'My sister's probably still a virgin.'

"Hey. I'm sorry. Had no idea. So are you?"

She turned in tears. "Dammit Johnny Lee, you say that like it's a disease. Just 'cause you been with all kinds of women—"

"Whoa now, it's not near as many as you think."

"Uh huh, so you have been with more than Mary Ellen. How many is it Johnny? Anybody I know? You already been with Paula?"

"Are you kidding me? How can you talk like that? No, I haven't slept with Paula. Can't say I've had the opportunity."

"Oh but if you did, you would?"

"You know, earlier you said something about me checking out all the women. Well guess what? I just happen to be a single man. That's what single men do until they find the right one. When I have me a woman of my own, that'll be that."

I waited for a reply but got none. "You realize you're the only woman that ever said 'I love you,' to me? That's what happened to me on the steps. About knocked me down when you said it. Think I didn't wanna crawl back in bed with you and pretend we weren't cousins? I'm kinda like your daddy; ain't saying it *is* love, but sure as hell ain't saying it ain't."

There I sat rattling on like a man in love and Jane knew it. Her frown turned into a smile, and she said, "So, not sayin' we *are*, but if we *were* dating, does that mean you wouldn't fool around with other women?"

"Yeah, that's what that means."

"Good, now I gotta ask you something else."

"Like what?"

"You think there's any way we could find my real mother's family? Might have a grandparent, or an aunt or uncle or even some cousins down there in North Carolina."

"Man, that's a tough one," I replied, amazed at how she could change the subject so easily. "We could try, but it sounded like either Little Rose deserted her family or they deserted her. Might not accept you if we did find them."

"You're probably right, but it would be fun to go down there and see some of them Indians. Who knows, maybe I'd fit in."

I knew right then she would never be satisfied until we drove down to North Carolina. "You know what, they had to bury that girl somewhere. Your mama, that is. If we don't do anything else, we surely can find her grave."

"Promise?"

"I promise. I will find that grave."

All of a sudden, Jane's smile went ear to ear as she came sliding across the seat. This time I saw it coming. We kissed like lovers, and it didn't take long until Jane's breathing grew heavy. When she began to whimper, it scared me to death. I pushed myself back and said, "Hold on, slow down. Ain't no way in hell your first time's gonna be right now, not in this old truck. I'm taking you back to the funeral home."

"Damn you, Johnny Lee."

"Hear me out. We gotta do this proper. Next week I'll come back, and if you haven't changed your mind, we can have us a real date. Then if you still like me, well, we'll see what happens."

"Until then, am I *your* woman?"

"Until then, you're my woman."

Chapter 34

Wanting no part of Mary Ellen's shenanigans, I passed on Bobbie's funeral and did not return to Grayson County until that Friday after work.

On our first real date, Jane and I went to a drive-in movie. It turned out not nearly as awkward as we had anticipated because no one there could really see or recognize us. I can't remember what movie showed, but the real plot unfolded in the cab of my old Dodge. No metaphor has been penned to adequately describe the delight I found in Jane's company. Her smile, her laughter, and her tears all touched my heart.

After the movie, Jane insisted we stop at the Dairy Dip in town. She'd been dying to introduce me to some friends. It made my day to have a girlfriend so excited about being seen with me.

That next day, we took a walk in the woods among all the brilliant autumn colors and along the creek where we once played as children. We enjoyed sharing stories of our past feelings for one another. Being together was our destiny. Apparently, we both knew it long before understanding.

Over the next few weeks I ran up an enormous long distance phone bill. Workdays were long and weekends didn't come quick enough. My feelings for Jane became certain. When she hurt, I hurt. In her presence, the birds chirped louder, and even the autumn breeze felt warmer. We were in love and there would be no denying it.

By mid-December, marriage became inevitable. We only spent one week planning our sacramental vows. Neither of us desired a fancy wedding, and St. Anthony's Catholic Church would be adequately sized considering most of our relatives were the same. I gave an open invitation at work for anyone willing to make the trip to Grayson County. Only Richard Barns and one of my bosses, Carl Jacobs, showed up. Paula Dawson agreed to be the maid of honor, and my old hunting friend Jerry Godfrey stood up for me. For a while, several of those who came to witness actually thought I planned to marry my cousin, causing some concern.

"Can't believe that boy couldn't find somebody to marry besides his cousin," complained my mother's brother, Uncle Henry.

"Ain't really his cousin," replied Mother. "She was adopted by James' brother and his wife."

Uncle Henry's wife Darleen walked in on the conversation, "Is it true Johnny's marryin' his cousin?"

"No he is not," snapped my mother, "Now you two stop talking like that. For heaven's sake, you'll have the whole church in an uproar."

"So," continued Aunt Darleen, "she won't even have to change her last name?"

"Well that part's right," Mother admitted.

Uncle Henry said, "Reminds me of the time Charlie Baker down in Edmondson County married his cousin. Said it didn't matter since they wasn't plannin' on having babies. Wound up having one anyway. Poor thing never was right bright. Wonder whatever happened to that kid?"

"Henry, would you please stop it. Them two's gonna have me some pretty grandbabies. Smart too I'll bet."

About that time, Father Michael O'Brian came to the vestibule stating, "Mrs. Smith, what is this I'm hearing about Johnny and Jane being first cousins? You know the law does not allow me to create such a union."

"Calm down, Father. They're not cousins. Jane was adopted at birth by Bart and Mary."

"Praised be the Lord! So we may continue."

As the truth of the matter spread through the church, a perplexed gathering made a united sigh of relief, and our vows received their blessing.

Afterwards, we had a reception in the church basement. Again, nothing fancy, just cake, beer, and a surprising amount of coaching from my uncles with respect to the wedding night activities. With Grayson County being dry, we hid the keg under a table in case the law should show up. As Jane and Uncle Bart finished their father-daughter dance, Sissy enticed me to join her on the floor. We'd just begun our own version of the waltz when she asked, "Who are those two men over there talking to Jerry?"

"They work with me, why?"

"The big one looks familiar," she answered in a concerned voice.

"You mean Carl. He's one of my bosses."

"Well, I've seen him before."

"You ever been to the packinghouse?"

"No. I've seen him in Indianapolis."

"Are you sure? Hell, he's at work all week."

Each time we turned in dancing, Sissy took another look. "He's staring at me. Johnny, I swear that's the same guy I've seen at home. Went to the convenience store across the street one night and he was there, standing right inside the door."

"No way."

"I saw him again a couple months later, sittin' on a bench in the park when I went for a run. Call me crazy, but unless he has a twin, that's the same guy."

"Well you know what they say; everybody has a look-alike somewhere in the world."

As we finished the dance and the crowd clapped, Sissy still had that look on her face. Something about Carl certainly did remind her of someone. I asked, "Want me to introduce you to him?"

"No, but I am gonna ask Mike if he's seen him before."

We parted, and in the excitement of the event, I forgot about Sissy until later when Paula Dawson approached me. "Hey there *Mr*. Smith. Was talking to your sister a few minutes ago. She sure has a feeling about that big guy. Said you told her he's your boss."

Three beers past my conversation with Sissy, I spoke freely. "She says he looks like someone from Indianapolis. Everybody has a twin, you know."

Paula asked, "What's his name?"

"Carl Jacobs."

"Carl Jacobs?" she repeated quickly, "That sounds like the guy that hangs out with Kelly."

Detective Kelly Rauschenberg. Surprised she didn't show up. "Yeah, that's him."

"Interesting."

Jane and I had reservations for the honeymoon suite at the Galt House in downtown Louisville. It seemed proper to speak with everyone, individually, at least once before leaving. I ended up with Richard Barns and Carl Jacobs. "You guys doing all right?"

"Doing just fine, Mr. Married Man," replied Richard.

"How 'bout you, Carl?"

He seemed preoccupied, "I'm okay, Smith. Congratulations on your new bride. She's a real cutie."

"Well, thank you very much. Means a lot to me, you guys coming all the way down here to my wedding."

Carl joked, "We just came for the free beer." He looked back while starting toward the keg and asked, "Richard, you ready?"

"No, I'm fine, still got half a cup."

When we were alone, I talked to Richard. "Hey dude, do me a favor. Don't leave until you see Carl get in his truck and drive off."

"Why, what's up?"

"Don't know, but my sister says she recognizes him from Indianapolis. Like he's been following her or something. Think she's mistaken, but you never know. Hell, of all the people at work, sure didn't think he'd show up tonight."

"Thought the same thing myself," Richard replied. "But don't you worry—I'll keep an eye on Carl. You just take that pretty little Indian on out of here before I steal her away."

I always thought differently of Carl Jacobs after that night. Already didn't trust him because of his underhandedness with Kelly Rauschenberg. We were friendly to one another at work, but that's about it.

Ron Gambrell

Chapter 35

For several years, all went quiet. No family business. No family meetings. Sissy seemed to be getting over her dilemmas, or at least she no longer mentioned them. Jane and I were married nearly five years before she got pregnant. In February of '83, little Christine Marie added a wonderful new dimension to our lives. My wilder side subsided. I can still recall the first time I backed off when some drunk insulted me and tried to pick a fight. Gabrielle's warnings, *Not worth it,* and *too much to lose,* somehow made more sense. My fear was that walking away would be embarrassing. It turned out not to be.

Things changed that summer, right after Sissy and her husband moved back to Louisville. Mike got a job in a local engineering firm designing sewer lines for new subdivisions. Around the last week in September, I got a call. There would be a meeting in the barn on Sunday morning. I skipped church and made the trip to Grayson County. Shortly after I arrived, so did my father and his brothers. We all had the traditional shot of moonshine before making our way to the family room via the storm cellar. Once we were there, Pop started.

"Guys, hate to call you all down here on a Sunday, but this shit can't wait. Johnny, I'm sure you know we ain't never quit looking for that third man who attacked your sister. If we'd got to them other two, they would have told us the name we needed. And you can bet your ass that's why they got killed. Whoever did it knew we were looking and wanted to keep 'em quiet."

"We already know this," chimed in Uncle Willie. "So what's new?"

"Yesterday Sissy told me she saw that same man checking her out again."

210

"Where?"

"At the grocery store."

"What man?" I asked.

"That big guy. The one that was at your wedding. Said she looked up, and there he was, standing at the end of an aisle, staring at her, just like he did in Indianapolis. She left her bascart full of groceries right there and went home."

"You're talking about Carl Jacobs," I said. "He's the one she complained about at the wedding."

"That's right," replied my father. "And I believe that bastard's the third man we've been lookin' for. Don't know what he's up to, but I can't wait around until he hurts Sissy again. Man puts his hands on her, swear to God I'm goin' off."

"Calm down, James," urged Uncle Bart. "Whatcha wanna do, call the cops? You know what they'll say. Just seeing someone at the grocery store don't mean nothin'."

Pop kept venting. "The man lives in the East End. What the hell's he doin' in a grocery store on the other side of town?"

I asked, "How'd you know where Carl lives?"

"Told you, boy, we ain't never stopped lookin'."

"Sounds like you guys have been doing things behind my back."

"It's not like that, Johnny," answered Uncle Bart. "We didn't involve you because you work with Jacobs. If he *is* the third man and he thought you suspected him, you'd be in danger."

"Well, he knows I'm Sissy's brother."

"All the more reason not to trust or turn your back on him."

"So you guys think Carl killed Pete and Joe?"

"Damn right," blurted my father. "Didn't you say they helped get him hired on at the packinghouse?"

"Yea. Believe they were high school buddies."

"And they all three raped my daughter." Pop seemed ready to blow his stack. "Guys, two of my kids are in danger because of this sonofabitch. What would y'all do if it was one of yours? I can't sit around and wait."

211

Uncle Bart held up his hand and said, "Before we go off here, we gotta think about the cops. That detective Paula talks to, the one that questioned Johnny, she ain't dense. Woman knows we been lookin' for this guy. We do the man in—she'll figure we did it."

"So, you think we should talk to her?" asked my father.

"Didn't say that. Didn't Paula say that detective woman is friends with Carl Jacobs?"

"Yes she is," I acknowledged. "Makes it hard to trust her, don't it?"

Uncle Samuel, who had been quiet, finally inserted his two cents. "She obviously knows more about Jacobs than we do. I for one would like to talk to the lady, see what she thinks about him stalking Sissy. Could be she's watching him."

I said, "Could be she's watching you guys watching him."

"Smartass," chuckled Uncle Samuel.

Uncle Bart said, "Don't laugh, brother. Johnny might be right."

"All the more reason then to talk to her," replied Uncle Samuel. "Feel 'er out. Weigh our options. Beats the heck out of doin' nothing."

Pop looked back at his brother Willie. "What do you think? Can we afford to talk to her?"

"Don't ask me. I told you years ago not to get the cops involved."

We all stood silently for a moment. Finally, Uncle Bart said, "James, it's your daughter. You decide."

"I wouldn't mind talkin' to the woman, seein' what she really knows about the man."

"See if she takes up for him," added Uncle Willie.

"Question is, where?" continued my father. "Can't have her coming here."

Samuel volunteered to set it up. "Guys, let me talk to Paula, see if she can't get her friend to meet us someplace. Maybe Grayson Springs. Hardly anybody goes in there these days. Do it soon, before all the leaves are gone, won't nobody passin' see us."

"Unless somebody has a better idea," replied Pop. Offering his hand he said, "Together?"

The rest of us all stuck our hands in and repeated, "Together!"

Uncle Bart looked at me. "I know we told you before to stay away from Jacobs, but things are different now. If you can arrange to be around him at work, it could be beneficial. That way we can have an eye on him. But to do it, you have to be disciplined, keep your mouth shut and your ears open. If you think for a second this guy ain't dangerous, you'd be wrong. Dead wrong. And don't try following him outside of work. One of us can take care of that as needed. Understand?"

"Yes, sir."

"Good."

Uncle Willie asked, "Johnny, you remember when you first came to us about those two that got killed?"

"Yeah."

"And remember what you wanted to do to them?"

I nodded.

"Well, there may come a time when we have to take care of this guy Carl. You gonna be alright with that?"

"Yes, Sir."

"And, what if it involves you?"

Before answering, I glanced at Pop. He stood wordless as if worrying about my involvement. "I'm alright with that."

"Not sayin' you will, but it is somethin' you might wanna be thinkin' about."

During the milking chores that evening, taking care of Carl was the only thing I could think about. Discussing the matter would have been nice. The hardest part of being involved with the family was keeping quiet.

Chapter 36

My father called me again the following Friday. Samuel had arranged a meeting with Detective Kelly for that Sunday, October 2, 1983 at the old Grayson Springs Inn. Planning the meeting for Sunday morning meant most folks would be in church, securing our privacy even more. Since the inn itself would be locked up, we'd have to do our business on the grounds.

I drove down with Pop that morning. The weather couldn't have been better. We all met first at Uncle Bart's, then everyone rode together in his LTD. The ride only took about twenty minutes. When we pulled into the Grayson Springs grounds there were no cars around and no signs of people. Uncle Bart drove all the way back to the building, and then turned around to face the gated entrance. I didn't much care for being stuck in the backseat between my father and Uncle Samuel.

I asked, "You guys mind if I smoke?"

"Hell yes, I mind," spoke my father. "Ain't sittin' in here with all y'all smokin'."

"Then let me out."

"Surely you can wait until they get here."

About the time he said it, a car pulled in off the main road. We all watched the vehicle's slow approach until it stopped next to ours. I recognized Paula as the driver, and sure enough, Kelly rode shotgun.

"Howdy," said Uncle Bart out the window. "Nice of you ladies to meet up with us today."

"It's our pleasure," returned Paula. "Mind if we get out, stretch our legs?"

"Not at all, we're a bit crowded in here ourselves."

After Paula eased a few feet further so our doors could open, both cars emptied. It looked like a smoke fest with everybody lighting up at the same time. I hadn't seen Kelly since our rendezvous in 1977. The lady still looked good. Her hair was longer and I liked that.

"How are you, Detective Kelly?"

"Fine. Hear you're married and gotta kid now?"

"Yeah that's right, and how about you? Still married?"

"Guess you could say that. Hey, is that sulfur I smell?"

"Sure is," answered Paula. Then she looked at Uncle Bart and asked, "Mind if we walk over by the sulfur springs real quick? Kelly ain't ever seen anything like that."

"Go ahead, but don't be long," warned Uncle Bart. "We'd like to take care of business and leave before church lets out up at Bear Creek."

As Paula and Kelly hurried toward the springs, Uncle Willie said, "Woman's got a hell of a tan. Bet a dollar she's got a black daddy?"

"You'd be right Uncle Willie. You got a problem with that?"

"No, not really. You?"

"No, sir."

Uncle Willie looked around and said, "Any y'all got a problem with this woman bein' half black?"

No one did. Pop said, "If Paula and Johnny trust her, reckon I do."

Uncle Samuel asked, "Damn, Johnny, you had a piece of that?"

"Which one?" I jabbed, knowing he had a crush on Paula.

"You little shit. Oughta cut your balls off."

"Not yet," joked my father. "Boy needs a son."

Uncle Bart pulled out a pint whiskey bottle with no label. That meant moonshine. We were passing it around as the ladies returned. Uncle Willie kept an eye on the ladies even as he took his swig. I wondered, *Is he admiring, or analyzing?*

Everyone sort of gathered around the LTD's front hood. It looked like the Knights of the Round Table with Paula and Kelly on one side, Uncle Bart, Uncle Samuel, and me along the front, and Pop and his brother Willie across from the girls.

Uncle Bart asked, "Miss Kelly, you got a last name?"

"Yes, sir. Just don't use it often."

"Well, I reckon since you know ours, we ought to know yours."

"It's Kelly Rauschenberg, sir."

"Lord have mercy," chuckled Uncle Willie. "Half black woman with a Jew name?"

"That's a little uncalled for!" snapped Paula.

"Sir," replied Kelly, "I didn't drive seventy something fucking miles to have some racist old white man criticize me for who I am."

"Hold on, honey."

"And, I am *not* your honey."

Pop said, "Easy ma'am. I can assure you Willie means no disrespect."

"He's right, ma'am. Hell, my wife is from a Jewish family. Truth is I could care less about who *or* what you are. Just found it amusing. That's all." As he spoke, Uncle Willie held out his hand.

"You sure about that?" Kelly asked.

"Promise," replied Uncle Willie.

Kelly grinned and then shook his hand.

Uncle Samuel shook his head, and Uncle Bart said, "If y'all are done with all this silly shit, I'd sure like to get down to business."

"Me too," said Pop. Who wants to start?"

Kelly said, "Tell you what gentlemen, let me explain where I am on this thing. Then you guys can ask questions or add to what I know."

"Sounds good to me," replied Uncle Bart.

"Hold on a minute," said Uncle Willie.

"Now what?" complained Uncle Samuel.

"With all due respect, how do we know this lady ain't wired?"

Kelly grinned and said, "It's because I'm black, right?"

"No ma'am. That's got nothin' to do with it."

Without hesitation, Kelly pulled her sweater straight up exposing both breasts, no bra. Even Paula's jaw dropped as Kelly turned to show her back and then faced us again, nipples perked up in the cool October breeze. "Convinced?"

Six Little Scars

Uncle Bart pulled out his bottle and took another quick snort. Uncle Willie said, "Paula, we trust you. How 'bout you and Ms. Kelly step behind the building there so she can show you the rest."

"Sir, I'm not shy." With that said Kelly pulled her sweater back down and dropped her blue jeans.

In unison, Pop and Uncle Willie moved toward the front of the car for a better view. Turning around in her underwear, showing off her well-rounded ass, Kelly said, "Guys, that's far as I go. Hope you're satisfied." Then she pulled up her pants.

Paula joked, "Seems to me Kelly's the one who should be worrying about a wire. How 'bout all y'all drop your drawers?"

The detective answered for us, "That won't be necessary. Wouldn't be here if I didn't trust 'em."

Uncle Bart said, "Appreciate that, ma'am."

While Pop and Uncle Samuel seemed to be in shock, Uncle Willie still had that look of suspicion.

"Okay then," started Kelly, "First of all, as you guys probably already know, at one time I suspected it was you who killed those two men from the packinghouse, Peter Metcalf and Joe Simpson. Couldn't help but think that, since their deaths occurred so close to the note Paula left on my desk. I knew it had to be family wanting to check those boys out in connection to the rape of Patricia Smith in '72."

"Told you before," I butted in, "we call 'er Sissy."

"Anyway," Kelly continued, "after spending some time with Johnny—"

Uncle Samuel kicked my leg.

"—I at least pretty much knew it wasn't him. Then after checking out all of your backgrounds—"

The elders glanced at one another with looks of surprise.

"—figured you guys were too smart to do such a thing that close after sending me the note. So then I started thinking, since there were three men involved in Patricia—Sissy's attack, the third man might have killed the other two to guarantee their silence. Question was, how'd he know someone overheard his accomplices talking about the crime? Truth be known, I'm the culprit—"

We all looked at one another again.

"—Paula left me that note before I cut it off with Carl. Actually, I'd been trying to cut it off, but he kept bugging me about getting together. Still does on occasion. Anyway, I mentioned Paula's note to Carl because he works at the same plant. At that time, he let on like he didn't know Metcalf or Simpson. Of course, we know better now. They were listed as references on Carl's application at the packinghouse. Always did figure the shooter knew his victims. Hard to walk up and shoot two hunters carrying guns if they don't know you. And now Paula tells me he's been following your Sissy. It all adds up. In my heart, Carl *is* the shooter, which would also make him the third man in Sissy's rape. Problem is we have absolutely no evidence to connect him to their murders or her rape. Remember, he used to be a cop himself. The man's extremely smart and not about to incriminate himself."

"But why would he be following Sissy?" asked Pop.

"That worries me. If he is the man we're looking for, your daughter could be in real danger. You guys might not know it, but we have more than a hundred rapes annually in the city. Out of that number, one a year since '72 has had an MO that reminds me of Sissy's case. He always brands his victims with a cigarette. Instead of it being three guys, it's only one. Leaves two scars—one on each arm."

"Is that right?" commented Uncle Willie.

"Yes, sir. It could be that one of the three who attacked your niece enjoyed what he did to the point of wanting more. Over the years, this guy has become a real sicko. Turned sadistic. Loves torturing both mentally and physically before the rape. The way he brands them with a cigarette led us to believe the rapist probably did time. Convicts like to mark their victims. Peter Metcalf did a year for robbery, so we first suspected him. Then I realized he did his time after your Sissy's rape. Of course that didn't completely rule him out, at least not until he and his partner got murdered and the rapes with cigarette burns kept occurring. That leaves only Carl, providing he is our man."

"So you really don't know?" asked my father.

"Not for certain. But I'll tell you this. Someone took evidence from the property room on your daughter's rape case, and that someone had to be a cop. The sign-in sheet is missing for one day in '74. That's the year Carl was on the force. My guess is he knew the evidence could incriminate him, so he destroyed it."

"Well then," I asked, "how can we find out for sure if he is our man?"

"Hate to say it, but we're going to have to wait for him to screw up. And he will eventually; they all do. But in the meantime, you have to wonder how many he'll brutalize before he slips."

"You still haven't said why he'd be watching my daughter. If he already raped her, why would he keep comin' around?"

"Mr. Smith, at this point it would be speculation for me to analyze what makes the man stalk. You can bet his drive is not entirely sexual. Rapists get off on overpowering and humiliating women. This one goes even further. He enjoys scaring the hell out of them before he does anything. He attacks from behind; pulls a cloth sack, probably a dark pillowcase, over their head; and then puts handcuffs on them so he can have his way."

"Handcuffs?" I thought out loud, "That oughta tell you something."

"Sure does," she replied, "since Carl used to be a cop. Another thing: the whole time he's with his victim, the man never speaks out loud, only whispers. Swears he'll let them go if they don't scream, but guarantees a slow painful death if they do. So far, we haven't found any bodies that appear to be related to this particular case. If it is Carl, and if he murdered those other two boys, you can bet it's only a matter of time until he starts killing his victims. It's one thing to rape a woman, but this man's MO makes him a special case. He's sick for sure. Probably went through abuse himself as a child. Criminal psychologists struggle to figure out what makes a man like him tick."

Kelly hesitated long enough to light a cigarette. Most of us followed suit. Then she continued. "Probably shouldn't be telling you guys this stuff. Hopefully you'll all keep what I'm saying to yourselves. We don't normally expose details until the case is solved. Captain finds out, I'll lose my job."

219

"Just tell us what you know, lady," insisted Uncle Willie. "We ain't gonna tell nobody."

Kelly took another draw, blew it into the air, and went on with her story. "Tell you right now, this one's got discipline. Only rapes one a year. Spends eleven months fantasizing and planning the next attack. Down at the station, they call him the December Rapist. The man does his work same month every year. Could be the stalking is part of the planning stage, which is even more reason to be concerned in Sissy's case."

"Maybe it's got something to do with Christmas," I interjected.

"Thought about that," replied Kelly.

"But this don't make sense," my father said. "He's been following my Sissy for over five years. Indianapolis, then at the wedding, and now here. If he plans on doin' somethin', what's he waitin' for?"

"You're right, it doesn't make sense. But nothing this rapist does makes a lot of sense. Maybe he just likes taking chances. Could be he wants your daughter to see him. At a point, some of these sickos actually have a desire to get caught. Personally, I don't think that's the case with this one. Be more inclined to think the asshole gets a thrill out of returning and looking at his victims. Sort of like living trophies."

"Sick bastard," snapped Uncle Bart. "I've got a trophy for him."

"Guys, LPD only has so much manpower and resources to devote to crimes like this. But since this prick is serial, and because of the nature of his crimes, they've got my partner and me working the case continuously. Everything comes through us. And I'm telling you, there is no evidence. The sonofabitch has his own ritual, perfected to the point of leaving no evidence. No sperm, no hair, no blood, nothing. He either doesn't ejaculate or is wearing a rubber because there's never any sperm. Strangely, he uses a lubricant before penetration. Probably for his own comfort or to kill biological evidence. Don't think he cares about hurting the woman."

"Can't you trace the lubricant?" asked Uncle Samuel.

"Basic KY jelly. Lots of people use it."

"You sayin' this is the only case you work on?" asked Uncle Willie.

"No sir, we're always working on new cases, but what I *am* saying is that this case never gets put on the back burner. Always on my mind. I lay awake some nights just thinking about how Carl might have used me to get information. It makes me want to get his ass no matter what." Kelly's voice began to tremble with anger as she rattled on. "I've seen his dirty work first hand. The trauma and the way he brands his victims so they can never forget what he does to them."

For a moment, it appeared no one wanted to speak. Then, practically in tears, Kelly finished. "Gentlemen, this man likes playing games. His once a year ritual seems to be done in a way to tease and torment the police. Looks to me like this might be Carl's way of getting back at the LPD for kicking him off the force. And with him being so smart, I'm afraid this is one of those cases where, short of a signed confession, the law's just not gonna get the job done. At least not until after he hurts or kills someone else. I'll admit, for me, stopping Carl has become personal, and not as much about punishment as prevention."

"So," asked my father, "What can we do to help stop this guy?"

Kelly dropped her cigarette, stepped on it, and said, "I want him stopped before he hurts another woman, period. You want him stopped for what he did to your daughter and before he has a chance to do it again. Guarantee you right now, if he grabs Sissy again, it'll make the first time look like a picnic."

Father's shoulders tightened as he shivered and shook his head. I feared the thought of that man touching Sissy again might cause him to have another heart attack.

"You okay, Pop?"

"No," he replied while wiping his eyes. "Lady, let's get to the bottom line here. Can't take much more of this."

"Mr. Smith, for the next two months we'll be watching close. I'll probably lose sleep and drink a lot of coffee staying close enough to make sure he doesn't attack your daughter or anyone else. If necessary, I'll go beyond the line of duty. I wish we had an excuse to put him behind bars, but without evidence, that's not going to happen."

"So what can we do?" I asked.

"We need to know for certain that Carl is going out of his way to follow Sissy."

"Why?" asked Uncle Willie. "What difference is that gonna make?"

"Well," said Kelly, "might or might not be enough to arrest him, but I know what difference it would make if it were my daughter."

Uncle Bart wasted no time. "Lady, what *are* you sayin'?"

"Sir, I'm saying without evidence, it doesn't look like the law's going to stop this bastard by December. If we could set something up to satisfy *my* mind that he is indeed stalking Sissy ... then, if you guys feel sure enough to act?" Kelly nervously paused, looked the other way, and said, "You know what I'm saying."

We all looked at one another in amazement. There stood one of Louisville's finest, apparently admitting that our form of justice may be the best answer to stopping Carl Jacobs before he returned to victimize Sissy again.

Paula spoke, "Listen guys. On the way down here, we were talking and maybe, just maybe, we have an idea, a way to at least tell for sure that Carl is following Sissy. But it's going to involve getting them both in the same room."

"No way," insisted Father. "You're not putting my daughter in the same room with that bastard. I'll kill the man myself before that happens."

"Easy James, let 'er finish," begged Uncle Willie.

Kelly stressed, "I have no intentions of putting your daughter in a position where she and Carl would be alone. Thinking more like a public place, maybe a restaurant, and you could all be there with her. All we need is some sort of an event where you folks are having dinner out together. Let Johnny drop the hint at work as to where and when, and we'll see if he takes the bait. If the man shows up uninvited, that'll pretty much do it for me. I'd bet money the only reason he drove all the way down here for Johnny's wedding was because he knew Sissy would be there."

"So," I asked, "you're saying he already knew Sissy is my sister?"

"That's my guess," Kelly answered.

"Don't think he knew that before Pete and Joe got killed," I continued. "Wonder when he figured it out?"

"Probably didn't take long to put your last name and hers together. Especially after we asked to interview you."

Uncle Willie butted in, "Ma'am, you said you were willing to go beyond the line of duty. Couldn't you just plant the evidence you need?"

He seemed to stump Kelly. After a few seconds, she answered, "No sir, really don't want to do that. Think too much of my job."

"He lied to you about knowing them other two. Ain't that enough to lock him up?"

"My word against his. And, since we dated...."

I could almost see Uncle Willie's mind wallowing in the details. For me, Kelly's speech had only increased my anger toward Carl, and judging from his face, my father felt the same. "Dad, let's do this thing. If we're all there, ain't no way he'll hurt Sissy. Maybe it'll lead to his arrest, or at least convince Kelly to turn her head."

"Under those conditions, it sounds worth a try, James," added Uncle Bart.

Kelly took a deep breath, crossed her arms, and stood listening.

"Course, I'd have to be there," Uncle Bart continued. "Like the lady says, if he shows up uninvited, that ought to say somethin'."

Pop looked at the others and asked, "What do y'all think?"

"Sounds good to me," replied Uncle Samuel.

"First," demanded Uncle Willie, who had seemed skeptical from the start, "we have to have this lady's word that she's the only cop knows what's going on."

Kelly looked him in the eye. "Mr. Smith, you have my word."

Uncle Willie stared back hard and said, "Lady, you do know if this guy shows up, it's all over. The man will disappear."

Without saying a word, Kelly again turned her head the other way, as if to say that's what she'd do in the end.

After a few seconds and without speaking, Uncle Willie nodded his okay.

"All right then, it's a deal," said Uncle Bart as he pulled out the pint bottle. After taking a swig of the 'shine, he handed it to Kelly. "Here you go, lady. If you're with us, you're with us."

"What is this?" she asked.

"It'll put hair on your chest," I joked. "But more than anything, it'll mean you're part of what we're doing here."

"Sure it won't kill me?"

"Only if you take too big a swig."

Kelly took a small drink and a slow exhale. The rest of us followed, except Paula since she had to drive. We said our goodbyes, and the two women returned to their car. Before pulling away, they backed up. Kelly had more to say.

She leaned against Paula and spoke out the driver's window. "Hey guys, if we intend to do this, we need to do it soon. December's coming quick. Figure out when and where, and then let Paula know. She can relay the message to me. After today, I don't want to be seen talking to any of you. And please, if Carl shows up, don't any of you go off and do something we'll regret. Can't turn my head if you do something stupid in a public place."

"Damn," grinned Uncle Samuel, "I was planning on pluggin' his ass right there."

"I mean it, gentlemen," preached Kelly. "No screwing up. We've got to be smart about this. Okay?"

"We hear ya," said Uncle Bart.

The ladies drove off, leaving five grown men standing there like schoolboys.

"Hope you dumbasses are happy with what we just did," grumped Uncle Willie. "Woman shows her tits and y'all fall apart. Ain't never had a stranger share in our drink, and I wanna ask, have any of you ever met a cop you could trust?"

I said, "Hey, already told you I don't trust her, but what else we gonna do?"

Uncle Willie, still not satisfied, asked, "So answer me this; how can a woman, a cop who's not willing to plant evidence, stand here and basically conspire to commit murder?"

No one gave an immediate answer, though we all admitted Uncle Willie had a good point. On the way back to the farm, we discussed when and where to have the family event.

Chapter 37

Christine's baptism provided just what we needed for getting the family together. Sissy and Mike had already agreed to be godparents. On the second Sunday in October, we would all gather at our church in Louisville for the christening. Instead of meeting back at the house afterwards—as originally planned—the family would go to Masterson's Restaurant near the University of Louisville campus. Dropping a hint to Carl Jacobs involved help from my co-worker Richard Barns. He could be trusted to play along without questions.

Filling vacations in the order room put me in Carl's department. On the Friday before the baptism, several of us stood in the lobby right after lunch. As always, Carl came in for his cup of coffee and to run us all back to work. I waited until he had a seat and then gave Richard a wink. He said, "Hey Johnny, goin' fishin' on Sunday. You wanna go?"

"Sounds good, but that's the day we're gettin' Christine baptized."

"What about afterwards?"

It took effort not to look at Carl.

"Can't. We're all going down to Masterson's. Sissy and Mike's gonna be the godparents. Promised 'em a steak."

"Smith, how old is that baby now?" asked Carl.

"Hell, she's almost eight months and growing like a weed."

Richard improvised. "So when you gonna have another one? I'd say that little girl needs a brother."

"Sounds like you been talking to Jane. She's ready, but I'm not. Gotta save a little money first."

"You know what they say," he continued, "if you wait until you can afford 'em, you'll never have 'em."

"Okay guys," Carl ordered. "Time to get back to work."

As we walked out into the department, Richard asked, "How was that?"

"Perfect. You did good," I replied. "Thanks for your help."

"Don't know what you're up too, but you'd best be careful."

"I will. You just keep all this to yourself."

That evening, I gave Pop a call to let him know everything was on schedule. He informed his brothers and, of course, they contacted Paula. She called Kelly. We decided it would be best not to tell Sissy and Mike about our plan. They might have a problem with being used as bait. On that Sunday morning, little Christine Marie Smith got baptized as planned. The church was unusually crowded with all my family packed in among the regulars. Josh no longer lived at the farm, but he and his new girlfriend, Anna, had agreed to help Jake with the milking so Uncle Bart and Aunt Mary could attend and bring Grandma Smith along.

After Mass, we headed to Masterson's. Whether Carl showed up or not, it would be a good time. Our tables were arranged so everyone could be seated together. A child's seat for Christine had been placed at one end. I took the first seat next to her, against the wall. Then it was Mike, Pop, Ray, and all the elders who, like me, wanted a seat facing the door. Jane sat across from me, then Paula, Sissy, Mom, my aunts, and Grandma. The other children filled up what was left at the end opposite Christine.

We were not the only diners in the room. Masterson's had a regular Sunday after-church crowd. I looked for Kelly on the way in but didn't see her, or Carl.

Everyone ordered drinks, and the small talk began.

Sissy said, "Johnny, y'all didn't have to do this. Gonna cost a fortune."

"Thank Mom and Pop. They're payin' for it."

"Is that right? Daddy, you gonna do this for my babies?"

My mother didn't give Pop a chance to answer. She said, "Sissy honey, you have a baby, we'll be glad to."

"So, Mike," asked Uncle Willie, "how you liking that new job?"

"Great so far," he answered.

"Do you make a lot of money?" asked Ray's eight-year-old son Phillip, loud enough for most in the room to hear.

His daddy scolded, "Boy, you best lower your voice, and don't be asking questions like that. Ain't none of your business what the man makes."

Ray said, "That's okay. Don't mind admitting I'll never get rich where I'm at. But, it is more than they paid me in Indy, and at least we're back in Kentucky."

"Amen to that," chimed in Mother.

"How about you, Sissy?" asked Aunt Mary. "You working anywhere?"

"Not yet, but I'm looking. Might go back to school part time. Like to learn computers. Mike says that's the thing of the future."

Pleased with my sister's comments, I said, "Sounds great. You oughta consider the community college. Thinking about enrolling myself."

"About time," added Ray.

After serving drinks and bread, our waitress began taking meal orders. It seemed to take forever as she made her way from one end of the three tables to the other. For a while, the family sat drinking coffee and shooting the bull. Then, as my father leaned over, telling me something I can't remember, Carl Jacobs walked through the dining area door. I winked, and within seconds the elders all knew of our uninvited guest.

It didn't take Carl long to spot us or to head our way. He walked right up to my end of the table. I guarantee at least three were dying to pull out their guns and do him in right there on the spot. Carl stopped directly behind Sissy and spoke to me across the table.

"Hey Smith, saw you coming in. Couldn't leave without saying hi."

"Good to see you," I replied. "Who you with?"

"Nobody. Supposed to meet a friend here in a few minutes. Gonna play golf over at Seneca."

Suddenly short for words, I asked, "Who you playing with?"

"One of my old friends from the police force. Should be here any minute." Then, looking down at Christine, he said, "Is this that baby girl you keep talking about?"

"Yes sir, that's her."

"Well, she sure is a real cutie."

Sissy, without looking back at Carl, spit coffee half way across the table, put her cup down, and sat there with a terrified look.

Mike stood immediately, saying, "You okay honey?" as he pushed past the back of my chair.

Pop kept his seat, but he looked like a rubber band ready to snap. Mother wore a strange look, as though she knew something bad had just happened.

Sissy said, "Believe I'm gonna be sick. Y'all excuse me please."

Carl moved over as Sissy slid her chair back, stood, and took off toward the ladies room. Paula followed Sissy, and Mike wound up standing face to face with Carl. By then the elders all had their hands under the table. Mike looked like he knew exactly what bothered Sissy. He probably recognized Carl from the wedding. I could sense my brother-in-law weighing his options. Afraid there might be a scene, I said to Carl, "My sister doesn't seem to be feeling well."

Mike tried to speak, "Mister—"

I cut him off. "Mike, have you ever met my *boss*, Carl Jacobs? Carl this is my sister's husband, Mike."

"Glad to meet you, sir," Carl said while reaching out to shake hands.

Mike refused the offer. "Believe I've seen you a time or two before."

At that moment, I wished I'd let Mike know what we were up to. Mother, in moving away, slid up against Aunt Mary's chair. Jane scooted closer to Christine and then sat there staring, as did the other women. Pop attempted to diffuse the situation.

"Mike, can you pass me that basket of rolls?"

Standing there dwarfed by Carl's large structure, Mike appeared to catch the hint, but he still didn't move. Poor guy either had no idea as to what he might be up against or simply didn't care. Luckily, Carl excused himself.

"Didn't mean to interrupt your meal, Smith. Guess I'd better go look for my partner. See you at work."

Carl walked away as the elders whispered in one another's ears, and the ladies all sat confused. His showing up assured our suspicions. If looks could kill, Carl would have been dead as Mike stared him all the way out the door.

When the men began to sit back down, Uncle Willie said, "Hey Mike, what say you and me go out for a little fresh air?"

Mike glanced back toward the restrooms.

"Don't worry," I said, "We'll check on her."

Uncle Willie slid behind the others. When he rounded the end of the table, I leaned close. "Remember what Kelly said. Don't do anything we're all gonna regret."

After answering with a nod, he and Mike walked away, leaving a table of frustrated men and confused women. Aunt Mary spoke first. "Suppose it would be out of line to ask what the heck's going on here?"

"You'd be right about that," answered Uncle Bart.

The whole scene had become chaotic, and Uncle Willie's deciding to take a walk didn't help matters. Jane, while tending to Christine, said, "Johnny, go check on your sister."

The elders' heads all nodded in agreement.

I watched Mike and Uncle Willie move out of sight before walking away. Sissy and Paula were standing in the hallway next to the lady's room door.

"What's going on?" I asked.

"Is he gone?" replied Paula.

"Yes, he's gone."

"Johnny, you ain't gonna believe this," continued Paula. "Sissy recognized his voice."

"Do what?"

Sissy, nearly hyperventilating, blurted, "What that man just said—about Christine being a—a real cutie. That's the same thing he said the night they raped me."

"You sure?"

"Yes, I'm sure. They held me down and put something over my face so I couldn't see 'em. When they pulled my clothes off, that sonofabitch said, 'Damn boys, she sure is a real cutie.' I'll never forget that long as I live. Johnny, that's one of the men that raped me, I just know it, and he's the same one that showed up at your wedding. I told you then that he's been following me."

"Calm down, Sissy. I believe every word you're saying, but for now, I need you to go back in there and act like nothing ever happened. Carl's gone, and you're safe. I promise. And I swear to you, with God and Paula here as my witness, I'll take care of Carl. Understand?"

Sissy put her arms around me. "How can I act like nothin' happened? How am I gonna live or sleep knowing that bastard's around? And what about those other two? Where are they? Johnny, I need me a gun. Man comes around again, I'll shoot."

It seemed like a good time to fill my sister in on Carl.

"Paula, can you go back and tell everyone that Sissy's okay? We'll be there in a minute."

"Sure," she replied and gave Sissy a hug before walking away.

When Paula had gotten out of hearing distance, I said, "Listen sister, I've never known you to be scared of anything, but I can see this shit's got you terrified. So I'm about to tell you something you're not supposed to know, and you damn sure better not repeat it, no matter what. Not to Mike, not to Mom and Dad, not to anyone. This has to be our little secret. Understand?"

"Talk to me."

"You need to know that we're on to Carl and have been for some time."

"We, who's we?"

"I'm not saying. You should be able to figure that out on your own. And, if you do, keep it to yourself."

Sissy huffed, "Oh, my God!"

"Just listen. We didn't say anything before because we were afraid you and Mike wouldn't come today. And we had to let this thing play out to make sure Carl was the one. Promise you one thing, the man's gonna get his due real soon. And those other two bastards, well, you don't have to worry about them. They're already dead."

"Johnny, you didn't?"

"No, it wasn't me. Believe Carl killed 'em to keep 'em quiet. It's a long story, and we'll talk about it later. But for now, you just keep your doors locked and don't go out by yourself until this is over. Can you do that for me?"

"We'll see, but I still need me a gun. Man comes around, I'll shoot to kill."

I said, "That's fine. Matter of fact, I'll get you the gun. Just don't go shooting the wrong person."

Sissy squinted. "So, what are you gonna do about him?"

"We've already talked to the police."

"The police? They never did anything before!"

"I hear ya, and if they don't, we will. But listen, if something goes wrong, you have to pretend this incident never occurred. Understand?"

"No, but I hear you."

"Good," I replied. "Now, let's you and me go back in there and act normal. Okay?"

"All right, but I'm still scared," Sissy answered while giving me another hug. "Little brother ... hope you know ... I ... I do love you."

It choked me up to hear her finally get the words out.

"Love you too. Love you a bunch."

On our return to the table, Sissy said she'd felt queasy, afraid she might throw up. Of course, that little statement set Grandma off, forecasting a possible pregnancy. My mother and the elders knew better. Uncle Willie and Mike had returned to the table. As we continued our celebration of Christine's baptism, the air hung heavy with uncertainty. Jane knew something was up but kept quiet.

As the party broke up, my father whispered, "Next Saturday, noon." It would be a long week.

Chapter 38

Five days after Christine's baptism, on a Friday evening, Jane, Christine, and I drove down to spend a weekend at the farm. Jake being out of school and back at home helped keep my mind off Carl Jacobs. Still, each time Uncle Bart and I were alone, the urge to speak surfaced. He knew it. At one point, he looked me in the eye and just shook his head. No matter what, I'd have to wait until the next day, when the others would be there, and we could talk in the barn.

At daybreak, while doing the milking, Jake asked, "Hey Johnny, you wanna go squirrel huntin' after breakfast? Seen where they been cuttin' hickory nuts up on the hill."

Uncle Bart looked up from attaching suckers to one of the Holsteins and said, "Rather you boys didn't do that today. Got somethin' else in mind."

"What's that?" asked Jake.

"Let's just say it's a surprise and leave it at that."

I thought to myself, *Wonder if he's talking about our meeting?*

"Hope it's a good surprise," Jake speculated.

"Let you decide that for yourself later."

"But Dad, can't you give me a hint?"

Uncle Bart answered with his silence. Jake understood.

Jane helped Aunt Mary prepare a breakfast fit for royalty. Grandma Smith was off visiting one of her sisters. Little Christine got her first taste of biscuits and milk gravy. After we stuffed our guts, Uncle Bart and Jake headed to the porch while I stayed behind to help the ladies clean up.

"Go on now, Johnny," urged Aunt Mary. "You did the milking this morning; we'll take care of this mess."

I gave Jane, Christine, and Aunt Mary each a kiss and then headed out for a smoke. Jake had already kicked back in one of the rockers with his feet propped up on an old milk carton, cap pulled down over his face, trying to sneak a nap. Uncle Bart puffed on a Winston, and old Max barely moved his tail at my approach.

After taking a seat, I joked, "If we'd gone squirrel huntin', he'd leaned up against a tree and fell asleep, guarantee it."

"Kiss my ass," grumbled Jake from underneath the cap.

The sound of tires on the blacktop at a distance drew our attention. As the vehicle neared, Uncle Bart flipped his ashes and said, "Looks like we're gettin' a visitor."

"Or two," I said when the truck turned into the lane. "Uncle Willie, and I believe there's someone with him."

Again without looking up, Jake commented, "Bet my left nut it's part of that surprise."

"Jake, you need to keep that to yourself for now. No more comments, you hear?"

"I hear ya'."

Before Uncles Willie and Samuel made it to the porch, my father's pickup came into sight. He had Mother with him.

Jake sat up in his chair. "Ain't sayin' a word. Just keepin' my mouth shut."

"Good," replied Uncle Bart.

A whole bunch of howdies got passed around as my parents and two uncles joined us on the porch. Pop looked tired. After reminding me of my need for a haircut, mother entered the house to join Jane, Aunt Mary, and the baby.

For the better part of an hour, we menfolk filled that porch with more bullshit than you could shake a stick at. Weather, fishing, hunting, and politics got debated as Jake squirmed in his seat, anticipating his surprise. With his patience running out, he stood as if to walk away, but stopped when Uncle Willie said, "How'd you gents like to join me in the barn for a little drink?"

Immediately, my cousin knew his wait had ended. "Little early for that, ain't it?" he asked with a grin.

"Oh well. We've been known to make exceptions," smiled Uncle Samuel.

Like a church congregation, we all stood at the same time and began our exodus from the porch. Holsteins grazed in the south field. Old Max's tail quickened as he trotted along. Before reaching the barn door, Uncle Willie moved close and whispered, "Just play along. It's Jake's day." Knew exactly what that meant.

Inside the barn, Jake stepped next to me and quietly asked, "Hey, you ever been out here for one of these meetings?" I realized then that Jake already had suspicions about the gatherings. After all, it would be hard to grow up there and not have a clue.

Before I could answer, Uncle Willie began speaking. "Okay guys, we're here this afternoon for a reason. We as a family have business to consider, and for the first time, our beloved Jake attends."

Immediately my cousin leaned close and whispered, "So, this ain't your first time."

Uncle Bart glared with a look of both pride and concern as he prepared to reveal secrets kept from his own sons for their entire childhood. I wondered if Josh or Ray would ever be invited.

Uncle Willie removed the Mason jar from its resting place in the cabinet. "Jake, you ever had any 'shine?"

"Of course."

"Shoulda figured that," commented his daddy.

"Well," continued Uncle Willie, "this here batch is for special occasions. We take a drink at the beginning of a family meeting and another at the end."

My gut feeling was that Cousin Jake had seen the jar before. Probably discovered it on his own.

Pop chimed in, "Jake, before we start, we'll let your daddy lead us in a prayer."

Uncle Bart intoned the ritual, starting with the sign of the cross. "Lord, we thank you for this day as we come together to discuss family matters. Give us wisdom, knowledge, and understanding in our endeavors. And please forgive us for any mistakes we might make along the way. Amen."

I thought, *These guys are good Catholics. They use the same words every time.* Even Uncle Willie's part remained the same, other than replacing my name with Jake's. "And one more thing, Lord, help Jake understand that in a man's darkest moment he just needs to have faith and follow directions. Amen."

Uncle Willie pulled me to the side and whispered, "Johnny, we want you to lead the way in the tunnel. You okay with that?"

"No problem. Be glad to do my part." Figured the elders were getting too old for crawling around in the tunnels anyway. "Is the path same as before?" I had to ask, knowing many hay cuts had come and gone since my last crawl through the tunnels.

"Yeah, basically the same, maybe a bale or two deeper at the beginning."

"How you guys expect Jake's big ass to get through the part where all those roots hang down?"

"Don't worry, we took care of that. He'll fit. Now listen," he continued, "You'll need to scoot along quickly when you get goin', gotta lose Jake."

"No problem, already know the way."

"Well, you're right except for one thing. Remember down in the lower level, coming to an intersection where you can go left or right?"

"Yeah, I took the right turn."

"Exactly. Now this time you need to go left. You'll go about 15 feet before comin' to a dead end. Feel around for another door in the floor. It'll open the same way as the other one."

"Isn't this getting to be pretty deep in the ground?"

"Somewhat."

"Is it the tunnel Uncle Samuel dug?"

"Yes, it is."

"So where's it lead?"

"Leads to another room. And when you get there you'll find some things left especially for you."

"You're kidding? Thought this was Jake's day."

"Today's important for the both of you." Uncle Samuel seemed serious about what he said. "When you get to the room, carefully feel around for a table. There is no electricity down there so we left an oil lamp. Be matches in an ashtray on the table. Light the lamp and everything will be clearer."

"Well, that makes sense."

"You know what I mean," he continued. "You won't have to stay too long. Just follow directions and you'll wind up joining us in the family room. And by the way, when you go down into the second level, after closing the door above you, reach up, put your finger back in the hole, and pull down hard. You'll hear a click. That'll release the door for Jake."

"You guys gonna join us for a drink?" interrupted Uncle Bart.

"Sure," Uncle Willie replied as he stepped away. For a second, I stood there wondering if there would be any surprises on my way to the room, and dreading the tunnels for Jake.

When I moved next to Pop, he wrapped his arm around my shoulders and whispered, "You okay with everything?"

"Yes sir. How about you?"

"Ain't slept good all week." He squeezed tight, and then let go to accept the Mason jar from Uncle Bart.

Jake seemed excited as everything went just the way it had for me. Then it came time for Uncle Willie to give his spiel.

"Now Jake, we're about to show you something no one has ever seen except for those in this room and your grandfather, God rest his soul. You must never reveal this to anyone, and you don't speak about it, not even to one of us outside this barn."

With that said, Pop began removing the bale of hay, giving Jake his first glance of the tunnel.

"How long's that been there?"

"Long time, son," answered his father.

"Well, I'll be damned. Right under my nose."

Uncle Willie continued, "This tunnel will lead you to a place you've never seen. Johnny's gonna go first, then you, and we'll come in behind."

I spoke to Jake before entering. "Hope you're not afraid of the dark."

"Don't worry 'bout me," he said. "If you can handle it, I can."

Chapter 39

I crawled in and moved on to allow Jake access. At the first turn, I waited until Uncle Willie began giving directions, and then scurried onward. It seemed logical that my uncles would hold Jake back long enough to give me an adequate head start. My mind was on locating the mysterious room described by Uncle Willie. From directly ahead came those familiar sounds of skirmishing rodents. Unlike last time, they were in front of me instead of behind. I began to worry they might be waiting at the end of the first tunnel.

Approaching the door cautiously, I listened, but heard no rats. They evidently had another exit in the hay. Jake probably got his final directions about the time of my descent into the lower level. After closing the door, I put my finger back through the hole, pulled down and felt the release.

Moving along much quicker this time, I reached the intersection, turned left, and easily found the second door. It had been designed exactly as the first. From that point, I cheated, using my lighter to navigate the tunnel's descending slope. Twenty feet later, with my Zippo overheating, the narrow passageway widened into the room described by Uncle Willie.

Right in the middle sat the table. On it: an oil lamp, a box of matches, an ashtray, and a note. I lit the lamp and took in the room. One chair sat on the other side of the table. The room itself measured about 12 feet square. A six-foot ceiling allowed me to stand up straight. On one side stood a tall metal cabinet. Close to it, three more folded chairs leaned against the wall. I took a seat, picked up the note, and began reading. It went something like this:

There comes a time when a man has to do what a man has to do. Several years ago, you spoke of three men who abused someone we love. You had the names of two. We now know the third. A while back you were told to consider the task of taking care of this guy.

We will provide assistance, but the chore will be yours. Your father wanted to take care of this himself, but he's in no condition.

The cabinet here contains non-traceable equipment. You will not use your own. If you can, bring back what you use. If you need to dispose of these items along the way, that's OK. Don't leave fingerprints. All items remain here during your planning. We'll decide later when you should pick things up.

In exception to our rule, you may talk to Samuel. When we leave the barn today, there will be two horses saddled, one for you and one for Samuel. Ride with him and he will consult with you on this matter.

Take a moment to look in the cabinet, then return to the tunnel you came from and continue as in your original visit to the family room.

Burn this note.

For a moment, I just sat there considering the reality of what the elders asked. My hands began to sweat and shake slightly while opening the cabinet. Its heavy, metal door had a lever-type handle with a key lock. It had been left unlocked. I removed and opened a two foot square, 4" thick gun case. It held the unassembled parts of a 12-gauge automatic shotgun and a box of 00-buckshot. A holstered Redhawk .44 Magnum pistol hung from a hook on the inside of the door. A box of twenty bullets lay in the bottom of the cabinet. Other items there included a military knife, rope, small binoculars and not one, but two sets of handcuffs.

Standing there breathing an awful air of mildew and burning oil, I thought about how the tiny room must be similar to those used by the Viet Cong. How they planned their attacks or perhaps tortured American GI's. I struck a match and lit the note. While it burned, my mind's eye saw Pete, Joe, and Carl on the floor, tied, gagged, and awaiting a butcher's sentence for what they'd done to my sister.

The note turned to ashes, ending my daydream. I returned the shotgun case to the cabinet, blew out the light, and started my ascent back the way I'd come. Returning to the intersection in the tunnel only took a couple minutes. I stopped there and sat for a moment, crouched, leaning against the cool dirt wall and thinking about Uncle Willie doing the same in the '60s. How he drank and cried away his worries for his little brother, Samuel, away fighting in Vietnam.

Something made noise in the tunnel beyond the next turn. Assuming it was Jake, I cautiously backtracked a few feet past the intersection. Huffs, puffs, and grunts drew closer as I crouched perfectly still. My own pulse raced in a short moment of anxiety until the collision.

"Ahhhhhhhhhh!"

"Jake, settle down, it's me."

"Damn you, Johnny. Why'd you leave me? How the hell'd you get behind me?"

"Take it easy, buddy. You're okay," I said while striking the lighter. The small flame revealed my cousin's wide eyes. Perspiration beaded on his forehead.

I asked, "How far'd you go in the tunnel?"

"Far as I could," he answered between heavy breaths. "Made it past that sorry excuse for a bridge, and then came to a dead end. Tried all those little holes on the sides along the way, but none went anywhere. I knew there was another direction back here somewhere. Wondered if I mighta took the wrong turn."

"Did you check up for a door at the dead end?"

"You gotta be kiddin'," he complained. "Don't tell me that."

"Didn't you get the clue saying that the second way would be the opposite?"

"Yeah, and that's the way I went."

"Well think about it: instead of the door being below you, it would be above. Shoulda figured, to get out we gotta go up."

"Sonofabitch. So you have been there?"

"'Afraid so, my friend. Now listen, why don't you go back that way and complete the trip. I'll give you a head start. They'll never know you needed help."

"Aw hell, Johnny, no need to do that. I'm not ashamed of being stupid. Let's just get the heck outta here."

"Okey dokey," I said, "That's fine with me. So let's go, I'm tired of squatting."

Jake chuckled and said, "Tell me about it."

My cousin outweighed me by about 60 pounds, making it harder to maneuver in the tunnels. He had to use the intersection to turn around.

"You go first," I suggested. "Want you to find the door yourself."

The elders had indeed increased the size of the smallest opening to accommodate Jake's bulk. Roots still hung down, and of course it seemed unreasonably tight to him.

"Almost turned back right here a while ago," he complained.

"I hear ya. Thought the same thing my first time." While speaking, my mind wrestled with flashbacks of the ants crawling all over me. For some reason, there were none present this time. Jake stopped when we reached the pit.

"Somebody needs to take a class on buildin' bridges. This thing sucks. Damn near fell off goin' and comin'. Wonder how deep it is?"

"Deep enough you don't wanna fall in. Don't worry though, smell the hay?"

"Yea."

"They put that down there to pad your big ass should you fall."

"Good thing," he replied while hanging from the rope and inching across the wobbly board.

I waited in the dark until Jake reached the other side, then followed. One minute later, we were back at the end of the tunnel.

"So it's up above," Jake mumbled to himself. "Anything special, or do you just push?"

It only took him a few seconds to figure it out. As with my initiation, the elders were waiting patiently in the dark. Most likely, they could already hear us in the tunnel before Jake opened the door.

His saying, "Is this it?" brought about everyone's encouraging laughter. Lights came on, and Jake stood there staring up out of the hole, covering his eyes and speaking frankly. "Hell, I might never got here if it weren't for Johnny. Ran into him on my way back the other direction. It was so dark I couldn't see. About shit my drawers when he grabbed me."

Growing impatient, I pushed him. "Would you move on out of the way? Be nice to get out of this hole."

"Sorrrryyy," he answered while my uncles gave him a hand up. Then they helped me. As Jake got barraged with questions about his trip through the tunnels, Uncle Samuel moved close and quietly prodded, "Find my room?"

"Sure did."

He held up a finger to his lips as if to say, "ssshhhhh."

I thought, *Why the secrecy?*

Uncle Willie said, "Now Jake, as you know, the reason for bringing you here today is simple. You asked to be included in our family's business. We didn't come to you; you came to us. Johnny here can attest to the fact that we never recruited him. When he found himself in need of family help, he came to us. Our purpose is not to look for trouble or to interfere with people we don't like. We only get involved in situations where someone in our family has been wronged and justice, for one reason or another, has not been served. When we pray to God, our purpose is clear. We ask forgiveness for our mistakes, and we also ask forgiveness for the sins of those who have wronged us."

Jake seemed to want to say something, but Uncle Bart motioned to him to remain silent. Uncle Willie continued, "Never, and let me repeat, never, are you to assume that you can use this family to bully someone or to show power over an adversary. And never are you to use this family for financial gain. We're not here to make or take money from anything we do. Is that clear?"

Before answering, Jake looked at his father, who in turn nodded his head as if giving permission. "Yes, sir," he replied, like a child afraid to say anything more than what his parent wanted to hear.

Next, my dad said, "Because of your interest, we discussed it and decided you were trustworthy enough to join. Do not abuse our trust. Never speak to anyone, not even your brother, about what is said in this room, and do not come here without first speaking to one of us. Is that clear?"

Jake acknowledged with a curt nod.

Uncle Bart put his arm around Jake's shoulders and said, "Son, there are going to be times when you think we are hiding stuff from you. Don't worry about it. We do things in steps around here. Johnny came to us several years ago. To this point, we have never asked anything of him. We will, and when we do it may or may not involve you. Eventually it will. By then you'll understand more about how we work. For now, we are mostly concerned with your ability to keep our business in this room. Understand?

"Yes, sir."

"You okay with everything we've said so far?"

"Yes, sir."

"If we should need your help, could you handle that?"

"Yes, sir."

"You know how to say anything else besides yes, sir?"

Jake smiled and said, "Yes, sir."

Uncle Willie gave him a friendly punch in the chest. We all laughed, and then Pop explained how we'd be leaving through the storm cellar.

Jake shook his head and said, "Can't believe all this existed without me finding it."

Back inside the barn, everyone welcomed the traditional closing drink. Jake winked at me before taking too big a swallow. The burning result was obvious. Uncle Bart said, "Easy, son, if you wanna get drunk, we can do that later. This here's more about tradition."

Chapter 40

Two horses—the old mare, Becca, and her latest colt, Trick—were tied to the hitching post, all saddled up and ready to go. Jake seemed to understand why he wasn't invited along.

"Have a good time," he said. "See you when you get back."

I mounted the mare and waited for Uncle Samuel's lead. Once in the saddle, he offered me his pouch of Red Man. Feeling brave from the moonshine, I accepted.

My father opened the gate, directing us to the north field.

Uncle Samuel urged his mount forward. As he moved away, the mare knew her role and instinctively followed.

"Enjoy the ride, son."

"Thanks, Pop. See you later." I waved back at him and the rest of the crew, then trotted up next to Uncle Samuel, waiting for his lead.

He spit juice, grinned, and said, "Let's ride!" When he kicked Trick in the loins, that darn colt stood straight up like Silver on *The Lone Ranger*. Uncle Samuel held on and ordered, "Gid-up!" Dust flew as the wild young horse dropped down and vaulted like a bat out of hell.

I thought, *What in the world?* and then hollered, "Come on girl, let's get 'em," teasing the old horse up to high gear. In the background, fading voices of the others whistled, whooped and hollered like cowboys in the old west. For half a mile, we ran those horses across that field like two bank robbers leaving town in a hurry.

As we approached timber I assumed things would slow down a bit, but it didn't. My uncle knew his way well. He found a gap in the trees and continued throwing dirt on a cattle trail. It required all my riding skills to dodge tree limbs and keep up. When we started downhill toward bottomland, the horses got a breather. Uncle Samuel pulled up to a walk and patted his mount on the neck. "Good boy," he praised.

I slowed the mare and in jest did the same, "Goooood oooldd girl. Is Uncle Samuel trying to kill you?"

"Hell, that old horse has a lot of runnin' left in 'er."

"If you say so."

"Not bad ridin', boy. Didn't think you had it in ya."

"Hey, this ain't the first time me and Becca went running."

"Well, you did good. Now let's give 'em a drink," he replied while stepping his horse into the creek.

As our rides lowered their heads for a sip of the cool running water, we both remained in saddle, silently taking in the beauty of our surroundings. From that vantage point, you could not see a single man-made item.

"Beautiful, isn't it?" I said, high on moonshine and fresh air.

"Sure is. This place ain't changed a lick since the first time my daddy rode me down here on the back of his saddle."

Bright sunshine filtered through trees, warming my face. It felt great to be alive. A whitetail doe, nervous from our presence, bolted from her bedding spot twenty yards away. She snorted all the way up the hill and out of sight. Though I was enjoying the moment, I knew we weren't there just for fun. "So, don't we have something to talk about?"

"Yep, we do," Uncle Samuel answered, "but not right here. Follow me." He pushed Trick onward, crossing the creek and starting uphill through a narrow strip of woods. We came out into pasture and made our way to a high place in the middle of a forty-acre field. Broomsedge bent in the breeze as we stopped at a spot marked by two stumps. "Good place to talk," said Uncle Samuel as he dismounted.

I scanned the landscape, still in saddle. "Won't anybody hear our conversation, that's for sure."

"Precisely the reason we're here. Never know who might be standing in the woods."

As Uncle Samuel took a seat on one of the stumps, I had to ask, "Sure there aren't any snakes hanging around there?"

"Sat here many times. Ain't ever seen one yet."

"All y'all got your own little place where you do your thinking? Uncle Willie showed me his hill the other night, the place where he meditates."

"Reckon every man needs a place to get away. This just happens to be mine."

I slid off the mare and said, "Shoulda brought a bottle."

Uncle Samuel laughed. "Never underestimate a Smith. Look there in my saddle bag and see if they ain't a half pint of somethin'."

Sure enough, he had a full half pint of Jim Beam. "Oooh, the good stuff."

"Now, join me on that there snake-free stump."

Taking a seat, I passed him the bottle. While breaking the seal, he said, "Tell me, Johnny Lee, now that we're alone, what do you think about all this?"

"Not sure. It seems like a movie to me. Like I'm watching, but not really in it."

He took a snort of the whiskey, and then asked, "Do you really wanna be in it?"

"Oh yeah."

"Sure you don't want me to do it instead?"

"Why, you got doubts about me handling it?"

"No, just got doubts about you wantin' to kill a man. Ain't as easy as you think."

"You trying to talk me out of it?"

"No, not at all. Just wanna make sure you know the score before we go any further. Things ain't the same as when you first came to us. You're married now and got that little one to think about. A lot more to lose if you should get caught."

"Just give me a swig of that whiskey and I'll tell you how much I hate that sonofabitch that raped my sister."

Uncle Samuel took a shot himself before handing me the bottle. He began speaking as I had me a Jake-sized swallow.

"You and your daddy both got a lotta hatred for this fellow. Could get in the way...cause you to think too fast...make bad decisions. Reckon you can forget the hate long enough to do the job?"

I blurted out, somewhat proving my uncle's point, "Gonna do whatever it takes to get rid of that asshole."

He hesitated before speaking. "Learned one thing in Vietnam: those who looked at their mission as a job seemed to last a lot longer than those who saw it as a personal vendetta. Back in history, men who fought with their hearts died in droves. They were willing to line up a few hundred feet apart and shoot at one another in a gentleman's war that almost guaranteed their death or injury. Today's soldier shows less chivalry and more brains. It's better to hide behind a tree and shoot your opponent than to attack in hand-to-hand combat. You may wanna face this man Carl and let him know why he's dyin', but that's not always the smartest way to do business. Remember, we're not in this for personal satisfaction. It's about serving justice."

"Thought a lot about how I could torture that bastard."

"Avoid becoming that which you choose to destroy."

After turning the bottle up again, I said, "Won't be easy."

Chapter 41

It seems that throughout history, man has had an obsession with high places, especially when gods, or spirits, or philosophy in general were involved. When Uncle Samuel rose from his stump on that hill and began slowly turning, staring into the sky, my first thought was that I'd upset him with something said. After his first 360 degrees, my thoughts changed. I began to see him as some sort of receptor. It was as if he were absorbing his thoughts from somewhere out in space. Not daring to speak or join him, I only watched in awe as the southwestern sun outlined his figure with a blinding radiance. Completing another full revolution, he said, "Listen to your soul, Johnny. It'll tell you what to do."

Does Uncle Samuel have his own form of Gabrielle? Looking up, I shaded my eyes from the sun and asked, "You suppose a man's soul is the same as his conscience?"

Apparently pleased with my question, he returned to his stump and replied, "Never thought about it like that."

"You always been religious?"

Uncle Samuel scratched his chin. "Guess you could say I got religion in Nam."

"What? Are you like a Buddhist or something?"

"No. That's not what I'm sayin'. I *learned* about religion in school and church on Sunday. Of course, outside that I didn't think much about it. Then in 1965, Uncle Sam sent me to Vietnam. For the most part of two years, that's where I went to sleep and woke up every day. Didn't get to see my parents. Didn't get to see my brothers. Couldn't even get a piece of ass. Got so homesick, when no one looked I cried.

Like a baby sometimes. Then, like a lot of others, I got to drinkin' and smokin' pot. Eventually, I did the hard stuff. LSD and heroin. Told myself it would be a break from the ugly shit we had to do."

"How could you function on LSD and heroin?"

"Didn't really. Heroin put me in another world. Mind driftin'. Sittin' around smokin', lookin' at the lights, rubbin' my legs. I swear, sittin' here right now, I can still see that needle, flickin' it to get the bubbles out."

Uncle Samuel seemed to be going off into his own little world. I asked, "How could you fight like that?"

"Couldn't. Had to straighten up before goin' on guard duty or out in the field. Everybody thinks we did drugs out in the field, but I'm telling you right now, I'm the only one in my platoon that made that mistake. It was like a pact. We covered each other's asses. If you were messed up, you weren't any good to the rest. When the guys saw I was gettin' hooked, they warned me, said they'd shoot me if I got high in the field."

"So, why did you?"

"After a while ... don't know ... it was like I didn't care anymore. At first, shootin' the Cong was sorta like shootin' stray cats, the ones that kill the young rabbits and quail. Something you didn't really wanna do, but knew you ought to. And so I did. But then as more and more shit happened, I got to hatin' 'em, and it ate at me. Made me careless and almost got me killed. Went after those little shits like they wasn't real people, just animals. And, that's what some of 'em were. No good sonofabitches took one of the guys in my platoon, Mark, and strung him up on a pole. When we found him, blood was running down and dripping off his feet. Ants crawling on him. Johnny, I can still see the look in his eyes. Had tape over his mouth. I pulled it off and he was chokin' on his own dick. He spit it out and started screaming, 'Shoot me! Shoot me!' Couldn't no one do it. Hell, it didn't matter. We cut him down and a couple minutes later he was gone. Done bled to death. Found his balls layin' on the ground. About half of us threw up right there. After that, I hated those little slant-eyed gooks so bad. Stayed drunk and tore up for days."

Though disgusting, Uncle Samuel's story had me mesmerized. I took another little swig of the whiskey. He downed what was left before continuing.

"Normally on Wednesdays they took us to a drop zone. Don't know how it come about, but that next week after Mark died, when time came to go back out, I was still a mess. Strung out, comin' off the heroin. Knew I was about to do the unthinkable, but in my mind it didn't matter. Somehow I managed to get my gear together and climbed on that chopper. In the rush, nobody paid attention to my condition except this one guy, a big, black dude named Spencer. Remember him staring at me through the smoke of his own cigarette. Man knew I was messed up. Never said a word, just stared.

"When we got there, it was a hot LZ. Fell about four feet just gettin' out of the Huey. As I rose up off the ground, someone grabbed me by the collar, jerked me to my feet and shoved me in the right direction. That's when I realized just how bad I'd screwed up. Hit the brush like always. Found a spot where I could hide for the moment. Sat there on the rotting decay of a tree trunk, hidden inside undergrowth, panickin'. When the slick shoved off and things began to settle down, it got scary."

"Slick?" I asked.

"The chopper, a Huey, that's what we called 'em when they were sneaking in and out of a hot LZ—"

"And a hot LZ is?"

"A loading or unloading zone under fire. Anyway, smoke from napalm somewhere up on the hill made it hard to see. Spencer found me there, balled up, shaking, and sweatin' like hell. Thank God the boy understood. Shoulda shot my ass and walked away, but instead he took me under his wing and helped me through it. Spencer Bishop, that was his name. Boy prayed over me like some kinda holy man. Don't know how to explain it, but in those next three days, that's when I got religion. Spencer saved my life, and I never forgot it. And I gave up the drugs."

"All except pot?"

"All except pot."

"I hear ya. But how about that LSD? What was that like?"

"Some of it made you see things, ugly creatures. One boy swore he saw a twelve foot chicken running through camp. Grabbed his gun and unloaded a clip at nothing. It's a wonder he didn't kill somebody. When I did it, it made me hyper. Wanted to fight. Guarantee you one thing, you don't never wanna fight a man who's on it. You couldn't hurt him, and he'd kill you with his bare hands."

"It says a lot that you were able to quit the drugs, come home, and live a good life."

"A couple of my buddies couldn't quit. One's dead. The other one lives on the streets, still stuck back in the '60s. Some folks look down on him. Me, I understand. Hell, we all became men in Vietnam, killin' human beings and seeing our partners blown up or cut to pieces. Tell you right now, that shit affects a man for life. Some can handle it better than others. Guess I'm one of the lucky ones. Could say havin' religion and listenin' to the soul helps keeps me straight."

"Well, I'm proud of you for serving your country."

Uncle Samuel got kind of quiet for a few seconds and then said, "Johnny, we're gettin' too sidetracked. Let's don't forget what we're here for. You need to tell me all you know about this man, Carl Jacobs."

"Sure, but first let me ask, why don't you guys want Jake to know what's going on?"

"Jake came to me asking questions about our family meetings. He'd evidently figured out some of it on his own. We didn't really wanna bring him in right now, with all that's going on, but we damn sure couldn't afford to have him walking around asking questions. Bart says Jake's ready, but shouldn't be involved in your situation. We all agree. Too many people know about it already."

"But why the note? Why not just wait and tell me that stuff here?"

"Could have, but you'd already asked about the other room. Decided it was time you saw it, and some of the things we keep there. Oh, and in case you're wondering, there is another way out of that room."

"Figured that."

"Behind the gun cabinet, there's a tunnel that comes up in the storm cellar floor."

"That seems about right."

"And there's something else you need to know. While waiting in the family room for you and Jake, we decided against involving Detective Kelly in our plans. Willie says that when he and Mike went outside the other day at Masterson's, they saw Jacobs getting in a car with someone. Put his golf clubs in the backseat. Willie said the driver was small and wore a cap. He's afraid it might have been Kelly."

"Well, that don't make sense."

"That's what I said. Nonetheless, we agreed to leave her out. No need takin' a chance on gettin' set up. If she's legit, she'll keep her mouth shut."

"So," I asked, "did Paula tell you about Sissy recognizing Carl's voice and what he said?"

"Yea. Pretty much seals the deal, don't it?"

"Does for me."

I told Uncle Samuel everything I knew about Carl. Then he said, "For now, I just need you to keep your eyes and ears open. We need to find or create some sort of situation where Carl will be alone and unsuspecting. And it all needs to be done on our terms, not his. You hear anything at all that we can use, let me know. But you can't call me. Call your daddy. Tell him you need to work on your brakes. He'll know that means to contact me. After he and I talk, he'll stop by your house to give you a time and place for us to meet. Next time you need me it will have to be something other than brakes. We'll discuss that before we part at each meeting."

"Sounds good to me, but I have to ask, why am I working with you and not my father?"

"Your daddy gets too emotional about this. And we understand why, it being his daughter and all that. Another reason is, even though he don't want to admit it, this shit could give him another heart attack. Best keep him away from the details. We'll tell James what he needs to know, and that's it. You okay with that?"

"Sure, I understand."

"And let me tell you, Johnny, we debated on using you for this. Done said you're a lot like your daddy, too emotionally involved. Only plus I see is that Jacobs might not be suspicious if he sees you. Not like he would with one of us. Reason I'm working with you is because if for some reason you quit, I'll take over and do the job."

"Don't worry, I'll get it done."

"I believe you. But if at any time you should change your mind, don't think for one second that we'll think bad about you for backing out. We're a family, and you don't have to prove anything to us."

"Thanks. I'll keep that in mind."

Uncle Samuel repeated that all details should remain in my head and never be written down. My anger toward Carl had not diminished one iota, yet in light of our conversation on that hill, the anger felt less like hate.

We rode more leisurely back to the house, taking in all the details that had blurred by earlier.

"Hey," I asked, "suppose the rest of the world knows what they're missing?"

"Only those that have seen it," he replied.

That evening, during the milking chores, I worked side by side with Jake, and we spoke of multiple topics without ever mentioning the day's experiences. Later that evening, as he and I fished for bluegills in Uncle Bart's pond, we were joined by Jane and little Christine.

"Daddy gonna teach you how to catch a fish?" Jane asked.

"See the little fishy," I said, holding one up still hooked to my line. Christine reached and touched the slimy critter. "Yeah baby, someday soon I'll teach you how to fish."

I found myself in a numb moment, thinking how lucky I was to be there on the bank of that pond enjoying my wife and daughter, my cousin, and even the sunset. For the first time, I began to wonder if serving revenge on Carl would even be worth the chance of getting caught and possibly having my good life taken away. Then it dawned on me that what happened to Sissy could very well happen to my own daughter someday. How it must have made my parents feel to know what those bastards did to Sissy. While I had a lot to lose, for the family and in the name of justice, the job would get done.

Later that night, after Jane had put the baby in bed, she joined me on the porch steps. We sat looking up at millions of stars sparkling on an endless black background.

"Beautiful, ain't it?" I asked.

"Sure is," Jane answered. "Just like when I was a little girl. Used to sit out here for hours on end, looking up there and wondering who else might be doing the same, somewhere else in the world."

"You mean like down there in the mountains of North Carolina, where your people are?"

"Why you gotta bring that up?"

"Why? Because I promised I'd find your mother's grave, and because someday Christine's gonna ask where you came from. Can't be letting her think you and me are cousins."

"So we just tell her the truth."

"Which is?"

"Stop it. I've got plenty time to figure that out."

"I don't get it. You used to say you wanted to go looking for your people. What changed your mind? Believe we ought to at least go find your mama's grave."

"Johnny, my mother's dead. Goin' lookin' won't change that. Ain't nobody down there that cares about me anyway."

"We don't know that. You've got to have people somewhere in those hills."

"What people? You talkin' about the ones that wasn't there when I was born? Where were they when my moma needed 'em the most? You say I should go down there lookin' for them. Well, I ain't never seen 'em come lookin' for me."

"Jane, you're being silly. Your people don't have a clue where you are. At least we have an idea where they live. This ain't about who was or who wasn't there all those years ago. People make mistakes. You don't give up on family just because they make mistakes."

"Family?"

"Honey, it's all about family."

Jane didn't reply, just sat staring up into the heavens. I put my arm around her and said, "They're probably sitting out there somewhere looking up at these same stars as we speak."

"I said stop it, Johnny Lee, and I mean it." Jane threw my arm from around her. "Ain't going down there right now. Got my hands full just takin' care of Christine. We can go later on. Just not right now." She got quiet.

For a moment I sat there observing Jane as she stared off into the sky trying to read her mind, and thinking, *This is what Sissy meant when she said we all have scars.*

Still gazing away, and without looking at me, Jane said, "Honey, do you really love me?"

"Yes, I do."

"Why do you love me?"

"Because you love me."

"How much do you love me?"

"I love you more than alllll those stars in the sky."

She turned, kissed me on the cheek, and said, "I love you too, more than you'll ever know."

Jane entered the house, leaving me and old Max alone. That made three times she'd turned down my offer to go and locate her people. I knew a part of her wanted to go, but something inside would not let her.

Chapter 42

Purposely bidding on jobs in the order room provided me the opportunity to be around Carl Jacobs. I listened to his big mouth day after day, hoping to hear something useful. Toward the end of October, I overheard him and a couple of his buddies from second shift planning their annual deer-hunting trip. When they revealed the location, it excited me. The farm they planned to hunt, about a hundred rough acres bordering Nolin Lake, wasn't much good for anything else. It belonged to the Hendersons, an old couple now living in Clarkson. They left the farm back in '63 when the Army Corps of Engineers dammed the river. I'd met them through Bobbie Davis. They'd allowed Bobbie, Jerry Godfrey, and me to hunt squirrels on the property. A nephew of theirs, Jimmy Henderson, worked at the packinghouse and was one of the two planning to hunt with Carl. I had disliked the man ever since he posted the farm and stopped our access. Jimmy sucked up to supervisors, hoping to be a boss someday, and that's how Carl wound up hunting the Henderson place. This would be his second year. The other guy, Steven Brown, an old friend of Jimmy's, had only been at the packinghouse for a short time. I knew little of him. Nonetheless, with the farm being where it was—not too far from Uncle Bart's place—it did seem there might be an opportunity for me to do a little hunting of my own. I'd walked that entire area many times. From Daddy's perspective, that farm could indeed be my backyard.

I met with Uncle Samuel and told him about the hunting trip. To my surprise, he didn't care for the idea. "Boy, you're talking about the old Henderson place. If Carl Jacobs and those other two are coming down here to hunt, you know they'll be packin'. Don't like your odds, three on one. And I sure as hell don't want some innocent bystander gettin' hurt."

"But December's almost here, and we may not get another opportunity. I know those woods like the back of my hand. Bet I could shoot the bastard right out of his deer stand without anybody ever seeing me."

"No way, Johnny Lee. Opening mornin' there could be hunters sneakin' in there that you don't even know about. And they won't be makin' noise. Might see you without you seein' them. Just not worth the chance. Guarantee the others aren't gonna go for it, especially not your daddy."

My uncle's reasoning made sense, but I still left the meeting disappointed. Then, like a gift from heaven, a few days later, Carl began talking about taking a personal day on Friday before opening day of deer season so he could go down early to set things up. His friends were on the second shift and would drive to the farm that night after work. *Bingo*, I thought. *Could give me several hours alone with Carl and most likely no other hunters.* I had my father arrange another meeting with Uncle Samuel.

"Think about it," I said. "If he arrives that morning, I'll have at least ten hours before those other boys can get off from work and drive all the way down there. That's more than enough time."

Uncle Samuel scratched his chin and admitted, "Well, time is runnin' out. I don't like the fact that he'll have guns with him. But, with a little planning, believe we can make it work."

I grinned and said, "Hell yes!"

In my mind, it would be easy to sneak up on Carl and simply blow him away with the 12-gauge shotgun provided by the family, but on second thought I wasn't sure that would satisfy me. Just didn't seem right to kill the man without letting him know why and for whom it was being done. So, just like in the bad-guy movies, I made the mistake of wanting a face-to-face conversation with my target. Why shouldn't Carl see me and clearly understand the reason for his fate?

The man ought to be thinking of his participation in my sister's attack as he received proper penance.

Uncle Samuel scorned my intentions. "Boy, you're making the exact mistake I warned you about. You take this shit personal, it'll get you killed."

"But this isn't war," I pleaded. "Believe there's a difference between shooting a man who's shooting at you and executing an unarmed criminal. Our government wouldn't execute a man without first hearing his side of the story, and neither should we. And I'd like to get me a confession out of the sonofabitch. Believe Sissy and my parents deserve that much."

"Not gonna happen, Johnny. Even if you could figure a way to tie him up, all you're gonna do is give the bastard a chance to talk you out of killing him."

"So what are you saying? You don't think I can handle it? Afraid I won't kill the bastard?"

"No, kid, I believe you could shoot him, just don't like the idea of him gettin' a chance to talk to you beforehand. He's smart, and he'll fool you if you let him. Besides, ain't no way you wanna face it off with a guy that size. No offense boy, but he'd kick your ass in a heartbeat."

"Not if I sneak up and knock him out. Then I could put those handcuffs y'all got on his hands and legs and—"

"Forget it, Johnny. Can't afford to let you get that close to him."

"Well, what about you? Could you do it?"

"Do what?"

"Could you figure out a way for *you* to get him down long enough to put the handcuffs on?"

"Sure, if I had a dawgone tranquil ... izer." Uncle Samuel cut himself off and then stood there as if thinking.

"What?" I asked. "What's on your mind?"

He continued standing there silently, barely shaking his head.

"Come on, dammit, you've got an idea. Tell me about it."

"How bad you wanna do this?" he asked.

"Real bad, why?"

"If I can get hold of a tranquilizer gun, think you could sneak up close enough to shoot him with it?"

"How close you talking?"

"I'd say no farther than seventy-five feet, and even that would be a long shot."

"Well, hell yes! I could do that."

Uncle Samuel continued, "Few years back, I had this young bull. Good stock. Paid a fortune for it. One day it busted out of the fence and stepped in a trap. Wild-ass sonofabitch wouldn't let us get close to him, let alone take the trap off. Then I remembered one of my old war buddies sayin' he had a tranquilizer gun. Said he used it on black bears that got too rowdy in the campgrounds when he worked as a ranger down in the Smoky Mountains. Now he works at the Mammoth Cave National Park. Lives in Caneyville. I drove down there and got the gun. Did a good job on the bull. Knocked it out long enough to take the trap off and patch up that leg."

"So, if it works on a bear and a bull, it oughta work on a man."

"That's what I'm thinkin'," replied Uncle Samuel. "Question is, does he still have the darn thing and the chemicals it uses? Believe it would at least knock him out long enough to handcuff his hands and legs. But Johnny, after going to all that trouble, you still have the same result in the end, and for what, your personal satisfaction? Why not just shoot the man?"

"Told you, it's not just for me. I wanna do it for Sissy and my parents. Besides, the way I see it, having me a confession might be a good thing in the event something goes wrong. What jury would blame me for blowing away the so-called December Rapist? This is a guy who brutalized my sister and God knows how many others. And he killed two men!"

Uncle Samuel thought about it and said, "If we do this, tell you right now, it'll have to be our little secret. No way in hell my brothers are gonna stand for it. Can you swear to me if anything goes wrong, you'll just blow that bastard away and be done with it?"

"On my mother's grave."

"Your mother ain't even dead, stupid."

261

"Okay then, on my grandpa's grave."

Uncle Samuel stood there for a few seconds and then said, "Let me think about it and see if I can find my old friend. Can you ride back down here in a couple days?"

"Sure, after work. Be near five o'clock your time."

"That'll do."

"Another thing. If you go after Carl on a Friday morning, how you gonna get off from work that day?"

"Don't worry, I'll bid into another department for the week. Won't nobody think anything of it if I call in sick. Believe me, I won't be the only one calling in the day before deer season. Guys do it every year. And I seldom miss work."

"Good."

Two days later, I again met with Uncle Samuel, this time without my father's knowledge. He had the tranquilizer gun and a dozen warnings about the chances involved. It turned out the suggested range was 45-50 feet. I took a couple practice shots at 75 feet and found that it dropped 2 inches at that range. Suddenly my options had grown. What could I say or do to Carl after he woke up, handcuffed hand and foot? From that day on, details of how, when, and where became easy.

Chapter 43

For an hour and a half, while driving, I had wallowed back through all the details leading up to my dilemma. Nothing had changed my mind. High-pitched noise coming from the dirtied, borrowed Jeep's off-road tires decreased as I slowed for the Leitchfield, Kentucky exit. It was twenty-four hours before gun season for whitetail deer. Hunting season for Carl Jacobs had already begun.

It suddenly seemed unbearably quiet, sitting at a stop sign where the ramp met State Road 259. Approaching headlights turned into a sheriff's cruiser. My heart rate increased as he passed toward town, staring my way. I took a deep breath, exhaled slowly, and then turned the opposite direction, toward Nolin Lake.

My destination was now only minutes away. I plugged in a tape of Bach's piano concerto, hoping to get fired up. In my head, I started repeating, *The man is no good, he'll do it again. He hurt your sister, now you can hurt him. The man is no good, he'll do it again. He hurt your sister, now you can hurt him.* That feeling began to creep on me, like the day I stood on the wood's edge some seven years earlier and shot at the assumed cattle thief. I felt anxious, short of breath, and wondered if deer fever, or in my case, man fever, might cause me to fall apart.

No one raised me to be a killer of men, but I had indeed been taught to kill. Rabbits, squirrels, birds, and rats were my childhood prey. As an adult, shooting a deer or killing cattle and hogs had become second nature. On that cold day, for the first time, my quest would be a human being. I'd heard several men, even my father and his brother Willie, say, "Know what I'd do if it were someone I love." *When it comes right down to it, how many men actually would?*

My religious upbringing taught me against taking the life of a man. Therefore, like Uncle Samuel, I would consider Carl Jacobs to be a wild, rabid animal that needed to be destroyed. After all, his actions were beastly the night he and his friends attacked my sister.

About six or seven miles out of Leitchfield, high-beams from a distance reflected in the Jeep's rearview mirror. I checked my gauges, making sure not to speed. Whoever drove behind me obviously was speeding and gaining ground quickly. In about half a mile the road would end at a stop sign. I'd be turning left toward a small community called Peonia. *Could it be the sheriff's cruiser? Did he turn around?* I did a quick scan of the Jeep's interior, making sure nothing incriminating lay visible. Two hundred yards behind me, emergency lights came on, verifying my worst fear. Worried there might be a lingering smell of homegrown, I rolled down the driver side window. Bach's concerto continued as I prepared for the worst.

It didn't make sense. *Why would the sheriff pursue me? Is he simply checking out a stranger on the early morning road?* All the planning and my best possible opportunity to deal with Carl Jacobs was about to get ruined. *If he runs a make on the Jeep's plates, I'm screwed. Should I try to outrun him? No way. What the hell did I do wrong?*

When the deputy turned on his siren, I braked, pulled to the road's edge, and stared into the mirror, expecting him to pull up behind me. Instead, the lights changed lanes and that sheriff's cruiser passed me in a flash, practically leaving the road as it turned right and sped away. "Jesus, Mary, and Joseph," I chanted out loud.

With my heart beating like a bass drum, I remained there, engine idling, for a few seconds. My whole right leg shook nervously as I held down the brake pedal; watching the deputy's lights fade away, I thought, *This is where Pop would have had a heart attack.*

Gabrielle scorned, *Wouldn't be shaking if you weren't breaking the law.* But then I remembered what Sister Mary Theresa once said about performing on piano in front of strangers: *Being nervous is half the excitement.*

At 6:10 a.m., I raised the volume on the stereo, turned left, and continued driving, trying to focus. I could not afford to keep drifting back. Like a college football player in the moments before a National Championship game, the time had come for a pep talk. On that cold November morning, Johann Sebastian Bach would be my coach.

For one day, I needed to become a different person. A killer. Surely for an hour or so, Johnny Lee Smith could become an aggressive beast. An animal. The animal I would be had God not placed spirits in the animal man, creating human beings. A part of me needed to go back thousands of years to a time when revenge wasn't even a word, just a reflex. Maybe the whole world should be that way. Then perhaps people would think twice before going out of their way to hurt someone. Why have we become a docile species that allows weakness to prevail? Why worry about the law when it comes to retaliation for evil acts? Perhaps revenge should be a given. Then no one would hesitate to destroy a bastard like Carl. If a dog goes mad, we shoot it. When a man goes mad, we make excuses. We blame the madman's actions on his past and ignore the fact that the best detriment to such behavior might be equally inhumane retribution. Thank God for Bach!

Even before reaching Peonia, I could see the towering steeple on top of Saint Anthony's Catholic Church, the place where Jane and I exchanged our sacred vows. The moon's light illuminated hundreds of gravestones speckled across the hillside. At the intersection, I turned right onto State Road 88. Twenty-five minutes and fifteen winding miles later, the entrance to the Henderson place came into sight.

I turned off Johann's melody before leaving the blacktop. About a hundred yards down the gravel entrance, an old logging road provided passage to a perfect hiding spot for the Jeep. A small buck and two does greeted my arrival. *Today you're safe,* I thought, slowly driving closer. All three bolted away, snorting, their white tails zigzagging out of sight.

After creeping another hundred yards or so into the woods, a small cedar and pine thicket provided concealed parking. Evergreen branches rubbed against the Jeep as I backed in for an easy, quick exit, should one be needed. Lowering the window allowed cold air to heighten my senses. According to the radio, it would warm up into the low 40s by mid-day. That would be tolerable for my wait. The night's dew had turned into a heavy frost, covering most everything in sight. When I killed the headlights and shut off the engine, it was quiet. Dark and deadly quiet.

I lit a Marlboro, and for a moment, sat trying to ignore nature's call. Then, as with a woman in labor, the recurring pains became too close together to ignore. Stepping out of the Jeep with a pocket full of paper towels, I quickly found a nearby log for leaning, dropped my Levi's, took the primal position, and exploded. After wiping, I burned the used paper and covered my steamy excretions with leaves, just to be on the safe side.

It would soon be daylight, granting me the opportunity to survey the area around the hunting cabin. I'd been there several times in the past, but of course things change. It would be beneficial to learn as much as possible before Carl's arrival. I would need to look at the cabin—in the cabin, if possible—and then find a perfect observation point for my wait. Potential target spots had to be considered. My plan involved using the tranquilizer as Carl unloaded supplies from his truck. Ideally, I would position myself within seventy feet of the cabin's entrance. If there were no good hiding spots available, one would have to be created.

The thought of sitting on the ground for a long period of time didn't worry me. It would be no different than waiting three or four hours in the cold for a shot at a deer. Proper clothes and an occasional cigarette make it bearable.

After drugging Carl, I planned to both handcuff and tie him to whatever solid object might be available. No chances would be taken with a guy who had once been a cop. He was ornery enough and smart enough to be evasive. After the tranquilizer wore off, it would be my turn to be creative.

I sat in the Jeep drinking coffee until around 7:00 a.m. Louisville time when dawn began to shed its soft light on the woods. It was time to get moving, survey the cabin area, and return to the Jeep for supplies and something to eat before taking position. After sliding into the camouflaged jumpsuit, I replaced my sneakers with combat boots, traded the hunter-orange cap for one in camo, and then strapped the Ruger Redhawk .44 Magnum around my waist. An army knife had already been clipped to the belt. My backpack contained a rope, a small hunter's saw, plastic sheeting, a hatchet, and an old blanket. I slipped it on my shoulders and wiggled it to a comfortable fit.

Nature provided a perfect morning for hiking. The woods had grown up considerably, making it difficult to recall my bearings and the easiest path to the cabin. After locking up the Jeep, I slipped on my gloves and began walking at a hunter's pace, one step at a time as though stalking deer. I knew I'd have to watch along the way in the dim dawn for possible poachers trying to bag an early buck. It took twenty-two minutes to cross about a hundred and seventy-five yards of woods.

The lack of leaves on the trees allowed visibility of the cabin long before reaching the clearing. The small-framed building had a metal roof and a stone chimney on one end. Its siding had been constructed with wormy chestnut boards from a nearby dilapidated barn, one that partially collapsed long before my time. A narrow clearing through the woods provided a route for an electric line from the blacktop. One single-bulb light shined by the door. *Surely they don't leave that on all the time?* I hesitated for several minutes, scanning, until confident of being alone. Moving in for a closer look, I found the door was locked, but still managed a dim peek inside through one of the windows. Wasn't much there except a stone fireplace, chairs leaning against the wall next to a table, several folded cots, and one of those old beds with the metal tubular headboard and footboard. Its bare mattress had been damaged by rodents. Crude cabinets hung on the wall next to the bed. With no cook-stove visible, I figured they'd be bringing a portable propane unit. A metal locker standing on the left side of the fireplace obviously provided mouse-free storage for essentials. In the corner, on the right side of the fireplace, sat a portable Salamander kerosene heater with its electric cord wrapped perfectly around the handle. A five gallon kerosene can sit next to it. From the ceiling, there hung a two-bulb light fixture. An outhouse positioned some thirty feet to the north of the cabin, at the edge of the woods, pretty much guaranteed there was no running water in the cabin.

After one trip around the building, I picked out my vantage point. Approximately seventy feet from the entrance, several small cedar trees growing close together would offer an adequate blind. I stepped off the distance. From the cedars, I should be able to get a decent shot at Carl. It should be easy enough to sit upright until his arrival and then lie down for a clear view under the low branches.

Layers of sandstone rock directly behind my makeshift blind would provide a leaning spot for waiting. Removal of a few small stones and some debris from the trees helped create a near-perfect accommodation. I spread the plastic sheet and covered it with my blanket, folded in half. This would keep me dry, warm and quiet. After several practice tries of rolling over from a seated position to my stomach, I lay in shooting readiness, scanning the area for potential problems. To my relief, there were none. Glancing at the time—8:28 a.m.—alerted me of a need to start back toward the Jeep. Satisfied with my preparations, I stood, covered the entire mess with leaves, and then moved away a few paces to admire my efforts. As I began my trek back to the Jeep, I heard the words of Sister Mary Theresa speaking to me in my childhood. *The world outside is full of trouble. You must listen to Gabrielle.*

"Jesus Christ, what am I doing?"

Chapter 44

Getting ready to hunt Carl Jacobs didn't seem much different from getting ready to hunt deer. The same camo clothing, face paint, boots, gloves, and hat would be used. In the backpack there would be the rope, water, a small, battery-powered cassette tape recorder, and, in case my stomach should start growling, some peanuts. Also, in the jumpsuit pockets, I had compact binoculars and, of course, two pairs of handcuffs wrapped in cloth to keep them quiet. Their key had been added to my key ring. Having smoked more cigarettes than usual that day, I had less than half a pack left. About three-fourths of a good joint remained hidden between the Marlboros.

At around 9:15 a.m., I had a bologna and cheese sandwich for an early lunch. I considered a shot of whiskey with my RC, but figured it might cause me to doze off or make some other mistake. I decided to take the half-pint along anyway, just in case.

The reality of my endeavor hit home upon opening the first of two gun cases. In movies, I'd seen assassins carry weapons in similar containers. Their firearms were always designed for long distance shots. Mine, of course, were not. The first, a short-barreled shotgun, should only be used at thirty feet or less. After assembling it, I loaded it with five rounds of 00-buckshot. One would do a messy job at ten feet.

The second case held the tranquilizer gun, something I'd only shot twice in practice. It reminded me of the CO_2 air rifles we used as children, only heavier. The gun had open sights. With my blind at 70 feet, there would be an inch-and-a-half to two-inch drop. Who knows what chemical I'd been given to load it with? Uncle Samuel provided just one chance at sedate-and-restrain, insisting that if one didn't do the trick, the shotgun should be used immediately. There would not be enough time to consider reloading the single shot rifle.

Using a syringe, I added chemicals and pressure to the dart. A small rubber sleeve held the anesthetic solution in place until penetration. CO_2 would propel the miniature missile at the pull of a trigger, just like shooting any other rifle. Upon impact, Carl's skin and clothing should push back the rubber sleeve on the shaft, thus releasing the active ingredients into his body. Uncle Samuel said it could take from one to three minutes for the drug to totally take effect. Then, according to Carl's weight and physical condition, it might take an hour to completely recover. And yes, there was the possibility Carl would die of a reaction to the drug.

While driving that morning, I had tossed all my cigarette butts out the window. An aggressive wipe of the steering wheel, dash accessories, and even the door handles, both interior and exterior, eliminated any existing prints. The gun cases could remain, as they too contained no prints. At the last second, I decided to pack my cassette tapes into the backpack. Left behind, they could be used to identify me.

Everything had been done. "Time to go." My heart began racing again. After eleven years, the moment of revenge for Sissy's suffering had arrived. With a deep breath, I slipped on the backpack, shut the Jeep's hatch, picked up a rifle in one hand, shotgun in the other, and started my hike.

Twenty feet later, my dry lips made me think about lip balm. "Not in my pocket. Shit." It would be impossible to sit in the open air for two hours without something to coat my lips. Back to the Jeep I went. I remembered using Chap Stick on the way down and decided it must have fallen out of my pocket. A thorough search produced the tube and a silver dime, both hiding down in that spot between the bottom and back of the seat. *Damn, now there's a fingerprint item that could have gotten me in trouble.*

Wasting no time, I applied a liberal coating on my lips while glancing through the interior for other mistakes. There were none.

I finally got away from the Jeep at 9:45, fifteen minutes behind schedule. As result, I caught myself a couple times moving too fast in the woods. *Slow down, dammit.* Even walking at a slow pace, my heart rate seemed rapid. Halfway through the woods, a sick feeling churned in my stomach. *Thought all these years this would be easy. Now look at me.* The nagging continued into convulsions. Quickly, I laid down the guns, moved away and bent over, violently throwing up bits and pieces of my bologna sandwich. I used water from the canteen to wash out my mouth. Still, my stomach was in knots. *Boy, deer hunting never did this to me.*

I knew only one sure way to settle my stomach; the joint hidden in my cigarette pack. Even though the use of marijuana went against the wishes of my elders, at that point it didn't matter. I simply could not afford to be sick. My mind drifted back to Uncle Willie's story about why he smoked pot. *Surely he'd understand.* Hands shaking slightly, I lit up and, like an asthmatic sucking on an inhaler, took a long, hard draw. The smoke expanded in my lungs and busted back out as I disturbed the woods with coughing. I tried again with a smaller hit, holding it in for as long as possible before exhaling. Two more tokes and something said, *Stop.*

After gulping water, I lit a cigarette and remained in that one spot for about five minutes, waiting for relief. The nausea began to diminish. *They say every man has two sides. Question is, which one of yours is a killer? Certainly not the one throwing up.* I closed my eyes and whispered, "Dear God, I've come here today to take care of a family matter in the fashion of my ancestors. Like my elders, I pray you'll have mercy on my soul come judgment day. Give me wisdom. Give me knowledge. Give me the understanding needed to succeed. If my actions are less than you desire, just show me a sign. And, please make it obvious. Amen."

Upon opening my eyes, things did seem brighter. Sunshine peeking over the eastern hills reflected through the naked treetops, creating millions of tiny crystals at the ends of frost-tipped branches. For the moment, it felt as though my actions were being orchestrated in heaven. The woods came to life. Little insignificant noises were all of a sudden amplified. The birds, the wind moving dead pin oak leaves still clinging to the wintered branches, and even the sound of a single-stroke John Deere tractor way in the distance. My mind wandered all over the place. I felt like Moses before he ordered his men to commit genocide on the Midianites, contemplating whether it was God telling him to kill or if he was simply using God as an excuse to slaughter. Each time I considered reconsidering, the words of my elders urged me onward. *The man is no good. He hurt your sister and may do it again. He needs to be stopped.*

A support team rallied as Bach reached down from heaven and directed his own pieces of encouragement. Those rattling oak leaves became percussionists while I hummed a classic march and began moving my feet once again, in the direction of the cabin.

In this game of life, I'd become both player and coach, grabbing for anything that might fire me up to do the unthinkable and to hopefully get away with it. Problem was, the more thinking I did, the less sense it made. *Me* walking around with guns, intending to kill someone. *Boy, if Sister Mary Theresa could only see me now.* Thoughts of her made me feel guilty. Never in her wildest dreams would she approve of my intentions against Carl. I knew exactly what she would say. *This is why I gave you Gabrielle. Why aren't you listening?* I tried to hear Gabrielle. I really did, but her comments were absent.

Nothing made it any easier. My burden grew heavier. A battle raged within me. *Should I keep thinking like a wimp, or have a drink and become numb to the task at hand?* I walked on with the booze burning a hole in my pocket. Step by step, the whiskey became my apple and the woods my garden. Too frigid for the presence of a snake, the cold alone became temptation enough, my excuse to fall. With both long-guns on the ground, I sat on a rotten oak stump, pulled out that half pint of Kentucky straight bourbon, and stared at it. "Should I or shouldn't I?" My hands began to shake, and I felt weak, less of a man than my father and his brothers expected. The devil tempted, *So, what you gonna do? Sit here like a baby or take a drink, be a man, and go kill that sonofabitch?*

Against all better judgment, I broke the seal and swallowed half the small bottle in one drink. My throat and stomach, raw from vomiting, were scorched by the whiskey. My head shook reflexively as I made a face that no one would see. I capped the bottle and returned it to the deep front pocket of my jumpsuit.

Did God look down upon me? Did he see a weak man sitting there between Satan and Gabrielle's silence, emotionally naked, waiting for the whiskey's venom to help justify his actions? Eventually, it did. I shivered away my fears and felt a tingle in my hair. I was suddenly calm, no longer shaking, and things began to focus. "That's better, no wimpy thoughts. Bring on the low-life that raped my sister."

Is this the way my uncles felt when entering a hot war zone in Vietnam? I picked up both guns and continued sneaking through my own little jungle.

Chapter 45

After ten more minutes and a thousand thoughts, I stood in the woods at a distance, observing the cabin. The light by the door had gone off. *Must be on a timer.* Nothing seemed to be out of place, so I moved to the nest, swept away enough leaves to accommodate my body, and crawled in. My watch read 10:21 a.m., well behind schedule. I took a few minutes to again practice my moves and then strategically place weapons for easy access: shotgun to the left, tranquilizer on my right, handgun on the ground within easy reach. From a comfortable sitting position, I'd be able to smoothly and quietly slide my legs back, lie flat, and shoot.

The temperature, cool enough to eliminate the threat of copperheads hiding around the rocks, would keep me alert. No ants, no mosquitoes, no insects at all. I sat quiet, listening to the woods. A slight trickle of water ran in the nearby wet weather creek. Not too far off, a gray squirrel scavenging through leaves in search of a meal made more noise than a 10-point buck. Blue jays screamed an alert to the approach of a red fox that seemed to catch wind of me in passing. The squirrel ran up a hickory tree shaking its tail and chattering, loud and continuous, until the fox and its threat had moved on.

Road noise from a vehicle rose gradually as it groaned and grunted up and down hills, eventually passing, and then fading away at a different pitch, as slowly as it came. When the woods settled back to the sound of water trickle and shuffling leaves, I found myself so relaxed that falling asleep became a threat. My mind had begun drifting into that soft dreamy state between consciousness and unconsciousness when the sound of another vehicle snapped me back.

The level of noise increased, drawing closer, and seemed to be louder than the last. Then, as it approached the lane leading to the cabin, the sound lowered. No doubt, someone slowed as though about to turn in. *It had better be Carl.*

Engine noise and tire crunches started down the winding lane, nearly taking my breath away. It scared me, not enough to quit or run, but enough to shake me into alertness. I removed the glove from my shooting hand while rolling into position for the short wait. Then came a shock that nearly brought back nausea. Carl's truck came through the woods, but he wasn't alone. A car followed him. *Could it be the other guys didn't work today?* Carl pulled up parallel to the front of the cabin, and as the other vehicle made that final turn into the clearing, I recognized its driver.

"Kiss my ass," I whispered. "What the hell's she doing here?" It was Detective Kelly Rauschenberg. She did say she'd go beyond the line of duty, but I never expected to see her in the backwoods of Grayson County. *Did she somehow know I'd be here today?*

Recalling Uncle Willie's doubts, I began to think, *Can Kelly be trusted? Could she in some twisted way be in cahoots with Carl? Have I been lured? Could they be planning to kill me?* None of my thoughts made sense. While there were things about Kelly I didn't like, deep down she seemed sincere. One minute earlier, I'd have sworn the lady truly wanted to rid the world of Carl and his threat to women. Now I watched, befuddled, as she pulled up next to the truck. Carl emerged first, walked around to Kelly's car, and stood there a few seconds waiting for her to get out.

Girl, if you suspect the man to be a rapist, why come all the way down here, deep in the woods, where he can do anything he wants with no witnesses? Unless, of course, you plan on killing Carl yourself. After all, we had left Kelly out of our plans. *Could it be the woman made her own?*

When she finally got out of the car, the two wasted no time before adding to my confusion by embracing and kissing like long-separated lovers. Carl lifted Kelly onto the warm car hood. She dropped her purse, and they went at it. I felt like a peeping Tom, staring as he felt her up in a way that from a distance reminded me more of an officer's frisk. *Hmm*, I thought, *don't trust her, do you?*

The longevity of their embrace convinced me that neither suspected my presence. Kelly, a cop, and Carl, an ex-cop, would never make themselves an easy target. Therefore, I chose to believe one or both had come to eliminate the other. I hoped there wouldn't be a need for me to rescue Kelly.

For what appeared to be a lack of oxygen, they broke their lip-lock and began talking as Carl moved toward the cabin. Then he stopped. "Hey, would you like a drink?"

"Sure," answered Kelly, staring at her reflection in the car window, fixing her hair. "Whatcha got?"

"Brought some whiskey for the guys."

"Oh hell yes, that'll do just fine."

Carl retrieved a brown bag from the front of the truck and said, "Need a chaser? Got one in the cooler."

"No, thanks," she replied. "I have one in the car."

Kelly continued her primp while Carl unlocked the cabin door. Once he'd made his way inside, out of sight, she reached back into the car and pulled out more than her drink. In a quick move, she placed what looked like a small revolver into her purse which, still sat on the hood.

Carl stuck his head out the door. "Come on in."

"Be right there, can't find my lighter."

"Don't worry, got matches in here."

Kelly picked up her purse, closed the car door, and walked around Carl's truck to the cabin entrance. When she disappeared inside, my heart beat fast. I didn't know what to do. One thing was for sure: with Kelly present, all plans were on hold. I needed a cigarette badly, but couldn't chance it.

About the time I figured they were getting it on, Carl returned outside to grab a blanket and pillow from the cab of the truck. *You guys gonna get comfy on that old bed?* I practiced following his movements with the tranquilizer gun as he returned toward the cabin door. My plan had been to shoot Carl in the butt while he unloaded gear from the back of the truck. Even if Kelly should for some reason leave, I still wouldn't be able to do that. In picking the spot for my blind, I assumed Carl would back his truck in for easy unloading. For some reason he hadn't. *Perhaps it's because of the way Kelly pulled up next to his truck.* Instead of looking at his taillights, I was staring at his headlights. Regardless, should the opportunity arise, my only shot would be frontal, somewhere in that short, narrow path between the truck and cabin. And this would mean a moving target—not my original plan.

Carl only hesitated for a second at the door before shoving it inward, not long enough for a good shot. The old door slowly shut itself most of the way, creaking as it did. I wondered, *Could there be another option? What if I make a noise or call his name just before he enters. Might do the trick. Surely he'd hesitate to investigate. For that moment, a shot at one of his legs could be available.* Without the butt shot, it would have to do, unless of course I decided to simply shoot him with the .44 Magnum.

My position allowed me to see through one window, and I caught a flash of Kelly. By the time I raised the binoculars, she'd moved away. After about another minute, both came out, walked to the other end of the cabin, and gathered several pieces of firewood before re-entering. *Why didn't they just use the kerosene heater? Could the fuel can be empty, or do they just want to be romantic?*

Moments later, Kelly came back out alone and scared the crap out of me when she began collecting twigs, obviously for kindling. She called back to Carl, "Probably find small stuff in the woods!"

Again, my heart began racing. I couldn't be sure she was on my side, and therefore didn't want her to know of my presence. *If she comes my way, I may have no choice but to shoot her with the tranquilizer. Carl comes looking, I'll use the shotgun on him.* For a quick plan B, it seemed doable.

I slid the safety off and began following her movements with the rifle. Each twig gathered brought Kelly closer to my position. If she got within twenty-five to thirty feet, I'd have to shoot or risk being spotted. It felt the same as watching a deer for just the right shot, only I gave up good opportunities, hoping this doe might go away. I held my breath, fearing she would see its condensation in the cool morning air. With no other choice, my finger moved to the trigger and started squeezing.

Carl came to the door and hollered, "Hey, how much you got?"

Kelly turned to show what she'd gathered. "Think this is enough?"

To my relief, Carl answered, "Should be plenty. If not, we'll fire up that stinking-ass kerosene heater."

"Good," mumbled Kelly, turning and stepping toward the cabin.

When I let off the trigger and released a long overdue exhale, I'll be damned if she didn't stop and look back as though my breath had caught her attention. At that moment, the face paint and camo certainly paid off. I lay there not moving, not breathing, watching her nostrils twitch like a bird dog on point, and began to worry she could smell my deodorant.

Carl, still at the door, asked, "You okay?"

"Yeah, thought I heard something out there."

"Might just be a deer. Woods'll be full of 'em today. Tomorrow we won't be able to find one anywhere."

"Really? Don't guess I'd know what a deer sounds like anyway," replied Kelly.

"Want me to check it out?"

"No, don't worry about it. My luck, it's a big ol' bear," she joked, while trying to hold the kindling with her left arm and brushing bark chips from her long coat with her right hand.

I snuck another breath as Carl said back, "Hate to tell you this honey, but there are no bears in these woods."

Kelly hesitated again and looked back in my direction. No doubt, the woman suspected something. She scanned the woods one more time before returning to the cabin, twigs in hand. Walking through the entrance, she began chattering about something. When the door shut, I took a deep breath and a sigh of relief. For a moment I thought about giving up, sneaking away, and leaving the two of them alone. *Kelly wants to kill Carl, fine, she doesn't need my help. And, if she's not here to kill the bastard, woman owes me and my family an explanation.*

While looking around, contemplating my exit, it felt as though the elders were telling me to stay, to wait and see if she would leave early enough for me to do my job. *Worst comes to worst, we can blame it on her.*

I decided to be patient, at least for a while. A few seconds later, while I was monitoring the window with my binoculars, Kelly popped into sight, staring out as though still not satisfied. *Girl, you sure don't look happy.* Suddenly, it appeared those detective eyes were looking right at me. Cautiously, I tilted the binoculars, fearing she might see the lenses. When Kelly finally moved away from the window, I switched guns until I was certain she and Carl weren't coming out after me.

Eventually, smoke rose from the chimney. After a while, more movement from inside the window caught my attention. With the binoculars, I got a dim view of Kelly, perhaps on top of her lover. *Been there.* Adjusting the glasses gave me a better view. I couldn't see a lot of movement, but every now and then Kelly turned as though looking out the window, like she knew someone watched. She still didn't look happy, at least nothing like the night we were together. *So why are you doing this? Why sleep with the enemy?* It just didn't make sense.

While cuddling comfortably in my jumpsuit, ugly thoughts entered my mind. *What if I stormed through the door of the cabin, unloaded the buckshot on two lovers, and left the entire mess looking like a jealous husband had discovered their affair?* Without knowing Kelly's intentions, it would be a bad idea. Besides, I couldn't do that to Mr. Rauschenberg. For all I knew, he might be a nice person.

The cabin door opened, with Carl's voice directing Kelly to the outhouse. As she turned the corner in that direction, he stepped to the other side of his truck and took a leak. I remained perfectly still until she reached the shitter, then rolled back to my shooting position. While waiting on Kelly, Carl started removing items from the back of the truck. *Damn, not yet.*

Kelly apparently lit a cigarette, as smoke seeped through the cracks of the outhouse. *Thought you couldn't find your lighter.* I could almost feel her staring from within, between the boards, looking for me. I tried to stare back with the binoculars, but couldn't see a thing. Lowering the lenses, I attempted to keep one eye out for Kelly and the other on Carl.

The outhouse door creaked open, and out popped the good detective. On her way back toward the cabin she continuously glanced around as though aware of my presence. When she walked around the corner of the building, Carl joined her, carrying a bag of something, and they both went inside.

Come on now, if you're gonna kill 'im, kill 'im, or get the hell out of here so I can.

My patience wore thin. I lay there wishing I were back home and in bed. Detective Kelly had certainly messed up my day. Clouds rolled in, and the breeze caused a sudden drop in temperature. I pulled the blanket up close and felt like taking a nap, but knew better. "Help me out here, Lord." No sooner than the whispered words left my mouth, the cabin door opened and it became evident that Kelly did not intend to kill Carl. She wore her coat and had the purse hanging from her shoulder, apparently ready to leave. She also had her drink cup in hand. *Musta made one for the road.*

I could read Carl's mind as he stood there chatting in the cold without a jacket. He'd gotten all he needed from Kelly and wanted her to get the heck out of Dodge. Without even holding her hand or putting his arm around her, he walked her to the car. He then offered a goodbye kiss, which she accepted, but with much less enthusiasm than earlier.

Chapter 46

It made no sense. Why would Kelly come to the cabin, and then leave without making some sort of an attempt on Carl's life? Regardless, her exit did at last provide me an opportunity to carry out my own plans. While Carl stood watching Kelly's car disappear through the woods, I wondered, *Did she spot me? Did she forget anything? What if she comes back in the middle of my killing Carl? Do I stop, finish, or what?*

With time running out, I knew I'd have to quit worrying and simply take a chance. *If she comes back, she comes back. Just have to hope the woman's on my side.*

Carl remained still until the sound of Kelly's vehicle faded away on the blacktop. Finally, he shrugged his shoulders as if he was cold, opened the topper door, lowered the tailgate, and began removing gear from the back of the truck. When he started toward the cabin, I tried again to follow his legs with the dart gun, but couldn't pull the trigger. The man simply moved too fast. No doubt, my only choice would be to make a noise and hope he stopped.

I used deep breathing to calm myself while awaiting Carl's next trip to the truck. After a couple minutes, he hurried back out, this time wearing his jacket. He dragged a huge cooler to the tailgate, struggled to lift it, and shuffled toward the cabin door. *Damn.* The cooler blocked a shot to his upper leg. I had to wait again, hoping he had more gear.

"Patience," Pop would say when deer hunting. "Get in a hurry, you'll miss the kill."

Seconds turned to long, anxious minutes. Finally, I saw Carl at the window. He stared out much like Kelly had earlier.

Is he looking for me?

After a while, he left the window and then reappeared out the door, returning to the truck. After removing a gun case, he closed the tailgate. When he moved close to the cabin's entrance, I shouted his name. "Carl!" The man stopped dead in his tracks, looking my way. Aiming high on his left leg, I pulled the trigger and could actually see the dart as it flew through the air, dropping with distance and striking Carl mid-thigh.

Immediately, he dropped the gun case and howled, "Goddamnnnn!" The heavy container landed with a thump. Without hesitation, he reached down, pulled the dart out and threw it. Instead of stepping inside of the cabin, my prey turned, opened the door of the truck, and jumped in.

Not good, I thought, *he might have a gun.* Rising to my knees, I dropped the rifle and grabbed my shotgun. Carl was clearly visible in the cab but too far away for the buckshot. When he started the engine, I jumped up and burst through the branches, hoping to get a shot before he could get away. Walking quickly toward the truck, shotgun tight against my shoulder, ready to fire, I noticed Carl's head disappear from sight. *Is he hiding or did the drug take effect?* Afraid to take a chance, I took cover by the corner of the cabin and waited. The truck's engine continued running. *If you're conscious, why aren't you trying to drive off?*

Rather than approaching head on, I decided to circle the cabin and come in from the back. Slipping and sliding on rocky ground covered by loose leaves, I made it to the other end. A slow peek around the corner revealed no movement. Squatting like a duck, I waddled ten feet to the back of the vehicle and then raised up just enough to look through the topper into the cab. Only the tip of his shoulder was visible. Moving along the driver side provided Carl's reflection in the outside mirror. After inching forward to the door, I looked in but still couldn't tell if he was out or pretending. As if disabling a bomb, I slowly opened the door. Carl made no attempt to move. He was breathing. "Good," I said out loud. "Now you're mine."

I needed to work fast at getting him into the cabin and restrained. Uncle Samuel had predicted he'd be out for close to an hour, but that was no guarantee. I turned off the engine. At that point it seemed safe to prop my shotgun up against the cabin. "Okay big boy, this ain't gonna be easy, but you're coming out of this truck."

Leaning in, I slid my hands under Carl's armpits and curled his bulk in my direction. The steering wheel got in the way, but eventually his dead weight rolled out onto the ground. Using one set of handcuffs from my pocket, I quickly secured his wrists. Then, to my surprise, his ankles were too large. "Damn. Shoulda brought shackles."

Checking his jacket, I found a .380 automatic in one pocket and a snub-nose .38 Special in the other. "Well, well, what have we here? Bet you lifted this revolver out of Kelly's purse." After tucking the pistols into separate pockets of my jumpsuit, I picked up Carl's gun case and shoved it inside the cabin, next to the door. At that point, a cigarette would have been great. Instead, I unzipped my jumpsuit to release heat and began tugging Carl toward the door. It was only three or four feet, but seemed like a mile. Once there, I tried to drag him inside but couldn't. He weighed a ton. Going in backwards, I managed to get his head and shoulders up the single step. Then I stepped over his lifeless heap, back onto the ground outside. Grabbing both legs, I lifted his butt clear off the step and shoved him on in.

Now, how do I wanna do this? With very little to tie to, I chose the largest object in the room. Somehow, I manhandled Carl to the end of the bed, propping him upright against its metal frame in a sitting position. By removing the handcuff from his right wrist, I was able to secured his left to the bedpost. I attached his right hand on the opposite side using the other set of cuffs. Carl now sat in a slump, back against the bed with arms stretched out from post to post, facing the fireplace. Out of breath, I stood for a few seconds, looking down at my handiwork and talking to myself. "Better tie his legs."

I hurried back to the blind for my gear. After a long-overdue bladder relief, I grabbed the backpack and .44 Magnum and then headed back to the cabin, leaving the rifle lying there on the blanket.

Using rope from the backpack, I slip knotted one end to Carl's left ankle while scanning the room for something to tie off on. The metal cabinet would tip too easily, and there simply wasn't anything else solid or secure enough to use. Inside the cabinet, someone had left a hammer and a coffee can full of 8 penny nails. "Voila. These oughta do the trick."

Working as if timed like a rodeo rider securing a calf, I took slack out of the rope and drove two nails through it into the floor about three feet from Carl's foot. The excess length worked perfectly to secure the other ankle. I nailed it also, spreading Carl's legs in the process. Then, cutting off what rope remained, I wrapped it around his waist and secured each end tightly to its adjacent bedpost. Upon awakening, he'd find himself fixed firmly upright against the bed.

Chapter 47

A small table, which sat near the door cattycorner to the bed, held nothing but an ashtray, a box of matches, and Carl's fifth of whiskey. I added my backpack, unfolded a chair, and took a seat on the side nearest the fireplace, facing Carl. The two pistols in my pockets made sitting uncomfortable. I placed both on the table and then lit a cigarette and stared at the mess I'd created. *What the hell you gonna do now?* A strong cup of coffee would have been nice, but the only thing available was a can of Coca-Cola from my captive's cooler. I popped the top, took a long drink, and set it down next to the whiskey, resisting the temptation to mix the two.

The waiting nearly drove me crazy. I picked up the snub-nose .38 Special, pointed it at Carl's head, and imagined finishing him off before he woke up. It would be the most humane way to end his life— almost like sticking a hog after shocking it unconscious. *So why didn't Kelly use this thing?*

Logs crackling in the fireplace caught my attention. The flickering flames reminded me of the picture of Dante's hell, an image embedded in my brain as a child by the Church. I laid the gun back down and finished my cigarette while contemplating several things: *How to kill Carl. Getting caught. Going to hell. Not getting caught. Still going to hell.*

"Sissy," I mumbled, "this is for you. You can put your gun away, it's about to be over. And Gabrielle, you're just gonna have to turn your head."

With my patience running thin, I decided to try shocking Carl awake with cold water from the cooler. It didn't work at all. Other than

285

breathing, he remained lifeless. "Bullshit. It always works in the movies."

After another twenty minutes of my fighting random thoughts and the temptation to get drunk, Carl began moving. He moaned a little, forced his eyes open, and gradually realized his dilemma. He tried to move, but appeared to be weakened by the drug. Recognizing me through my face paint, Carl spoke with difficulty. "Smith, what's going on here?"

"Take it easy, big boy, and I'll explain."

"Take it easy my ass," he slurred.

"You mean your *big ass*. Damn you're heavy."

"You little sonofabitch. Untie me right now or—"

"Or what? Hate to tell you this, pal, but you're not getting untied. Got a couple bones to pick with you. Then I'm seriously considering skinning your sorry fat ass alive."

"For what?" he asked. "Ain't done nothing to you!"

"Don't play dumb, Carl. You know it's not about me. It's about my sister and all those other women you been raping."

Carl moved his head back and forth as though still trying to focus. "You got me mixed up with somebody else."

"Is that right, and you ain't the December Rapist?"

"Never heard of that ... whatever you said. I'm not a rapist."

"Yeah right, and you and your buddies Pete and Joe didn't rape my sister back in '72?"

Carl suddenly had nothing to say.

"What's wrong, cat got your tongue? Proud of what y'all put my sister through?"

He didn't answer. Just sat there, head hung, silent.

"Tell you what, Carl. I went to a lot of trouble so we could have this little chat. You don't wanna talk, that's fine, but I'm still gonna kill ya."

Trying to focus, he said, "You've got the wrong person."

"Bullshit. My sister recognized your voice at Masterson's. That little thing you said about my daughter being a real cutie. Same thing you said about Sissy that night when you took her clothes off, right before you raped her."

"She remembered that?"

"Sure she did. How could she not after you burnt her arms so she wouldn't forget?"

"Smith, not saying I wasn't there. Not saying I'm innocent either, but you got it all wrong. I didn't take your sister's clothes off, and I didn't have anything to do with burning her."

I couldn't believe he admitted to being there. Maybe it was the anesthetic making him careless. "Then who did?" I asked.

Carl squirmed, weakly tugged at his restraints, and said, "Give me one of those cigarettes and I'll tell you about that."

I didn't trust him, but I wanted to hear what he had to say. "You try something, anything, I'll blow your brains all over this bed you and Kelly been screwing around on."

"Don't think you have to worry," he slurred. "Case you haven't noticed, I'm all tied up."

I removed the .44 Magnum from its holster and laid it on the table, just to be safe, and then got just close enough to stick my cigarette in Carl's mouth. Lit me another.

"Now start talking."

"Smith, I didn't burn your sister. Swear to God, neither did Joe. It was Pete. He was into that, not us."

"But you *admit* you raped my sister?"

He sat there a moment, puffing on the cigarette. "No, not really."

"Bull. Know damn well you were in on it."

"Only way I raped your sister was by not stopping those other two. Made me sick to watch."

"You know I don't believe that."

"Don't expect you to, but that don't change what really happened."

I thought to myself, *Kelly warned he'd be smart. Probably just trying to lie his way out of trouble.* "If you were there and didn't stop it, you're just as guilty as them."

"Think I don't know that?" he spoke quicker, the drug wearing off. "Think I don't know it was wrong? Hell yes I do, but believe me, it wasn't supposed to happen. Pete said we were just gonna rough her up a little for what she did to his cousin."

"You talking about Beth?"

Carl's eyes opened and closed as though trying to focus while he continued, "Shit, I don't know, guess that's her name. Never even met her. All I knew was the girl we grabbed supposedly beat up Pete's cousin real bad. Said he just wanted to pay her back. Didn't have a clue they'd rape her."

"Oh yeah? Well, you shoulda stopped 'em. Instead, you went along with it, and that makes you no better than them. Your sorry butt oughta be in prison."

Holding the cigarette with his teeth, he leaned his head back to avoid the smoke. "I was young and stupid and too afraid to stop 'em. Feel like killing me for that, go ahead. Got any idea how bad I've felt ever since that night?"

"Big sonofabitch like you, scared of Pete and Joe? Don't believe that."

"Pete had a gun. Guess I was a pussy. Afraid he'd shoot me."

"Bullshit, believe you were in on it then; believe you ain't never quit, Mr. December Rapist."

"Rapist? You need to listen to me. I'm not a rapist. Get that through your thick skull. Never was and never will be. Ain't ever touched another woman like that since your sister."

"What do you mean '*like that*'? How *did* you touch my sister?"

"You gotta remember, I was scared. Pete told me I had to do her so they wouldn't have to worry about me rattin' 'em out. Didn't know what to do. By that time, your sister appeared unconscious. I got on top of her and pretended, hoping Pete wouldn't shoot me. Dick wasn't even hard."

"Yeah right, you expect me to believe that?"

"It's the truth, I swear. You can't call it rape if I didn't put it in her."

I stood there dumbfounded, wondering what to do. Couldn't tell if I was hearing a sliver of the truth, or if he was just a damn good liar?

This sure as hell ain't going right. Can't shoot the man if what he says is true.

With my plan unraveling, I picked up the whiskey bottle and took a couple big swallows. I chased it with the Coke and sat back down in the chair. "So, let me ask you this. Did you kill Pete and Joe?"

Carl spit the remainder of his cigarette out on the floor. I raked it in with my boot and squished it out. After sucking in a lungful of air, he exhaled hard and said, "Knew from talking to Kelly that someone had overheard those boys talking about what we did to your sister. When Joe told me they were gonna go huntin' on that Sunday, I decided to meet 'em out there and talk about it. I found their truck, then caught up with 'em out in the field. Soon as I mentioned the police were investigating them on your sister's rape, Joe got excited, started screaming that we were all about to get caught. He said the police were still looking because Pete had raped someone else. Pete told Joe to shut up, but he wouldn't, so he just shot the poor bastard, right in the face. Man never had a chance."

"And I guess you just stood there?"

"What could I do? Scared the shit out of me. Had a .380 in my pocket, but I knew if I went for it, he'd blast me like he did Joe. Played it off for a little bit, acting glad that we didn't have to worry about Joe's big mouth anymore. When Pete laid his gun down to light a cigarette, I grabbed Joe's. I asked him if it was true he'd raped other women. He denied it, of course. Said Joe didn't know what the hell he was talking about. So I asked, 'Then why'd you shoot him?'

"He didn't say a word, just grinned. Same sick face he had the night he raped your sister. Told him I was gonna have to turn him in for killing Joe. He said he'd tell the cops I shot Joe to keep him quiet. You don't know how much I hated that sonofabitch. He ruined my life. Standing there at that moment, I felt nineteen years old again, only this time *I* had the gun. I told him, 'Shoulda stopped you that night. Shouldn't have let you hurt that little girl. You ruined her life, my life, and Joe's. Now you killed him!' About that time, Joe's dog came running up and it startled me. When I turned that way, Pete went for his shotgun. I didn't even think. Blasted him just like he did Joe. Tore half his face off. One shot and the evil bastard was dead."

"And you just left 'em there?"

"Couldn't think of nothing else to do. Let me tell you something, Smith. Killing Pete does bother me, a lot, so much I can't stand myself anymore, but it still don't bother me nearly as much as what happened to your sister."

"So, you're telling me you ain't the December Rapist?"

"Noooo. Done told you that."

"Well, then how come those same kind of rapes keep happening every December?"

"What kinda rapes you talking about?"

"You know what I mean. Kelly says the girl gets beat up, raped, and has the same burns on her arms. Said cops first thought it might be Pete, but since he's dead now and it keeps happening, she thinks it must be you."

"Woman's gotta be lying. She's a better detective than that. You got any idea how many rapists are out there? If I was into all that, it'd be her tied up here instead of me."

I thought, *Uncle Samuel warned me Carl would try to lie his way out, but that part there makes sense. If he is the December Rapist, and if he thought Kelly suspected him, why didn't he kill her? Maybe he thought she was trying to set him up. Is that why he was staring out the window?*

No doubt, the man had been there when my sister got raped, and he did kill Pete, maybe Joe too, hard to tell. But nothing he'd said explained his following Sissy.

"So why you been stalking my sister? Guarantee that's part of why Kelly suspects you."

Carl seemed to be thinking and speaking more clearly. "Wasn't stalking her, at least not the way you think."

"Bullshit! Know damn well you didn't drive all the way to Grayson County just to see me get married. You came down to see Sissy. And what about all those other times you showed up for no reason, even in Indianapolis?"

"When Kelly told me somebody'd been asking questions about the rape, I knew it had to be family. After all that time, wouldn't nobody else be interested. When she said someone overheard Pete and Joe talking, I figured it mighta been at work. Then you getting all nervous and telling me lies when they wanted to interview you about Pete and Joe's deaths, well, knew something was up."

"So what's that got to do with you following my sister?"

"You might not believe it, but every single day I think about what happened to your sister. Always feeling guilty. It's the reason I've never got married. After killing Pete, it only got worse. Couldn't sleep. Started drinking too much. Figured my life's over anyway, might as well try and get close enough to your sister to ... you know ... somehow tell her I'm sorry. Let her know the guys that did it are dead. Might at least end *her* nightmares. Then, who knows, maybe she could forgive me for not stopping 'em."

I stood up, started pacing, and said, "You can forget that, she won't wanna talk to you."

"You were right. I did go to Indianapolis to see her."

"How the hell did you know where she lived?"

"Still have friends on the force. They can find anybody."

"So how can you say you weren't stalking her?"

"You can call it stalking if you want. Went there three times. All I wanted to do was find the guts to talk to her. First time I got close enough to see those scars on her arms, it made me sick, almost threw up right there. Chickened out and drove home. Hated myself so much that night I burned my own arm just to see how bad it felt."

"Bullshit! Bullshit! Bullshit."

"Swear to God, I did."

"Then you *are* a sick bastard."

"When I came to your wedding, it wasn't about wanting to see her. And I had no intentions of hurting her. Just wanted a chance to talk. Still couldn't. Even tried again when she moved back to Louisville. Each time I went home and burned my arms."

"Yeah right?"

"Push my sleeves up. You'll see. Scars on each arm, just like your sister."

"No thanks, I'll take your word for it. Sounds to me like you needed a psychiatrist *and* a priest. If it bothered you that much, how come you didn't just turn yourself in? You were a cop. Don't you think they would have gone easy on you if you told your side of the story?"

"Thought about that, but it would wind up being my word against theirs, Pete and Joe. Couldn't take the chance. Kept thinking about what they do to ex-cops in prison."

The longer we talked the more confused and frustrated I got. Carl sat staring as I drank more whiskey. The sweaty dampness of my clothes caused me to shiver. Charred wood glowed red in the fireplace, but not enough to keep the place warm. On my way to add another log, I noticed the Salamander heater.

"How come y'all didn't use this?"

Carl didn't answer. I pulled the heater out to the middle of floor, unrolled the electric cord from its handle and plugged it into a wall socket. The fan began roaring immediately. Within seconds, fuel ignited and extremely hot air blew from the front.

"Turn it the other way!" pleaded Carl, over the noisy heater. "You're gonna burn me!"

I rotated the heater toward the back wall, took a seat, lit me another cigarette, and waited for the room to warm. Carl continued his stare. He was too quiet, and it worried me. *What's he thinking? Plotting?*

After three or four minutes, the heater started sputtering and ran out of fuel. The small room had gotten comfortable by then, so I just pulled the plug. A nasty kerosene stench filled the room as Carl watched my every move.

"Tell me something," I asked. "What's the deal with Kelly? Why's she so convinced you're a serial rapist?"

"Hell, I don't know. Maybe because I lied about knowing Pete and Joe."

"Or because you stole the evidence in my sister's case, you piece of shit."

"She told you that?"

"What do *you* think?"

Carl's chin fell to his chest. After a few seconds, he looked toward the fireplace and said, "When I met Kelly, we hit it off. Problem was, when we got in bed I, I couldn't do it. Couldn't get it up. Couldn't get rid of that disgusting image of your sister lying there on the ground, helpless. Even today, I tried here but couldn't. Being a detective, I'm sure she thinks there's a reason, and she'd be right, except it ain't the way she thinks. And, if you told her I've been stalking your sister, well, guess she's just adding things up. Telling you though, the woman's got me all wrong."

"Well, no wonder she thinks you were involved, you were."

"Told you I was there with your sister, but swear to God, I ain't got nothing to do with those other rapes you been talking about. Thought it was funny when Kelly suggested coming down here with me today. Been giving me the cold shoulder for a long time. Now it makes sense. She just lured me in for you."

"No, it's not like that. She surprised me showing up. I thought maybe she came down here to kill you."

Carl glanced at his jacket pockets, as if looking for the guns I'd removed. "Looking for the pistols?" I said, reaching for the .38. "This one belongs to Kelly, doesn't it? Went through her purse, didn't you, while you had her out there pickin' up sticks?"

"Think you got it all figured out, don't you?" Carl huffed. "Best be careful. Kelly could be playing you like a fiddle."

"Is that right?" I asked as if it didn't bother me.

"Might be waiting out there for you to do her dirty work. When she asked me to come down here early, could have been setting up me and you both. Stayed here just long enough to make sure you were here, then left so you could take care of business."

"What makes you think she knew I was here?"

"Said she heard noises out there in the woods. Kept looking out the window."

Carl's theory almost made sense, especially if Kelly invited herself down. Realizing my doubts, he continued, "Wondered why Kelly cleaned up after herself. Put all her cigarette butts in a cup and took it with her. Made sure she didn't leave any evidence. And if you kill me, chances are she'll nail you for murder."

I didn't answer, just sat there.

"Tell you what, Smith, untie my feet, take these cuffs off, and we'll figure this thing out together."

"Hell no. You think I'm crazy? Ain't about to let you loose."

Carl began tugging on the handcuffs.

"Kinda funny, ain't it, ex-cop like you being cuffed. How's it feel? Been beating up on any black folks lately?"

"Screw you, Smith. And Kelly too. She the one told you that?"

"No, didn't hear that from Kelly. Got my own sources."

Carl knew I referred to his getting kicked off the force for what he'd done to the black guy.

"Sonofabitch was a drug dealer. Sold drugs to kids. I didn't do nothing but rough him up."

"Yeah, but then you took his money."

"Who cares, it was drug money. Wasn't that much anyway."

"Still wasn't yours."

"Tell you right now, half the cops on the force would have done the same thing, given a chance."

"Sure, and I guess they'd rape my sister too, given a chance. You're a no-good bastard, and that's all there is to it. Don't believe any of this bullshit you've been feeding me. You're nothing but a liar."

"Tell you what, you take me to the local sheriff's office, and I'll turn myself in for my part in your sister's rape."

I took a swig of the Jim Beam, lit another cigarette, and began venting. "You got any idea how many times I visualized cutting your jugular vein just like one of those hogs at work? Or what it would be like to throw your big ass, live and kicking, down in the pre-auger and listen as the grinder cut you to pieces? Ain't never tortured anybody. Believe I can do it though."

"Listen, this needs to stop right here, before you get in too deep. My guys are gonna be here any minute."

"Is that right? I could swear I overheard them saying that they wouldn't be coming down until after work this evening. Seems to me they oughta be pulling in here about midnight."

"They took off today."

"Bullshit. If they took off, they'd been here already. All you do is lie."

Carl's face turned blank. His scared eyes stared at the heater.

I asked, "Are you cold?"

He shook his head as I stood there contemplating my next move. I turned the heater back around and shoved it up between Carl's spread legs, with the fan pointing directly at his chest. "Ever read the Bible Carl? There's a passage that says, 'do unto others as you would have them do unto you.' And since you and your buddies saw fit to burn my sister after having your way with her, well you know."

"Told you I didn't burn your sister!"

"Yeah, but you mighta lied about that like you just lied about what time your friends are gonna get here tonight."

"Don't do this, Smith. You're not that kind of person"

Ignoring Carl, I retrieved the five-gallon kerosene can from the corner and began refueling the heater. "Don't think I can do it, huh? Well, believe I've got just enough whiskey in me. But then, who knows, might not have to go that far." I set the can down, had a seat at the table, and said, "Perhaps we can cut a deal and spare your pathetic life."

"What?" Carl asked. "What kinda deal you talking about?"

"Well, let's say you was to make a confession, telling everything that went on in the attack on my sister. The rape, the beating, the burning of her arms until she went unconscious. Can you do that for me, big boy? If you do, I just might spare your sorry ass."

"Sure. I'll tell exactly what happened that night, sign anything you want. Just let me loose, and I'll write it myself."

"Oh no, boss, got a better idea."

Reaching in the backpack, I pulled out the little tape recorder. "Need this to be in your own voice so I can play it for my sister and my parents."

"No deal," he snapped. "You want a confession, it'll have to be handwritten. Ain't doing it for your damn tape recorder."

I knew of course what he wanted and wasn't about to release his hands. Not for one second. "Okay then. At least I gave you a chance." Standing back up, I stretched the heater cord to the wall socket and plugged it in.

As soon as the blower started, Carl shouted, "Turn it off!"

Entertaining the idea of watching the heater burn Carl's clothing before spreading to his flesh and hair, I waited until the flame ignited.

"Turn it off! Start the recorder! I'll give you your damn confession!"

I unplugged the heater, returned to my seat, and said, "Thought you might see it my way." Then, picking up the .44 Magnum, I pointed it at his crotch, and said, "If you hesitate to give a total, truthful, believable confession. If you even make it sound like you're being forced to give it, I'll blow your balls off and watch you bleed to death. You understand?"

Chapter 48

As Uncle Samuel had predicted, all the time I spent arranging an opportunity to speak with Carl only caused problems. Simply shooting him would have been a whole lot easier. By the time our visit got to the point of asking for a taped confession, I had enough whiskey in me to do just that. I took another drink from the bottle and even offered him one. Whiskey ran out around his mouth, dripping, as I let him get all he wanted.

"When I turn this thing on, you are to say your name and tell me the whole story of what happened that night you and your buddies attacked my sister."

With his eyes closed, Carl mumbled, "Let's get it over with."

At the sound of the record button, he took a deep breath and started. "My name is Carl Jacobs, and I'm making..."

He didn't speak loud enough to suit me, so I kicked his foot. He opened his eyes and saw my hand next to my ear. Raising his voice, he continued, "I'm making this confession to let the world know what happened one night back in 1972 when I was just nineteen years old. Me and a couple other guys—"

"Names," I mouthed.

"—their names were Pete Metcalf and Joe Simpson. We'd been drinking all afternoon when we saw this girl heading toward us on the sidewalk. It'd just gotten dark. As she walked under the streetlight, Pete said it was the girl who beat the shit out of his cousin. Said we should rough her up a bit, just to teach her a lesson. Didn't see the harm in that, but when he said he wanted to take her clothes off and leave her naked like she did his cousin, that worried me. It all

297

happened so fast, didn't really have time to think about what we were doing. We hid behind some bushes until she reached us, then Pete and Joe grabbed her. Pete put his jacket over her head so she couldn't see us, and then they dragged her out of sight. Girl started trying to scream. Joe hit her a couple times through the jacket, just to shut her up. Pete whispered he would kill her if she kept making noise. Girl got quiet."

Listening to Carl's description made me sick and angry. He tried to blame everything on Pete and Joe. I wanted to shoot him right then, but couldn't. At least not until he finished his confession.

"Pete threw her down on the ground and told me and Joe to hold her while he took her clothes off. Thought that's all we were gonna do, just pay her back, so I helped Joe hold her down, and I kept the jacket over her head. When Pete pulled off her shoes and started on her pants, she started kicking and screaming. Really pissed Pete off. He smacked her head two or three times through the jacket until she quit moving. Then he started using his knife to cut off the rest of her clothes. Before you know it she wasn't wearing anything but the jacket over her head."

Carl took a couple deep breaths before continuing. "And yes, even I commented on how good she looked. But then Pete started saying he wanted to screw her, and Joe said go for it. When Pete pulled his pants down, I let go and stood up. Scared me to death. Told him he shouldn't do it. He didn't listen. Joe held the girl's arms and kept the jacket over her head. Poor little thing tried to fight but wasn't strong enough. I just stood quiet, like a fool, like a coward. She tried to hold her legs closed, but Pete forced his way. While he was doing it he moved the jacket up enough to try and kiss her. Believe she bit him because he went crazy like an animal, started biting her all over, her lips, her neck, and her tits. After he got done, he told Joe to keep her down while he lit a cigarette. He kept puffing on it until it got real hot. Then he said, 'Now, bitch, I'll make sure you never forget this.' He started burning her arm. Told him to quit, but he wouldn't. She started trying to get loose again, but they held her down. Burned her on both arms. Girl moaned and growled, but she never once screamed. I felt sorry for her but didn't have the balls to stop 'em. Could see Pete was crazy and knew he had a gun. Guess that's why I stood there like an idiot, afraid he would kill me. Then Joe decided he wanted to do her too, and so he did. When he was done, Pete burned her again on both arms. After a while, she seemed to give up, and she quit moving. Pete wanted me to do her too. Said if I didn't they wouldn't be able to trust me."

After hesitating for a few seconds, Carl continued with his voice breaking. "Poor girl looked pitiful lying there, not moving. Didn't even need Pete or Joe to hold her. Went ahead and got on top of her like I was doing it. Never even got a hard on. Figured if it looked like I was doing it, they'd leave me alone. Heard her crying under the jacket, and it made me sick. I whispered I was sorry and rolled off. Threw up right there. When I looked back, Pete was already burning her again with the cigarette. Could smell it. I begged him to quit. He stopped after one arm. Said I didn't deserve two anyway. Girl quit moving. I thought she might be dead. Pete said she was passed out. He rolled her over on her stomach and stuck the cigarette to her butt. She still didn't move, so he picked up his jacket, and then he stood there and pissed on her. When he was finished, we just walked away and left her, naked, behind the bushes."

Carl's face looked different, like a kid confessing to his daddy, knowing he's about to get the shit kicked out of him, tears running down his cheeks. He seemed to be done, but then he added, "I was glad to hear she didn't die. Been hating myself for what she went through. And if I could talk to the lady, Sissy, I would try and make her understand that those times when she saw me, I didn't mean her any harm. Just wanted to tell her how sorry I am for what I did, for not stopping Pete and Joe from raping her. I wish there was a way she could forgive me. And that's all I've got to say."

When he finished, his head bobbed up and down. Carl cried like a baby with me watching, sick and stunned. I turned off the recorder and stuck it into my shirt pocket, under my jumpsuit.

At that moment, I didn't like who, what, or where I was. Carl's story wasn't what I expected. Part of me felt sorry for the man, but another part knew he'd lied about his involvement. Was there truly remorse, or did he just want me to let him go? If I did, would he try to kill me? Between all the bullshit and the whiskey, I didn't know what to think. My body and mind were drained as I stood, took another swig, slammed the bottle down, and went to the door for fresh air.

Looking out, everything was perfect—the sunshine, the woods. *The beautiful woods. My backyard.* Behind me lay what was maybe the ugly truth of what happened to my sister, maybe a pack of lies. At that moment, I didn't know what to believe.

Gabrielle whispered, *Would you know the truth if you heard it?*

Her questioning seemed like Sister Mary Theresa speaking in person. Without thinking, I raised my head and mumbled, "Don't know what to do. Said I might not kill him if he told the truth. But, did he? Can't believe *everything* he said. Hard to believe any of it."

"Smith, who the hell you talking to?"

I turned to see Carl's glare. The one he used at work. The one I couldn't stand.

"Looks like you're not cut out for this kind of shit," he continued. "Gettin' confused, aren't you?"

"Screw you, Carl. Only thing I'm confused about is why you didn't try harder to stop 'em."

"What would *you* have done?" he snapped back.

"By God, I'da ran. I'da ran like hell. Bastard couldn't shoot you when he was raping my sister. You should have took off and said you were going to the police. Asshole would have stopped right then, and my sister might not'a got burned. Joe would have been too scared to rape her. Your sorry ass could have gone to the cops. Then you wouldn't be here facing me."

Carl didn't answer.

Thinking about how easily he could have stopped them angered me to no end. I could hear a buzz, not like the ringing in my ears, but something mechanical. Looking around, I realized it came from the motor inside a little timer plugged into a wall outlet. It apparently controlled the outside light. The unit had a round object similar to a clock that made a revolution every twenty-four hours. Pins placed on the wheel controlled the start and stop of current. Suddenly, I had an idea.

I could set the timer to come on after my departure, unplug the light, and replace it with the cord to the Salamander heater. When the timer started the current, the heater would come on and within minutes, it would burn Carl to a crisp. That way he could get what he deserved for his part in my sister's attack, and I could be long gone when it happened.

For the first time that day, rage got the best of me. I started yelling at him, "Tell me, dammit, why didn't you run? How could you just stand there and let it happen? Turn this around. What would you be doing to me if I had let that happen to your sister, or mother, or daughter? What would you do?"

Carl didn't answer. His silence pissed me off even more. I stood there looking down at him, ready to explode. "You know Carl, I'm afraid I can't believe a word you say. Guess I'm gonna have to leave you tied up until after your friends get here."

"But you said you'd let me go."

"No. Said I'd consider letting you live if you told the truth."

"But I did tell the truth," he pleaded in an oddly calm voice. "Told you the whole story, just like it happened."

As he spoke, I reached down, picked up the plug from the heater, and took it to the timer on the wall next to the door.

"What're you doing?" Carl asked.

"I'm giving you a chance to live and a chance to die. If you told the truth about your friends arriving soon, you've got nothing to worry about. Right now this thing shows about ten 'til two." Looked at my watch. "Yep, set on slow time. Tell you what, I'm gonna set this timer for 2:30." Carl watched quietly. "If your friends arrive as you say they will, they can release you, and you'll live. I'll give Kelly a copy of your confession, and she can tell the police you killed Pete and Joe to keep 'em quiet. Maybe my family can live with that. Course, if you lied, around forty minutes from now you'll get the sentence you deserve."

"You're letting the whiskey do your talking. What if they have a flat tire? What if their car breaks down? What if—"

301

"What if I don't give a shit? A while ago, you said they'd be here any minute. Well they're not here yet. Were you lying? I believe you were. Surely they'll be here in the next forty minutes. Unless, of course, you lied. Did you lie, Carl? Have you lied about everything?"

"Listen to yourself. What's the difference between me and you? I killed Pete for what he did to Joe and for what he did to your sister. Now you wanna kill me for not stopping them, or for what you *think* I might have done. What makes you any better than me?"

"See there, believe you lied again. Don't think you killed Pete for what he did to my sister. Believe you killed him because you were afraid he'd kill you or tell the cops you killed Joe. It won't be me killing you, it'll be your lies."

I finished setting the pins for 2:30, plugged in the cord from the heater, and let it hang visibly. "Think we're done here," I said while putting the two small handguns into my backpack.

"You're making a mistake. Don't do this."

"Bet that's what my sister said when you were holding her down for Pete. And you know what they say; what goes around, comes around."

"You're screwing up. You kill me, and you'll regret it for the rest of your life. You gotta think about your wife and kid."

"Listen, you sonofabitch, I've done been thinking about all that. Been thinking about it for a long time. You, Pete, Joe, y'all got away with this shit for too long. If Pete and Joe were here right now they'd be lying too, trying to stay alive. Sure, a part of me wants to let you go, but sometimes a man's gotta do what a man's gotta do."

"You're gonna get caught." The man spoke as though he'd accepted the fact that he was going to die. "In the end we all do. Won't take homicide five minutes to see you've been here. Kelly knew it, and they will too. Hell, bet she knows right where you were hiding out there. They'll have you nailed in a heartbeat. Who'll take care of your wife and that little girl when they send you to prison for the rest of your life?"

"Shut up, dammit, or I'll shoot you right now." Though I didn't like hearing the things Carl had to say, he did remind me of one thing. I needed to clean up in the cabin and outside. After gathering all my cigarette butts, I wiped off the whiskey bottle, cabinet handles, and anything else I thought might have fingerprints. Then I grabbed my backpack and stepped out the door. My shotgun still leaned against the cabin.

Carl yelled, "Better not leave anything, Smith! They'll nail you for sure!"

I walked quickly to the blind, glancing around to see what, if anything, the cops might catch. At first, I thought only the rifle, my blanket and the plastic under it. Then, while folding and stuffing things into my backpack, I noticed half a cigarette next to the rocks. "How dumb can you be?"

By the time I finished spreading leaves and several branches, the area looked pretty much the way it did before my arrival. I slipped on the backpack, picked up the rifle, and started back to the cabin. Time was running out. I needed to grab my shotgun and get moving toward the Jeep before the fire started.

Back at the cabin, I pushed the door open and couldn't believe my eyes. In the short time I'd been gone, Carl had pulled the bed away from the wall about three feet, creating slack in the ropes on his legs. "What the hell are you doing?"

It didn't make sense. He had pushed the heater aside and had his legs wrapped around the kerosene can, jerking it toward himself, splashing fuel onto his jacket. When I yelled, he stopped, leaving the can to rest directly in front of him.

I dropped both rifle and backpack, drew the .44 Magnum, and said, "Damn, Carl. Don't know what the hell you're up to, but it's only gonna make you burn faster."

"Smith," he said, "don't shoot me. If I have to die, you surely can give me a chance to say my piece."

Cautiously, I stepped inside the cabin, leery of what he might be up to, and thinking, *Maybe he dowsed himself with kerosene hoping he'd die quicker?* Curious, I listened.

"Been around you enough to know you're not a bad person. Do this and it'll ruin your life, and you'll be just like me. Sure, I should have tried to stop Pete, shoulda ran, shoulda got the cops, but I didn't. It's always easy to look back. But when you're there, and everything happens so fast, it's hard not to panic. I got scared and made a big mistake, and now look. Look at what it's cost me. No wife. No kids. Nothing. And you're right, I *am* a sick man."

Carl turned his head, stretched his neck as far as he could and began tugging at his coat sleeve with his teeth. And yes, he did look like a wild, sick person as he gnawed and pulled. Within seconds his purpose became obvious as he managed to expose some of the burn marks he'd spoken of. Little white scars like Sissy's.

He turned back to face me, wild eyed, and said, "See there, it's not a lie. Got more on the other arm. It is sick, ain't it? Think about it Smith, I can't even get it up for Kelly, the only woman I ever really cared about. But you, you have it all. You have a beautiful wife, a precious little girl, and a life I could never have."

With a lump in my throat, I listened as Carl rattled on. What he said made sense, but it still sounded like one last attempt at getting me to let him live.

"Hard enough just having your sister on my mind, but then I went and killed Pete. Since that day, my life's been over. And look at you, all pissed off and about to make the same mistake. We both know it's time for me to die. Been wanting to do it myself, just ain't had the guts. But I can't let you do it. Can't let you ruin your life like I did. Kill me and it's all over for you. We shouldn't both go to hell over this shit."

Before I realized what he was doing, Carl used his feet to shove the kerosene can forward, hard, away from his body. It seemed like slow motion, standing there watching the five gallon can slide across the cabin's wooden floor toward the fireplace. Upon hitting the stone hearth, the can tipped forward, splashing kerosene into the hot embers. Flames erupted, spreading quickly as fuel emptied onto the floor, running back toward Carl.

"Get outta here!" he screamed. "Save yourself!"

In all my preparations, I never dreamed the man would attempt suicide to prevent me from executing what in his mind amounted to murder. I had longed to see Carl die and yet in the moment of truth, I instinctively began thinking of how to save him. I holstered the gun and pulled out my knife. I went to his feet, one of which was already burning. Cut the right rope. Before I could reach through flames to the other, Carl kicked me in the chest so hard I fell backwards.

"Get the hell out of here!"

Fire reached the ceiling. Burning kerosene spread up his pants like a fuse. "Tell Kelly I loved her!" He squirmed in pain. "Tell her I'm not the monster she thought I was!"

I climbed back to my feet and watched Carl's fuel-soaked jacket ignite.

"Tell Sissy the scars are gone. I'm burning them awa—"

Flames engulfed his body, and he bawled out like a dying steer.

I stood there helpless, just as he had on the night of my sister's attack. Smoke began to fill the room, and I squatted, staring. The moment I'd fantasized became a terrifying reality. Gabrielle's words ripped through my mind. *This is what you wanted. You played God, and this is the hell you created.*

The wall behind me caught fire, spreading over the doorway. Coughing, I pulled the door open and crawled out, glancing back at Carl's lifeless body burning. I quickly gathered my gear and fled. Fifteen feet into the woods, I stopped to look back. Flames blazed in the window, smoke seeping out. In my mind, Carl floated, free, away from his tortured past. One minute, I was like Lot's wife, frozen, staring, tasting my own salt. The next, I ran. Ran like the chicken I accused Carl of being. Ran like the criminal Carl sacrificed himself to prevent me from becoming.

Chapter 49

Bare branches beat me all the way to the Jeep. With hands shaking uncontrollably, I dug the keys from within the jumpsuit, opened the hatch, and threw in my gear.

Still coughing and breathing heavily, I sat in the driver's seat trying to gain composure. With the sleeve of my jumpsuit, I wiped my face. Anxious moments flashed by as I started the Jeep's engine, shoved it in gear, and bounced through the woods. Right before the blacktop, I stopped and rolled down the window to listen for approaching vehicles. There were none. Somehow, I forced myself to drive away at a normal speed.

Reaching the curve at the top of the hill, I looked back at smoke rising above the leafless woods and began wondering how long it would take before someone noticed. Another quarter mile down the road, a pickup truck drove in my direction. I returned a wave to the old man driving, hoping he wouldn't remember me or the Jeep. *He surely will see the smoke.*

It only took a few minutes to reach Uncle Bart's place. Two more vehicles had passed along the way. I didn't recognize either one. I spent those fleeting moments trying to convince myself that regardless of how it happened, Carl was dead, and I had his taped confession. His final screaming words were stuck in my head as I scooted up Uncle Bart's gravel lane. Max, not recognizing the Jeep, left the porch and started barking. I drove right past the house and made a beeline for the tobacco barn's open doors.

Max remained outside, continuing his tirade as the V8 ceased, popping and crackling its relief. Within seconds, Uncle Bart appeared in the rearview mirror, closing the barn doors. It got dark, but only long enough for him to reach the light. He came to the Jeep and stood, staring through the window. I sat exhausted, with no desire to face him or Aunt Mary. When he opened the door, I asked, "You got a cigarette? Mine are all gone."

"Goddamn boy, you smell like a burnt whiskey barrel," he said while offering me a Winston. "Hope you didn't mess things up."

Without getting out of the Jeep, I lit the cigarette and said, "Believe everything's gonna be all right."

"Believe? What the hell's that mean? You either did it, or you didn't."

Jesus, he wants details. "It's been a rough day. Can you give me a few minutes?"

"Oh, my God, this don't sound good. Come on out of there, boy. Gotta see if you can stand up."

I crawled out of the Jeep. "Where's that bottle of 'shine? Believe you and me oughta have a little drink."

"Huh, I'd say you've done had enough. Need to go to the house and clean up. You look like shit. Never can tell when someone might stop by."

We left the barn, walking together toward the porch. Halfway there I stopped to look north. Dark smoke ascended in the distance.

Seeing my stare, Uncle Bart looked also. "Don't tell me that's the Henderson place."

All I said was, "It's over."

"Goddamn boy, did you have to go and burn the place?"

Without answering, I started toward the house. As I neared the porch, Aunt Mary came to the door.

"See any deer?"

I tried to look straight. "Sure did, saw one small buck and some does."

"Looks like you're beat," she added.

"Yes ma'am, I am. Thought I might go clean up and lay down until milk time."

"You go right ahead," said Uncle Bart.

"Are you hungry?" asked Aunt Mary. "Got some good salami and a hothouse tomato."

"Sounds good. My stomach's empty."

As Aunt Mary headed off to the kitchen, Uncle Bart stood wordlessly, staring at the distant smoke. A few seconds later, we both looked up at the sound of a roar coming from the main road. Soon a pickup sped into sight, closely followed by another. Both honked their horns loud and long as they drove by.

Uncle Bart said, "Looks like the word's out. Reckon I oughta head that way. At least offer a hand."

"Won't be anything left."

"Good, now you go on in there and get cleaned up."

Aunt Mary came back to the door. "What's all the noise?"

Uncle Bart answered, "Looks like a fire burning up north. Reckon I oughta run up there and see if there's anything I can do."

"Gonna take Johnny with you?"

After looking back at me, he said, "No, boy looks beat. Probably ain't much we can do anyway."

Uncle Bart took off in his truck with Aunt Mary and me standing on the porch watching. When he made the turn out of sight, she gave me a long, hard look.

I tried to ignored her stare. "How about that sandwich?"

Without saying anything, Aunt Mary entered the house and headed toward the kitchen. I flicked my cigarette into the gravel, took one last glance at the smoke, and then followed, stopping at the bathroom.

Bloodshot eyes and smeared face-paint stared back from the mirror. "Jesus." The warm water felt good on my face. I needed a bath but didn't have the energy.

In the kitchen, Aunt Mary remained standing, staring as I ate the salami sandwich. It was obvious she had something on her mind. Finally, she speculated. "Probably ain't none of my business, but I want you to know I'm not dense. You coming in here all liquored up, smellin' like smoke. Know damn well you ain't been out huntin'. *Hope* you ain't out there carryin' a gun and drinkin' at the same time. Know your daddy taught you better than that."

She waited for a comment, but I had none until she said, "Tell me Johnny, you know somethin' about that fire burnin' up north?"

"You were right, good salami. And not bad for a hothouse tomato."

Aunt Mary caught the hint and simply said, "Want another?"

"No ma'am, think I'm gonna take a nap."

As I stood to leave the kitchen, she gave me a hug. "Trust you ain't done nothin' out of line. You feel a need to talk, I'll be here."

I kissed her on the cheek and said, "Thanks, love you, and I'll remember that."

She squeezed me tight, let go quick, and said, "Damn, boy, you need a bath."

"Yeah, believe I'll wait 'til after my nap. Make sure you wake me up before milk time."

"We'll see."

On my way up the stairs, Aunt Mary hollered from the kitchen, "Jane called a little while ago, said she and the baby gonna be down by six."

"Good."

In the upstairs bedroom, I opened the curtains to get a view of the skyline. The smoke had lessened, but still continued. Apparently the flames had been contained to the cabin clearing.

It was all I could do to slip out of my boots and the jumpsuit. Leaning back on the bed, I pulled the tape recorder from my shirt pocket and held down the rewind button for a second. Hit play and heard Carl's voice. "And that's all I've got to say." Rewound again, "that's all I've got to say." Again, "And that's all I've got to say."

As I stared at the recorder, my mind drifted. *Do I really wanna let Pop and his brothers hear this? No one's gonna believe Carl set himself on fire. If they hear this, they might think I killed the man needlessly. And, I just might have.* I rolled over on the bed and stuck it between the mattress and box springs.

Chapter 50

Jane shook me once and then opened the shade, allowing in way too much sunshine. I lay there in the bed, slightly moaning.

"Wake up, honey," She tried to bring me around. "You been asleep so long I'm beginnin' to worry. We done got the milkin' finished and Mama's puttin' a late breakfast on the table. You oughta come on down and eat."

Breakfast?

"Come on Johnny, brought you a cup of coffee. Now you get your sorry butt up out of that bed."

"Okay, okay, go away. Be down in a minute." As she left the room I said, "Hey, I'm all out of cigarettes. Got any on you?"

"Mine are downstairs. Believe I seen a pack of yours out in the car, in the console."

"Good. Love ya. Where's Christine?"

"She's in the kitchen with Mama, wonderin' where her daddy is."

Yawning, I said, "Tell her I'll be down in a minute. And, thanks for the coffee."

"You're welcome. Now don't you lay there and let it get cold."

For a minute or so, I remained in bed, visualizing events from the day before—flashes of the burning cabin and Carl's face engulfed in flames. Although I was still in my clothes, somebody, probably Jane, had covered me with a quilt. I sat up shivering, and not just from the cold. Christine's sweet giggle rose from the kitchen. *Gotta get moving. Gotta talk to Uncle Bart, find out what he saw or heard.*

I rolled off the featherbed and looked through the window as though expecting to see smoke. Nothing but clear skies and sunshine so bright I had to squint.

Back on the edge of the bed, I pulled on my boots. *Jane didn't mention the fire. Does that mean her parents avoided telling her about it?*

Hot coffee hit the spot. "Aaaugh, need about a gallon of this." Finally I headed downstairs, cup in hand, hung over as hell. On my way out the front door, I called toward the kitchen, "Be right back, gonna smoke a cigarette."

Sunshine knocked off some of the November chill, and a lack of wind made it even better. Shaded spots of frost still lingered across the yard. I sat my cup on the porch next to the steps before walking to the car. The pack of Marlboros lay right where Jane said they'd be. "Thank God."

I fired one up before stepping to the side of the house. I heard a gunshot blast from the direction of Uncle Willie's place. *That's where I should be this morning, out huntin' deer.* Standing there empting my bladder, I noticed my feet were wearing western boots instead of my combat boots. That's when it dawned on me that I hadn't seen my jumpsuit in the bedroom. *Must have been Uncle Bart covering my ass.*

At the porch, Max had his nose down, sniffing my coffee. "Back off, pal, I need every drop of that." I sat on the porch, feet on the steps, and the old dog laid his head in my lap. "What's wrong, buddy, nobody give you any attention this morning?" I scratched Max's head while finishing my coffee and cigarette.

On my way back into the house, I stepped into the bathroom long enough to wash my hands and face. A glance in the mirror revealed little change from the day before. *What a mess.* Whiskey eyes, hair looking like Einstein on a bad day, and a neck full of two-day-old whiskers.

The aroma of Aunt Mary's breakfast lacked its normal appeal. I pushed myself to the kitchen anyway. Christine's pretty little face greeted me from a high chair. Rubbing my beard into her neck brought smiles and giggles. I patted Jane on the butt. Poured myself another cup. Everyone took turns saying, "Good morning."

The table was full of biscuits, gravy, sausage, and scrambled eggs.

Uncle Bart said, "Don't believe I ever known a man to sleep that long."

"Sorry about that. Didn't mean to miss the milking."

"Mama says you come in all liquored up," nagged Jane. "Thought you and your daddy were goin' lookin' for deer."

Both Uncle Bart and Aunt Mary sat waiting for my lie. Fortunately, the phone rang, and Jane, of course, jumped to answer.

"Hello.... Is that right? Okay, Uncle Willie, we'll do that. Bye, bye." Such a short conversation seemed odd. We all waited like schoolchildren for an explanation. Jane spoke while turning on the radio. "Uncle Willie says we should listen to the news."

"Why's that, honey?" asked Aunt Mary.

"They're supposed to talk about some hunter that got burnt up in a cabin yesterday not far from here."

I buttered my thumb instead of the biscuit, thinking, *Here we go.*

Uncle Bart reached over and wiped the butter away with a napkin.

"Believe I can do that myself."

"That's okay, I'm gettin' used to cleaning up after you."

Jane stared at Uncle Bart's comment.

When the Leitchfield station finished its commercials, a newsman started. "Goooood Saturday morning, this is David Clemons with local news. Last night we reported that a man had died when a cabin off Highway 728 near Nolin Lake burned to the ground. State Fire Marshal Leroy Adkins says they are investigating to see if arson might have been a factor."

Aunt Mary turned my way. I avoided her stare as I listened to the newsman.

"State police are revealing only that the vehicle found at the cabin is registered to a Louisville man. They suspect the vehicle belongs to the deceased but are withholding details pending identification. Officials are asking anyone who has information that might assist in the investigation to call the Kentucky State Police in E-Town or the

Grayson County Sheriff's Department. In other news, Jake Colepepper, from Big Clifty, has filed a lawsuit against his neighbor Charlie Boone. Colepepper says his prize-winning Angus gave birth to a spotted calf. He blames Charlie Boone for allowing his Holstein bull to gain access to the Angus herd. Mr. Boone of course blames it on Jake's fence being down. And now, for a look at today's weather."

"Turn that thing off," scoffed Uncle Bart. "Don't care to hear about the Hatfields and McCoys feudin' over that damn spotted calf. Done heard all about it last week in town at the barbershop."

Jane switched off the radio. "Daddy, you know anything about that fire?"

"Yeah, I do. Matter of fact, I went up there and helped keep the flames from spreading into the woods. Wasn't nothin' we could do about the cabin. Whoever started the fire made sure of that."

"Did you see the dead man?"

"No. Roof was sittin' down on the ground when I left. Reckon they had to wait for it to cool before gettin' inside."

I wished someone would change the subject. Jane looked my way and asked, "You go help daddy with the fire?"

"Hell no," answered Uncle Bart quickly, "Boy was near ready to pass out when I left."

Jane scolded, "Can't believe your daddy let you get all liquored up like that. And why didn't he stay to deer hunt this morning? Did he even come over here? Ain't like him to run back to Louisville so quick." Question after question.

Aunt Mary said, "Jane honey, you mind if we eat in peace? We can talk about all this later. I'm sure it'll be all over the TV news this evening."

Jane gave me a glare. "Well, all righty then. But we *will* talk about this later."

Uncle Bart led us in grace, and we had our breakfast without further mention of the newscast.

Distant gunshots rumbled throughout the morning. Thoughts kept popping up in my mind of Carl and his friends and how they would be hunting were it not for me. It worried me half sick, thinking I might have left something in or around the cabin that could be used to identify me. I wanted to drive back over just to see, but knew better.

That evening, Channel 11 news reported, "A Louisville man, identified as Carl Jacobs, burned to death yesterday in a cabin in Grayson County in what police and fire officials now consider a case of arson and homicide. Jacobs and two other men were to share the cabin for the opening weekend of deer season. A spokesperson for the State Fire Marshal's office says area residents spotted smoke around 2:30 p.m. Central Time. State police say Jacobs had been handcuffed to a bed in the cabin and apparently dowsed with kerosene before the fire started. The deceased and his two hunting companions worked together at a packinghouse here in Louisville..."

Right away, Jane asked, "Is that the same Carl Jacobs who came to Masterson's?"

Uncle Bart looked like a deer in headlights. I had to say something. "Hang on honey, wanna hear this."

"...According to the Grayson County Coroner, Jacobs' body had been burned so badly that it had to be sent to Louisville for identification using dental records. Steven Brown, one of the two men who planned to hunt with Jacobs, stated that Jacobs came down earlier in the day to set things up, but may have been meeting with a woman."

Uncle Bart looked at me as if to say, "*Woman?*"

"State Police were called to the scene, but declined to elaborate pending investigation."

I thought, *Huh, guess they'll be looking for a woman?* Then I saw Jane's stare.

Later that night, as we prepared for bed, she asked, "Honey, you know something about what happened to that man yesterday?"

"Why would you ask such a question?"

"When I gave you a kiss this morning, I noticed your hair smelled like smoke, and it wasn't no cigarette."

I hesitated and then asked, "Do you trust me?"

"Depends."

"On what?"

"Did you and your daddy kill that guy?"

"No, we did not."

For a moment, she stood silently in front of the window, as if staring out into the darkness. While I lay there trying to read her mind, she turned, let her gown drop to the floor, slid into the bed, and kissed me."

I returned her kiss and whispered, "I love you."

"You better, by God."

The next afternoon on our way home, I expected Jane would bring up Carl's death, but she didn't. A few days later, however, she dropped the newspaper in front of me as I drank my morning coffee. Pointing at the headline, she said, "You need to read this."

Louisville man burned in cabin
Apparently executed

In the case of a local man, Carl Jacobs, found burnt to death last week in a hunting cabin in Grayson County, the Coroner's office reports finding signs of the victim having been injected with a drug sometime in the hours before his death. Toxicology reports revealed alcohol and traces of a sedative commonly used to tranquilize animals, in Jacob's system. Police suspect the drug may have been used to subdue the victim long enough to restrain him. His charred body was found handcuffed to a bed. A spokesperson for the Kentucky State Police said, "Jacobs, a former Louisville Police Officer had been under investigation for several rapes in the Louisville area, and was also a suspect in the double murder of two fellow packinghouse employees in 1977." Police suspect Jacobs' execution-style death may have been in retaliation for one or more of these crimes.

As I read, Jane pretended to clean the stove. When I lit a cigarette, she said, "Reckon your sister can sleep better now." After that, Jane never mentioned Carl Jacob's death again.

Chapter 51

About three weeks after Carl's death, I was working 2nd shift when I got a call from Kelly Rauschenberg. She wanted to meet for a drink at a Louisville nightspot called Jim Porter's. It was a conversation I'd been dreading, though expecting. I phoned Jane to let her know I'd be stopping after work. I arrived at Jim Porter's at around 11:30 p.m.

Thursday night drink specials had provided a huge crowd of middle-aged women being wooed by a bunch of horn-doggin' men. While staring over my first sip of whiskey, I spotted the good detective and someone else sharing a booth. From that spot, I could not identify the other person. Memories surfaced from my 21st birthday when the sexy Kelly shared a booth with me. I asked myself, *How can we talk about Carl with someone else present?*

Kelly's expressions led me to think she might be on the prowl for, well, for something. By moving several feet down the bar, I was able to recognize the other person; Paula Dawson, minus half her hair. I found the new look attractive, yet a bit disappointing. While watching the two, old suspicions resurfaced, and for a moment I fantasized about them being together. A tug of war ensued between Gabrielle and Jim Beam. Jimmy won.

Alcohol had obviously not dampened Kelly's senses. She spotted me well before I reached the table and alerted Paula, who turned to look my way. They were dressed similar in blue jeans, western boots, and a black shirt.

"Well helllooo, Johnny Smith. Nice to see you," Kelly said as she slid over, allowing me a seat.

I sat down, drink in hand, looked across the table at Paula and said, "Damn, almost didn't recognize you."

"Well, what do you think?" she asked.

"About what?"

"My *hair*, silly. Do you like it?"

"Looks nice, but as you know, I'm partial to long hair."

"Speaking of," she slurred, "where *is* that hot little wife of yours?"

"Home. Sleeping. She has to get up early."

Kelly spoke again, "So while the wife sleeps, you're out looking for trouble?"

"Not really. Wouldn't be here if you hadn't called."

Paula, with her blouse half open, continued with a tease from the past. "So, can you come outside and play? Maybe we can make it worth your while."

I set my drink on the table, lit a cigarette, and replied, "That mean you've got another joint you'd like to share?"

"Noooo honey, but I've got somethin' better. I've got Kelly. And *I* know that *you* know that she's better than any ol' joint."

Paula seemed to be confirming my earlier suspicions about the two of them. Kelly appeared pleased with the idea and began running an index finger up and down my pants leg. Ignoring the rub, I joked, "Daggonit, Paula, think I'm gonna have to pass, even though I must say you and I have always had the same taste in women."

"My, my," chimed Kelly, "the boy still has a wit."

It surprised me that neither lady spoke of Carl's death. When Kelly's fingers got too close for comfort, I began looking for a way out.

"You know, a few years ago I might have taken y'all up on such a good offer. But things just aren't the same as they were back then."

"Your wife should be pleased to have a good boy like you," Kelly sassed.

"Thanks. I'll take that as a compliment." I downed the rest of my drink and said, "Guess I should get out of here and leave you two alone."

317

"Hold on now," Kelly snapped in her cop tone. "Don't you think we need to talk about something?"

"We?" I asked, glancing toward Paula.

"Shit Johnny, she knows what's going on. Don't be so uptight."

I grinned and joked, "Either of you ladies wearing a wire?"

Paula popped two more buttons on her blouse and pulled it open exposing most of what I always had wanted to see. Fortunately, our booth provided some privacy. While staring at Paula, I said, "So, Kelly, what is it you wanna talk about?"

"Well, let me start by saying I figured it was you or one of your people hiding out in those woods. That's why I didn't kill Carl myself."

Sure, I thought, *that and the fact that Carl stole your gun.* I listened as Kelly rambled on, surprised at her speaking so boldly.

"Couldn't do anything knowing someone might be watching. Had to hop in the sack with him before leaving, hoping he wouldn't become suspicious. Certainly didn't want to mess things up for whoever hid in the woods. Believe now it must have been you. Your uncles or daddy wouldn't do it that way. They would have shot the bastard and been done with it. Of course, you had to tie him up and talk a while, didn't you?"

Not wanting to answer, I said, "Can you keep it down a bit? Don't think we want people hearing this stuff."

Paula listened quietly as Kelly continued in a loud whisper. "Tell me, Johnny, what'd ol' Carl have to say? Did he confess?"

Still not knowing for sure if Kelly could be trusted, I tried to pick my words wisely.

"So, how *is* the investigation going? Police got any suspects? Are they looking for that woman the newspaper talked about?"

She grinned. "Told you they would look the other way on this one. Won't be any serious investigation. They're just glad to have that bastard off the street. You can tell your sister it's over, nothing to worry about. All three of those dirty sonofabitches are dead."

"That's a good thing , I guess. But now that it's all over, there are some things that still bug me."

"Like what?" Kelly asked.

"Like the day you interviewed me at work, back when Pete and Joe got killed. How'd you know that it involved me? Paula wasn't supposed to mention any of our names."

"And I didn't," blurted Paula.

"Then how did Kelly already know their deaths somehow involved my sister?"

Kelly spoke quietly, "Thought I explained that at our meeting at Grayson Springs."

"Refresh me."

Kelly described exactly what was in Paula's note, reassuring me that the only names on it were Sissy's, Pete's, and Joe's. She spoke in detail about discovering that the evidence had gotten stolen from the property room and how she couldn't trust any of the men in the department. When her boss mentioned the deaths of Pete Metcalf and Joe Simpson, she simply put two and two together.

Paula told me her side of the meeting at Iroquois Park with Uncle Samuel, and then Kelly described her meeting with Carl at the river; how she had mentioned Pete and Joe's names without dreaming he was involved.

Kelly finished saying, "All makes sense now, doesn't it?"

"Somewhat," I replied, "but there *is* something else you need to know." I glanced at Paula and then back at Kelly. "Both of you. But you gotta swear you won't repeat a word of it." I looked at Paula again and said, "Not even to my family."

Paula leaned toward the middle of the table to hear me better.

"Carl did give a confession. Said he was present but didn't actually rape my sister. Said he didn't burn her either. Claimed he just stood there, scared to death, afraid to try and stop them or to run because Pete had a gun."

"No, he lied," Kelly mumbled.

"Hear me out," I continued. "I asked him about stalking Sissy, and he said he wasn't stalking her, just following, trying to get up the nerve to talk to her. He wanted to apologize for his part in the attack and for not stopping what happened to her."

319

"Give me a break," Kelly said out loud. "I don't believe a word of that."

Paula added, "Mighty convenient for him to say them things when there's no one alive to dispute it."

"I didn't believe him either until it was too late. Now I do. Listen, if I told y'all everything, you wouldn't believe me. But I will tell you that Carl didn't mind dying. Just wanted it all over with. Said his life wasn't worth living anyway, what with feeling guilty about what happened to my sister and then killing Pete."

"What about the other guy, Joe?" Kelly asked.

"Carl says Pete shot Joe because he wouldn't shut up. Kept accusing him of raping other women. When Carl told Pete he was gonna turn him in for shooting Joe, well, one thing led to another. Pete tried to shoot Carl. Carl shot Pete in self defense."

"Still sounds too convenient," reasoned Kelly.

"I hear ya, but there's more." I took a deep breath. "When Carl sat there burning, knowing he had only seconds to live, he shouted out, 'Tell Kelly I love her, and tell her I'm not the monster she thinks I am.' It appeared that in his final moments, the man worried more about you and my sister than himself. He swore over and over that he never raped Sissy or any other woman. And another thing. Carl told me he couldn't have a normal relationship with *any* woman because of his involvement with my sister's attack. Said every time he tried, he thought about Sissy and couldn't do it. So, is there any truth in that statement?"

Without speaking Kelly nodded, nervously lit a cigarette, and said, "Sounds like he had you convinced."

"Not at first, but now that I've had time to think it over, don't know how to explain it. But, I've got a gut feeling that we all made a big mistake."

Neither lady spoke. Both seemed suddenly sober. I picked up my cigarettes to walk away but hesitated long enough to ask, "Did you know he had scars on his arms? Said he burned himself every time he saw Sissy, some kind of punishment for what he did or didn't do."

Paula looked at Kelly for an answer. "Well?"

Kelly shook her head, "No, I never saw scars. Carl never took his shirt off. Guess now I know why. But think about it, if I *had* seen burn marks on his arms it would have only made me more suspicious."

She had a good point, but it didn't change the truth, and I could see the worry in her eyes. I couldn't stand any more. I had to leave. Paula had glassy eyes. I bent over, gave her a hug, and said, "Nice to see you again. I'll tell Jane you said hi."

Then I remembered the gun. Leaning close to Kelly, I whispered, "By the way, that little snub-nose .38 of yours is in a safe place, and my family thanks you for looking the other way."

Kelly squinted and said, "I kept my word. Expect your family will do the same."

She had a tear running down the side of her face. I wiped it away gently with my thumb and said, "They will. And I hope they never know the whole truth. But you and I, we have to live with what we've done."

With no more to say, I turned and walked without looking back.

Chapter 52

That Christmas, I invited Sissy out to my car. After telling her what Carl said in his final moments, I played the tape. What should have been closure seemed more like a reminder. It about killed me, watching her, eyes closed, apparently reliving the awful experience while listening to Carl's voice. By the time he was done, she wept uncontrollably. I cried too as Sissy curled into my arms and rocked like a baby.

Eventually she sat up, wiped her face, and said, "Me and Mike saw that on the news, about him burning up in a cabin. Knew right away it was him."

"Figured you might make the connection."

"But," she added, "they said two more men came down there to hunt with him. You sure they're not the other two that raped me?"

"Yes, I'm certain. Done told you once, those other two guys are dead. Have been for some time."

"Oh God Johnny, I'm so sorry you had to go through all this."

"Girl," I replied, "don't you worry about me. I'll be fine."

"Did you play that tape for Mom and Dad?"

"No, and I really don't want to. I'm just glad it's over. But I do need to ask you something. Did Carl lie in his confession? Was it like he described it? Did he rape you?"

Sissy closed her eyes again, tears squeezing out the edges and running down her cheeks. "I'm sorry, but that man just described things I've tried to forget."

"But did he lie?"

She began rocking again, staring out the side window. Her voice trembled as she said, "No. He didn't lie. It was just like he said it. I tried so hard to erase that night. Completely forgot about that man saying he didn't wanna do it. I was hurtin' so bad by then, didn't matter. Just wanted 'em to kill me and get it over with. But Johnny, that man helped 'em take my clothes off. Why didn't he stop 'em?"

Though my sister's tears ran freely, I still had to ask, "Can you remember, did he really whisper, 'I'm sorry,' while he was on top of you?"

Sissy didn't speak, only closed her eyes as if thinking. After a few seconds she nodded yes and then covered her face with her hands.

She'd had enough. I wanted to ask about the scar on her butt, but I couldn't. If it wasn't true, she would have told me. I held her for the longest time until Mike came looking. When he opened the door, Sissy struggled to be strong. She raised her head, wiped away tears, and said, "I'm okay. No more worrying."

Mike understood without questioning.

Two days after that same Christmas, my guilt was confirmed, and I shed my last tears concerning Carl Jacobs. A headline in the Courier Journal read:

FBI takes over Louisville case
December Rapist strikes again

I knew what it meant even before reading the article. Carl Jacobs was not the December Rapist. Using my pocket knife, I cut the article from the paper, folded it, and slid it under items in my wallet.

For the longest time, I anticipated the elders would summon me to the barn to discuss the article and to grill me about what had happened at the cabin. They never did. To this day, I do not know if Paula told them about my conversation with her and Kelly at Jim Porter's.

Generations of honorable men from Grayson County, Kentucky have served justice as needed for their next of kin. Cousin Jake and I may well be the last to crawl those underground halls of justice created by my uncles. As our elders grow old and go to sleep on Bear Creek Hill, may they rest in peace with the belief that someone remains ready and willing to protect our families.

Fortunately, it has been years since any of us felt the need to practice backwoods law. For you my son, I can only hope that after reading these pages, you will consider the consequences of taking the law into one's own hands. Like me, your roots are in Grayson County. The blood of my ancestors flows through your veins. I pray the day never comes when a family member has been wronged and justice goes unserved, for as sure as I am alive at this moment, you will have the instinct to act.

My advice is simple: always, always allow the law to work in the way it is intended. In today's world a man must think long and hard before crossing the line. Consider all consequences. Never act in haste. If in doubt, don't act. Avoid becoming that which you strive to destroy. Be wise; learn from the mistakes of others. Make damn sure that you are accurate in your assessment of another man. Do not become judge and jury without all the facts. Even when you think you have all the facts, you probably do not.

When Carl Jacobs killed Pete Metcalf, he did the world a favor. Carl may have deserved punishment for his part in the attack on Sissy, but certainly not the death penalty. Mistakes were made. Kelly Rauschenberg, a sincere woman, wanted to protect other women so badly that it clouded her judgment. In analyzing an odd set of circumstances, she falsely associated one man's strange behavior with the crimes of another. The elders accepted her reasoning and did not confront the accused before condemning him. If they knew the whole truth, my father and his brothers would likely blame themselves. For that reason, I never volunteered the details of that day.

As November 11, 1983 unfolded, I sensed something was wrong, yet I continued. In my uncertainty, I failed the test of reason. I choose to believe that in the end, Carl sacrificed himself so that I might not wind up like him. Unfortunately, in a way I have. December lies where the snakes should have been.

Six Little Scars

From time to time, you may hear fathers and brothers say, "I know what I'd do if it were someone I love." While their intentions are sincere, such words should be heard as evidence of love and pain. Most are simply venting.

Keep in mind that life is short. What's done is done. If it is a matter of securing your family's safety, you may want to act. Otherwise, it might be easier to live with the scars of someone else's wrong than to create your own. Anger diminishes over time, but guilt never goes away. Do not jeopardize your own well-being, or that of a loved one, for a careless moment of revenge. It will never be worth the sacrifice. Regardless of my efforts, Sissy still carries her scars.

John L. Smith
October 30, 2006

Ron Gambrell

PART III

Matthew Smith
After re-reading my father's story.

Chapter 1

Like father, like son. Here I sit scribbling, thinking. When I was young, following Dad around like a puppy, he used to say, "A smart man learns from his own mistakes, but a wise man learns from the mistakes of others." It made sense that he would want me to read about his past so I could learn from it. When they found Carl's charred body, who would have believed Father's version of what had happened? That he hadn't tortured and killed him. He was always a careful man. That's why he wanted me to burn his yellow tablets to protect those involved directly or indirectly: Mother, Sissy, the Elders, Paula Dawson, and Detective Kelly Rauschenberg. In Mother's secret readings, I hope she read what I thought were the best parts, the twists and turns of her and Dad's relationship and how fate had brought them together.

During my second reading I found myself focusing more on the details of my mother's ancestry: how she'd been adopted and how my father had promised to find the grave of her real mother, but never did. For years, both my parents had buried their pasts. I guess you could say Father dug his up by writing it all down in those final months. On his deathbed, drugged and delirious, when Dad uttered the word, "promise," either he was reliving his promise to my mother or he was attempting to pass it on to me.

When I had finally finished the second reading and returned to the bedroom, sunshine bled around the blinds. My wife, Lori, sat upright, back braced by pillows against the headboard, nursing the baby.

"Can't believe you're just now going to bed," she mumbled.

Instead of acknowledging her, I crawled under the covers and attempted to use her legs to warm my cold feet.

"Damn you," she protested. "You did that on purpose."

Stretching my neck, I kissed the back of Daniel's hungry little head and then Lori's arm before rolling over to face the windows. Within seconds, I fell asleep, without whiskey.

Six hours later, when I came back to life, Lori vented. "If you think I'm going to raise my son with a man who drinks all night and sleeps all day, you're wrong."

I deserved every slashing word, but was in no mood to hear it.

"I lived with this shit when I was a kid," she continued, "Now it's beginning to feel like I married my father."

Somehow, I kept my cool. Moments later, Lori stormed out with Daniel, saying she was going to her mother's. Actually, her leaving gave me an opportunity to research some of what I'd read the night before. With a fresh pot of coffee brewing, I dived into the internet.

At around 4:30 p.m., as I spoke on the phone, a rapid knocking startled me. "Could you hold just a second, please? I have a visitor."

When I opened the back door, my mother walked right in accompanied by a blast of cold air.

"Mom?" I motioned for her to sit at the table. Speaking into the phone, I said, "I'm sorry. My mother just stopped by. Could I call you back later? Sure. Thank you very much for your time. Bye."

I hung up, turned, and said, "Well good morning, I mean afternoon. Didn't expect you."

"Is it good?" she replied, while removing her jacket.

Without answering, I poured us both a cup of coffee, took a seat, and said, "You can add your own sugar."

Still standing, she said, "Don't you act like nothing's wrong. I just got off the phone with Lori."

"Is that right?"

"She says you're a mess, and from the look of you I'd say she's right."

I hadn't shaved, my hair was uncombed, and I wore yesterday's wrinkled jeans and t-shirt. "Wasn't anticipating any company," I explained.

Finally sitting down, she spooned in sugar and began stirring her coffee. "I've heard Lori's side of this."

Mother has that habit of speaking half a sentence and expecting you to figure out the rest. "She's mad at me. Says I've been drinking too much."

"And?"

"She's right. Been having trouble sleeping. Every night I wake up dreaming or thinking about Dad. It's the only way I can go back to sleep."

"Don't give me that. I miss your daddy too. Day and night Matthew, but I'm not gonna let it turn me into a drunk."

"I'm not a drunk."

"Then quit acting like one. Lori's just had a baby. Her world's in an uproar. Instead of you helpin' her out, you stay up all night drinkin'? You're scarin' 'er."

"She said she's scared?"

"Matthew, you know what her daddy was like. She ain't gonna sit around here waitin' on you to become him. Lori's a good girl. You wanna keep her, you'd best fix whatever's bothering you."

I got up, stepped into the front room, and retrieved Father's tablets from next to the computer. On my way back into the kitchen I said, "You wanna know what's wrong with me?" I dropped the boot box onto the table. "There it is."

"Matthew Lee!" Mother jerked back in her chair. "I can't believe this. You were supposed to burn it."

"I've tried, I swear."

"Didn't I warn you about keepin' that?"

"Yes, you did." I sat back down and said, "Mom, I've got to ask you something about what Dad wrote. How come he never took you to find your birthmother's grave?"

"You don't know that."

"I read what he wrote. You saying Dad lied?"

Mother's face told me her secret readings had not gotten that far.

I laid my hand on the box and continued, "In here it says he promised to find your mother's grave."

Mother dug out a cigarette, lit it, and said, "That's what he was trying to tell you the day he died."

"I know, Mom. Just figured it out last night."

"The man was dying, and that's all he could think about; some stupid promise he made almost thirty years ago."

"It wasn't stupid. Dad was all about his family. What about yours? And how many times did I hear him say, 'A promise is a promise'?"

Mother reached for Father's box, pulled it to her, and opened it. When she removed the top tablet and held it against her face, I nearly broke down.

"Mom?"

"Ssshhhh," she said.

After half a minute, Mother lowered the pages to her bosom and held them tight as if she was hugging the man she missed. "Back then," she said quietly, while staring at the ceiling, "when I was young, the idea of finding something, anything to do with my real mother, seemed so important. Your daddy called down there where I was born. He said there wasn't anybody left that knew anything about it. The priest named Father Christopher had died, and the nuns were all gone. Only choice we had was to go down there and look for ourselves."

"So why didn't you?"

"Hard to say. Wasn't your daddy's fault we didn't go. He asked several times. I always chickened out."

"Chickened out? That doesn't sound like you. What's to be afraid of?"

Almost in slow motion, Mother placed the pages back into the box. She stared at them as she answered, "Don't know, Matthew. Sittin' here right now, I still don't know. Guess if my parents here hadn't been so good to me, mighta been more in a hurry to go lookin'. Can't say I don't think about it. But, like I told your daddy, we don't know why my mama wound up at that church. Who knows what her parents were like? Did she run away, or did they run her off? Either way, they weren't there when she needed 'em the most. If they had been, she might still be alive."

"And you never would have met Dad, and Christine and I wouldn't be here."

"Suppose that's one way to look at it."

"Well, I still think you and Dad should have gone down there. Stubborn as you are, I can't believe you let a fear of the past stop you from finding out all you can about your ancestry. Hell, it's not fair to Christine and me. We deserve to know."

"Your daddy warned me about that. Said you two'd be asking questions some day."

"We did, Mom. You just played it off. Always found a reason to change the subject."

Mother took a deep breath. "Guess I treated y'all like I did your daddy. Over the years, especially when you kids were little, I thought about my real moma, but didn't feel like we had the time or money to go lookin'. We were so busy just trying to make ends meet. Every time your daddy asked me to go lookin', I found a reason not to. Eventually he quit askin'."

"Well he obviously never forgot about it, and he knew darn well you didn't either. So now it's up to me to fulfill his promise to you."

"You don't have to do that. Not after all these years."

"It was his dying wish. You said it yourself. And I believe that's why he keeps waking me up at night."

"Matthew honey, you're letting this get to you."

"Damn right I am. And I plan on finding that grave."

"And how you gonna do that?"

"It's called the internet, Mom. Did a search for St. Johns Church in Waynesville, North Carolina."

Mother's eyes widened, "That's where I was born."

"That's right, and I called down there. That's who I was talking to when you knocked on the door."

"You didn't?"

"Mom, there's an old nun living there named Sister Mary Peter. She remembers a Cherokee girl who died while giving birth at Saint John's."

Mother's lips quivered as she remained silent, listening.

"The woman knew the girl you call your real mother. She was there the day you were born. And she knows where your mother's buried." Still no comment. "You know I have to go down there. Now, do you wanna go with me or not?"

"Why?" Mother blurted, "What for? What are you telling me that I didn't already know? My mother's dead." Turning away to hide her tears, she said, "Don't need no nun to tell me that."

"Mom, I didn't mean to upset you. But this did mean a lot to Dad."

"Oh well."

"Mom, I intend to fulfill his promise. You have to go with me. You and Christine."

"Don't have to do nothin' I don't wanna do!"

"Okay, listen. You don't have to, but *I am*. And, I'm sure Christine's gonna want to. So please just think about it. We can make a day of it. Might do us all good to get away, see the mountains."

Mother got up and started pouring herself another cup. With her back to me she spoke. "Can't believe I'm standin' here thinkin' about goin' down there after all these years. Shoulda went when your daddy asked me. Now he's gone. Don't know which is worse, losin' my mother without ever gettin' to know her, or losin' your daddy after all these years. Told myself it would be easier, not havin' to watch him suffer. But it ain't. I still dream about him."

"Just like me."

Mother ripped a paper towel off the roll and began drying her face. She turned back toward me. "Woke up a couple nights ago thinking he might be alive, layin' there next to me, but all I had was his pillow. Still smells like him."

I stood and put my arms around her. "I know how you feel, Mom. We all miss him."

"You have no idea," she cried.

"Believe I do," I whispered as her face lay against my chest. "And I'm sure it's killing Christine too. We're all just gonna have to grieve and mourn until the hurt goes away."

"Guess that's the way it's supposed to be," she whimpered.

I leaned back, looking into her face as I said, "You're right Mom. But think about it, that's something we never got to do for your birthmother, my grandmother."

She released me and turned to get her coffee.

I asked, "What would be wrong with going down there and paying our respects? You, me, Christine, we owe it to ourselves."

Mother sat back down, picked her cigarette out of the ashtray and said, "So you think that's what your daddy had in mind?"

"Mom, I know it is. If you think he didn't know how much all this means to you, you're lying to yourself. And I believe he'll be right there with us all the way."

"Long gave up on learnin' about my people. Thought for a while your daddy mighta went down there without me, but I don't reckon he did. You and Christine wanna go, I'll ride along. Just this one time."

"Great, Mom. We'll have a good time."

"If you say so."

Chapter 2

Two weeks passed before Christine and I could get the same day off from work. Mother had been working part-time in the evenings for a small grocery store as a cashier. They understood and said, "Go anytime you want."

On Wednesday, December 12, Mother, Christine, and I began our journey around 4:00 a.m. My sister complained about the early start and the 31-degree temperature. However, leaving at that time allowed us to beat the morning rush-hour traffic. Since my truck would be too small, we took Mom's SUV. I drove. Snow flurries sprinkled the window but disappeared altogether by the time we reached the Tennessee border. After driving four and a half hours, we stopped for gas and breakfast near Knoxville. The route we took from there wasn't the shortest, but it would allow us to pass through the Cherokee Indian Reservation, home of Mother's roots.

As we approached Gatlinburg, the Great Smoky Mountains stood majestically ahead, their peaks touching the clouds. I couldn't imagine how early settlers ever crossed over them. An abundance of tourist shops, wonderfully decorated for the holidays, attracted the attention of my mother and sister as we drove through town. Determined to reach our destination at a reasonable hour, I drove on, agreeing to stop for shopping on the way home.

For the next twenty minutes we climbed. The absence of leaves actually provided a good view and feel for the rugged terrain. Right after we crossed into North Carolina and began our descent toward the land of our forefathers, Mother suddenly said, "Pull over, Matthew."

"Pull over? Right here?"

"Anywhere," she answered, "think I'm gonna be sick."

"Oh Mama," Christine asked, "You all right?"

"If I was all right, wouldn't be sick."

Wasting no time, I took advantage of a pull-off provided for sightseers. Mother, still wearing her brown fur, mid-length winter coat, quickly opened the door and climbed out. When she stepped across the guardrail I expected to see her bend over and throw up. Instead, she took a few steps, lit a cigarette, and remained upright, staring out at the vast wilderness. Her breath steamed in the cold air.

Christine complained. "She's not sick. Just wanted to smoke a cigarette."

About a minute later, Mother called back, "Turn it off. Y'all get out. Come join me."

The late morning sun had burned away some of the cloud cover lingering between the mountain crests. Cold wind from the north blew Mother's long hair over her shoulders, partially covering her face. Standing at the road's edge, Christine asked, "Mom, what are you doing?"

Without an answer, we both crossed the guardrail and stepped closer.

Christine repeated herself, "Mom, what *are* you doing?"

"I'm listening," she spoke softly.

"To what?"

"Just close your eyes and tell me what you hear."

"Mom, it's cold out here."

"Just try."

My sister and I both tried. Seconds later Christine said, "Don't hear anything."

"Sure you do. Tell 'er Matthew, what do *you* hear?"

"Blue jays," I answered. "Way down there."

"What else?"

"The wind."

"That's it," replied Mother. "The wind is talking. When I was a little girl, used to stand up on Daddy's hill listening to the wind talk. Difference was, except for late at night, I could always hear other things, cars, trucks, tractors. Here, there's nothin' but the wind and the birds."

We stood there a while longer listening to the sound of silence. For as far as the eye could see, nothing man-made, only wilderness. I'd never seen anything make Mother so content.

Christine whispered, "God, I wish she'd quit smoking. Gonna wind up just like Dad."

"Leave her alone," I said. "This is her day."

We allowed Mother to enjoy the moment. As she finished her cigarette, rubbed out the butt, and stuck it in her coat pocket, I said, "Time to go, Mom. Sister Mary Peter's expecting us."

When her trance continued, I put my hand on her shoulder. "Come on Moma, let's go."

Without speaking, she turned and made her way to the Blazer.

As soon as we got moving again, Christine said, "Like it here, don't you Mama?"

While navigating the winding road toward Cherokee, we listened to Mother's enthusiastic explanation of her childhood love affair with nature. Already, our trip seemed to be bringing out the best in her. I thought to myself, *Without us, who would Mom have to talk with about things that make her happy?*

Nearing the reservation, my thoughts switched from Mother's actual childhood in Grayson County to the one she might have had in the mountains of North Carolina. When we passed an old homestead that had been preserved as a tourist attraction, she stared silently at the log buildings and split-railed fence nestled in the flat bottomland surrounded by mountains.

"You wanna stop?" I asked.

"No. Let's keep going."

As we continued into Cherokee, I longed to read her mind. She looked out at the terrain, the people, chimney smoke rising randomly from the hills, and what might have been home. Mother and I both were disappointed as our anticipation of an Indian Reservation wound up being a more modern, commercialized version.

I commented, "Probably need to find the back roads to see any real Indian culture."

"Might not be any left," Mother replied with frustration in her voice.

"What'd you expect," added Christine, "teepees, horses, and leather-clad natives?"

Mother's glance met mine. We both grinned, and she said, "That would be nice."

In a three-or four-mile stretch, we saw about all there was to see in the little tourist town of Cherokee. The only obviously Native Americans were a woman and a little boy and girl coming out of a store. While we waited for the light to change, the girl in her long braids, seeing my mother staring out the window, waved like she knew her. Mother smiled big and waved back as we pulled away.

At a tee in the road, I took a left on Highway 19. A short piece later, we drove past the area's largest facility: a gambling casino.

I said, "They tell me the Cherokee own it."

Mother mumbled, "Wonder what my ancestors would think of that?"

Christine replied, "Guess even Indians have to keep up with the times."

I had my own opinion. "Purely economics, Mamma. How else are people gonna make money down here?"

"Money," Mother added. "Everything's always about money."

Chapter 3

Forty minutes beyond Cherokee, North Carolina, we reached the quaint town of Waynesville. A cemetery appeared on our left.

"Is that it?" asked Mother.

"No," I answered, "Should be on the other end of town. We'll get to the church first. Are you nervous?"

She took a deep breath, exhaled, and said, "Yeah."

As I grinned at Mother's honesty, Christine said, "Mom, this place is so beautiful. It's like going back in time. Hard to believe this is where you were born. And where my grandmother grew up."

"Honey," Mother replied, "your grandmother didn't grow up here. Believe she was raised back there on that Cherokee reservation."

I used my cell phone to call ahead. A woman answered with a soft Southern accent, "Saint John's Church, this is Joyce Edwards."

"Hello, could I speak with Sister Mary Peter?"

"May I ask who's calling?" the lady said back.

"Yes ma'am, this is Matthew Smith from Louisville, Kentucky. I spoke with Sister yesterday evening. Told her I'd call when we got into Waynesville. Should be at the church shortly."

"Hold on, sir."

After a few silent moments, Miss Edwards came back. "I'll walk Sister out when you pull in. What type of vehicle are you driving?"

"Dark blue, four-door Chevy Blazer, ma'am."

"We'll be watching. Bye."

"Bye, ma'am."

I closed my phone just as we crossed a railroad track. "Damn, people say we have a country accent. Wait 'til you hear *this* lady talk."

Looking around, Mother said, "Bet most of this town hasn't changed much since I was born."

"You're probably right," I agreed.

A few blocks and a couple turns later, we found St. John's perched up on a little hill. I pulled in and waited, thinking Sister Mary Peter would come out of the church. Instead, a door opened on a large white-board house that shared the same parking lot. Two women exited. One wore a heavy winter coat with a hood and helped the other along. That woman, obviously Sister Mary Peter, was dressed in a black habit and covered with a heavy black cape. Nearing us, the younger, a middle-aged woman, looked at me and said, "Hello, I'm Joyce Edwards. And you must be the folks from Kentucky."

"Yes, ma'am," I answered. "I'm Matthew Smith. This is my mother Jane and sister Christine."

"Well, you can call me Joyce, and this is Sister Mary Peter. Most folks just call her Sister Mary."

The nun was old indeed, but her eyes were young and blue as the winter skies above.

"Should we go inside to talk?" I asked.

Sister Mary shook her head and then faced my mother. "So, your name is Jane. How appropriate. And, you do look native."

Mom stood there silently in her jeans and fur coat with her long dark hair parted in the middle, grey roots showing slightly, and a worried look.

"Your son told me your husband passed last year. Please accept my condolences."

Mother didn't speak, but she nodded in appreciation.

"He also tells me you might be the little girl born here back in '56," continued Sister Mary. "Is that right?"

Mother looked as though she wanted to answer, but she didn't.

"It's okay dear, I won't bite," encouraged the old woman as if speaking to a child.

Finally Mother spoke. "My parents ... adoptive parents, told me I was born here and that my mother died giving birth."

"And your birthmother's name?" quizzed Sister Mary.

Instead of answering, Mother pulled from her purse the small black and white photo she'd been given years earlier. She handed it to the nun face down with the name showing and waited for her reply.

Sister Mary whispered the words out loud, "Little Rose," then turned it over and looked at the image. "Always wondered where that went. Took the picture myself on her birthday with Father Christopher's camera. Girl told us she was sixteen. We took her word for it. Nobody really knew for sure." Sister Mary took a couple long breaths. "Mind if I ask, if you didn't know your mother, just who did they list as parents on your birth certificate?"

It was a question even I'd never thought to ask. Mother said, "Still have it at home. Says, 'parents unknown.' Daddy said it had to be done that way for adoption purposes."

"Well, let me tell you, that is the way Father Christopher filled it out. Saw it myself." Sister Mary seemed relieved. "So you are that little baby girl. Still remember it like yesterday. Came in from school, heard you cryin'. Your mother done bled to death, all over my bed. Poor girl had that baby, you, snuggled up tight. Father Christopher had to force her arms apart just to pull you out."

Mother stared at the old nun's story wanting to cry, but holding back. Christine took Mother's hand in hers, worried what toll the moment might take.

Sister Mary handed the picture back and said, "Come here, dear. Let me hold you again."

Uncomfortable at first, Mother allowed the embrace.

Sister continued, "Knew you went to Kentucky, but I never heard anything else until your son called."

Mother stood silently while Sister Mary held onto her. Miss Edwards remained quiet, watching.

Sister Mary leaned back a little and said, "Cried myself to sleep that night after they took you away. Wanted to keep you here, take care of you, but Father Christopher said it could never happen."

With the wind blowing Mother's long hair, Sister hesitated. She used her hand to softly brush the strands away from Mother's face back over her shoulder. "I was young then and at a time in my life when I still questioned my vocation, my decision to deny myself children. Asked Father if we could at least try and find the grandparents, but he said no. Said we had to honor Little Rose's wishes. She'd told us if something happened to her, we should find you a good home."

"Why?" Mother asked, finally opening up, unleashing the questions she'd held back for years. "Why was she afraid of her people? Why did she come here in the first place?"

Sister Mary released her hold on Mother and stepped back a little. "Don't know that she was afraid of her people. Believe she ran away out of respect. There's a very strict Christian congregation up in the Big Cove area of the reservation. Back in the fifties, they had no toleration for a girl getting pregnant out of wedlock. Especially from a white man. And I'll tell you something else. Little Rose's father might have held a seat on the Tribal Council. If so, her condition could have shamed him and the tribe."

Sister Mary pulled a handkerchief from under her cape and used it to dry her face. "Those were tough times for a young girl in her situation."

"You say my father was white. Did you know him?"

"Oh no. But I'd bet he had green eyes."

Mother's head tilted backwards as if she were trying not to cry. After a few seconds she looked back at the nun and asked, "So are you saying my mother's people still wouldn't accept me because I have a white father?"

"No child, I'm not. Always believed that given the chance, I could have found Little Rose's parents, and they would have taken you in, raised you and loved you. Honey, you're their blood. If your grandparents are still alive, they would be old now, like me, and a whole lot wiser, I'm sure. Believe if you could find them, they'd be happy to see you. Think if it were you and you'd lost your daughter. Wouldn't you be missing her? Chances are they have no idea what happened to Little Rose. Maybe God sent you to tell them. Even if they are dead, you're sure to have siblings."

Miss Edwards politely interrupted, "Sister Mary needs to get off her feet and out of the cold. You folks plan on visiting the cemetery?"

"Yes, ma'am," I replied. "Believe I can find the cemetery, but was wondering if you could direct us to the grave."

"It's easy," explained Miss Edwards. "From here, you'll end up taking a right into Green Hill Cemetery. As you drive through, those indigent graves will be up on the hill to your left. Shouldn't take long to find what you're looking for."

Sister Mary added, "Haven't been up there in ages. Wish I could walk better, I'd love to go with you."

"You're welcome to join us," I replied. "We'd be glad to help you along."

"I'm afraid my hill climbing days are about over. Maybe in the spring when it's warmer."

"Well," I replied, "we sure do appreciate your meeting with us like this. It feels good to talk with someone who actually knew my grandmother."

Sister Mary took Mother by the hand and said, "It's good to see things turned out just fine, and I'm glad you found your way back here like I always prayed you would."

The old nun turned her attention to Christine. "Don't say much, do you dear? Suppose sometimes it is better just to listen. Can I count on you to bring your mother back to see me?"

"Yes, ma'am. I'll try."

Mother asked, "Sister, my husband told me years ago that he called down here, and there was no one left who remembered anything about my mother. Why would he say that if you were here?"

"Oh no, don't think your husband lied to you. When the school closed down, I had to leave. Went to Charleston. Just recently came back. Always did plan on retiring in Waynesville. Part of my heart remained here the whole time I was gone."

Relief swept Mother's face. "Wanna thank you for caring so much about me *and* my mother."

"And thank you for coming here in answer to my prayers. I do hope to see you again real soon."

Sister Mary and Miss Edwards turned and started to walk away. After two steps, they stopped. The elder looked back and said, "You know dear, most folks give up on God too soon. They get upset when he doesn't answer their prayers the way they want. When you were born, I prayed against Father Christopher's decision to send you away. Wanted you here, where I could see you growing up. But I see better now. Wasn't Father Christopher's decision. God had his own plan. He had a reason for sending you to Kentucky. Don't believe you wound up there just because you needed a new family. I believe God put you there because someone in Kentucky needed you. Open your heart, see God's little miracles. Look at these two beautiful babies you brought into the world. And look at us, standing here together after all these years. Do you think it's an accident God brought me back to Waynesville? Do you think it's an accident your son called when he did? Believe God had a reason for taking you away. And now he has a reason for bringing you back. You go on up there and find your mother's grave. She's been waiting a long time. Little miracles. It's days like this when I see God's hand at work."

Sister Mary reached to touch Mother's hand again. "Don't know about you, but before I go to sleep tonight, I'll say a little prayer thanking God for this day and for bringing you back to me."

"What time do you go to bed?" Mother asked.

"About ten," the old woman answered, as if she knew Mother's thought.

"Then at ten, I'll be thinking of you and saying the same prayer."

Sister Mary grinned and nodded her acknowledgement. Then she turned away as she and Miss Edwards continued their walk.

Mother stood still, watching until Miss Edwards had accompanied Sister Mary Peter up the steps and into the house.

After getting back into the Blazer, Christine said, "Hope you realize how much that woman cares about you. She loves you, Mama. All this time you thought there wasn't anybody who missed you. Well, now we know at least one."

Mother remained quiet for a few seconds, staring out the window. Then asked, "You kids mind if I smoke a cigarette on the way?"

"After all that," I replied, "you deserve one."
Christine smacked me on the head from the backseat.

Chapter 4

A short drive later, we arrived at the Green Hill Cemetery. Halfway back the main road, there were several cars parked in succession. Nearby, mourners gathered around a burial site. I looked up and to the left at the area described by Joyce Edwards and said, "Has to be them right up there."

Christine questioned, "What'd she call 'em? Indigent graves?"

"That'd be the poor folks. The ones that didn't have enough money to bury themselves," answered Mother, a sad tone in her voice.

With the Blazer parked behind the other vehicles, we began our trek uphill. The sun shined bright, but the breeze remained near freezing. Along the way, we passed numerous markers from the late 1800s and early 1900s. When the gravestones started getting smaller, Mother said, "Looks like we're in the right spot."

For ten minutes or so, we continued examining stone after stone. Then our search halted temporarily, as from the burial site below, we could hear the barking sounds of a sergeant directing his honor guard. Mother, Christine, and I stood at our own form of attention while seven riflemen, decked out in their Class A's, shot off three volleys for a twenty-one gun salute. We then held our stance as the sweet sound of "Taps" drifted uphill from a soldier's bugle. Shortly after his last note, the crowd began to disperse. As they did, one gentleman, wearing a long dark overcoat, began walking in our direction. He limped slightly but managed his way to the top of the hill. We watched his approach, worrying our presence had somehow disturbed the funeral service.

"How you doing, sir?" I asked.

"Doin' fine, young man. Just wanted to come up here and thank you folks for your respect during our service."

"No problem. Heck, we were afraid we might have been a disturbance."

"Not at all," he replied. "My name is Johnny Puckett. I'm the funeral director. Don't recall seeing you folks before. Anything I can help you with?"

Christine spoke up. "Yes, sir, maybe you can help us find a gravestone."

Mother said, "Hold on, honey. Don't you think we oughta introduce ourselves first?"

I figured it was my duty. "Sorry, sir, this is my mother, Jane Smith."

"Nice to meet you, ma'am," spoke the gentleman as he reached for a handshake.

Mother accepted, saying, "Likewise."

"I'm Christine Smith," added my sister.

"And I'm Matthew."

"Nice to meet you all," repeated the old fellow. "Now, just whose grave are you folks lookin' for?"

"Sir," I answered, "we're looking for a grave marked 'Little Rose.'"

Before the man could answer, Christine asked, "Got any idea where it might be?"

"Well now dear, you gotta understand, most people gets buried up here 'cause they got no money and no kinfolk. In all these years, don't recall a single soul that come lookin' for that little girl's grave. So if you don't mind me askin', just what is your business here?"

I didn't know if the man was suspicious because we were strangers or what, but I sure didn't like the change in tone of his voice. Suddenly, standing there on that hill, I felt what Father meant in his writing when he wrote about family matters and family taking care of family. Mr. Puckett might not have realized it, but to me, he'd just insulted my family.

"Listen here mister, didn't nobody invite you up here."

"Matthew!" Mother snapped, "You're outta line, Son."

346

"Maybe so Mama, but I'm gonna say my piece. Now Mr. Puckett, sir, you might notta meant to, but the way I see it, you just insulted me *and* my mother *and* my sister."

The old man looked shocked, as did Mother and Christine, but I continued anyway. "That little girl, as you said, *does* have kinfolk. That'd be my grandmother you're talking about. And right now, you'd be standing in front of Little Rose's daughter and granddaughter. So how about a little respect, and by God, if you know where that grave is, we'd appreciate your help."

"Oooowee," exclaimed the old guy. "Boy sure does have the temper of a Cherokee."

Mother begged, "Please excuse my son. Looking for this grave was his daddy's last request, and he's been so excited."

"Ma'am, you don't have to apologize. Down here we appreciate a young man willin' to stand up for what he thinks is right. But now, I know for a fact Little Rose only had one child. So, you telling me you are that little baby girl born over at St. John's all those years ago?"

"That's what they tell me, sir. Been carryin' this here picture around for a long time waitin' for this day."

Mother handed the picture to Mr. Puckett.

"Well looky there," he said. "Believe it is her. So where in the world did you get this picture?"

"My daddy had it in his wallet."

"Your daddy?"

"Well, my adoptive daddy. He said a priest named Father Christopher gave it to him the night they came down here and got me."

"I'll be damned. And I'd have to say there is a good likeness between the two of you. Guess maybe I do owe you folks an apology."

"So how about that grave, mister?" asked Christine.

"Well young lady, let's just say if it were a snake, it'd done bit you. All your mother's gotta do is turn around and take about three steps, and she'll be there."

In unison, we turned that direction and moved in front of a small, vertical stone that, like others in the area, had winter-browned, overgrown grass nearly hiding it.

"That's it right there, ma'am," ensured Mr. Puckett. "Sorry it's so grown up. I'm the one usually keeps things trimmed around here, but since my leg got hurt, ain't been able."

Mother appeared weak as she went to her knees in the frozen grass and began pushing away the vegetation. We were all shocked. The marker read, "Here lies Jane-Little Rose-?. Born November 5, 1940. Died November 10, 1956."

Christine said, "Oh my God Mama, her name was Jane, same as yours."

By some odd coincidence, Mother's adoptive parents had given her the same name as her birthmother.

Mr. Puckett looked at me and said, "Thought it was odd when you introduced your mother as Jane and then said she was Little Rose's daughter."

I heard the man's voice but didn't reply. Mother pulled up grass, roots and all, trying to groom the grave. Christine joined her, then so did I. With Mr. Puckett standing by, the three of us joined hands, and I prayed out loud, the way I knew my father would have.

"Lord, we've come here today to deal with family matters. While we kneel here in this graveyard, a place of death, we celebrate the life of one of our ancestors. We are grateful that in her dying, she provided life for us. May Little Rose rest in peace knowing there are those here who care and appreciate and remember her. In heaven, let my father's soul unite with hers, that they may hold hands and watch over us until our time comes and we join them. Amen."

As my sister and I stood, Mom prostrated herself on the grave and, for a moment, even laid her face against the cold stone itself. She then began rocking and weeping and moaning. Frightened, Christine leaned into my arms.

Placing his index finger to his mouth, Mr. Puckett whispered, "Leave her be."

My mother's years of holding back were released with sounds more animal than human. Finally, the strong woman who rarely cried erupted into soulful sobbing.

"Mr. Puckett," I whispered, "Do you think there's a chance my mother has people living on the reservation?"

The old man took my arm and drew me back a few steps. "Young man, yes, she most likely does have people up in those hills. But keep in mind, that little girl came from the Big Cove area. Even today, those folks up there don't set too well with outsiders. It's up to you, boy. Course, I know what I'd do if it were my mother."

A chill went through me, and for an odd moment, Mother's moans seemed distant. I closed my eyes and somehow saw myself, from a distance, standing there not as Matthew Lee Smith, but as one of the Native Americans whose blood ran in my veins. Right then I knew the sounds emerging from my mother weren't taught. They were born in her, passed on from those whose generations of listening to the wind had preserved a culture unseen by most. The day I was conceived, the blood of my great-grandfather Robert Smith, a simple man and a warrior of his own right, mixed with that of Jane-Little-Rose-somebody's father's father.

After finishing his writing, and when it was too late to add more, my father must have realized the one person whose scars he'd forgotten. My mother. The woman to whom he'd long ago made a promise to find her people or at least the grave of her mother. So as he lay on his deathbed, he attempted to pass that promise to me. Standing on that hill in North Carolina, I wondered if my Father's spirit could finally rest in peace.

In 1956, a scared Native American girl left her home, her loved ones, and her heritage. Did she fear her father and her elders, or did she simply fear she'd shamed her people? My gut feeling is that she would have some day returned *with* her child. In dying, Little Rose left behind a precious, loving human being, my mother. In dying, she left scars of the unknown. In dying, she may well have left a void in the hearts of those on the reservation who loved her. In his passing, my father left a final wish to bring the love of his life, the mother of his children, the daughter of Little Rose, back to the place of her birth. A place where she could begin to find answers to some of the questions that had haunted her for many years.

Chapter 5

It all seemed different in the dark as I slowed at Bear Creek, pulled off Highway 88, and started uphill. My Aunt Sissy, sitting next to me, said, "Ain't been up here since we buried your daddy." The truck's headlights illuminated gravestones, throwing long, narrow shadows that rotated in unison. "Kinda creepy," she mumbled.

I parked in a gravel spot at the hill's crest and rolled down the window, breathing in cold air. Aunt Sissy pulled her hoodie up over her head and said, "Couldn't you pick a warmer night?"

Ignoring her complaint, I sat staring out at the tulip poplar. As it had in my father's youth, the old tree stood alone like a sentry over the graves of our ancestors. Its bare branches looked as dead as the bones it guarded. About a hundred yards away, a single fixture on a pole in front of St. Augustine's Church spread soft light over a scant portion of the graveyard.

"Come on," I said, "let's do this." I carried my backpack. Aunt Sissy grabbed a couple of old blankets from behind the seat. We made our way to the spot next to the tree where Father had sat in his story. Aunt Sissy spread a blanket and took a seat while I retrieved a wooden crate full of sandstone rocks that I had gathered from my backyard. I placed them in a circle over Father's grave, stared at it for a few seconds, and then looked back at Aunt Sissy. In the dim light she looked young and mysterious, the white of her eyes glowing and her long dark hair streaming out from under the hoodie. She patted the blanket next to her and said, "Sit with me, Matthew. Please."

After I was seated, she spread the other blanket over our legs and said, "This reminds me of when your father and I were kids. We'd sneak out to the back yard, snuggle under a blanket, and share one of Mama's cigarettes."

It about killed me when Aunt Sissy lit a cigarette and then scooted up against me. I said, "Wish he could be here with us."

She put her arm around me, pulling me closer, and said, "He is, Matthew."

To avoid bawling, I began emptying the backpack: a felt bag that held my great-grandfather's gold pocket watch, the cardboard box containing Father's story, a bottle of lighter fluid, and a small Mason jar, half-full of moonshine that I had found in the cabinet over Father's workbench. I twisted off the jar's lid, releasing a wild odor somewhere between vodka and rubbing alcohol. "You ever drink any of this?"

"No," Aunt Sissy replied. "Never really had the opportunity."

Holding the jar up in a toast, I scanned the graveyard and said, "For you, Dad, and all the Smith men who carried on the practice of protecting their own." My first taste of moonshine went down smooth and then burned. I must have made a face.

"That bad?" Aunt Sissy asked.

"All I can say is it *will* warm you up."

"Well, give it here then. I might as well try it." She took a bigger swig than I did, swallowed, choked, handed it back to me, and said, "Jesus Christ! How the hell do they drink this shit?" I took another small drink. When I started to cap the jar, she said, "Hold on," while reaching for it.

As she continued sipping moonshine, I loosened the drawstrings of the felt bag. Our family heirloom slid out. Aunt Sissy stared at the gold watch and said, "I wondered where that thing went."

"Grandpa gave it to me after Dad's funeral."

The gold chain swayed as I applied several twists to the winder stem. No sound. No ticking. "Dammit."

"What's wrong?" Aunt Sissy asked.

A good shake jolted life back into the old Hamilton as its second hand started moving. "Nothing," I replied. "It's working now."

Six Little Scars

Fifteen feet forward and six feet under lay the remains of Robert J. Smith, the man who carried that same pocket watch across Europe during World War II. I held it up to my ear to hear the ticking. Aunt Sissy leaned closer, laying her head on my shoulder, and for a while we sat leaning against the tree and relaxing to the peaceful sound of the watch's tick. I said, "Dad wrote about sitting here drinking whiskey, smoking marijuana, and missing his grandfather. The way I miss him."

"We all miss him," replied Aunt Sissy while sucking down another swig of the shine.

"You best take it easy on that stuff."

"Don't you worry none about me."

As she capped the jar and set it down an owl hooted somewhere in the woods across the road. I turned that direction, thinking, *No way!*

"What now?" Aunt Sissy asked.

I hesitated and then said, "You know, I first thought about coming here by myself. Then I considered asking Grandpa or one of his brothers. But then I got to thinking how no one could appreciate more what I was about to do than you. And ... well ... I would like to believe that if it were my sister, I would do the same as dad did."

"Matthew honey, your daddy had good intentions, but he made mistakes along—"

"I know he did. I read it all. He did what he thought was right."

"Yes he did. And you have no idea how much I appreciate the things he went through on my behalf."

Not sure if it was the moment or the moonshine, but I had to ask. "Aunt Sissy, the night dad died, can you remember what you were saying to him when Lori and I came in? He seemed upset."

"He wasn't upset. He was havin' a hard time speakin'. He was reminding me of what I had once said. 'We all have scars'"

"And, 'some are just more visible than others,'" I finished.

"He wrote that?"

"Yes he did. He never forgot. It was a great statement by you." Instead of replying she sat quietly. I said, "You always seem to wear long sleeves. Is that to cover up the scars?" When she nodded, I asked, "Could I, like ... see them?"

"Are you shittin' me?" she growled while throwing off the blanket and struggling to her feet. Without speaking, she removed her hoodie.

"You're gonna get cold," I said.

She ignored me while sliding up the sleeves of her sweatshirt. "Look, Matthew. See these little mother fuckers—"

"I'm sorry—"

"And there's another one on my ass! Wanna see it too?"

"No, Aunt Sissy. I said I'm sorry."

"You're sorry? Dammit, Johnny Lee—"

"I'm not Johnny Lee."

"Matthew, then!" she huffed down at me while turning away and stomping off toward the truck. "You know what I mean!"

I was in shock and sat there speechless. Was it the moonshine, the memories, or both? I began to think it had been a mistake to bring her along. While she leaned against the truck smoking a cigarette, I continue without her.

Dad's promise to my mother had been fulfilled. It was time to take care of family business. I placed twigs inside my circle of sandstones and then set the old boot box on top of them. After dowsing it with the lighter fluid, I stood silently, thinking back. When we were children, Dad would drag Christine and me to church. Mother rarely went. After taking communion, he would always go to his knees, close his eyes, and pray silently, so intensely that sometimes his head would shake. When I asked him what he prayed for, he said, "Forgiveness of my sins." Preparing to burn his past, I understood.

A gentle breeze began, and I could hear its whisper—little gusts of comfort, so close to words it had to be real. Standing there among the dead, I realized we all have it: the wind, our conscience speaking, or God himself. Those little whispers of wisdom that help us determine right from wrong. I felt saved.

The owl across the way continued its call. Looking back down at Dad's gravestone, I took a deep breath and said, "The man in this box may not be the man I grew up with, but I do recognize him. He's in me." I turned my attention to the stars and spoke as though father were up there somewhere listening. "The day you died, I believe you worried more about Mom, Christine, and me than yourself. That's the man I want to remember. That's the man I want to be."

As I spoke, I felt arms reaching around my waist. "I'm sorry, Matthew."

"Don't be," I whispered.

"I stood back there watching you, and I swear it was like watching him. Honey, you *are* your daddy made over."

She released her hold and stepped in front of me. Her hand touched my cheek, and then she ran her fingers through my hair. "You are the same sweet, honest man he was. Don't you ever change."

I wiped my face and said, "Thank you."

Aunt Sissy reached for my hand and said, "I'm ready."

Looking skyward, I said, "Dad, I want to remember you the way it was when you took me fishing and hunting, and the way we all laughed at your bad jokes. The way you picked on Mom, just for the fun of it. Her acting like she got upset, knowing darn well that everyone in the room knew better. I remember one day when you came home from a hard day of construction work, dirty sweat on your face and arms, clothes all soiled, fatigued to the point of slumping. Mom said, 'You're gonna be sore in the morning.' You said, 'Someday when I'm eighty years old, I'll be wishing for the opportunity to be young, working my ass off, and feeling sore again.'"

Aunt Sissy looked skyward and cried out. "Didn't make it to eighty, did you little brother?"

I could feel her suffering. "Dad, it took me a long time to figure out your promise to Mom, but I did, and I fulfilled it for you. Mom's happy. Now it's time to fulfill my promise to you. I know you're out there somewhere, watching. I hope you don't mind my bringing Aunt Sissy along. She deserves to be here. Your story never would have been written had it not been for what she went through. She's going to be with me when I burn your words. Your good and bad memories."

As I spoke, Aunt Sissy went to her knees, much like my mother had on the hill in Waynesville, NC. Thinking back to the day we buried

Father, Aunt Sissy never cried. That night with me on the hill, she did. For the longest time, I just stood there watching. Finally, still bawling, she looked into the sky and began ranting. "Damn you, Johnny Lee! Damn you! How could you leave me? I didn't get to thank you enough for all you did! I was so hard on you, and you were right! You put your life on the line for me! You risked everything." Her shoulders jerked up and down as she wept. "I miss you little brother. I miss you so, so much."

I knelt next to her, kissed her on her cheek, and said, "Let's do this together." I fumbled with the butane lighter. Unlike the night in my backyard, this time, it remained lit. No gusts of wind. No distant howling. No more empty feelings. Aunt Sissy and I both held the lighter while we touched the tiny glow to the box. As flames erupted, we rose and stood side by side holding hands. Within seconds, the box's lid drifted away in weightless ash. Yellow tablets became yellow flames as my father's words disappeared. Aunt Sissy's hand gripped mine tightly. I whispered to her. "This is closure for dad *and* me. My sleepless nights are over. You too can be done with this shit. We've burned away the bad memories right here tonight. And, all three of those men are dead. May God have mercy on their souls? Especially the man named Carl." Aunt Sissy's tears ran freely as I stared into her eyes. "Those scars inside of you. Let them go up in this smoke. Let them drift right out of you and into this cold dark night. Let the sun shine on you tomorrow and forever. Let the scars on your arms *only* be a reminder of the love between my father and you."

Startled by a whooshing sound, we looked up. That hoot owl with its four-foot wingspan glided toward us, right through the glow, the smoke, and ash. We both stumbled backwards as the big bird arced upward to the tulip poplar's lowest branch. Majestically perched, its eyes glowed, staring down at our efforts.

Aunt Sissy asked, "Do you feel what I feel?"

"It's the owl," I said. "The owl holds my father's spirit."

Aunt Sissy looked up at the big bird and said, "I swear ... I can feel his presence."

"Me too."

Still focused on the owl, Aunt Sissy said, "It's over little brother. Because of all you went through, I finally feel free. This is for you, Johnny Lee." Before I could speak, she removed her hood, shook out her hair, placed her hands behind my head, and kissed me in a way that I still cannot explain. I was so shocked that I allowed her to do what she felt she needed to do. It was so perfect that it could not be wrong. I had no idea that closure could be so passionate.

When it was over, she looked into my eyes as if waiting for my reaction. I said, "That was the most perfect thing I've ever experienced."

She looked up at the sky and said, "Forgive me Lord as I forgive those who have trespassed against me."

I stepped to the tree and picked up the Mason jar. Returning to Aunt Sissy's side, I put my arm around her. My heart raced as I raised the Mason jar toward the owl and whispered, "Together."

Matthew Smith
December 15, 2007